Select praise for Kristan Higgins

NOW THAT YOU MENTION IT

"Higgins is in top form. Many readers will relate to the family saga and rough past, and the light romance and humor sprinkled throughout will suit a wide audience. Readers won't want to put down this highly recommended read."
—*Library Journal*, starred review

"Kristan Higgins adds humor at every opportunity to *Now That You Mention It* and proves that it is possible to deal with our past demons without losing our minds." —*BookPage*

ON SECOND THOUGHT

"Emotional depth is seared into every page along with wry banter, bringing readers to tears and smiles. Another hit for Higgins." —*Library Journal*, starred review

"Higgins' complex, witty characters will seem like close friends, and readers will savor each and every page as they find that love comes in many different flavors and forms. Demand will be high for the latest from this women's-fiction star."
—*Booklist*, starred review

IF YOU ONLY KNEW

"The kind of book I enjoy the most—sparkling characters, fast-moving plot and laugh-out-loud dialogue. A winner!"
—*New York Times* bestselling author
Susan Elizabeth Phillips

"This emotional journey is filled with drama, laughter and tears and squeezes the heart. It should be on every bedside table in the country!" —#1 *New York Times* bestselling author Robyn Carr

KRISTAN HIGGINS

Waiting

on

You

ISBN-13: 978-1-335-44800-2

Recycling programs
for this product may
not exist in your area.

Waiting On You

First published in 2014. This edition published in 2023.

For questions and comments about the quality of this book,
please contact us at CustomerService@Harlequin.com.

HQN
22 Adelaide St. West, 41st Floor
Toronto, Ontario M5H 4E3, Canada
www.Harlequin.com

Printed and bound in Barcelona, Spain by CPI Black Print

This book is dedicated to my beamish boy, Declan, who makes me laugh every single day. This is the part where I'm tempted to get mushy and sentimental and use a lot of nicknames, but I'll try to keep it dignified. Let's just say that you're everything a mother could ever hope for in a son, and I love you. Tremendously.

Waiting

on

You

CHAPTER ONE

"DRINKS ARE ON the house!"

A cheer went up from the gang, not just because Colleen O'Rourke—the bartender and half owner of the best (and only) bar in town—had just offered free booze, but because Brandy Morrison and Ted Standish had just gotten engaged.

Colleen hugged the happy couple once more, then went behind the bar and accepted high fives from her regulars as she pulled beers and mixed martinis, poured wine and slid glasses down the bar. After all, Brandy and Ted were her doing. That made…hmm…fourteen couples she'd set on the road to matrimony? No, fifteen! Not bad. Not bad at all.

"Good job, Coll," said Gerard Chartier, accepting his free Cooper's Cave IPA. He sat at the end of the bar, where the fire department was having a "meeting," the agenda of which seemed to be O'Rourke's list of microbrews. She wasn't complaining. They were good for business.

"Your sorry single state hasn't gone unnoticed," she said, rubbing his bald head. "Not to worry. You're next."

"I'd rather stay single."

"No, you wouldn't. Trust Auntie Colleen, ever wise and all-knowing."

"Colleen!" her brother, Connor, yelled from the kitchen. "Stop harassing the customers!"

"I'm part of our charm!" she yelled back. "Gang, are you feeling harassed?"

A satisfying chorus of *no* answered her. She breezed into the kitchen. "Hi, Rafe," she greeted the backup chef, who was making one of his famous cheesecakes. "Save some of that for me, okay?"

"Of course, my truest love," he said, not looking at her. He was gay. All the good ones were.

"Brother mine," Colleen said to her twin, "what bug is up your ass?"

"You just gave away three hundred dollars' worth of booze, that's what," he said.

"Brandy and Ted got engaged. Beautiful ring, too."

"Your work, Collie?" Rafe asked.

"As a matter of fact, yes. They'd been eyeing each other for weeks. I gave a gentle shove, and voilà. I expect I'll be a bridesmaid. Again."

Rafe smiled. "And when will you work your superpowers on your own self, lovey?"

"Oh, never. I'm too smart for all that. I like to use men for purely physical—"

"Stop! No one wants to hear about your sex life," Connor said.

"I do," said Rafe.

She grinned. Tormenting her brother, though they were both thirty-one, was still one of the great joys in life.

"It seems like such a waste. All that, unclaimed." Rafe gestured to her torso and face.

"She got burned when she was young," Connor told Rafe.

"Oh, please. That's *not* why I'm single. Besides,

you're single, too. It's all part of our dysfunctional childhood, Rafe."

"Don't even try," he said, adding the sour cream layer to the cake. "I was a gay boy born to Jehovah's Witnesses and grew up in East Texas with five older brothers who all played football. It was *Friday Night Lights* meets *The Birdcage* meets *Swamp People.* No one can compete with me in the land of dysfunctional families."

"You totally win," Colleen said. "Con and I only had a cheating father and—"

"Isn't tonight your night off?" Connor interrupted.

"Yep. But I came in because I sensed, using our magical twinsy bond, that you missed me."

"You sensed wrong," he muttered. "Get out of my kitchen. Your posse just came through the door."

"He has batlike hearing," Rafe said.

"I know. It's creepy. Bye, boys! Don't forget my piece of heaven, Rafe. Connor, come say hi. Everyone loves you, for some reason."

She went back out into the bar and sure enough, there were the girls: Faith Holland, her oldest pal in the world (and a newlywed, and while Colleen couldn't claim that one as her idea, she'd nonetheless helped keep them together); Honor, Faith's older sister (bone-dry martini, three olives), someone Colleen had *definitely* helped with sweet Tom Barlow—their wedding would be in early July; and Prudence, the oldest Holland sister (gin and tonic, now that it was spring), married for decades.

"How's tricks, Holland girls? Honor, you want your usual? Pru, a G&T? And what about you, Faithie? I have some strawberries I've been saving for you…a little vodka, a little mint, splash of lemon…want to try one?"

"Just water for me," Faith said.

"Oh, lordy, are you pregnant?" Colleen blurted. Faith and Levi had gotten married in January, and from the way he looked at her, those two got it on like weasels. And you know what they say about weasels.

"I didn't say that." But she blushed, and Honor smiled.

"Well, I hope you are," said Pru. "Nothing like the blessing of kids, even though I thought I would kill Abby the other day. She asked if she could get her tongue pierced. I said sure, I'd get a hammer and a nail and we could do it right now if she was that dumb, and the conversation devolved from there."

"Hi, girls," Connor said dutifully, having emerged from the kitchen.

"Con, bring Pru and Honor their regulars, and a big glass of ice water for Faith here."

"I thought you wanted me to say hi, not to wait on you," he said. "Faith, are you pregnant?"

"No! Maybe. Just shush," Faith said. "I'm thirsty, that's all."

"Connor Cooper would be a great name," he suggested.

"I think it sounds pretentious," Colleen said. "Colleen Cooper, or Colin for a boy…now we're talking. Con, how about those drinks? And some nachos?"

Her brother gave her a dark look but left obediently, and Colleen settled back in her seat. "Guess what you missed? Brandy Morrison and Ted Standish just got engaged! He got down on one knee and everything, and she was crying, and it was beautiful, ladies! Beautiful!"

Hannah, Colleen's cousin, brought over their food and drinks, and Prudence launched into a story of her latest adventure in keeping things fresh in the old conjugal bed. Very entertaining. Coll scanned the bar as Pru talked, making sure all was running smoothly.

It occurred to her that spending her night off at work was maybe not 100 percent healthy. Granted, options were limited in Manningsport, New York, a town of just over seven hundred. She could be home, reading and cuddling with Rufus, her enormous Irish wolfhound mutt, who would love nothing more than to stare into her eyes in adoration for several hours. One couldn't rule out the ego boost that provided.

Or, Colleen thought, she could be out on a date. Rafe had a point.

It's just that every guy she met seemed to be lacking something. She hadn't felt the tingle in a long, long time.

As the proprietor of the only year-round alcohol-serving establishment in town, Colleen saw a lot of relationships blossom or end in a fiery crash. When things went right, it was generally because the woman had cleverly manipulated the guy into good dating behavior. He'd call when he said he would. Put some thought into dates. He'd ask questions about her life because she didn't vomit up all her personal history in the first ten minutes.

Far more common, however, was the fiery crash model, when Colleen mixed a sympathy cosmo or poured an extra ounce of Pinot Grigio into a glass for a woman who had no idea what went wrong. Colleen could tell her, of course, and sometimes did… *Maybe you shouldn't have talked about your ex for two hours,* or *Is telling him you were just cleared for fertility treatments a good idea on the first date?*

Happily, the now-engaged Brandy had asked Colleen for advice from the start. *Should I go out with him again tomorrow? Is it okay to sleep with him yet? How about if I text him right now?*

The answers: *No, no* and *no.*

"Colleen," said the bride-to-be now, "I just wanted to thank you again for everything." She bent down and gave Coll a hug. "Bridesmaid?"

"Of course!" Colleen said. "You two…mazel tov! I'm so happy for you!"

"Thanks, Coll," Ted said. "You're the best."

"My fifteenth couple," she said to the Holland sisters as the happy couple left for some monkey sex, one presumed.

"You have a gift," Faith said, taking a slab of nachos onto her plate.

"And yet just last night, there was some poor woman in here, begging the guy she was with not to dump her, and I took her aside and said, 'Honey, if you have to beg, do you really want this loser?' But of course, she kept crying and begging, and it was agony, I tell you." She finished her drink, one of the strawberry thingies Faith had passed on. "Maybe I should teach a class. Pru, when Abby starts dating, you send her to me."

"Will do. And thanks, because God knows, she's not listening to me these days."

"Excuse me," came a voice, and all three of them looked up.

"Hey, Paulie," Colleen said. "How are you? Have a seat!"

Paulina "Paulie" Petrosinsky pulled up a chair, swung it backward and straddled it. She'd been Faith and Colleen's classmate—not quite a friend back in the day, but really nice. She came into O'Rourke's once in a while, usually after a workout at the gym, where her weight lifting skills were the stuff of legend.

"Um… I overheard you say something about, uh, teaching people? Women?" she asked.

"Slut University," Pru said, and Faith and Honor snorted.

"Very funny," Colleen said. "My reputation is greatly exaggerated."

"And whose fault is that?" Faith asked. "You should stop spreading rumors about yourself."

Colleen smiled. Had she in fact written something flattering about herself on the men's room wall just last week? She had. "Ignore my so-called friends," she said. "What's up?"

"Um…can you really help a, um, a person? With, uh…you know. Love and men and stuff?" Paulie's face turned deep red, then purple.

"Are you all right?" Honor asked, frowning a little.

"Oh, that. My face. It's called idiopathic craniofacial erythema. I… I blush. A lot."

"Wish I could hang around," Prudence said. "We farm people have to get up early. Good luck with your man, Paulie! See you, girls!"

"So are you interested in someone in particular?" Colleen asked, scooching over into Pru's vacated chair to make more room at the table.

Paulie swallowed. "Yeah," she whispered, glancing around.

"Who?" Faith asked.

"Um… I'd rather not say."

Colleen nodded. "What do you like about him?"

"He's…he's just so nice. I mean, really kind, right?

And he's cheerful and good and smart, I think, too. I mean, he...well. He's great."

Colleen smiled. "And do you feel sick when you see him, and then hot, and then nauseous?"

"Exactly," Paulie said, her face purpling again.

"Do you imagine conversations with him, holding hands and moonlit walks and all that other mushy stuff?"

"I—yes. I do." Paulie took a shaky breath.

"Does he make your danger zone tingly? Does your skin get hot, do your knees wobble, does your tongue feel swollen—"

Faith stood up. "I miss Levi," she announced. She gave Colleen a kiss on the cheek and squeezed her sister's shoulder. "Good luck, Paulie! Take Colleen with a grain of salt."

"I'm going, too," Honor said. "Bye, matchmaker. Do no harm, mind you. See you, Paulina."

"So who is this guy?" Colleen asked when they were gone.

Paulie shot a nervous glance back to the bar. Aha! A hint. "You know what?" Paulie said. "Never mind. He's...he's out of my league."

"No, he's not!" Colleen cried. "Paulie, you're so nice! You are! Anyone would be lucky to have you." Besides, Colleen always felt a little guilty where Paulie was concerned.

"Thanks," she muttered.

"It's true," Colleen said firmly. Granted, Paulie hadn't been blessed with great beauty. And her dad was a little odd—Ronnie Petrosinsky, owner of four small restaurants called Chicken King that served fried chicken thirty-eight different ways, all of them very, very bad for you. He was locally famous for his commercials, where he pranced around dressed as a rooster wearing a crown. Poor Paulie was also featured in a fluffy yellow chick suit, wearing a crown—the Chicken Princess. Try getting out from under that title, especially in high school.

"Listen, Paulie. No one is out of your league. Go ahead, tell me."

Paulina sighed gustily and drained her Genesee (first order of business: get her to drink something more feminine). "It's Bryce Campbell."

Oh. Okay, so that might be tough.

Bryce was gorgeous. Jake Gyllenhaal DEFCON 4–gorgeous. He got his share of tail, as Colleen knew all too well. Bryce was a regular. Not the sharpest tool in the shed, but sweet. He had a certain charm, and women threw themselves at him all the time.

Lots of women.

"That's fine," Colleen said, realizing she hadn't spoken for a moment. "Not a problem."

Paulie gave her a despairing look.

"I'm serious. We can work with this. So, tell me more about you and Bryce."

Paulie's expression grew dreamy, the severe blush fading. "He volunteers at the animal shelter, you know?" Colleen nodded; Bryce had in fact helped her choose Rufus the Doofus. "And the animals, they all love him. I go in a lot. I, um… I've adopted two dogs and four cats in the past year."

Colleen smiled. "That's a lot. But go on."

"And the other day, I was getting gas, and so was he, and I didn't even plan that! He just smiled at me and said, 'Hey, Paulie, how's it going?'" She sighed at the memory of the magical words. "It was amazing. I mean, that smile, right?"

Yes. Bryce had a beautiful smile. That was true.

"He's never in a bad mood," Paulie went on. "Never has a bad thing to say about anyone. Not that I talk to him. Not much, anyway. But sometimes we lift weights at the same time, and…well, I try to talk to him. But my mind goes blank, and I never think of anything good to say. But last week? I had to walk past him, and I said 'Excuse me,' and he said, and I quote, 'No problem.' Colleen, he smelled *so* good."

The woman had it bad.

"And when we were in high school, he never made fun of me."

Colleen's heart gave a squeeze. Paulie had a solid, athletic build and held the school record for the number of push-ups, beating even Jeremy Lyon, football god, a record that stood to this day. Her father's business didn't help her social status; he'd started out as a chicken farmer, and Paulie hadn't grown up as comfortably as most of the kids in town, though not as poor as others. And then, when the Chicken King became so successful, well, that was different, too, and it was hard to be different at that age.

Though she was now the chief operating officer for the Chicken King franchises, Colleen had never seen Paulie out of gym clothes, and she always seemed on the fringe of things, as nice and smart as she was.

With a pang, Colleen realized Paulie reminded her of Savannah, her nine-year-old half sister.

"You know what? Let's forget about it, okay? I'm sorry," Paulie said now.

"Absolutely not," Colleen said. "He'd be lucky to

have you. I'm serious. You're great, you have so many nice qualities…it's not gonna be that hard, Paulie. What have your other relationships been like?"

"Um… I… I've never had another relationship."

"That's fine. So, no experience with men?"

"I'm a virgin," she said.

"No worries. Nothing wrong with saving yourself for true love." Colleen herself had, after all. Not that hers was an exemplary story.

"It's more like no one's ever asked me."

Oh! Poor lamb! "Not a problem."

"He'd probably rather go out with you," Paulie said.

"Oh, please," Colleen said with a flinch. "Bryce? No. We're not… He's a sweetheart, but not my type. But you guys…you'd be great together."

Paulie's face lit up. "Really? You think so? Honest? I'll do whatever you say. You think I have a shot?"

"Absolutely."

Connor was back. "Dad called. Wants you to babysit. Apparently, Gail needs a break."

Ah. Gail Chianese O'Rourke, their stepmother, four years their senior, not so lovingly known as Gail-the-Tail-Chianese-Rhymes-with-Easy-Hyphen-O'Rourke.

"A break from what?" Colleen asked. "From spa appointments? From shopping? A break from having breaks?"

"I don't know. Ask him to call you on your cell next time. Hey, Paulie, anything else for you?"

"Uh, I'm good, thanks," she said, shifting to take a ten from her pocket.

"On the house," Connor and Colleen said in unison.

"Thanks." She stood, tripped a little over the chair; Con grabbed her arm and Paulie flushed again. "Well.

Thanks, Coll. You rock." With that, she headed out into the beautiful spring night.

"I'm fixing her up," Colleen said.

"Oh, God," Connor muttered.

"What? You have something against true love?"

"Do you have to ask?"

The bar was emptying; the sidewalks, few that there were, tended to roll up early in Manningsport. Connor sat down with her. The only folks left were on the volunteer fire department, who felt that O'Rourke's was their home away from home.

"Con, you think Mom and Dad screwed us up forever? I mean, neither one of us has a significant other."

Connor shrugged. He hated talking about their parents.

"You should go out with someone. Jessica Dunn, maybe. Or Julianne from the library. Or I could fix you up."

"I'd rather hang myself, but thanks."

"If you do, can I have your car?" She gave him a look. "What aren't you telling me?"

He grimaced, but hey, the twin telepathy was alive and well. "Don't have kittens, okay? But actually, I'm seeing someone."

"What? Since when? Who?"

"No kittens, Colleen."

"Well, you're my twin, my family, my coworker! We share a house!"

"Another life mistake."

"Connor," she said more calmly, "how are you seeing someone and I don't know about it? Who is she? How long has this been going on? Why didn't you tell me?"

"Because of this. I didn't want you to go crazy and give me advice or start naming babies."

"When have I ever done that?"

"An hour ago. You told Faith to name her baby after you."

"Well, so did you."

Her brother crossed his arms. "It's not serious. Not yet."

"I can't believe you kept this from me. God, those three minutes you have on me ruined you. I should've been born first, and I would've been, if you hadn't shoved me out of the way."

"Okay, we're done here. You wanna kick out the fire department, or shall I?"

"Get out, people!" Colleen yelled, and the various and sundry members of Manningsport's bravest started reaching for their wallets.

Hello. Bryce Campbell was there, too. He must've come in when she was with the girls. He was watching the fire department with an almost wistful look on his face. Boys. They never got over the thrill of their first shiny red truck.

Well, no time like the present.

"Hey, Bryce," she said, ambling over.

"Hi, Colleen." He looked at her and smiled, and yes, Paulie had a point. Bryce was cute. That wasn't news, but still.

"How's your dad?" Smiling Joe Campbell was one of Colleen's favorite patrons, though he hadn't been in much in the past year.

"He's great!" Bryce flashed another look at the MVFD, who were now filing out the door, laughing.

"You should join the fire department," she said.

"Yeah. I doubt my mom would approve of that. I might get hurt."

"You probably wouldn't, though. Their safety record is stellar, even if they are a bunch of goofballs." She took his empty glass and wiped the counter in front of him. "So, Bryce, you seeing anyone these days?"

He raised a friendly eyebrow. "You asking?"

"No."

"Right." He gave a mock grimace. "Nope, no one special. I wouldn't mind having a girlfriend, though."

This was going to be easier than she thought. "Really? What's your type?"

"Aside from you?" He winked.

"None of that, now. Answer the question."

"I don't know. Pretty. Kind of…pretty and nice and hot, you know? Like Faith Holland, except maybe taller and skinnier, and don't tell Levi I said that, okay?"

"Bryce Campbell. Looks aren't everything, you know." And if he had a problem with Faith—who was built like a 1940s pinup girl—she was going to have to tread carefully with Paulie. "How about personality?"

"Really outgoing. Like me, kind of. You know anyone?"

"Hmm. No one leaps to mind." Actually, four women leaped to mind, but Bryce was a typical man—he didn't know what he needed; he just knew what he liked. "But I'll think about it, okay?"

"Thanks, Coll! You're the best!"

"It's true. Now get out, we're closing."

Half an hour later, Colleen walked to the yellow-and-red Victorian she shared with her brother. A duplex, so it wasn't quite as dysfunctional as it sounded. Connor had left a little earlier, and the first-floor lights were out. Colleen's apartment was on the second floor—a staircase in the back led to a small deck and her door.

She wondered if this mystery woman of his had visited the house yet.

"It's all good," she murmured to herself as she opened her door. "After all, we have somebody to love, too. Right, Rufus?"

One hundred and sixty pounds of scruffy gray canine agreed. She allowed him to maul her, scratched his rough gray fur, gazed meaningfully into his eyes, and then extricated herself. "Who wants a cookie? Is it us? I want an Oreo, and you, my beautiful countryman, can have a Milk-Bone."

Some bozo had bought Rufus as a puppy, then, shocker, learned that the breed tended to get a wee bit large. But the idiot's loss was her gain, because, as Bryce Campbell had suspected, Rufus and Colleen were kindred spirits.

She called Rushing Creek and talked to Joanie, the night nurse in her grandfather's wing, and ascertained that Gramp was having a good night. Then, with a sigh, she got the snacks, made Rufus balance his cookie on his nose before allowing him to inhale it, then flopped down on the couch with the box of Oreos. Because really, no one had just one Oreo.

Love was in the air. It was all around her, as a matter of fact—Faith and Levi maybe percolating a baby; Honor and Tom getting married; Brandy and Ted now engaged. Paulie and Bryce (complicated on several levels…but maybe a chance for Colleen to do something good).

Connor and someone.

That one gave her the biggest pang. Granted, there'd

been many times over the years when Colleen would've cheerfully sold Connor to the gypsies (and had, in fact, put him up for adoption when they were twelve and he announced the fact of her period in the cafeteria). When their parents went through their ugly, horrible, terrible divorce, she and Connor had become closer than ever. They often called or texted each other simultaneously. Saw each other every day.

It was strange, thinking of her twin married, a dad. She certainly wanted him happy, of course she did. It was just that she always pictured it in the happy, sunny future, in which she would have a great spouse and adorable tots.

But that picture always held a dreamlike quality, the image overexposed, as if the sun shone too brightly, and her husband's face was blurred.

Once, she'd known exactly who the face belonged to, and it hadn't been blurry at all.

CHAPTER TWO

"MOMMY SAYS YOU'RE emotionally shut down." The voice came from the child standing in the doorway of Lucas Campbell's office at Forbes Properties. A female child of the smallish variety. One of his four nieces, specifically.

"That's adorable. I thought I banned you from visiting me," Lucas said. He pressed the intercom to his assistant. "Susan, please call Security and have my niece escorted from the building."

"She's five years old," Susan said.

"Have them send a team."

Chloe grinned, flashing the gaping hole in her teeth. Too soon for dentures, probably. "Mommy says you're constibladed."

"I'd have to agree," Susan said, then clicked off.

He leveled a stare at his niece. "The word is *constipated*. If you're going to talk about me, you need to up your game. Why are you here? Didn't I pay you not to bother me?"

"I spent your money."

"So?"

"So give me more." The kid had the soul of a Beverly Hills trophy wife. She skipped over to him and climbed onto his lap.

"Don't think this show of affection will win you any points," he grumbled.

"What are you looking at?" Chloe said, settling back against him.

"Mr. Forbes is building a new skyscraper," he said.

"I want to live in the penthouse."

"You're broke. And you have no earning potential, I might point out. You can't even drive. Not very well, anyway." This earned a giggle, and Lucas smiled into his niece's hair.

"Is that a princess you have there?" came a voice.

"Hi, Frank!" Chloe scrambled off Lucas's lap and charged into Frank Forbes's legs. "Uncle Lucas showed me your new skyscraper, and I want to live in the pent-house!"

Frank picked up Chloe and laughed. "Well, you can stay overnight before we sell it, how's that? You and your sisters?"

"Hooray!"

"Little girl, whatever your name is, go see Susan and tell her to let you answer the phones," Lucas said. "You can be her boss until your mom comes to get you." Steph, Lucas's older sister, worked in Accounting seven floors down, and often sent her youngest up to bother him. Chloe was in the after-care program that Forbes offered its employees. Cara, Tiffany and Mercedes—Chloe's sisters—had all been in the same program, though they were now extremely mature at ages fourteen for the twins, and sixteen for Mercedes.

Chloe stampeded for the reception area, the promise of power the best bribe possible.

"When can we hire her?" Frank asked, sitting down in the leather chair in front of Lucas's desk.

Lucas smiled and waited. Frank only came by to talk about one thing these days—why Lucas should stay with Forbes Properties and not leave, as he planned to, once the Cambria skyscraper was finished. But Lucas was done here, as grateful as he was. Frank Forbes, his boss and former father-in-law (and yes, a relation to *that* Forbes) had been good to him.

"I wish you'd stay, son," he said, almost on cue. "There's no need for you to leave."

"Thank you. But I think it's time. More than time."

Frank sighed. "Maybe. It won't be the same without you, though."

The truth was, it was still hard for Lucas to believe he worked here—him, a kid from the South Side, taking an elevator to the fifty-third floor every day. He'd first worked for Forbes Properties the summer of his freshman year of college, doing grunt-work construction, mostly cleaning up after the union carpenters and electricians, schlepping supplies, then working his way up being able to drive nails and cut wood.

Four years later, he'd been given a promotion, a health care package and a title.

That's what happened when you knocked up the boss's daughter.

And despite the fact that Frank had forgiven him for that transgression, had treated him far better than he deserved, had truly made him part of the family— and not just him, but Steph and her kids, too—Lucas couldn't stay anymore. His debt to the Forbes family was paid as much as it would ever be.

"Have you seen my daughter lately?" Frank asked now.

"We had dinner the other night."

There was a pause. "She looks good, don't you think?"

"She does."

Lucas's intercom buzzed. "A call for you on line three," came Chloe's voice.

"Did you get a name?" Lucas asked.

"No," she answered. "Get it yourself."

Frank smiled. "I'll see you later, son."

"Thanks, Frank." He waited until Frank left; the guy would stop to talk to Chloe, no doubt, who collected souls like a tiny Satan.

"Lucas Campbell," he said into the phone.

"Lucas? It's Joe."

"Hey, Uncle Joe," he said. "How you doing?"

There was a pause. "I'm not so good, pal."

Something flared in Lucas's chest. "Are you okay?"

"Well…the tumor's getting bigger, and I think I'd like to…you know. Wind down."

The words seemed to echo. Lucas looked out his window, automatically noting the Sears building, the Aon Center. "What can I do, Joe?" he asked, then cleared his throat.

"Can you come home for the duration? Bryce…he'll take this hard. And there are some things I'll need help with."

"Of course."

For the past eighteen months, Joe had been on dialysis; once a week at first, then twice, and now every other day. The kidney disease made him tired, but dialysis would keep him going almost indefinitely.

Unfortunately, a routine scan had discovered something more ominous—stage IV lung cancer, which would take him long before kidney failure, and Joe wanted to die on his own terms, as much as he could.

Joe was his only uncle, the older brother of Lucas's late father. Joe's wife, Didi, wasn't the nurturing type. Bryce, their son, was an overgrown kid, sorely lacking in pragmatism. Not like Lucas, though they were almost exactly the same age.

"Is Bryce still at the vineyard?" he asked. His cousin had gotten a job at one of the many small vineyards in the Finger Lakes area, where Joe and Didi lived.

"No, he left there. It wasn't for him," Joe said.

Ah. Lucas tried to remember if Bryce had ever had a paying job for more than three months and came up empty.

"I'd like to see him settled before…before long," Joe added. "You know. Employed. Happy. Stable."

Adult, Lucas thought. He'd spoken to Bryce a couple of weeks ago, but it was mostly about the White Sox.

Lucas hadn't been back to Manningsport in years. It wasn't as if it had ever been home—just a place he'd lived for four months.

"I'll make some arrangements, then," Lucas said. "Call you tonight, Joe."

Very gently, he hung up the phone.

So he'd be going back to Manningsport. Once more, he'd do his best to look out for Bryce. Once more, endure his aunt Didi, who'd only found him worthy of attention when he'd married Ellen Forbes, and still hadn't forgiven him for divorcing her.

And once more, he'd see Colleen O'Rourke.

CHAPTER THREE

"Hey, sugarplum!" Colleen said as her little sister wriggled into the first booth at O'Rourke's. "Nachos grande, coming up!"

Savannah's face lit up, then avalanched. "Oh, no thanks," she said, tugging at her formfitting purple shirt. "Maybe some water and a salad? Dressing on the side?"

Colleen paused. "You don't like Connor's nachos all of a sudden?"

It was a Friday evening tradition that Savannah came to the bar for supper while Dad and Gail went out on a date. Colleen, Connor and their sister would eat together, because even if Connor couldn't stand the sight of their father and didn't speak to Gail, he wasn't an ass. Both twins loved Savannah quite a bit. Tons, in fact.

But it was fair to say that the universe had been paying attention to Gail-the-Tail-Chianese-Rhymes-with-Easy-Hyphen-O'Rourke when she was pregnant with Savannah.

Nine years ago, Colleen had been visiting her father and the Tail, despite her father's infidelity and Gail's fertility, and had overheard Gail saying this: *If Colleen is pretty, imagine what our daughter will be like. Think it's too early to call a modeling agency?* Warm chuckles between the parents-to-be ensued, and Colleen had to stay in the cellar, where she'd been sent to hunt for a bottle of wine, until the bile surge subsided.

She imagined the baby *would* be beautiful. No such thing as ugly babies, after all. But she knew what Gail was saying. Colleen was pretty, something her father used to point out with great frequency…but Baby Girl 2.0 was going to be even better.

However, the karmic gods want to hear you praying for healthy children, not children with superior bone structure.

Savannah was not beautiful.

Colleen adored Savannah from the second she'd seen her at the hospital, with her little tubular head and snub nose. She changed diapers and took the baby for walks and rocked her and kissed her and sang to her, and Connor did the same, though with a lesser degree of fervor, being that he was a guy and all. But Colleen was in love.

Gail…not so much. Not enough, it seemed.

Savannah was wonderful and happy and funny, but she wasn't beautiful. Not like Gail, who was a mere four years older than Colleen, and not like Colleen. Savannah was stocky and pale, whiter even than most Irish, which was saying a lot; while Colleen had creamy skin and rosy cheeks, Savannah was practically translucent. Her face was dotted with giant freckles, rather than a sprinkling of cinnamon, and her pale eyes were set close together. Instead of Gail's Irish setter–auburn hair, Savannah's was a pinkish strawberry-blond.

She walked heavily, despite Gail trying to teach her to tiptoe through the house, a strong, strapping girl with a low center of gravity that made her a great catcher on O'Rourke's softball team, which Colleen managed in the town league. But she wasn't what Gail had expected.

Gail wasn't a bad mother. She made sure Savannah ate her veggies and got enough sleep, went to all her school activities and drove her to trumpet lessons, though Gail had petitioned hard for the flute or violin or something "more feminine." It was clear Savannah confused her. *She,* after all, was a size two. *Her* hair was long and glossy and straight. Green eyes, of course. Perky boobs (Savannah had not been a breast-is-best baby) and a great ass. She bought micro-shorts and cropped tops for Savannah, who preferred Yankees T-shirts and sweats.

"A salad, huh?" Colleen said now.

"Mom says I should lose some weight."

Colleen blinked. Savannah was solid. Sure, she had a little pudge. She was *nine.* Any second now, she'd shoot up five inches and things would balance out a bit more.

"Listen, sweets," Colleen began. "Eating healthy is smart. Your mom is right about that."

"I had a grilled pork chop for lunch. And broccoli," her sister said. "And water. No carbs."

For crying out loud. "Very nutritious. But everything in moderation, right? Nachos once a week isn't going to ruin you. And life without nachos, you know? Why bother?"

Her sister's smile lit up the room.

Ten minutes later, Connor set down the nachos and slid in next to Savannah, and all was as it should be. Savannah chattered happily about gym class and baseball (they were Yankees fans, of course). Connor let her come into the kitchen and drizzle sauce on the cheesecake desserts that were flying out of the kitchen, and Colleen let her take orders. All the regulars loved Savannah.

When Gail arrived to pick her up, she gave the girl a

hug, then inspected the salsa stain on her shirt, shooting Colleen a dirty look.

"Nachos," Colleen said. "It's our girls' night tradition."

"Mmm," Gail said. "Well. Good night." Savannah waved, grinning.

So, yes. There was a personal parallel between her sister and Colleen's other mission tonight: Paulie Petrosinsky and Bryce Campbell, Step One.

Like Savannah, Paulie lacked certain attributes deemed important by some. But it didn't mean Savannah and Paulie were any less deserving of true love with the man of their dreams (though, yes, Savannah would have to wait quite a few years for that, thank you very much). Tonight's mission: get Paulie on Bryce's radar.

Speaking of Paulie, in she came, wrapped in what appeared to be a dirty sheet that went past her knees. Colleen had said "soft" and "feminine" and "bright" when Paulie asked what to wear. Not "gray." She hadn't said the word *gray* once. The word *sheet* had also not been mentioned.

"How do I look?" Paulie asked. "The salesman said these worked on every figure so I bought six of them."

Colleen grabbed Paulie's arm and hustled her into the office in the back. "Get out, Connor. Wardrobe emergency."

"Then I should stay, don't you think?" he asked, not even looking up from the computer, where he was doing God knows what.

"Is something the matter?" Paulie asked. "Crap. You know what? This isn't gonna work. I think I'll go home."

"No, you're not, no you're not," Colleen said. "Courage, my friend. Just let me fix your hair a little, okay?

We're going for a soft, gamine look, and you used just a little too much product." Ow. Paulie's hair was stiff with gel. Colleen broke through and tousled it a bit for a slight improvement. "Let's ditch this, uh…this sweater, is it?" Colleen plucked at the gray fabric that swathed Paulie's muscular figure.

"No! It's a multi-look sweater," Paulie said, clutching it closed. "I have six of them."

"So you said."

Paulie's face was bright red, so Colleen reached across Connor to grab a folder and began fanning her, smiling encouragingly. "That's fine. The sweater can stay. It's…it's an interesting piece." Confidence, she well knew, was the key to true beauty.

"You can wear it seventeen different ways," Paulie said. "Like this, my favorite, just sort of flowing—" And it did flow, almost all the way to the floor, since Paulie was about five-one. "And then you can take the ends and wrap it around your neck—"

"Why would you do that?" Colleen said. "To hang yourself?"

"And then you can make it even into a dress, see, like this. Or a scarf. Even a skirt."

"'It's a sock, it's a sheet, it's a bicycle seat,'" Connor said in a singsong voice. "Remember that, Coll? *The Lorax?* What was that thing they made from the Truffula trees?"

"A Thneed," Colleen said. "Here. Let me drape it… um…great. There!" Okay, it was a weird sweater, but if Paulie thought she looked good in it….

"It hides a lot of flaws," Paulie said.

"You don't have flaws. You're very strong and healthy-looking."

"I heard you can bench-press two twenty-five," Connor said, earning a kick from Colleen.

"True," Paulie said proudly.

"And that's great," Colleen said. "But tonight, let's focus on femininity. No, don't panic. We're just planting the seeds, that's all. Just planting seeds."

"Or Thneeds," Connor said.

"Shut it, Connor. Why are you still here, anyway? Go cook something."

He obeyed (finally).

"No need to be nervous, Paulie," she said more gently. "You've known Bryce for aeons—"

"Tell me about it," she muttered, her face going blotchy.

"—and he already likes you."

"He likes everyone."

True. Bryce didn't have a mean bone in his body. Or an ugly bone, either. Which was why women launched themselves at him like hypersonic missiles.

"Now tonight," Colleen said, "you just want to get his attention, okay? As a woman, not as his buddy. Don't talk about sports, don't mention how much you can bench-press. Just say something like, 'Oh, hey, Bryce! You look really handsome tonight.'"

From Paulie came the sounds of a dry heave.

"Now, now," Colleen said. "It's gonna be fine. Bryce *is* handsome. We all know that. So you just remind him that you're here and female and fabulous. I want you to just brush against his arm, like this, just a little swoop of the breast, okay? A breast-swoop." She demonstrated, pressing the girls lightly against Paulie's shoulder.

"You smell great," Paulie said.

"That would be a perfect thing to tell him."

"No, I meant you. You smell really nice."

Colleen paused. "Thanks. Now take a deep breath." She looked down at Paulie's kind, flushed face. "This is just the shark-bump test. Just to bring you onto his radar."

"Got it. Shark. Radar." She was hyperventilating.

"Breathe in for four, hold for four, exhale for four, that's a girl. I know Bryce's usual type, and guess what? They're not right for him, are they, or else he'd be married right now. Just imagine that he's been waiting for you all his life."

"No need to sell it that hard, Coll."

"It's called confidence." She squeezed Paulie's hard shoulders. "I'll be right behind the bar."

"What if I screw up? What if he laughs at me? What if I puke and—"

"Calm down. Remember, you're smart, you're an executive at a successful company, you have what, an MBA? Everyone likes you, Paulie. Bryce just needs a little…strategy, and he'll see you for the amazing person you are. And if you really love him, he's worth the effort, right?"

"Yeah. He is." Paulie stood up a little straighter.

"So let's go. I hate to be cliché, but I want you drinking a martini or a mojito. No more Genesee."

"Feminine, fabulous, martini, mojito."

"Perfect. And next time, wear a girly color. Not gray."

"It's fog."

"It's gray, Paulie. You came to me, remember? I'm the expert. So no Thneed next time."

Paulie cracked her neck. "What if—just putting this out there—what if I panic?"

"Um… I'll give you a sign."

"Really? That would be so great, Colleen!"

"I'll do this. See?" She tossed her hair back in the time-honored fertility gesture women used to get men to notice how shiny they were. "Hair flip equals abort, abort. You pretend your phone is ringing and you just step away. Okay?"

"Roger that."

Colleen took the shorter woman by the shoulders. "You're special, and he'd be lucky to have you."

Paulie smiled, even if her breathing was labored. She really did have a sweet smile. "Okay. Thanks, Coll. If you say so."

"I do. Now get out there and make me proud. Don't forget your lines."

"Hi, Bryce, you smell so hot."

"No, no, we don't want him to think he smells like meat on a grill. It's, 'Hi, Bryce! Don't you look handsome tonight.'"

"Hi, Bryce, don't you look so beautiful tonight."

"Handsome." Colleen smiled firmly.

"And handsome, too."

"You look handsome tonight, Bryce."

"So do you."

"Close enough. Go get 'em," Colleen said. "I'll be eavesdropping."

She held the door for Paulie and went behind the bar, pulled a Guinness for Gerard, automatically smiled at his compliment because he was a schmoozer of the first class, and watched her protégé.

There weren't too many people here; it was a Tuesday in late May, and the summer season hadn't really begun yet, so she had a great view.

She really hoped this went well. She owed Paulie a little happiness.

When they were in sixth grade, something happened to Paulie. Her hair turned greasy, her face broke out and she thickened without growing in height. Not a big deal. After all, Faith had epilepsy, Jessica Dunn wore hand-me-downs, Asswipe Jones's dandruff could've been covered by The Weather Channel. Paulie's awkwardness wasn't that big a deal.

But then came The Smell. A not-very-good smell that wafted from Paulie. The other kids noticed it but didn't say anything. Not at first. But then whispers started, and Paulie seemed completely unaware, smiling, blushing, always being so damn nice.

One day, several of Colleen's crowd decided to talk to their English teacher about it. Mrs. Hess was young, pretty and nice and had a Southern accent, which they all found terribly exotic. Sure enough, the teacher listened sympathetically.

"I hear what y'all are sayin'," she said. "And here's what I think should be done. It'd be a genuine favor if one of y'all took Miss Paulie aside and just told her the truth. Otherwise, how's she gonna know, bless her heart?"

Colleen was immediately elected as the bearer of bad news. If anyone could say it, it was Colleen. Personally, Coll thought Faith would be even better at it, but no, the other girls said Colleen was good at that sort of thing. And so, the next day, Mrs. Hess asked Paulie to stay in at recess, and then said, "Colleen here has something she'd like to discuss with you, Paulie," she said with a smile, then slipped from the room.

"What's up?" Paulie asked. There was a hopeful look

in her eyes, and Colleen felt her heart spasm a little. She'd been sick with nervousness all day long as it was, and the greasy cafeteria pizza at lunch hadn't helped.

Colleen was popular; not mean-girl popular, just really well liked. She had the glamour of being a twin, not to mention her prettiness and ease with boys. Paulie had none of those things (except that everyone thought she was nice). But already, before she said a word, Colleen *knew* this wasn't going to go well.

"So," she said, sitting next to Paulie, who was clad in rust-colored corduroys and bedazzled sweatshirt. Damn. Faith would've been perfect for this job… Faith the sweet, the kind, the slightly tragic, would've had just the right touch. "Okay, well, here's the thing, Paulie."

"Yeah?"

Colleen's stomach didn't feel so good. She could almost taste the bitter smell. Didn't Paulie's mother talk to her about stuff? She cleared her throat. "Some of us were talking," she said, biting her thumbnail. "And… uh, it was about things that, um, happen to some people when you're a teenager and stuff."

Paulie frowned. "Oh."

Colleen's stomach lurched. "It's nothing bad, Paulie. You're really nice and smart and stuff. But, um… well…there's a certain…smell? There's a funky smell around you." She winced. "I'm sorry."

Paulie looked at Colleen a horrible, long minute, then bowed her head. "I don't smell," she whispered.

Colleen swallowed. There was that taste again. Why had the other girls elected her? Why hadn't Mrs. Hess said something instead, or had Paulie see the nurse, who could talk about hormones and whatever? "I'm sorry," she said again. "But you do. It's hard to sit next to you sometimes."

"Who was talking about this?" she whispered, and a single tear slid down her face and landed on the molded plastic desktop.

"Just…a few of us. I—we thought you should know."

"I don't smell!" Paulie yelled, then pushed back from the desk and ran out of the room.

And Colleen threw up. Not because of the smell… because of shame. Shame and greasy pizza. But the rumor flashed—Paulie smelled so bad that she made Colleen puke.

Paulie didn't come back to school for the rest of the week, and Colleen had never felt so small. She told only Connor about the conversation, and when he said, "Oh, Coll," she knew for sure she'd done something terrible.

Later that month, they learned that Paulie had bigger problems. Her mother had run off with another man, and Paulie would be living with her dad from now on. When she returned to school, she had a new haircut. Her clothes were better, and the smell was still there, but it was fainter. Eventually, it went away altogether.

A thousand times, Colleen wanted to apologize; a thousand times, she convinced herself that it was kinder not to bring it up. In tenth grade, they were assigned to the same group for a social studies project, and Paulie couldn't have been nicer.

So if Colleen wanted to help Paulie with her love life, who could blame her?

Paulie stood in the vicinity of Bryce's usual spot at the bar. Gerard said hi to her, but Paulie didn't answer, just stared at Colleen as if she was facing a firing squad.

"How about a mojito, Paulie?" she said cheerfully, tossing some mint into a glass.

"Sure," Paulie mumbled, rubbing her hands on her sweater.

And then in came Bryce Campbell, all easy male grace, tall and lanky, dressed in a white polo shirt and jeans. He waved and made his way to his usual place at the horseshoe-style bar. A strangled noise came from Paulie.

Colleen handed her the drink. "Hey, Bryce, don't you look handsome tonight," she whispered.

"Coll, you could whisper to me?" Gerard said. "I can think of a whole bunch of things I'd like you to say."

"Shush, child, I'm talking to my friend," she answered. She gave Paulie a firm smile. "Now's good."

"I'm not ready," Paulie whispered.

"Yes, you are."

"No, I can't. Can you do it for me?"

"Like we're in third grade, and you want me to tell him you like him?"

"Yes. Please."

"No. Come on now. Handsome, shark, boobs, smile. And then you're done. Now go."

With a faint groan, Paulie inched toward Bryce, who was at the end of the bar, talking to Jessica Dunn. Hmm. Jess was way too pretty, all blonde and super-model-esque, Bryce's usual type.

Paulie stopped just behind him and shot Colleen a terrified glance and appeared to freeze. Luckily, Hannah was behind the bar, too, so Colleen boob-skimmed her.

"Get your boobs off me. Sexual harassment and all that," Hannah said.

"Shh." She smiled firmly at Paulie, who took a deep breath, swung her shoulders and bodychecked him right off his stool, Jessica Dunn stepping neatly aside as Bryce sprawled on the floor. Colleen's view was all too clear. "Goddamn it!" Paulie said. She reached down to help him up, tripped on the dangling end of the Thneed, stepped on Bryce's hand and spilled her mojito right onto his head. "Shit! Shit!"

So much for soft and feminine. Colleen tossed her hair for the "abort" sign. Paulie didn't notice, Gerard was wheezing with laughter, one of those guys who loved nothing more than the physical pain of others (he was a paramedic, after all). Now Paulie was hauling Bryce to his feet, but she was too strong, and she yanked him not only up, but slammed him into the bar, causing the hanging glasses to rattle and sway.

Colleen tossed her hair again. Coughed. Coughed again more loudly. Tossed. Coughed. Tossed. Cough 'n' tossed.

"Wow, Paulie, easy does it, okay?" Bryce said, rubbing his arm at the shoulder. Paulie's face was broiling-red. She took both ends of the Thneed and twisted them in anguish.

Another hair toss, this one so hard Colleen thought she might've dislocated her neck, and still Paulie didn't see her. Colleen threw up her hands.

"What are you doing?" said a low voice behind her.

Colleen's heart froze, as though she'd swallowed a large ice cube, and it was stuck right over her heart.

She turned around.

Yep. Lucas Campbell.

None other. Standing approximately two feet from her, looking at her with those knowing, dark eyes.

Her skin suddenly felt tight. Mouth: dry. Brain: dead.

"What are you doing, Colleen?" Lucas asked again.

"Nothing," she said as if it hadn't been ten years since she'd last seen him. "What are *you* doing?"

"I'm here to see my cousin."

"So go see your cousin."

"What are you doing to my cousin?"

"I'm not doing anything to your cousin." So mature. And did they have nothing else to say to each other? Ten years apart? A river of tears (hers) and blood (his... well, she wished it was his blood).

Lucas just looked at her, his pirate eyes unreadable. Shit.

Of all the gin joints in all the world, she started thinking, then squelched a blossom of slightly hysterical laughter.

Lucas Damien Campbell was *here*. Here in her bar. You think he could've called? Would that have been so much to ask, huh? Hmm? Would it? *Hey, Colleen, I'm coming to visit my cousin, so be prepared, okay?*

Colleen took a ragged breath, then coughed to cover. Unfortunately, the cough became genuine, and tears came to her eyes as she hacked and choked.

"You okay?" he asked in that ridiculously sexy, river-of-dark-chocolate voice.

"Yes," she wheezed, wiping her eyes. "Just great."

"Good."

He dragged his eyes off of hers and looked over at the little knot of people at the end of the bar; Jess was laughing, Bryce smiling and Paulie looked like she was praying for a swift death.

"Are you trying to fix Bryce up with Paulina Petrosinsky?" he asked. Damn. She'd forgotten how…observant he was.

"No," she said, proud of getting that one word out.

"Yes, you are."

"No, I'm not."

"Yes. You are." He raised an eyebrow, and her knees wobbled. Sphincter! He was *here*. Here and beautiful, and damn it, older. A *decade* older than the last time she'd seen him, and yet it seemed like yesterday when he'd walked with her down to the lake and broke her heart. Irreparably, the bastard.

Her breath wanted to rush out of her lungs, but she held it in carefully, not wanting to induce another sexy choking fit.

She'd forgotten how he looked, like a pirate, like Heathcliff of the moors, dark and slightly dangerous…except for his eyes, which could be so sad. And so happy, too.

His black hair was slightly shorter than it had been years ago, but still gypsy beautiful, curling and black. He'd lost his boyish skinniness, had broadened in the shoulders. He hadn't shaved today, and he seemed taller now than he had back then.

Back when he loved her.

He seemed to read her mind, because something flickered through his eyes.

In the year after Lucas left her, Bryce would come into the bar and mention him occasionally. *Went to see my cousin last weekend,* or *Hey, Lucas is taking me and Dad to a White Sox game!* Finally, in a rare show of vulnerability, Colleen had asked him not to talk about Lucas anymore. And in an even rarer show of understanding, Bryce seemed to get it.

She knew he was married. No kids—surely Smiling Joe Campbell would've mentioned that. She knew he worked for his father-in-law. That was about it.

She had told him never to call her again, never to write, and he took her at her word.

And now, her heart was jackhammering in her chest, and though she hoped like hell her heart wasn't written all over her face, she was…terrified.

Lucas took a breath. "Colleen, I'm only back in town because Joe asked me to come. I imagine you know he's pretty sick."

Her heart gave an unwilling tug. "I do," she said, then, fearing that sounded a little too matrimonial, she added, "Know he's sick. I do know he's sick, I mean. He's sick, I know it, the dialysis, not easy, I guess, and I'm sorry." Her Tourette's of Terror, Connor called it when she babbled. Not that she was terrified often, but hell, she certainly was now.

"Thank you." He glanced again at Bryce—right, right, there was something going on with Bryce tonight, whatever—then looked at Colleen again. "It's good to see you."

"Can't say the same," she answered.

His mouth tugged on one side, causing a respondent tug in her special places. Five more minutes, and she'd be back in love.

"Bryce doesn't need more complications in his life right now."

"And by complications, you mean what, exactly?"

"The Chicken King's virgin daughter."

"Oh, cool! That sounds like a Harlequin romance. I would definitely read that." The Chicken King's virgin daughter was nowhere to be seen at the moment.

"And how do you know Paulie's a virgin, huh? Maybe she's the town slut."

Yeah. This wasn't going well.

"I doubt she's the town slut."

She bristled. "What are you implying, Lucas?"

He gave her a strange look. "Nothing. Just that Paulie doesn't seem like the type."

"Well, what if she *is* a slut, huh? Maybe Bryce likes sluts." *Time to shut up now,* Connor's voice—her conscience—advised sagely.

"I'm sure he does."

"So what's your problem, then?"

"I'm trying to have a rational conversation here."

"Yeah, and I haven't seen you in ten years, and you just waltz into my bar and start insulting me and bossing me around. I do know about your uncle and how sick he is, because guess what? I visit him. I like him. I bring him magazines and cookies, and he likes my dog."

"You have a dog?"

"Yes, I do, so just…you just, um, put that in your pipe and suck on it." *Smooth, O'Rourke.* She tried to look haughty and dignified. "Maybe I happen to think that Bryce needs someone to help him through this difficult time."

"Maybe he has other things to deal with."

"And maybe I'm right and you're wrong."

He tilted his head to one side. "I'm getting the sense that you're still mad."

"I'm not."

"Leave my cousin alone, all right?"

"Make me."

He rolled his beautiful (damn them) eyes and walked over to Bryce, hugging him.

Humph. He hadn't hugged her.

"Let's stop being stupid, shall we?" she muttered to herself.

Lucas said something, then smiled. Shit, that was a *good* smile. Hardly ever saw it, that was the trick. She, on the other hand, smiled like a pubescent monkey or jackal or hyena or some other animal that smiled a lot. "What do you think?" she asked Victor Iskin, a regular at the bar who had a well-documented love of animals. "Do hyenas smile more than monkeys?"

"Yes," he answered.

"Do I look like a hyena right now?"

"Can't say that you do, dear."

"Colleen! Leave the customers alone!" Connor called from the kitchen.

Lucas and Bryce were leaving, thank the sweet Christ child.

Her hands were shaking. She heard an odd sound; it was her, sucking air.

"Who was that?"

Colleen gave herself a mental shake. "Hey. Paulie. How'd it go?"

"I knocked him down, stepped on his hand, spilled a drink on his head, yanked his arm, hurled him into the bar and then hid."

"That's good," Colleen murmured.

Paulie frowned, then looked at Colleen more closely. "Who was that? The guy you were talking to. He looked familiar."

"That's…that's Bryce's cousin."

"Oh, man, I remember him! Lucas, right?" Paulie ran a hand through her hair. "You were together, weren't you?"

"Yeah." She closed her eyes.

"Well, shit. Are you still in love with him?"

"No!"

"Are your special places tingling?"

"Excuse me? No. No, that's…of course not. I mean…
he broke my heart. First love and all that crap. A long
time ago."

"Yeah, well, I'd give anything to have Bryce look at
me the way Lucas was looking at you."

"We were fighting."

"I'd give anything to have Bryce fight with me that
way." Paulie raised her eyebrows.

A change of subject was definitely needed. "Okay,
so tonight's Bryce encounter didn't go as planned," she
said. "The good news is, you got his attention, right?
That's the first step."

"The first step in his filing a restraining order against
me, maybe."

"Oh, come on. Bryce probably doesn't know what a
restraining order is."

"He's not dumb, Colleen."

Colleen winced. "No, you're right. Sorry. Anyway,
you were memorable, so it's not all bad."

As she and Paulie talked, there was another voice
in her head. Common sense, call it. *Don't fall for those
eyes again. Don't notice his hands, or his mouth. Those
are just tricks. We're not doing this again.*

Already, it felt like she was in a whole lotta trouble.

CHAPTER FOUR

THE FIRST TIME she ever saw Lucas Damien Campbell, Colleen fell in love.

Not that she was a believer in that kind of thing.

Even at the tender age of eleven, when her mother had sobbed through yet another sappy romantic comedy, Colleen pointed out the fact that the characters had known each other for only six days, so it was a little hard to buy into the whole everlasting soul mate philosophy. In seventh grade, Tim Jansen sent her a letter full of hyperbolic compliments ("your eyes are shinier than a mirror," which Colleen thought was creepy and hoped wasn't true) and anguished love ("I feel like my heart will explode when you smile at me"). She patted his hand and said he probably should take up a sport to channel some of that energy.

High school was no different, though the boys abruptly grew taller...despite the abundance of hormones, despite her abiding love for Robert Downey, Jr., Colleen remained above the fray. No, she'd rather hang out with her brother, laugh at his friends, and watch Faith and Jeremy, the perfect couple, with fondness and a satisfying bit of melancholy. By the time she was a senior, virtually every boy in Manningsport had asked her out and received a kindly "no." Love—especially the sloppy, frenching-in-the-halls type—was not meant for Colleen Margaret Mary O'Rourke.

"What do you mean, you're not going to prom?" her mother asked one night around the family dinner table. Con was going with Sherry Wong, a mathlete like himself. "Hasn't anyone asked you?"

"Nine guys have asked her, Ma," Connor offered, taking another shovelful of mashed potatoes.

"It's not for me," Colleen said easily. "Drama, rayon dresses, crepe paper, the inevitable tears. I'll pass."

"That's my girl," Dad said with an approving nod. Connor sighed, and Colleen could feel his mood drop several degrees. It was no secret that Colleen was their father's favorite.

People like them, Dad said once in a while, were too smart for that. Just what *that* was, Colleen wasn't sure, but she was flattered to be included. Her father's approval was everything. Connor was smart, too—smarter, at least according to his grades, but "we think alike," Dad would say.

Pete O'Rourke was still handsome enough to get stares from women of all ages—black Irish, the same clear gray eyes Colleen had, unlike Connor's blue. He was the youngest of his family, widely viewed to be the star of the family by his older sisters, who fussed over him at family gatherings, getting him plates of food as if he were an invalid, cooing over his latest real estate coup. In town, men shook his hand, laughed loudly at his jokes, came to him for advice—Dad owned six of the fifteen commercial buildings in town.

Mom was still sappily infatuated with him, which Colleen found both cute and annoying. When his car pulled into the driveway, she'd rush to ditch her slippers, shove her feet into heels and put on lipstick. If he commented on her appearance, "Jeanette, is that a new hairstyle?" she'd flush with pleasure. "Oh, thank you!" she'd say, not quite noticing that it wasn't exactly a compliment. And Dad would give Colleen a little wink of collusion, which made her feel simultaneously guilty and clever.

Mom never finished college, knocked up in the great tradition of the O'Rourke family. She worked part-time for an interior designer and actually could've joined the firm; her boss quite liked her, but she always said no. "Your father is such a good provider," she'd say.

Slightly overweight, she'd go on fad diets before the holidays or the annual Manningsport Black & White Ball, get her hair done, buy a new dress…but still, Mom always looked a little older, a little frumpier, a little less certain than Dad. Pete O'Rourke was, there was no mistaking it, one of those guys who got better with age, Manningsport's version of Pierce Brosnan: the graying hair, the extreme good looks.

To Colleen, the best compliment she could get was that she was her father's girl. Except when Mom said it, for some reason; there'd be a slight and rare tinge of bitterness in her voice. Then again, Mom loved Connor best. It was only fair.

So yeah, a high school romance, prom, and all that… leave that for the other girls: Theresa and Faith, who'd marry their high school honeys, no doubt. Let other girls worry over boys (or girls, in the case of Deirdre and Tiffy). Colleen would give advice to the girls, deflect advances from the boys, cheerful and observant and not at all lonely…not with a twin and a best friend and adoring father. It was exactly how she wanted things.

And then she met Lucas Campbell.

It was big news, of course. Manningsport had a tiny year-round population; just about any change was cause for excitement.

"Kids," said Mrs. Wheaton, their beleaguered English teacher, adjusting her corduroy (ouch) jumper, "we have two new students joining our class shortly." She consulted her paperwork. "Bryce and Lucas Campbell. Uh…cousins, it says here. Please be nice."

"Is Bryce a boy's name?" Tanya Cross asked. She wasn't tremendously bright.

"Yes," Mrs. Wheaton asked. "Now, getting back to *Hamlet*. Does anyone have an opinion on Ophelia?"

No one bothered answering. A ripple went through the class. *Two* new members of the senior class? Jeremy Lyon had transferred in last summer, and look how totally awesome he was! Could lightning strike twice? The girls began either whispering to or ignoring each other. Posture: improved. Hair: tossed. Legs: crossed. Lips: licked.

The guys in the class exchanged glances, aware that two new roosters in the henhouse would shift the dynamic. Well, not all the boys. Asswipe Jones was sleeping (hungover, probably), and Levi Cooper stared at Jessica with that hot look of his. Jeremy was running a hand through his own dark hair.

As for Colleen, she didn't need to sit up or lick or cross. She already had it going on. (False modesty—not one of her flaws.) Still, she too glanced at the door. Just because she didn't want to date anyone didn't mean she didn't want to be acknowledged as, yes, the prettiest girl in high school, the funniest and the most sought-after.

The door opened, and in came the newbies.

There was a stunned silence, then a collective murmur.

"Oh, my God," Tanya breathed.

Yep, the first guy was a looker. Blue, blue eyes, sweet smile, dark brown hair that was styled but not too embarrassing. Dimple in his left cheek. Were Colleen the dating type, she'd probably be all over that. His eyes stopped on her, his smile widened, which was gratifying. Colleen allowed a faint smile back. The not-quite-catty thought came to her—she could have him if she wanted. Which she didn't, but still.

Then she noticed the second guy. Her smile faltered.

Holy St. Patrick. Her face didn't change (she hoped), but her body was…was *doing* things. Stomach tightened, mouth dried, knees (and other parts) tingled. She acknowledged the feelings from afar because her brain couldn't quite function at the moment.

He looked a lot like the other boy, but he was darker. Not quite as good-looking…well, no. Not quite as perfect, but a *lot* more compelling. Black hair instead of brown, olive skin and deep, dark eyes.

He looked like a Spanish pirate. Like a Romany gypsy. Like Heathcliff in *Wuthering Heights,* and like Heathcliff, there was something about his expression that said he knew things, saw things, that he wasn't as sweet or as easy or as simple as the boy who stood next to him.

"Now, which one of you is Bryce?" Mrs. Wheaton asked.

"I am," said the blue-eyed guy. "This is my cousin Lucas. He lives with us." And even though Bryce made the introduction, it was Lucas who shook hands with Mrs. W. first, causing his cousin to follow suit, and Colleen could sense the dynamic: Lucas, the cousin who lived with "us," was in charge.

"Nice to meet you," the gypsy boy said, and Colleen just about slid out of her chair in lust. Because that *voice,* good God, did eighteen-year-old boys really get to sound like that? It was deep and mellow and just a little rough and caused a reverberation in Colleen's special places, and what the hell would happen if he actually spoke to her?

"Welcome, boys," Mrs. Wheaton said. "Find a seat, if you'd be so kind." There was a tremendous screech as the female half of the class pushed their chairs back to make room for the newcomers.

Lucas went past Colleen, and it was horrifying, embarrassing, *thrilling* to have her heart pound so hard. He smelled like soap and sunshine and wore faded jeans and black Converse, and that was all she saw because she didn't dare look at him. *Don't talk to me, don't talk to me,* her brain chanted. He didn't, just went past to the back of the room, the longest four seconds of her life. Her cheeks burned—honestly, a *boy* making *her* cheeks burn? This never happened!—and she stared at the words in her book. *I do not know, my Lord, what I should think.*

Preach it, Ophelia.

Where was he? Was he looking at her? Who was he sitting next to? A girl? Probably a girl. Jessica? She always sat in the back. She'd probably already given him her number. They were probably already planning a hookup, because everyone knew Jess just used Levi for sex. Would the Spanish pirate boy go for someone like that? Colleen would lose all respect, not that she had any just yet, but you know, she could already feel herself getting mad, boys were so stupid, and—

"How's it going?" Bryce asked. He'd sat down next to her, and she hadn't quite noticed.

"Great," she said. "I'm Colleen. Welcome to Manningsport."

"Nice meeting you," he said with an easy grin.

Where was Lucas? What was he thinking? Would he like her, too? Because it was obvious that what's-his-name, Bryce, already did, though he was now talking to Tanya, who was being super-duper helpful and sharing her copy of *Hamlet* with him, pressing her boob against his arm. Colleen hoped he liked the smell of Eternity perfume, because Tanya practically bathed in it.

She wanted very much to turn around and see the gypsy boy. Also, she should probably stop referring to him as *pirate* or *gypsy*. Even mentally.

She didn't turn. She was too smart for that, as Dad pointed out.

She didn't feel so smart now.

For the next thirty-one minutes, she tried to concentrate on *Hamlet*. Never before had she been quite so interested in the words coming out of Mrs. Wheaton's mouth. Not that she could actually understand them, mind you, but Colleen assiduously took notes, keeping her handwriting tidy, mentally repeating phrases like "preoccupation with death," "theme of decomposition." And in the meantime, her entire body pulsed with hot, almost painful throbs and a vague sense of danger, the same as last summer, when they'd gone swimming on Cape Cod the day after a shark attack. Just because you couldn't see it, didn't mean it wasn't there. Waiting.

"Come on, idiot," her brother said, nudging her head with his backpack. "Physics lab. Snap out of it."

Ah. Class had ended, then. Lucas and Bryce were

talking to Mrs. Wheaton. Colleen stood up and gave her brother a look. "I was taking notes. Thank me later when I save you from flunking the test."

"I don't need notes," Connor said, going on ahead.

She carefully didn't look at Lucas...well, not directly. Wouldn't want to give the impression that she *couldn't* look at Lucas, so she did the drive-by glance...gaze just skimming the face, looking away the instant before his eyes could meet hers, a faint smile on her face, so very pleasant. "Bye, Mrs. Wheaton," she said. "Bye, boys." Because Colleen O'Rourke wasn't bothered by the male species. She was too smart for that.

For the next three weeks, Colleen managed not to speak to Lucas Campbell. Bryce, she found, was as friendly as Smiley, the Holland family's Golden retriever, and about as smart. Bryce was quite beautiful and fun to look at, and she found herself flirting with him harmlessly, same as she did with all the other boys. He could volley it back pretty well, though most of her jokes went over his head. Still, he had long eyelashes and beautiful blue eyes and always seemed happy.

His cousin...well, Colleen didn't know what he was like. She gave him the occasional drive-by, not wanting to ignore him outright because of what that might reveal.

Tanya Cross who was as determined as she was irritating, asked Bryce to the prom. Bryce then sealed Tanya's bitchery by asking Colleen if she'd go with him, and could she give an answer because "that Tanya chick wants to go with me."

"Sorry, pal," she said, patting him on the arm like a fond auntie. "It's not really my thing. You go with Tanya. She's sweet." Which Tanya wasn't, but it wouldn't be nice to say so…plus, it would irritate Tanya all the more to know that Colleen had been totally classy.

Had Lucas asked her to go, her answer might've been a lot different.

He didn't.

Lucas wasn't going and had turned down four girls before it had been ascertained that no, he *wasn't* waiting for someone else to ask him; he just wasn't going. This, of course, was widely and voraciously analyzed every time two or more girls gathered in a classroom, hall, cafeteria, gym, bakery, school bus or mall and via phone, text, email, sign language and smoke signals.

Oh, the delicious and frustrating mystery of it! No one knew why Lucas lived with Bryce. Their fathers were brothers, and Bryce said only that "it worked out best." Bryce's mother worked for an insurance company that had a branch in Corning, a half hour away; hence the senior-year move from Illinois.

Bryce's dad was the one who showed up at Bryce's soccer games, sitting with his nephew, talking easily. The fondness between them was reassuring to Colleen. Lucas Campbell was no Heathcliff (thank heavens, because she knew how irresistible those types were).

Still, Lucas had a tinge of tragedy about him: his own mother dead; details of the father unknown, though speculated upon greatly—mafioso, movie star, eccentric billionaire, prison, gay, defrocked priest. Coll pretended not to listen but ate up every word.

The week before prom was consumed with talk of dresses, hairstyles, shoes and how to stop a guy from going too far. Despite her own utter lack of experience, Colleen was asked for advice and doled it out, sounding quite expert to her own ears—*tell him beforehand how far you're comfortable going, or just say, "that's far enough," no, don't french on the dance floor, it's so tacky, and whatever you do, don't have unprotected sex.*

On prom night, she took pictures of Connor, helped Sherry pin on his corsage because Sherry had it bad for Con and couldn't quite manage it as her hands were shaking. Colleen wished them a merry prom and waved with her parents as the limo pulled away, filled with the other four couples as well as Con and Sherry. "Kids today. They grow so fast," she sighed happily. "What are we doing tonight, parents?"

"I thought we'd watch movies," Mom said hopefully. "I made Rice Krispies treats."

"Oh, hooray," Colleen said. "Dad? You in?"

"I have to go to check on some properties," he said a bit tersely.

"Okay. I'll come and help," Colleen offered, a twinge of guilt at instantly changing plans. "We can watch movies a little later, Mom."

"Sure!" Mom said with forced good cheer. "I'll tag along, too." She frowned, her sweet face soft.

"No. I'll go alone. You girls stay here," he said in that voice he used when he was irritated.

"Roger that," Colleen said, keeping her voice light. Experience had shown that when Dad was in a bad mood, there was no point in arguing.

"Don't be silly. We'll go with you, and we can all get some dinner afterward, and it'll be really fun?" Mom suggested, her voice ending in a question mark. Colleen wished she wouldn't be like that.

"I said, I'll go alone. Okay? I have some business to take care of."

"Sure!" Mom said, and Colleen had to stifle an eye

roll. She loved her mom, of course, but…well. "Of course, Pete! We'll keep the home fires warm."

Dad forced a smile, then kissed Colleen's cheek. "I'm sure the other girls are glad you're not going tonight, honey. All their dates would be after you."

"Hmm," Colleen said. It was a slightly insulting insinuation—she'd never steal someone else's guy, and she liked to think that most other girls quite adored her—but she knew Dad meant it as a compliment.

And so she and Mom ate the sticky treats and admired Matthew McConaughey's abs, Mom sitting with the house phone *and* her cell on the arm of her chair, just in case Dad changed his mind.

He didn't, but around eleven, the phone rang. It was Faith, urging her to come to the after party at her boyfriend's lovely house.

"Okay if I go up to the Lyons', Ma?" she asked her dozing mother.

"Oh, sure," Mom said. "Did your father call?"

"Nope. Why don't you go to bed? Con and I will be home later."

"Want to take the car?" Mom asked.

"Nah. I'll walk." Jeremy only lived a half mile away from the O'Rourke house, and she could get a ride home.

"Okay. Make sure you're smart, sweetheart." Her code for "don't drink, don't do drugs, don't have unprotected sex, don't get kidnapped, don't eat tuna fish" (she had a strange fear of tuna, for some reason).

"I was born smart." She kissed her mother's cheek. "See you later."

The Lyon parents were exceptional hosts; nothing was more fun than one of their parties because they were the cool parents—the kind who knew how to be welcoming and funny and also how to disappear and let the kids do their thing.

The entire senior class was there, it seemed, and gourmet pizzas were being served, in addition to three kinds of green salad, ciabatta sandwiches and designer pop, and yards and yards of organic snack food and desserts. "Hi, Mrs. Lyon," Colleen said. "Thanks for having us!"

"Colleen, why on earth didn't you go to your prom?" she asked.

"I have an old soul," Colleen answered, getting a fond chuckle as a reply.

Most of her classmates were in the huge finished basement. 'N Sync played from the hidden speakers, and a fire crackled in the stone fireplace. Colleen saw Connor, who was nodding as Sherry talked. He shot her a look that she read perfectly, courtesy of their psychic twin connection—*I'm dying here, curse of the nice guy, please save me.* She blinked at him. *You should've listened to me, shmuck-o. Suffer on.* He responded with a subtle middle finger. But hey! She'd warned him. Sherry had had a crush on Connor since preschool, something Connor had refuted until a few weeks ago.

Faith and Jeremy were snuggled on the couch, the golden couple, prom king and queen, of course, as if anyone else had a chance. Some guys were playing pool while their dates gossiped or sulked in a gaggle nearby. Funny thing about prom; no one ever had as much fun as they were supposed to. Except Faith and Jeremy, of course.

Bryce Campbell, looking pretty beautiful in his tux, gave her a sloppy wave. Colleen instantly pegged him as being a bit drunk. Must've snuck in some booze, because the Lyon elders would've called his parents if they'd noticed he'd been drinking. Tanya added a sharp look and put her arm around Bryce's waist. Please. Colleen was so not the type to swoop in and ruin someone's night. She drifted over to them. "You look gorgeous, Tanya!" she said, getting a fake smile from the girl. "And you, pal, very handsome." She leaned in. "No more drinking here, got it?" she whispered. "And no driving."

"Got it, Coll," he said with a smile.

She got a bottle of Virgil's root beer, made the rounds, admired the gowns of the girls, winked at the boys and generally schmoozed, comfortable as the grand dame of the senior class. Part of things, but above them. A modern-day Emma, her favorite Jane Austen heroine. She ascertained that her brother was still trapped as Sherry moved in to try to kiss him, and once again smilingly rejected his silent plea for help. Revenge for the time he locked her in the cedar closet for six hours when they were ten.

At about midnight, it was decided by half the group that a visit to the lake was in order; for one, it was a gorgeous May night, the sky gleaming with stars, the air soft and gentle and just cool enough for cuddling; and two, those who wanted to have sex or drink could drift off to wherever without getting busted by Mr. and Mrs. Lyon. The good kids stayed put, and Colleen figured she would, too.

Until she saw Bryce Campbell fumbling for his keys.

"Hey, buddy," she said, earning yet another glare from Tanya. "You're not driving, are you?"

"Oh, I'm fine, don't even worry about me," he slurred. So much for her warning. Was there a creature on earth more stupid than an eighteen-year-old boy? "I'm totally fine, Colleen. You're pretty, you know that?"

"You're not driving. Let Tanya… Oh, right." Tanya had flunked her driver's test three times already.

Colleen could tell the Lyons, of course. But then they'd call Bryce's parents, and who wanted to be the kid who turned in a friend?

"How about if I drive, then?" she offered.

"No *thanks,* Colleen," Tanya said. She really was quite dim.

"Your date's not sober, sweets. Besides, it'll be fun. You guys can sit in the back and cuddle, and I'll be your chauffeur."

"All right," Bryce said. "That does sound fun." He smiled affably. Goofball.

Jeremy and Faith walked everyone to the door, already acting like a married couple, and Mr. and Mrs. Lyon waved good-night and told everyone to drive safely.

Colleen got into Bryce's car (a red Mustang convertible, really, did his parents *want* him to die in a fiery crash?), and Tanya and Bryce got in back. Bryce took a brown paper bag from under the seat, unscrewed the cap of the bottle inside and took a pull, then offered some to Tanya, who accepted.

"Underage drinking, children," she said mildly. "Illegal."

"Lighten up," Tanya said.

Kids today. No respect. Good thing they had her to watch over them and get them home. And sure, it was fun to drive the Mustang.

The gathering at the lake was on a private beach; the owner was a summer person who surely wouldn't mind if the Manningsport youth used her property. Colleen parked the Stang on the street and followed the path down to the lake, the sound of peepers shrill and sweet.

The party was already in progress; Asswipe Jones lit a fire on the small beach, and a radio was playing. Two or three couples were out on the dock, smooching. There was laughter and a shriek as Angela Mitchum's date, a kid from Corning, picked her up and threatened to throw her in the water.

Bryce and Tanya weren't the only ones drinking. Colleen made the rounds and ensured that those who were had a ride with a sober driver; most of the kids had come via limo; Colleen had seen one parked on the street, the driver smoking a cigarette and talking on the phone.

After a while, most of the couples left. It had gotten colder, and the night was winding down. There were still a few couples left—the drinkers, naturally.

Sigh. The curse of the designated driver. She'd volunteered, after all. She checked her phone, hoping to call Con to alleviate her boredom. No cell service down here, though.

Stifling a yawn, she sat down on the sand, which was a little chilly. The stars stretched and blazed above, and a comet streaked across the eastern sky, and then her eyes were closed.

She awoke to the sound of angry voices.

"Fuck you, pretty boy," someone was saying. Great. It was Jake Green, one of the too-privileged lacrosse players. He'd been the first of the nine who'd asked Colleen to the prom and was now talking to Bryce out on the dock.

Colleen got up. Tanya was sitting with her head in her hands, crying. "What happened?" Colleen said, putting an arm around her. "Honey? You okay?"

"My shoe broke," Tanya sobbed. "See?" She held it

up for inspection. "The heel just snapped. And they're so pretty!"

Colleen sighed. People who couldn't hold their liquor really shouldn't drink. "What's going on out there?" She pointed to the dock.

"I dunno," Tanya mumbled, tears falling on the wounded shoe. "I'm tired."

"I'll get Bryce and we can go."

"Good." With that, she lay down on the sand, her wounded shoe cradled against her chest, and closed her eyes.

The voices were louder now. The moon had risen higher, fat and full, shining across the lake in a wide path of white light, allowing Colleen to see who was out there with Bryce. In addition to Jake were his minions (because all irritating rich boys had to have minions)—Jase Ross and Chris Eckbert—Crabbe and Goyle to Jake's Draco Malfoy. Their three dates appeared to have left.

"I don't know why you're mad. I meant it as a compliment," Bryce said.

"Hey, guys," Colleen said. "What's going on?"

"Oh, you're here?" Jake sneered. "I thought you were too good for the prom."

"No, no, not too good, Jake. I'm only here as a designated driver. Speaking of that, Bryce, can we go? I'm tired, and Tanya is, too."

"Fuck you, O'Rourke," Jake said. "Mind your own business."

"He's mad at me," Bryce whispered (loudly). "I told him I thought he looked like Cameron Diaz."

Colleen bit down on a smile. Jake was indeed blond and blue-eyed.

"You're gonna be sorry you said that, idiot," Jake said.

"Oh, come on," Colleen said. "He's drunk, Jake. And you *do* look like Cameron Diaz, right, Crabbe? Right, Goyle?" She smiled at Jase and Chris, who, uncertain of how to respond, glanced at Jake.

"Bryce, let's get going," she said, starting toward him. He answered with a crooked smile.

"Hold on," Jake said, and then put his hand on Bryce's chest and shoved, almost gently.

"Dude," Bryce murmured. His legs buckled, and Colleen realized that at some point, Bryce had gone from sloppy to shit-faced. This was confirmed when he lay back on the dock. "I don't feel so good," he muttered.

"I don't feel so good," Jake echoed in a high-pitched voice. "I bet you don't, pussy." His minions laughed, and Jake gave a tentative kick to Bryce's ribs.

"Knock it off!" Colleen said.

"Hey," Bryce said faintly, sounding more surprised than hurt.

She took a step toward them, stopping as Jake turned and looked at her, a speculative expression drifting over his face.

The cold lance of fear that slid through her stomach was almost alarming.

Jake was in front of her. Jase and Chris were behind her.

Oh, shit.

That was the thing about life in a small town. Once, they'd all been friends, more or less—all forty-nine kids in the senior class, back in the day of Halloween parties and field trips to the local cemetery. But somewhere in high school, things changed. Cliques formed, circles closed, and before you knew it, you could lose track of a person.

And Colleen had definitely lost track of Jake. She'd rebuffed him a few times, starting in seventh grade, not liking his rich-boy superiority, his casual dismissal of the girls who liked him. Chris and Jase, too, had never been her favorites. Chris wasn't that bad, just kind of a jerk. But Jase had a mean streak, too.

Suddenly, they seemed…dangerous.

Without looking away from her, Jake gave Bryce another oddly gentle kick, as if trying to see if he enjoyed it. Bryce appeared to have passed out.

"You think he'd drown if we rolled him in the lake?" Jake asked.

The minions snickered

This night was heading south. Fast.

"Okay, that's enough, boys," she said briskly. "Help me get him to the car." Yes. Give them the chance to be on her side, to change the dynamic.

Chris and Jase didn't move, waiting for instructions from their leader.

"You think you're better than everyone, don't you, Colleen?" Jake said softly, looking her up and down.

And all of a sudden, Colleen was—there was no more denying it—genuinely scared. Her knees buzzed, and her heart kicked in her chest.

"Jake, come on," she said, and she hated the fact that her voice shook. "Let's call it a night."

"I don't think so. This prom sucked, and I want some fun." Another kick to Bryce, resulting in a soft grunt and nothing else.

"Don't hurt him," she said, her voice breaking.

"What will you do for us if we don't?" Jake asked.

Colleen swallowed.

There was no cell service down here.

Tanya was sleeping on the shore.

And no one else was around.

If only Connor had come, because she always felt stronger and smarter when her twin was around. Connor would die before letting anyone hurt her. If only Jeremy was here, because he was tall and strong and honorable. Or Levi Cooper, who was badass and had a protective streak. Or Big Frankie, or any number of nicer, more decent boys.

But they hadn't. She was on her own.

"I'm glad you came down here, O'Rourke," Jake said. "Guys, aren't you glad? Coll, so *nice* of you to come! Yeah, I think we can all use a little fun, sure. And everyone knows how much fun you are." His eyes drifted down her body, then up again, stopping on her breasts.

Jesus God in Heaven.

You read about stuff like this. Saw those awful reports on CNN. Stuff like this happened all the time, and it was beyond belief. But Jake wouldn't—and Jase and Chris, they wouldn't—

She could run...except Jase and Chris were blocking the way. Even if she managed to get past them, which was unlikely, she'd have to leave Bryce to their mercy. She could jump in the lake and swim, but the water would be cold, maybe cold enough to stop her from thinking clearly. What if she drowned, and even if she didn't, where would she swim? How far? Could she make it somewhere safe? What if they just waited for her wherever she came to shore?

This wasn't really happening. She *knew* these boys.

She'd gone to *kindergarten* with them. They wouldn't actually—

Jake took off his tuxedo jacket.

Oh, God.

The word she hadn't wanted to think now reared up in searing color.

Raped. She could end up raped. The image throbbed in her brain like a tumor, blotting out everything else. Three against one.

She turned around to face the minions. Jase weighed upward of two hundred and fifty pounds; he'd been a tackle on the football team. The regional division championship football team. Chris was smaller, but still had a good forty or fifty pounds on her. "Chris, remember that field trip to the glass museum? When we sat together?" For a second, he looked uncertain.

Oh, please, please help me, Chris, you weren't always a bad kid—

"Come on, Colleen, let's have a little fun," Jake said from behind her, and then he had her by the arms, jerking them behind her, and bile surged up in her throat, yes, yes, let her puke, maybe it would stop them.

"Bet you wish you'd been nicer to me now," Jake whispered, and he licked her cheek, and icy terror convulsed in Colleen's chest. "Let's get this party started, boys."

But then all of a sudden, Chris was down on his knees, looking stunned, and oh, thank you, thank you, God, someone had come to help her, was it Connor, had he somehow sensed she was in—

It wasn't Connor.

It was Lucas Campbell.

Chris tried to get to his feet, but Lucas simply put one

foot against his shoulder and pushed him into the water. There was a splash, then some sputtering and yelping.

"This is not your business, man," Jake said.

"Let go of her," Lucas said, and his voice was almost friendly.

Then Jase lunged at him, but Lucas made two very small moves, one punch to the throat and one to Jase's meaty face, and Jase, too, dropped to his knees, blood spurting from his nose. "Jesus!" he wheezed, his voice thick and wet. With that, he ran heavily down the dock, causing it to bob beneath his fleeing bulk.

Jake's grip loosened, and before Colleen could formulate the thought, she elbowed him as hard as she could. He reacted by grabbing her hair, yanking so hard she saw a flash, and there was a blur of movement. Then Colleen was free, and Lucas was holding Jake by the throat.

Jake's eyes bulged as he clawed at Lucas's arm, his feet scrabbling for purchase on the rough wood of the dock. Lucas, on the other hand, looked calm as a June day.

"You okay, Colleen?" he asked without looking at her.

It was the first time she'd ever heard him say her name, and if there was a whisper of doubt that she'd been affected by him before, it was gone now.

"I'm fine," she said, and her voice sounded strange.

Chris had made it to shore, she saw. He half staggered, half ran up the path.

"Is Bryce hurt?" Lucas asked, his voice low and calm even as Jake continued to struggle.

"He passed out," she said. "He's drunk."

It seemed as if Jake was about to strangle there; he was breathing, but he wasn't fighting anymore. "You should probably let him go. You don't want to kill him."

He glanced at her. "That's debatable." But he did let go, and Jake dropped right on his ass, hard, and sucked in air.

"My parents will fucking sue you," he gasped.

"They can try," Lucas said.

"You're going to sue *him?*" Colleen blurted in outrage. "Think about what my parents will do to you, you little shit."

"For what?" Jake said, his voice shaking with tears. "For horsing around?"

"You were going to rape me!"

"Are you kidding? You *wanted* it, Colleen," Jake said, and even while on his knees, there was a smug look of entitlement on his face. "Why else did you come on to me? To all three of us?"

Her hands turned into fists, and she took a furious step forward, fully intending to kick him in his Cameron Diaz face, but Lucas stepped between them.

Jake's voice took on more confidence and the nasty edge returned. "Are your clothes torn? Did I even kiss you!" He stood up. "This asshole, though…he has a violent streak."

"Yeah," Lucas said. "I do. I'm from the South Side of Chicago, and don't you forget it." He stepped forward, forcing Jake to step back. "If I see you within fifty feet of her, you'll see just how violent a Southie can get. Me and a hammer. You and a new orifice. You understand?"

Granted, being protected wasn't really Colleen's thing, as she'd never needed it before, but *damn.* Jake's eyes grew comically round with terror.

"I asked you a question, you little shit."

"I understand," Jake said, his voice shaking.

"Is there a problem here?" It was the limo driver, followed by Chris.

"This asshole grabbed me by the throat!" Jake said, his tone immediately sullen.

"Sounds like you deserved it," the driver said. "At least, according to him." He gestured to Chris, who gave her an ashamed nod. "Now get in the limo, rich boy. Party's over." The driver looked at Colleen. "Are you okay?" he asked.

She hesitated, then nodded.

"If you ever touch her again, Jake," Lucas said, his voice soft and matter-of-fact, "you'll be eating through a straw for weeks."

"Oh, yeah?" Jake said. "Just because you snuck up on me—"

Lucas made a small movement toward him, and Jake screamed and jerked back.

"Come on," the driver said.

"Oh, Jake?" Colleen said sweetly.

He gave her a lethal look.

"You wet yourself."

Jake looked down at his crotch, froze a second, then shuffled off the dock. He yelled at Jase, shoving him as he walked past.

"Stupid little dick," the driver muttered. He turned to them. "You guys all set?"

"Yeah. Thanks," Lucas said.

"Sorry, Colleen," Chris muttered, following the driver down the dock.

It was only when they were gone that Colleen looked at Lucas. "Thank you," she whispered.

"Sure." He took a few steps down the dock to his cousin. "Bryce, you okay?"

"Hey, dude," Bryce said. "What was that yelling all about?"

"What did I say about drinking tonight, huh? Someone almost got hurt, and you're shit-faced."

"Sorry, man. I had a little too much, I think."

"Get up, buddy." He helped his cousin to his feet.

"Remember when I saved you?" Bryce said.

"Yep."

Bryce took a weaving step toward her. "Oh, hey, Coll. How you doing?"

"Hey, idiot," she said gently. She put her arm around him, steering him down to the shore.

Delayed terror kicked in then, and she started shaking. "You cold?" Bryce asked.

"Little bit," she said.

Tanya was sleeping on the sand, and without bothering to try to rouse her, Lucas simply picked her up.

"I'm tired," she whined. No one bothered to answer.

A mountain bike was parked behind the Mustang. Lucas dumped Tanya in the backseat, then popped the trunk and loaded the bike in. "You rode here on your bike?" Colleen asked, though the answer was obvious.

"Yeah." He glanced at her. "Where's your car?"

"I was playing chauffeur. Tanya can't drive, and Bryce was already pretty sloppy."

He nodded once, then opened the car door for her.

No boy had ever held a car door for her before.

She gave him directions to Tanya's house, then walked Tanya to the door. Mrs. Cross was waiting up, her mouth falling open when she saw her daughter's less-than-sober state, then thanked Colleen for seeing her home and began laying into Tanya for her stupidity. Colleen waved and went back to the car.

Bryce was sound asleep in the backseat, his snoring soft and rhythmic.

"Does he drink this much all the time?" she asked.

"Once in a while."

Colleen nodded. Maybe she shouldn't have asked, because Lucas seemed tense. Then again, this had been a tense night, hadn't it? Holy Mary. There'd be fallout—Jake was not the forgive-and-forget type. She might have to make sure everyone heard about his pants-wetting. Then again, that could make matters worse. Don't poke a wounded snake and all that.

"You're gonna have to watch your back," she said, stealing a look at her driver's profile.

"Yeah."

She cleared her throat, uncharacteristically nervous. "You were really brave. Three against one."

He glanced at her. "Three against two," he corrected.

"Yeah, well, Bryce wasn't much help."

"I was talking about you."

The words brought a nearly painful heat to her cheeks. "I am pretty good in a fight," she said, forcing some bravado into her voice.

But she hadn't been good. She would've lost that one without Lucas, and the thought made her legs start shaking again. "Take this left, and we're the third house on the right," she said.

He pulled into her driveway, then turned off the engine and got out. She got out as well, all too aware of his presence behind her.

The house was quiet, but Mom had left the light on over the sink, her code for *everyone's in bed*. Colleen turned to Lucas. His eyes were steady on her, dark and mysterious in the moonlight.

"Thank you again," she said briskly.

He looked at her for a long minute. "You sure you're okay?" he asked.

"Perfect," she said, forcing a smile.

His dark pirate eyes narrowed slightly. "Don't do that. Don't lie."

Well, hell. Men—especially boys—didn't usually call her on her bullshit. "All right, then. I'm still shaking, and I probably won't sleep tonight, but I'm not hurt, and I'm really, *really* glad you came looking for Bryce." She wiped her eyes, which appeared to be tearing up. "I could say I don't know what would've happened if you hadn't come along, but I'm afraid I know *exactly* what would've happened if you hadn't come along. So thank you, Lucas Campbell, for coming along." She smiled, and it felt normal again. "And for being all badass and scary when you did. It was very hot."

He laughed.

She hadn't expected that.

It was a smoky, ashen sound, just a low scrape in his chest, and it filled her with lightness, somehow. But at the same time, she felt a little terrified, too, because she knew, somehow, that Lucas Campbell was different. He was dangerous to her, in ways that had nothing to do with violence and everything to do with the soft, hot feelings that pulsed and burned in her chest.

"Good night," he said. But he didn't move.

"Good night," she whispered.

And then he kissed her, so gently at first, as if he'd never kissed a girl before, and please, looking like that, like Heathcliff, like a pirate or a gypsy or a member of the Sharks or the Jets…please, he'd kissed *plenty* of girls before.

The kiss was soft and sure at the same time, and she felt his welcome heat against her cool skin, felt his hand go to the back of her head, his fingers sliding into her hair. His mouth moved against hers, testing and waiting to see if she'd respond, and she did, hoping she was doing it right, because it sure *felt* right. It was all instinct—all those tips and comments and methods she'd given lectures on to her classmates these past five or six years, hell, she had no idea what she was supposed to be doing. All she knew was that Lucas Campbell was kissing her, and it felt so, so good.

It took her a second to realize he'd stopped, and that his forehead was resting against hers. Her hands were on his wrists, clinging to him.

"You're with me now," he said softly. Then he pulled back to look at her. "Okay?"

She was too smart for all this. She had an old soul. She couldn't picture having a boyfriend.

But his eyes were steady, and his lashes were thick and dark. "Okay," she whispered. So much for her legendary comebacks.

"I wasn't sure you liked me," he said after a minute. "It's the whole white-knight thing."

There was that laugh again, and just the sound of it had her stomach tightening in a warm spiral.

"I'll see you around, hotshot," he said, stepping away from her, and the cold and emptiness he left was a little shocking.

He seemed to read her mind, because he was back, and this time his kiss was more insistent. She grabbed his hair and answered, her mouth opening under his, and God, this was better than food, better than breathing, and a lot more important than either, the hard press

of him against her, the silkiness of his hair, the taste
of his mouth—

"Go inside," he ordered finally.

"You're not the boss of me," she said, hoping her legs
still worked. He grinned, and hell, she nearly came.

They'd be sleeping together. Soon. It was as inevitable as morning.

A long time later, she lay in bed, her fingers tracing
her lips.

This night might've turned out horribly, horribly
wrong.

Instead, she was in love.

CHAPTER FIVE

THE DAY AFTER he saw Bryce at O'Rourke's Lucas pulled up to Joe and Didi's house in his rental car, turned off the engine and sat for a moment.

In the fourteen years since he'd left for college, Lucas had been back to Manningsport only a handful of times, and only once since he'd gotten married.

Here was the thing about Didi Nesbith Campbell, Lucas's aunt by marriage. She had a vision of how life was supposed to be, goddamn it, and when life didn't obey, she got mad. Was still mad, in fact.

She'd married Joe just after he'd sold the rights to a video game for a million bucks when he was twenty-four years old. Rat-Whacker got picked up by Nintendo, and Joe seemed on track to billionaire status, joining the whiz kids of that era who made their first million before they were twenty-five.

And, like most of them, Joe was a flash in the pan.

That first million turned out to be the last million, but by then, they had a big house in the suburbs and a baby boy. Much to her supreme dissatisfaction, Didi had to get a job. She found her niche at an insurance company, denying claims of horribly injured people. Even as she rose through the ranks, she never got over the bitterness of having married the guy who failed to become the next Bill Gates.

The other great inconvenience of Didi's life was in-heriting Lucas. She already had her only begotten son; she certainly didn't want the silent child of her slacker husband's criminal brother.

Well. Time to see Joe. Lucas took off his sunglasses and headed toward the house.

It was beautiful up here, that was certain. The leaves were fresh and green, glowing with good health, unlike Chicago, which was currently baking in a heat wave. But here, where the landscape was dotted with deep glacier lakes and waterfalls by the dozens, where green farmland spread out on the hills and the forests were thick and deep, it was cooler and more lush than the flat Midwest and its punishing summers. The air was heavy with the smell of lilacs, so painstakingly trimmed along the border of Didi's perfectly landscaped (and somewhat soulless) yard.

Lucas would be in Manningsport for a month, maybe two. He wouldn't be staying at Didi's, that was certain, no matter that the house had five bedrooms and a base-ment apartment. No, he'd rather amputate his own foot and eat it than do that. For the moment, he was staying at the Black Swan B and B.

He knocked on the front door. Nephew or not, Didi wouldn't like him coming in unannounced.

Sure enough, she opened the door. "Oh. It's you."

"Hello, Didi," he said. "How are you?"

"I'm quite well," she said, her lips tight. "You may as well come in."

"Is Bryce here?"

"No, he's at the gym."

Bryce still lived at home, though he'd bounced around a little bit after dropping out of college. He'd tried to live in Chicago for a short time, and Lucas had even gotten him a job with Forbes Properties, which lasted five days before Bryce quit. Bryce had also tried Manhattan, San Francisco and Atlanta, but all roads led him back to Manningsport, specifically, to the basement apartment that Didi had made for her baby boy, giving him the illusion of adulthood while remaining clamped under her thumb.

"How's Ellen?" Didi asked.

"Good," he answered. She waited for more. He didn't offer it.

The one thing Lucas had ever done that won approval from Didi was to marry Ellen Forbes. "Any relation to Malcolm?" Didi had immediately asked when he'd told them. No curiosity about why he was marrying someone he'd never mentioned, or what had happened with his longtime girlfriend, or why he wasn't going to law school. Just "Any relation?" Her eyes alight with a sudden, keen interest.

The answer, of course, was, yes.

And suddenly, Lucas was a beloved nephew. Didi wanted to help plan the wedding, just *loved* Ellen to death within seconds of meeting her, thought of Lucas like a *son,* wanted so much to have holidays together, one big happy *family,* the Forbeses and the Campbells, wasn't it *wonderful?*

Granted, Ellen and her parents saw right through her, but Didi was too busy trying to pretend she was completely at home with their vast wealth, the penthouse overlooking Lake Michigan, the maid who served dinner, the sailboat and cars and drivers and wine.

Once, Lucas had come upon her in Frank's study, where she was slipping a little glass statue in her purse.

"Please don't steal from my in-laws," he'd said mildly, and she'd flashed him a glare of such hatred, he'd actually smiled. She might want to kiss up to his in-laws, but it was almost reassuring to see that she still couldn't stand the sight of him.

When informed about his divorce, Didi's first question had been, "What about the holidays?" After all, if Lucas wasn't a son-in-law anymore, odds were low that his aunt and uncle would get an invitation to the famous Forbes New Year's Eve party, the amazing Thanksgiving dinner for thirty of their closest friends.

Frank and Grace Forbes—and Ellen—had stayed close with his sister, Steph, and her girls since the divorce, because they were really wonderful, not about to cut off five people—six, counting him—they loved. His divorce was more than amicable, not to mention Ellen's idea.

"How's Joe today?" Lucas asked Didi.

"See for yourself," she said, turning away. "Take off your shoes first."

He obeyed, then started upstairs.

"He's in your—the room off the kitchen," she said. "It was easier that way."

Of course. Joe was weak, that was true. Also, Didi was a bitch.

Lucas went through the vast chef's kitchen to the small hallway that led to the laundry room and his old room. Knocked gently on the door, which was open a crack.

The room was crowded: the hospital bed, a night table covered with the detritus of sickness—pill bottles, a half-filled glass of water, tissues, a magazine and Joe's silver pocket watch, which had been handed from

father to son since the Civil War. A desk with a large-
screened computer was wedged against one wall. The
room didn't have windows, and Lucas remembered how
dark it was in here. Like a grave, he'd often thought,
and now more than ever.

His uncle was sleeping. Lucas hadn't seen him for a
few months. The kidney disease made Joe appear tan,
and he was thinner than he'd ever been, though a little
puffy from fluid retention.

But now, even asleep, he looked old. And tired.

A lot like Lucas's father the last time he'd seen him.
The family resemblance was strong.

Joe was dying. The reality hit Lucas like a tanker,
and his eyes stung all of a sudden. Despite Didi's cease-
less resentment, Joe had always been a good uncle.

Joe stirred, then opened his eyes. "Hey," he said,
struggling to sit up. "How are you, buddy?"

Lucas gave his uncle a lean-in hug. Cleared his
throat. "Good to see you, Joe."

"You, too! You look great. When did you get in?"

"Last night."

"You see Bryce yet?"

"Sure did. Found him at O'Rourke's." And not just
him, either.

"Yeah, he goes there a lot." Joe smiled. "So."

"So."

"Don't tire him out, Lucas," Didi said, appearing in
the doorway, hands on her bony hips.

"He won't," Joe said.

"When's Bryce coming back? He wanted to do something with you this afternoon." Her eyes flickered toward Lucas. This was typical for her; any time Joe and
Lucas might have a bonding moment, she was there to

interrupt and remind Joe that he *had* a son, a wonderful son, a *real* son.

And the thing was, it generally worked. Joe was a nice guy, but he was no match for Didi. There were other terms for it, meaner terms, but it was clear that Joe generally did what Didi told him to do.

"Give me a few minutes with my uncle," Lucas said, and without waiting for an answer, got up and closed the door in her face.

The door flew open again immediately. "Just because you breeze into town whenever you like, I'm still the one who has to take care of him. My whole life is doctor's appointments and hospital visits these days. I don't have a minute to breathe—"

"Then breathe now," he said, and closed the door again.

Apparently Didi couldn't find a way to argue that. After a second, her heels tapped away down the hall, though Lucas would bet she'd tiptoe back and eavesdrop.

"What can I do for you, Uncle Joe?" he asked, taking his seat again.

Joe sighed. "Here's the thing, Lucas. Bryce…well, he's just not really grown up yet, you know what I mean?"

He nodded, his hand on his uncle's. Joe's arm looked odd, courtesy of the fistula he needed for dialysis.

"I'd like to leave this world knowing he had a plan, at least. I don't want him—" Joe glanced at the closed door and dropped his voice to a whisper. "I don't want her to have her hooks in him forever. You know what I mean?"

"I do."

"So maybe you could hang around for…well, till the

day comes. I know he's gonna take this hard." Joe's eyes filled with tears.

Yes. Last night, Bryce had acknowledged that his dad was sick, but he also talked about how much better Joe was looking these days. Dialysis was amazing! And besides, a kidney would come along any minute.

The fact that Joe wasn't on the organ registry—and indeed, wasn't eligible for a transplant, thanks to the tumor in his lung—was not something Bryce would admit.

"I'll stay however long you need," Lucas said. He owed it to Joe, after all.

"You can get off work that long?"

"Yep. I'm leaving the company, remember?"

"Right, right." Joe paused. "Where will you stay when you're here?"

"I'm at the Black Swan right now," he said. "Just called the Realtor about a short-term rental."

"You're welcome to stay here," Joe offered, but they both knew that he wasn't. Didi would hate having him here, and if Didi wasn't happy, no one was allowed to be happy.

"That's okay."

"So you think you could help Bryce? Maybe help him find work? He hasn't ever had a job he really loved, aside from the dog shelter stuff."

"I'll see what I can do."

"Just having you here is going to be great. He's always worshipped you. Always wanted to do what you did, whatever that might've been."

Lucas nodded. That was certainly true; from baseball cards to a paper route, if Lucas had it, Bryce wanted it. And Didi made sure he got it.

"There's another thing I need you to help me with,"

Joe whispered, and Lucas felt a flash of anger that the man had to whisper in his own home.

"What's that?" he asked, adjusting Joe's blanket. It was meat-locker cold in here. Another thing he remembered too well.

Joe glanced at the door, then picked up a notepad and pen. Wrote something down and passed it to Lucas.

I want a divorce before I die.

Lucas looked at his uncle. Back at the notepad. Back to his uncle. "Well, holy shit, unc," he said, then grinned. "I'll get right on that."

"Thanks, Lucas." Joe smiled, but his eyes closed. "I'm glad you're here," Joe said, his voice fading into sleep. Then his eyes opened. "Maybe you can see some old friends while you're here." He winked, the ghost of his old self, then fell asleep, just like that.

CHAPTER SIX

"OH. COLLEEN. IT'S YOU." Carol Robinson, one of the local Realtors, gave Colleen a jaundiced stare. "Fine, come in. I'm not showing you around, though. I know you won't be buying."

"Lovely to see you, too, Carol." Piña colada, very old-school, Carol was. "Bursitis flaring up again?"

"No. I just don't want to waste my time. Hi, Jeanette, how are you?"

Colleen's mother pulled her shirt away from her chest. "It's so hot in here, Carol! How do you stand it?"

"You're having a hot flash. I still get them," Carol said. "It's ridiculous."

"Satan's barbecue," Mom said. "Don't make that face, Colleen. You'll see."

"I can't wait. Carol, do you have a fact sheet on the house?" Carol handed her one with a sigh. "By the way, do you have to walk in the middle of the road every morning? I almost hit you the other day."

"Oh, that's right, I saw you speeding by. Jeanette, your daughter and that red car of hers…"

Colleen had brought her mother to an open house, and yeah, fine, she had a bit of a reputation with the real estate people. It wasn't her fault. Yes, she wanted to buy a house, very much, in fact. She was thirty-one, for heaven's sake. She didn't want to live above her brother forever. Their house was adorable; it was just that it was *their* house, and she wanted a place of her own. A place where, yeah, she'd have those adorable tots and Rufus could frisk and frolic, and her husband and she would have lots and lots of great sex.

And since Lucas Damien Campbell had walked into her bar the other night, she felt considerably more motivated to find that husband and bear those children.

Today, she'd taken her mom with her, because (a) she was a saint, and (b) it was one of Mom's many Significant Dates, of which there were many, 99 percent of them marking some dire event relating to Dad.

This house was a white farmhouse with a porch, a horseshoe driveway and big, beautiful yard. Not too big, not too small, not too new, not too old. Remodeled kitchen with white cabinets and glass fronts, lots of counter space, should she take up cooking (which she wouldn't but it could happen, if hell froze over). The living room had lots of windows and a really pretty fireplace.

Colleen and her mother went upstairs as Carol went back to reading her fat spy novel.

Coll felt a tingle of hope. If she was busy moving into a new place, painting and shopping for a new couch and plates, she'd have less time to lie in bed and think about a certain tall, dark un-stranger. "Black-haired boy, work of the devil," her grandmother used to say, and it was flippin' true. Lucas had black hair and had broken her heart. Jeremy Lyon had black hair, and he'd broken Faith's heart by coming out of the closet on their wedding day. Dad had black hair and broke Mom's heart.

Connor, on the other hand, had brown hair, taking after Mom's side of the family, with no broken hearts in his past. Levi Cooper, police chief and decorated veteran—dark blond, making Faith very happy these days. Gerard Chartier: bald, a cheerful man-whore and very well liked. Grandma had known what she was talking about.

The master bedroom was at the end of the hall and utterly gorgeous. Slanted ceiling, a long window seat, built-in bookshelves. Even space on the wall for a TV, if she was so inclined. Not that she approved of watching TV in bed; in her mind's eye, Tom Hardy would be waiting, naked and impatient, for her, his beloved wife. In reality, however, she and Rufus put in far too many hours watching HGTV and *Game of Thrones*. (Was Jon Snow too young to lust after? Probably and oops, another black-haired boy.)

"This is lovely. What do you hate about it?" Mom asked.

"Nothing," Colleen said.

"You'll find something. You always do."

"Thanks for the vote of confidence, Ma."

Her mother wandered into the bathroom. "Oh, Collie, come in here, sweetheart."

The master bathroom was vast—tiled floor, walled-in shower area and a huge, triangular tub, big enough for Colleen *and* Tom Hardy *and* his muscles.

"Uh-oh," Mom said. Her face flushed bright red, she began flapping her shirt again. "Oh, dear! Oh, man! I think I might be having another hot flash!"

"Really? You hide it so well." Mom had always been the type to detail her physical woes. "Bleeding like a stuck pig" had been popular back in the good old period days. "Ovaries the size of grapefruits" was another.

"That Chinese food went through me like a knife." One of the many ways Mom was so much fun.

Mom continued flapping, then climbed in the bathtub. "This porcelain feels like ice. Thank God, too." She lay there, red-faced and panting, and Colleen waited, used to her mother's menopausal adventures by now. After a minute, Jeanette lifted her head, her hair damp with sweat, and surveyed the tub. "So how many jets does this thing have?" she said speculatively.

"Icky, Mom." Quite a few, though. Handy, in case marriage to Tom Hardy didn't work out.

"Why? Just because it feels like tumbleweeds are blowing through my—"

"Hail Mary, full of grace," Colleen began. "The Lord is with thee. Blessed art thou who can make my mother stop talking, and blessed—"

Her mother gave her a martyred look. "You know, Colleen, just because I'm suffering through menopause, and just because your father left me for That Whore doesn't mean I don't have certain urges."

"Mom! Come on."

"What? Am I not a human all of a sudden? Not allowed to be lonely? Hey, did you know that John Holland got married a couple weeks ago?"

Another maternal habit: announcing facts known by everyone as if it was big news. Of course she knew. She was the best friend of the man's daughter, and if there was a more beloved man than Faith's dad, Colleen didn't know him. She herself wouldn't have minded being the second Mrs. Holland. Well, not really. But it had always been fun to flirt with him anyway.

"He's been widowed for twenty years," Mom said.

"Ma, I know. I grew up with Faith, remember?"

"Of course I remember. You girls were at our house half the time. The point is, both he and Mrs. Johnson are older than I am."

"True. Want to see the other bedrooms now?" Colleen asked. So far, the house had given her no reason to reject it. But the tingle was fading. This bathroom was possibly too large. It always seemed to her that when she found the right house, she'd know. Instantly.

Just as she'd known with Lucas the day he walked into her English class.

And look where that had gotten her.

Her phone buzzed with a text. From Bryce, no less. Think Jessica Dunn is a good match 4 me?

Oh, crap. First of all, Jessica Dunn would never go for a guy like Bryce; Jess had a very appealing edginess to her, and Bryce was as complicated as a chocolate chip cookie. Secondly, there was Paulie!

Not really, she typed back. Hang in there. I'm working on someone for you. She's special.

Pretty? appeared almost immediately.

Sigh. Paulie could not be described as pretty. Striking.

Awesome, came the reply. C u soon!

"I'm gonna lay here for another minute," Mom said. "But, Colleen, I was thinking. It doesn't seem like your father is going to come to his senses any time soon. I thought That Whore was a midlife crisis, just a little fling—"

"They've been together for ten years, Mom."

"And even after that child, I thought he'd come back to me."

"Savannah, Mom. Say what you want about Gail the Tail, but be nice about Savannah. She's my sister."

"Your half sister." Mom sat up, grabbed one of the

attractively rolled facecloths and ran some water on it, then held it against her chest. "Anyway, John Holland has adult grandchildren, he's in his sixties, but *he* found someone. I'm only fifty-four, and what do I have? Nothing. No grandchildren, not even a daughter-or son-in-law, and nothing on the horizon, either. What's wrong with you and Connor?"

A familiar refrain. "What's wrong with *you*, Mom? Why haven't you given me a nice stepfather? I wouldn't say no to Mariano Rivera, for example. Or George Clooney. Actually, I'd marry both of them myself, so take them off the list. Sean Connery, he'd do. Or Ed Harris. Why haven't you married Sean Connery or Ed Harris, Mom?"

"Your father married That Whore. John Holland married Mrs. Johnson. Cathy Moore turned gay and married Louise. And here I am, sitting in a tub having a hot flash. On the tenth anniversary of your father leaving me, no less."

"Well, you can get out of the tub, Ma."

"Wait till you hit menopause. I'll have no sympathy for you." Mom sighed. "I'm tired of things being the same. I want a life. I want to get laid."

Hail Mary, full of grace—

"Barb McIntosh said you told her you could fix up anyone. Does that include me, or don't I count?"

Colleen's head whipped around from where she was examining the showerhead.

In all the years since the divorce, Mom had not gone out once. Not once. "Really? You really want to date?"

"Yes. Why shouldn't I? Your father has That Whore, and if John Holland can find someone, I probably could, too. I'm not disgusting, am I?" Her mother climbed out of the tub and scooped her hair off her neck in a regal move, one that Colleen had copied as a kid.

Danger, she heard Connor's voice say in her head. He definitely was the logical twin. And yes, fixing up Mom could be the emotional equivalent of waterboarding.

Then again, Mom had waited *years* for Dad to come back to her. Denial, then bitterness as an Olympic sport. Maybe what she needed to get over Dad was another man. Certainly, Colleen had always thought so.

"And if I meet someone, maybe your father will get jealous and finally get his head out of his ass."

Crud. Using people to make other people jealous... that never worked very well. "Mom, if you want to date, maybe find someone, I think that'd be great. But Dad's not coming back."

"You never know. So? Will you help me? I need to set up an online profile."

Faith had done the same thing with her father last fall. It hadn't been a particularly good experience, though all's well that ends well. Also, Faith herself was sweet and naive.

Colleen was not.

If there was one thing she knew, it was men and how they thought.

"Oh!" Mom exclaimed, grasping Colleen's arm. "And guess what else I heard? Guess! Guess!"

"The sound of a butterfly's wings," Colleen said.

"No. Guess again."

"What, Mom?"

Mom let go of her arm, fluffed her hair and gave Colleen a triumphant look. "I heard Lucas Campbell is back in town."

"I know."

"Surprise! Isn't it great?"

"He's back because Joe Campbell isn't long for the world, so I'd have to say no."

"It is! It's great because—"

"Don't, Mom."

"Because you never got over him." Mom fixed her with a triumphant look.

"That's debatable." Granted, a debate she'd probably lose, but still. "Also, Mom, he's married."

"No. He's divorced."

Colleen blinked.

"Aha! I *knew* you didn't know that!" Mom crowed.

"Are you two done up there?" Carol called from downstairs. "I have other people here who might actually buy this place, you know."

"We'll be right down. She doesn't love it," Mom yelled. Colleen barely heard.

Divorced?

No, he hadn't mentioned *that* the other night. Questions surged into her head. Why? For how long? Was he heartbroken? Bitter? Had he cheated? Had she? Was he seeing someone?

Get a grip, she told herself. *He broke your heart. He fell in love with someone else, and he left you. Just. Like. Dad.*

"Colleen?" Mom asked. "You're not really interested in this house, are you?"

"It's almost perfect," she said, clearing her throat. "But there's not enough shade in the front."

CHAPTER SEVEN

A WEEK BACK in Manningsport, and Lucas had spoken to an attorney, who told him that a divorce for Uncle Joe was going to be just about impossible. Lucas wasn't giving up on that just yet. New York divorce law was a tangled, Puritanical web, but maybe there was a loophole somewhere. Then there were Joe's finances; he wanted whatever assets he had to go to Bryce. What exactly those assets were remained to be seen, because Didi kept a tight fist around the family funds.

In the meantime, Lucas found a short-term, furnished rental in a pretty building on the green, roughly two hundred feet from O'Rourke's front door. He'd been avoiding the pub, not wanting Colleen's panties to get into a twist (though thinking about her panties wasn't the worst way to spend time).

Today, however, he was stopping by the Manningsport Animal Shelter to see Bryce, and hopefully get his cousin to commit to a plan of action for a future that included more than playing video games in his mom's basement. Bryce loved animals; maybe Lucas could convince him to go to school to become a veterinary assistant or the like.

The shelter was a gray building on the outskirts of town, and Bryce's Dodge Ram pickup truck was parked outside, along with a cute little Porsche and a mountain bike with a wicker basket on the handlebars. Lucas went inside. There was no one in the waiting room, but he heard voices coming from behind a closed door. Some female murmuring, then Bryce speaking more clearly.

"Let's use a little lubricant, don't you think, baby? Don't be scared. I'll just ease my finger in like that and squeeze, nice and gentle."

Lucas froze.

"Doesn't that feel good, sweetheart?" Bryce went on.

A moaning sound came in response.

What the *hell?* Was Bryce having sex in an animal shelter?

"Bryce? It's Lucas."

There was a scrambling sound from inside, and then the door opened, and there was Colleen, her hair tumbled, cheeks pink.

A white-hot knife of jealousy slid between Lucas's ribs, and for a second, he couldn't see straight.

"Hey," she said calmly, though her eyes widened a bit.

"Colleen."

She raised an eyebrow at his tone, then looked behind her. "Your cousin's here, Bryce," she said.

"Hey, Lucas!" Bryce called. "I'm covered in slime. Be out in a second."

Colleen came into the waiting room, closing the door behind her. "We meet again. How are you, Spaniard?"

It was her old nickname for him…she had often said he looked like a Spanish pirate.

"I'm fine," he said tightly. "What exactly were you doing in there?"

She cocked an eyebrow, then grinned. "Sounded like

sexy time, didn't it? But no. Just Bryce expressing the anal glands of a very cute little dog."

"I—okay, I'm speechless."

"I know. There's just no good comeback for that."

"Is life so quiet here that this is what passes for fun?"

"Don't sell it short. Want to watch? He's *really* good." She grinned, and Lucas felt a responding smile start in his chest.

"So your dog required some, um, special treatment?" he asked.

"No, that would take the New York Giants and a very, very brave vet. It's Mrs. Tuggles, one of Paulie's recent acquisitions. Rufus over there is my baby." She pointed, and Lucas glanced over to where a gray, cow-sized dog lay on its side as if dead.

"Are you a good boy, Rufus?" Colleen asked.

The dog's tail thumped twice in confirmation.

"So these anal glands," Lucas said. "Your way of getting Paulie and Bryce together?"

"Mmm-hmm."

"How romantic."

"Hey. It's working. You see, Lucas, a lot of men don't appreciate what's right in front of them, so they have to be shown. In twelve-foot neon letters. With arrows pointing to it." She paused to let that sink in, lest he miss the innuendo (whatever it was). "Also, Mrs. Tuggles was blocked and kept scooching her butt across Paulie's rug. You get the picture."

The exam room door opened again, and there was Paulie, holding Mrs. Tuggles, a rotund little dog that looked extremely satisfied at the moment, her wide mouth grinning, tongue lolling. The dog yawned and closed her eyes.

"Looks like she could use a cigarette," Colleen said. "Bryce, what did you do to her?"

"I aim to please," Bryce said, drying his hands on the paper towel. "Hey, Lucas! You know Paulie, right? We went to high school with her senior year."

"Nice to see you again," Paulie said.

"Good to see you, too, Paulie," he said with a smile. Her face grew pink…then red…then blotchy. That was some blush.

"Mrs. Tuggles, say hi to Lucas," Bryce said. He bent down to kiss Mrs. Tuggles's head, bringing his own head in the vicinity of Paulie's chest. Her face went into the purple zone, and the dog licked Bryce's face with exuberant gratitude and slobber. Kind of disgusting.

"You got a minute, Bryce?" he asked when the dog was done frenching his cousin.

"Totally. Girls, it was great seeing you both," Bryce said. "All three of you, that is." He scratched the pug on the head.

"Oh, yes…uh, I mean, yeah. You, too," Paulie said. She cleared her throat and took a deep breath. "Colleen, thank you for coming with me." Her voice was loud and expressionless. "I was so concerned about poor Mrs. Tuggles, and it was good to have a friend." She took a shaky breath. "Bryce, you were so wonderful. Let me buy you a beer some night." Her face went nuclear.

Lucas would bet a hundred bucks Colleen had given her those lines.

"Sure. That'd be great," Bryce said, completely oblivious. Paulie's eyelids fluttered, and she took an unsteady step backward, looking as if she was about to faint.

Colleen gave her a little push forward and picked up a bike helmet from one of the chairs. "See you around, boys. Paulie, I'll walk you out. Come on, Rufie!"

The women and their animals left, and Bryce stretched his arms over his head. "I think Colleen might have a thing for me," he said.

There was that flash of jealousy again. "I'm pretty sure that's not it," Lucas said.

"You never know. She and I—" He glanced at Lucas as if just now remembering that Colleen had once been with Lucas. "Uh…nothing. We hit it off. As friends, you know? At the bar, just shooting the shit. Friends. You're right, there's nothing there." He cracked his knuckles. "What can I do for you, bro? You want a dog? Or a cat? My mom won't let me have one, which is probably why I work here, you know?"

"I can't have a pet, Bryce," Lucas said. "I'm only in town for a while."

"Right, right. Or you could move back."

"Not gonna happen, pal."

"Right. South Side forever."

Lucas smiled. "I figured you could show me around, since you said you spend a lot of time here."

"Sure! Come on back."

Another door led to the kennels. The usual suspects—pit bull here, Rottweiler there, with a couple of older-looking dogs. Bryce had a kind word for all of them, even the snarling black mutt in the last kennel. Then on to the cat room, where there were far too many felines of varying colors and sizes.

Bryce picked up a kitten. "Who's beautiful, huh? Who's so pretty? You are, sweetie!" The kitten batted Bryce on the nose and mewed.

Lucas had never had a pet. He could get one, he guessed; he just wasn't home a lot. Maybe now that he was leaving Forbes, he'd get a dog who could ride in his truck to job sites and lie at his feet at night. It'd be nice to have some company.

Well. He'd wait to get back to Chicago. There were plenty of animals waiting to be adopted in the city, he was sure.

"You ever think about becoming a vet tech, Bryce?" he asked. "You're really good with animals."

"Thanks! But not really, no. You need school for that."

"So? You could do it part-time, I bet."

"Well, whatever. Even so, the shelter can't afford to pay anyone. We're all volunteers, and Dr. Metcalf comes in when we need real stuff done."

"Could you work for Dr. Metcalf?"

Bryce shrugged. "He has this hot chick who works for him. She volunteers here, too. We hooked up once or twice." He scratched his head. "Maybe I should give her a call. I'm thinking about having kids."

Wow. "Yeah, you'd be a great dad," he said (and hoped). "But you need a job first. And possibly a place of your own, so you don't have to raise a kid in your mother's basement."

"True enough. You wanna get a beer? I think O'Rourke's is open."

"It's eleven-thirty, Bryce."

"Yeah, so they're definitely open. Oh, I get it. You don't want to see Colleen."

Lucas gave his cousin a look. "I have no problem seeing Colleen."

"Okay."

"I don't."

"Must bring up memories, though, right? Because you two were pretty hot and heavy."

"That was a long time ago. Anyway, about you getting a job, Bryce—"

"Shit! I forgot. I'm supposed to have lunch with my mom. I gotta run." Just then, the front door opened, and a *very* pretty woman came in. "Hey, Ange! Right on time."

"Hi, Bryce," she purred, sparing Lucas a glance (and giving him a gratifying double take). "Your brother?"

"Cousin. Lucas, this is Angie… Angie, uh…"

"Beekman."

"Right! Ange, I gotta fly, but listen. You wanna grab a drink sometime?"

Lucas couldn't help feeling a flicker of sympathy for Paulie.

"Sure," she said with a coy smile. "See you around, boys."

Lucas scrubbed a hand through his hair as Bryce tore out of the parking lot a few seconds later, going too fast, as usual.

WHEN LUCAS WAS FIFTEEN, his cousin saved his life.

"Remember when I saved you?" Bryce would say from time to time. And Lucas would have to say of course he remembered, and yes, it sure was lucky Bryce had been there, and absolutely, they were as close as brothers, and yep, they did look alike, since they both looked like their fathers—and Dan and Joe could've passed for twins.

It wasn't that Lucas disliked Bryce. No one did. Bryce Campbell, the adored only child of Lucas's aunt and uncle, was unendingly cheerful, up for anything and had an intense case of hero worship. He kept a respectful distance from Lucas's sister, Stephanie, who was six years older and called him only "kid." But he stuck to Lucas like a tick.

About three times a year, Joe, Didi and Bryce would

visit them (they, in return, were never invited to the wealthy suburb to the north of Chicago where Bryce and his family lived). And every time, Bryce would be glued to Lucas's side, wide-eyed with wonder at anything Lucas had or did—his tiny bedroom on the third floor of the two-family house they lived in, his second-hand bike, the stunts he could do on it. Lucas was a White Sox fan, obviously, being from the South Side; Bryce traded in his Cubs shirt to match Lucas's, which nearly got him stoned by his peers. Lucas would clear the crowded table after dinner because he was the kind of kid who did chores; Bryce decided that nothing was more fun and exotic than washing dishes by hand. And the thing was, he meant it.

Bryce couldn't get over the fact that Lucas was not only allowed to *have* a knife, but was allowed to use it as well, and viewed whittling as damn near miraculous. He peppered Lucas with questions about his late mother, who'd died of ALS when Lucas was six. Did he miss her? What had it been like to have a Puerto Rican mother? Did they ever see her ghost? It never occurred to Bryce that the subject might be a sensitive one.

Lucas liked his cousin. But Bryce could be tiring, like a puppy who just wanted to bring you a stick. At first, it's really cute. *Aw, hey, a stick! Go get it, boy!* But by the tenth time, when the puppy's enthusiasm hasn't been touched but yours is getting tired, you wish the dog would take a nap. By the twentieth time he brings you the stick, your arm aches. And by the fiftieth, you really wondered what you were thinking when you decided to get a dog.

It was always something of a relief to see Bryce get reluctantly bundled off into the car with his parents.

"My God, that woman is evil," Dad would say of his brother's wife, tousling Lucas's hair. Though it was clear Aunt Didi barely tolerated her husband's family, she never let them visit without her, even if she did brush off a chair before sitting on it. "But your cousin, he's a pretty great kid, isn't he?"

And Lucas would agree that yes, Bryce was really nice. Which he was.

Joe Campbell was the brother who'd made good; Dan never made it out of the careworn neighborhood where they'd grown up. Joe got into college, which was near-miraculous from the sound of it, whereas Dan became a mechanic, married the girl next door and moved into an apartment around the corner from where the brothers grew up.

It was clear that Joe viewed their childhood as far more idyllic than Lucas's dad did. Even when he was little, Lucas understood that, felt his father's edge when Uncle Joe would wax poetic about riding their bikes in the empty lot or leaving pennies out on the rail for the train to flatten. After all, Joe and his family got to leave at the end of the day.

When Steph was nineteen, she moved in with her boyfriend and had a baby girl. Another thing Bryce couldn't get over—how cool was it that Lucas was an uncle! How he wished he had a sister, too, so he could be an uncle! "Bryce, angel, a baby's not always a *good* thing," Aunt Didi said.

"This baby is," Lucas said, giving his aunt a dirty look. Mercedes was cute and smelled nice, most of the time, and Steph was a good mom.

Didi didn't blink. "Well, we'll see how things turn out, won't we?" she murmured. "Not all of us are thrilled that our tax dollars pay for Stephanie's lifestyle." And though he wasn't 100 percent sure what she meant by that, Lucas knew that it was a put-down just the same.

Visits from Joe and Bryce and Didi were rare, he didn't have to think about it much. Would it be nice to take a vacation in Turks and Caicos, wherever that was? Probably. Would it be fun to have a flat-screen TV in your room? Sure. But Lucas wouldn't trade places, that was for sure. Home always seemed a little nicer after those visits. Careworn instead of shabby, washed in the light of relief that they had each other, at least.

Until Dad was arrested.

Things Lucas Didn't Know About His Father:

1. He'd been arrested at age eighteen for grand theft auto (a Camaro left with the keys in it, so really, who could resist? Certainly not an eighteen-year-old American male from the wrong side of the tracks).
2. He'd been arrested at age twenty-one for breaking and entering and vandalism (Mrs. Ortega's place, where he and his buddy sat in the living room, watched Cinemax, drinking her schnapps).
3. He was $95,700 in debt, thanks to Mom's medical care during her unsuccessful battle with ALS.
4. He was a drug dealer.

Lucas was fifteen at the time of the bust. The cops showed up, flashed a warrant and searched the house while Lucas made frantic phone calls to the garage. It was too late; the police found several small bags of crystal meth in a shoe box in the back of Dad's closet.

Seemed like Dad had become a minor dealer in an

organization run by one of his old high school friends. It was the only way he'd found to stop the creditors from taking the house after Mom died; he already worked eighty hours a week at the garage. Because of Dan's "criminal past," the judge sentenced him to sixteen years.

"I'm sorry, son," Dan said to Lucas as the bailiff handcuffed him. Lucas hugged his father and tried not to cry. His father, who looked a decade older than he had that morning, didn't need to see that. Besides, they'd appeal, the public defender said. This wasn't forever.

Lucas wanted to stay with his sister, but Steph had tearfully turned him down. She and Rich lived in a tiny apartment, and she was pregnant again, this time with twins. Though Lucas swore he'd help, he could sleep on the couch, Mercedes loved him, he could babysit and everything, Steph said he'd be better off with Uncle Joe.

Joe and Bryce showed up as Lucas was packing. "This is so great!" Bryce exclaimed. "You can live with us now! We'll be like brothers!"

Lucas barely refrained from punching him. It wasn't *great*. His father was in *jail,* and even if he'd be getting out soon—please, God—this was far from great.

Being without a choice in the matter, he went, moving from the South Side, the run-down but tight-knit blue-collar neighborhood he'd lived all his life to a development made up of streets with saccharine names: Shadow Creek Lane, West Wind Way, Shane's Glen Circle.

Didi showed him his room, the smallest room in the house, jammed full with an unused treadmill (which Didi insisted stay in the room, rather than be moved to the basement), a broken computer from the early nineties and a twin bed under the eaves. Bryce had been hoping they'd bunk in together, but no. There was another unused bedroom, but Didi said it was for company.

It was horribly different.

There was a pool in the back, serviced by Juan the pool boy; he and Lucas would speak in Spanish together, which irritated Didi and filled Bryce with still more admiration. The lawn was mown by a landscaping company. They had a cleaning lady. Didi drove a Mercedes and shopped at high-end retail stores and, according to a receipt Lucas found, spent one hundred and fifty dollars on her hair every five weeks.

Lucas remembered his father asking Joe for money five or six years before. He'd been lingering in the bathroom, needing a break from Bryce's constant questions, and was washing his hands with much more care than usual.

"I hate to ask," Dad said. "And I wouldn't, except… well, the hospital hired a bill collector. I'm working as much as I can, but…"

"No, no, I understand," Joe said. "Um, I'll ask Didi."

A few nights later, Uncle Joe had called, and Dad's answers got shorter and shorter. "I understand. Of course not. Don't worry about it. Thanks anyway. No. Sure. Yep." He hung up the phone, sighed, such a weary, hopeless sound that Lucas must've looked stricken, because the next minute, Dad smiled. "Want ice cream for dessert?" he asked, and they both pretended things were okay.

A few months after that phone call, Didi and Joe took Bryce on a Disney cruise around the Mediterranean.

For the first few weeks he was living with them, Lucas kept his clothes in his backpack because he knew he wouldn't be there long. His father's sentence had been sixteen years, but come on. That was for rapists and murderers. Not for a mechanic who was trying to pay off his dead wife's medical expenses and support a family. Surely Dad's lawyer would get that straightened out.

But as the days turned into weeks, and the first month came around, Joe gently explained that it looked like it might be longer than Lucas hoped. He might as well make himself at home, right?

When it came time for back-to-school shopping, Didi bought Bryce's clothes from Hollister, and Lucas's from Kmart. Point taken. Joe bought him a new baseball glove for his birthday, the first never-been-used glove he'd ever had, despite playing for a couple of years already, and five minutes after he opened the package, Didi's tight lips and hissing whispers managed to convince Joe that Lucas didn't *need* a new glove. But Bryce did. Lucas could have Bryce's old glove.

And so it went. It was Didi's job that afforded the big house and tricked-out car in the garage ("Isn't it cool that your niece and our car have the same name?" Bryce said once). Didi was vice president of something, whereas Joe worked from home, and somewhat sporadically.

But despite his uncle's assurances that they were thrilled to have him, despite Bryce's adoration, Lucas had never felt so alone. He missed Stephanie, who was kind of a screwup, sure, but who was also funny and who let him have ice cream every night the year after Mom died, when Dad worked nights. He missed his niece, who smiled and drooled on him and babbled at him. Her first word had been *Wookus* and everything.

Being half–Puerto Rican was not a big deal in his old neighborhood, but here in the suburbs, he was the only nonwhite, as far as he could tell. He missed people knowing who he was—Dan's son, Steph's brother, widely regarded as a good kid. He missed his room with the poster of Yoda on one wall, one of Michael Jordan on the other.

Here at Didi's, the walls were bare. His bedspread was blue, the sheets new and stiff, the bed tightly made, unlike the nest of soft old blankets on his bunk bed back home. Didi asked him to throw out his battered feather pillow, saying she'd bought him a new pillow, and his probably had any manner of microscopic life growing in it. He obeyed.

If it had just been Joe and Bryce, it would've been easier. But Didi was constantly irritable when he was around, no matter how hard he tried to be polite. The fact that he needed a haircut or new shoes seemed like a personal insult, and she'd get a look on her face as if she'd just smelled a rotting corpse. When she had to introduce him, she always called him "Joe's nephew"— never *our* nephew. Never Bryce's cousin, even. One night, he overheard Didi describing his parents as "Southie trash," and he had to go for a long run to burn off the hatred.

Bryce was tiring, too, in a completely different way. Everything Lucas did still fascinated him, from the fact that he flossed his teeth every night (Dad had warned him about that—they couldn't afford a dentist, so Lucas had been instructed to take damn good care of his teeth) to the fact that he knew how to cook a meal.

He tried to stay out of the way. Kept his head down, showered at night after the rest of them had gone to bed because Didi made comments about the hot water running out. He never asked for seconds and always made sure his room was neat. He worked to catch up in school and wrote to his father and Steph, because a cell phone wasn't one of the items given to him. But he emailed from the library every day, sitting at the third computer in the second row. He also sent handwritten letters to Dad because Dad had said in one of their weekly phone calls (which Didi resented) that getting mail was really great. And he sure would love it if Lucas could visit.

Lucas asked. He waited until he could have a word alone with his uncle. "Sure, of course, I'll see when we can make it," Joe said, but nothing materialized. He asked again, and then again. Late at night at the end of his second month, he overheard Joe and Didi talking through the air-conditioning vent that made for excellent eavesdropping. "I think I'll take Lucas to see my brother tomorrow," Joe said affably, and Lucas actually jolted upright, his heart leaping in his chest.

Silence, then, "Excuse me?"

"It'd be good for him. He's having a tough time."

"Are you an *idiot,* Joe? You want to take a *child* to a *prison?* Can you imagine how that will impact your *son?* Lucas is a bad enough influence on him as it is. And I think I've bent over backward here, taking him in the way we've had to. This is *not* how I envisioned life, you know. Now you want to take him to see your criminal, drug-dealing brother?"

As usual, Didi got her way.

So the letters and emails had to suffice.

Then, after seven months, word came that Dan was being transferred. Overcrowding in Illinois prisons; Dad was going to a facility in Arizona next week. Joe broke the news at dinner, and Didi's pinched face froze even harder.

"Do you think you can take me to see him this weekend?" Lucas asked, his fork was clenched in his hand.

"You bet, sport," his uncle said.

"We'll see," Didi answered. "This is not really dinner conversation, though, is it?" She inclined her head toward Bryce, who was texting someone and smiling.

"Please, Aunt Didi." He hated calling her *aunt*. She didn't deserve the title, but maybe, please God, it would soften her up.

"I *said,* we'll see, Lucas."

That meant no.

Dad was being moved on Monday. It was already Wednesday.

That night, after the family had gone upstairs and no voices drifted down through the vents, Lucas packed his cheap backpack, made a couple of peanut butter sandwiches, taking care to wipe down the counter and put the knife in the dishwasher. Left the house, closing the door silently behind him.

His plan was pretty basic: he'd get to his sister's place and get her to borrow her friend's car. The prison was about three hours out of Chicago. If she couldn't take him, Tommy O'Shea's parents might. They'd liked him well enough back in the day. Once, Lucas had intervened in a fight on Tommy's behalf and got a black eye for his trouble. Maybe it'd be enough to get a ride. Or he'd hitchhike.

He made it out of the development and walked about a mile to the train tracks. It'd be perfect if he could hop a freighter like the hobos of yore, but the trains on this track were commuter trains and flew by at this time of night. But the tracks did lead into Chicago, so Lucas walked along them, his heart both heavy and light.

It'd be good to see Dad again. But it would be terrible to see him, too, because this would be the last time for a long time. A really long time.

Arizona…that was two days of driving, and Lucas didn't even have a learner's permit.

He was about two miles out of town when he looked over his shoulder.

Shit.

Bryce was following him. His cousin raised his hand and trotted to close the distance between them.

"What are you doing?" Lucas said.

"Hey! I should ask you that, right? Where are you going? You running away?"

Lucas took a breath. "I'm going to say goodbye to my dad. Don't follow me, okay? I'll be back in a day or so."

"No, it's cool! I'll come with you, in fact."

"Bryce, if you come with me, your mom will have the state police out looking for you. Go home, buddy."

"Why? It'll be fun! The two of us, together!"

"No. You can't come."

"Well, I'm not going back." Bryce grinned, but there was a hardness there, the stubborn tone of a kid who was used to getting his way. "He's my uncle. I wanna say goodbye, too."

"Then go back home and ask your mother to take you."

"Yeah, right. She'd never let me go to a prison."

"Exactly. What do you think she's gonna do when you don't come down for breakfast?"

Bryce shrugged. In the distance, a train whistle

sounded, as lonely and sad as the call of a wolf at this late hour.

Lucas turned his back and kept walking. Bryce fell in step beside him. "This'll be great. We'll go see Uncle Dan then maybe hitchhike back or something. Maybe we can stop at your old place and hang out."

For a flash, Lucas could feel how good it would be to punch Bryce. Hard. Hard enough to knock him down. To tell him to get his head out of his ass, to see things from someone else's point of view, just once, and not be such an idiot. To go home and enjoy his status as Perfect and Adored Son and not co-opt this one thing, this goodbye to his father. To acknowledge that the loss of his mother and father *hurt,* goddamn it. To recognize that this wasn't some sort of *cousins-ho!* adventure. It was Lucas's chance to say goodbye to his father, who'd worked so hard and been so stupid and wrong and was such a good guy even so.

"This is fun," Bryce said now. "I mean, I don't think I've ever been out this late at night." He smiled.

"Yeah," Lucas said.

The train whistle sounded again, and Lucas put his foot on the rail. A faint vibration hummed through it.

In a flash, he saw how he could lose Bryce. He could cross the tracks at the last minute; Bryce wouldn't follow him because he'd be scared of getting hurt. When they were little, he never tried the stunts Lucas could pull on his bike, wheelies and jumps and spins. He wouldn't even dive off the dock at the lake where Joe had taken them last month.

So Lucas could sprint across the tracks, and Bryce wouldn't follow. The train would come, and it was a long one from the sound of it; Lucas hadn't grown up two blocks from the tracks for nothing. Then he'd run ahead as fast and far as he could, hidden by the train, and duck out of sight. Bryce would give up and go home, and Lucas could make it up to him when he got back. He just had to wait until the train got close enough, so Bryce wouldn't dare follow.

It almost worked.

When he estimated that he had four seconds until the train passed, he bolted onto the tracks.

But instead of being on the other side, he jerked to a stop right in the middle. *You're supposed to be across by now,* a quiet part of his brain calmly informed him.

One Mississippi.

His foot was stuck. Wedged tight between two cross ties. He wore Converse high-tops, the kind that went up to the ankle. Laced up tight because Didi had fits if either boy had untied shoes. Which meant he couldn't just pull his foot out, and wouldn't have time to untie it. The laces were double-knotted.

Two Mississippi.

He yanked and yanked, and time froze, and thoughts flew through his head, as clear and cold as a January night on the plains.

At least it'll be fast.

Bryce is gonna freak.

Poor Steph, hope the kids will do okay.

All the while, he lunged with his entire being, but the shoe didn't budge.

Three Mississippi.

The light washed over him, blinding him, and the train whistle was screaming—*sorry, conductor, not your fault*—and he looked at it, all that whiteness and noise and figured this was it, it'd be okay, Mom would be there, and—

And then something crashed into him, and he landed hard and was rolling on the gravel and dirt and the train was roaring past, shaking the earth.

Four Mississippi.

When the train finally passed, the quiet took a minute to return. The sound of hard breathing filled the air.

"Jesus," Bryce said faintly, looking at him. A smile crept on to his face. "Jesus Christ, we're still alive, thank you, God!"

Bryce had saved him. Bryce had risked his own life to save him, had hurtled across the tracks, tackled him and knocked him free.

The kid had come through.

And even though he was glad not to be a stain on the tracks and the conductor's conscience, Lucas felt his heart slide down a little. "Thanks," he said.

"Are you kidding? I wasn't just gonna let you die! That was unbe*liev*able!"

Lucas's ankle was starting to swell from the force of being ripped out the shoe, which remained unharmed on the track. He tried to stand, but white-hot fire flashed up his leg.

"It's okay, I'll help you," Bryce said.

And he did. Three miles back to the house, Bryce kept hold of him, carried his backpack, never grew tired. Got an ice pack and an Ace bandage and some Motrin. He suggested they not tell anyone about this, and Lucas agreed. They told Didi and Joe he'd tripped, and when he still couldn't walk without pain a week later, Joe took him to the E.R., where the doctor told him he'd torn a ligament. Crutches for a month, physical therapy for two.

He never did get to see his father again.

Dan Campbell died nineteen months later, stabbed in the laundry room of his prison which, he'd said in his letters to Lucas, was much nicer than the one he'd left.

CHAPTER EIGHT

"So WE NEED a plan," Colleen said, scrubbing a countertop with Clorox Clean-Up. They were at Faith's new house, a snug little Craftsman bungalow two blocks off the town green. "A safety net. I need a man, Faith."

"I'm totally on board," Faith said.

"As you should be, since I'm your best friend and have been your maid of honor twice."

"And I appreciate it. Leave those counters alone, Coll. God, he really freaked you out, didn't he?"

"I have no idea what you're talking about."

Faith rolled her eyes.

Yeah, okay. Stress-cleaning. Colleen set down the sponge, took off her rubber gloves and turned her attention to unpacking a box full of photos. Here was one from Faith's sister's wedding, when Faith had been about ten. Gorgeous, all of those Hollands. The perfect family, unlike her own mess.

"About my new man," she said. "I need someone hot and romantic and intelligent with a great sense of humor who can cook and is also a cowboy or a firefighter."

Faith snorted. "Okay, I'm thinking…uh…cowboys are pretty scarce. And for hot firefighters, we only have Gerard."

"You know what would be great? A tragic widower

type, like Jude Law in *The Holiday*. Definitely my type. Or Hugh Jackman in *Les Mis*. Le sigh!"

"Right, right. Impoverished fugitives who burst into song. Coming up empty, Coll."

Colleen flopped onto the couch. "That's the entire problem with living in this tiny town. Fine. Will Jack date me? Can you make him?"

"Of course I can." Faith took the photo and put it on the mantel. "But you do really want to settle down, right?" Faith said. "I don't want you to break my brother's heart."

"Of course I want to settle down! This whole domestic bliss thing you and Levi have going… I'm burning with jealousy. In a loving, supportive way."

It was true. Levi was hot and grouchy and wonderful, and whenever Colleen saw the way he looked at Faith—that protective, alpha thing, *my woman, people, and yes, I have been banging her silly*...well, sure. She wanted that. Plus, she hadn't been banged silly in ages.

"Faith, what's wrong with me? How come I never found anyone? Anyone real, that is?"

"Huh. Let me think about that for a second. Plus, I'm starving."

"Eating for two?"

"It's not official yet, so don't say anything, and yes, of course you're godmother. Even if Pru and Honor will kill me for it."

"I hope they do kill you. Then I get your baby."

"I think Levi would have something to say about that." Her hand went to her belly in that primal, beautiful way.

"I can handle Levi," Colleen said. "Come on. I

brought you a salad. All that nice spinach is good for my godchild. And it's loaded with bacon for you."

They sat at the kitchen table and ate. Not only had Colleen brought the salad, courtesy of her brother, but also some whole-grain artisanal bread from Lorelei's Sunrise Bakery, sparkling water and Lorelei's famous carrot cupcakes for dessert.

The breeze came through the open windows that overlooked the small, precious backyard. Soon there'd be a little kid toddling around out there. It was nice to picture.

"I think the reason you haven't found anyone," Faith said carefully, "is that men are scared of you. They want you, of course, because come on. Look at this." She waved her hand in front of Colleen. "Beautiful. But it's intimidating. You have a smart mouth, you're successful and you know everyone's secrets. It's a lot. And then there's Connor."

"I know. I should euthanize him."

Faith shoveled in some more spinach. "Do you really like Jack?"

"Sure! Of course I do. He's hot."

"Gross."

"I know, I know, he's your brother. But he's got that crinkly eye thing going. Like your dad." Colleen took a bite of bread. "I wish your dad had married me instead of Mrs. Johnson. I'd make such a good trophy wife."

"I'll ignore that. Okay, of course I'll fix you up with Jack. And then you can get married and your babies will be my nieces and nephews. Not that I'm rushing anything."

"SORRY," JACK SAID two nights later as they sat at Hugo's on their first official date. "I'm not feeling it."

"Oh, shut up," Colleen said. "You don't know anything. Jessica!" She waved Jess down; though Jess worked at Blue Heron for the Hollands, she still waited tables here a couple nights a week. "Don't you think Jack and I make a great couple?"

Jess tilted her head. "I'm not really feeling it."

"Damn it!" Colleen drained her martini and sighed.

"You guys want dessert?" Jess asked.

"Sure," Colleen grumbled. "Bring us the lava cake, okay? We'll split it because it's more romantic that way." She tried not to mind as Jack looked at Jessica's ass as she walked away. For one, it was a great ass. For two, yeah...the chemistry thing might be a little hard to overcome. The past hour and a half seemed like six.

On paper, things were perfect. Jack obediently called her for a date, though he didn't pick her up at her house; she lived a stone's throw off the green, but he kissed her cheek in the restaurant foyer. He smelled nice. She'd been flirting with him for ages, and he always blushed and went silent, indicating high levels of attraction.

And then...fizzle.

Happened every damn time.

She stared at him. It wasn't that there was no chemistry. It was that there was a black hole where chemistry was supposed to be. Jack felt an awful lot like a brother right now. Picturing him naked...yuck.

"Jack, I don't get it. I've been flirting with you for five years now. Now here's all this—" she gestured to her torso and face "—and you're just sitting there like a mushroom."

"Maybe you're not quite as..." He let his voice trail off before he damned himself completely.

"Yeah, no. It's not that."

He smiled. She couldn't help smiling back.

"I think it's that you're like a fourth sister," he said.

"But you blush when I flirt with you."

"It's a flush of horror."

"Really?"

"I'm sorry. It seemed rude to say, 'Please stop, you're making my skin crawl.'"

"Jack! I didn't make your skin crawl!"

He grimaced.

"Oh, sphincter." She put her head on the table. "Well, what am I supposed to do? The man I once loved, who dumped me for someone else, is back in town and I don't have a boyfriend. You'd think you could just marry me out of decency. How many free beers have I given you over the years?"

"Four," he said.

"I'd give you more in exchange for your hand in marriage."

"It's not you, Colleen," he said kindly, even if he was being a jerk and not marrying her. "You know. The divorce. Trust issues and, uh, what else did my sisters say? I wasn't really listening. Anyway. Sorry."

"Well, this sucks." She paused. "Will you at least be my date for Tom and Honor's wedding? I can't go with Connor. He might have a girlfriend." Perhaps three martinis had been one too many. Then again, conversation hadn't exactly been flowing. Vodka had.

"I'll have to pass," Jack said. "I plan to be the handsome, single brother of the bride."

"Well, thanks for nothing," Colleen grumbled.

And then the door opened, and bugger it all, there was Lucas Damien Campbell, Prince of Darkness.

Alone. Black jeans. Black shirt. Black hair, black eyes (not in the hockey player way, but in the Heathcliff way). God, he was beautiful, a thuggish angel, the kind who did God's dirty work. Beautiful with a side of scary.

You need to stop with the hyperbole, Connor's voice informed her.

Colleen swallowed with an audible click, her throat dry as…as…something really dry, she couldn't think just now.

She forced her eyes to the blond-haired, blue-eyed Jack.

"As of right now, you're my boyfriend, Jack, and I will castrate you if you deny it."

"And we wonder why you can't find a man," he said.

"Excuse me?"

"I love you deeply, Colleen, and can't take my eyes off you." His words were undercut by the act of taking out his phone.

Lucas saw them, did a slight double take, and came over, all predatory masculine grace (now *that* was a great phrase, oh, mommy, yes, and even better live and in person).

"Hi," he said.

"Lucas, what a pleasant surprise, do you know Jack Holland, my boyfriend?" Alas, Jack was texting. Colleen kicked him under the table.

"Ow!" he said. "Stop kicking me. I already have three sisters."

Lucas smiled. The special places squeezed. The men shook hands, and Colleen couldn't help being jealous of Jack, having Lucas's hand squeeze his, that big, swarthy, beautiful hand, strong and sure and—

"Here's your lava cake," Jess said, setting it down. "Hey," she added, looking at Lucas. "Did we go to school together?"

"No," Colleen answered. "I mean, yes, but it was only for a little while."

"Oh, right," Jess said. "You guys were together. Nice to see you. Luke, right?"

"Lucas," he corrected.

"Like George Lucas," Colleen said. "Not like Luke Skywalker. Personally, I like Luke better, you know, like 'Use the Force, Luke, the Force is strong within you,' but Lucas isn't bad. I'm not judging."

"You're cut off," Jess said. "And here's the check, whenever you're ready."

"Jack?" Colleen said. "Our cake is here, punkin." She took a bite.

Unfortunately, lava cake tended to be, well…lava-hot. As her tongue shriveled in agony, Colleen reacted. Spit that cake right out.

"Pretty," Jack murmured as she scraped her tongue free of the molten dessert.

"Thut up," she said.

She gulped some ice water, some dribbling down her chin in her haste. Lovely. No napkin, where the hell was the napkin? She looked like a drooling freak. Fine. She used the tablecloth to dab her chin. And neck. And bosom, for the love of St. Patrick.

Lucas was watching the show, his eyes holding an irresistible hint of smile.

"Okay, fine. Lucas? Is there something I can help you with?"

"No," he said. "Just getting something to eat."

"Good. Because Jack and I want to get back to our romantic dinner, right Pooh Bear?"

Jack looked confused. "Are you talking to me?"

"You're Faith's brother, right?" Lucas asked.

"Afraid so. And Prudence's, and Honor's. Have we met?"

"I used to date him," Colleen said. She took another forkful of cake, careful to blow on this one.

"Right," Jack said. "You were talking about him in the bar the other—"

"No, I wasn't," she said. "Shut up, Jack."

Jack sighed. "Babe? Sweetie-pie? Cuddlebuns? Can I leave now?"

Okay, so this wasn't working. Time to surrender. "Just get out of here, Jack, and thanks for nothing."

Her un-husband grinned, shook Lucas's hand far too cheerfully and stopped to chat with Jess. "You better pay for dinner!" Colleen added.

He did. He might not want to marry her and sire three gorgeous children (possibly four, if one pregnancy was a set of twins, as Colleen would prefer), but he did pick up the tab.

"Can I join you?" Lucas asked.

"Sure," she muttered. He slid into Jack's vacated chair, and the air seemed to shimmer with the sheer force of...of *them*.

"I thought we should talk."

"Are you stalking me?"

He gave her a slight smile. "Would you like me to?"

Yes, please. "Such an ego. Good to see that hasn't changed."

"There are two restaurants in this town, Colleen.

You own one. I showed up here as a courtesy to you. Not to stalk you."

"You can come to O'Rourke's. I have no problem with that. I'm totally over you."

Another almost-smile. The special places began to purr.

Jessica came over and cleared the table, her movements precise and efficient. Lucas ordered a glass of 2010 Fisher Cabernet Sauvignon that Robert Parker had anointed with a 96. It went well with Lucas's whole fallen angel thing. He might as well have been drinking a soul.

Colleen looked around the restaurant, automatically smiling at the familiar faces scattered among the tourists. Hugo's was the fancier restaurant in Manningsport, white tablecloths and flowers and a view of the lake. The sun was setting, the sky purple and slate, the lake darkening. A few boats glided toward the marina, white sails sharp in the dimming light. Hugo's was busy tonight, and if Hugo's was busy, it meant O'Rourke's would be mobbed. She should go help out after this, even if it was her night off.

She didn't move. Her skin felt too tight. "So you're here," she said, "and I'm here, and obviously we'll run into each other now and again."

"Yes."

"You look good, Spaniard," she said. "The years have been kind."

His eyes smiled. His face didn't move; it was like a magic trick or something, the way he could smile like that. Those dark, dark Latin eyes. Lucas never said too much, but his eyes did. Always had.

Never once had he ever said he loved her. Never.

But she would have sworn it was true anyway, hell's to the yes, she thought she'd seen it in his eyes a thousand times.

She wondered if his wife had thought the same thing.

Her throat was abruptly tight.

"I need to walk my dog," she said. He could just stay here and eat and brood and be by himself.

"Can I come?" he asked.

"What about your dinner?"

"It can wait."

Dang it. "Sure."

He left a few bills on the table, and they went out. Better. The cool May air was welcome against her hot face.

They crossed the town green. O'Rourke's looked safe and cheery; she could see the mob through the windows, the soft, golden light and gentle tide of voices and music from inside. The pub's slogan was simple and heartfelt, and one Colleen had come up with the first day she and Con bought the place: *O'Rourke's: You're very welcome here.*

And now, Lucas one step behind her, she wanted very much to go into the bar, see her brother, flirt with Tom Barlow and Gerard Chartier, chat up Cathy and Louise, give a hug to Mel Stoakes, whose wife had just died. She wanted to be the person behind the bar, because she knew what she was doing there.

They went down the block, away from the green and into the Village until they were in front of her house. "I'll be right back," she told him, and ran up the stairs, past the landing where she'd just planted her porch garden, and up to her cheery blue door.

Rufus, her faithful pup, was waiting. "Come on, big

guy," she said, and he bounded down the stairs in two strides.

Lucas took a step back, she was happy to see, and Rufus did what most dogs did—rammed his snout right into Lucas's crotch.

"Easy there, boy," he said.

"He likes you. Then again, he tried to hump a tree the other day, so don't take it personally."

Lucas's teeth flashed in the darkness. "You need a leash?"

"Nope." Rufus stuck to her side like a guardian angel as they walked to the park down by the lake. "Go ahead, boy," she said, and he loped off to sniff and investigate.

The air smelled coppery and sweet—lilacs and lake water—and the hum from O'Rourke's was audible on the breeze. Small waves slapped the shore and dock. There were a few people out, but it was fully dark now, and most were on their way home.

The tingling feeling was back, and her whole body thrummed with that invisible connection to Lucas, as if they were circled by electricity.

She wondered if he felt it, too.

This is pathetic, she told herself. *He was your first love. Big deal. Get over it. He'll be gone again soon, anyway.*

She sat down on one of the benches that overlooked Crooked Lake. Lucas sat next to her, not touching, but close enough.

He smelled the same. That clean, sharp smell, like the outdoors. She used to tell him it was ironic, he smelled like the mountains, her city boy—

Well. He wasn't a boy anymore. And he wasn't hers.

Funny that she'd felt buzzed earlier. She was stone-cold sober now.

"Well? You wanted to talk," she said, her voice sounding terse to her own ears.

"Yes." There was a long silence, the wind gusting. It was getting chilly. She should've brought a sweater. Or he could put his arm around her, and she'd feel perfect.

Stop it.

Rufus came up, and she rubbed his rough head, then tugged on his ears. He smiled happily and flopped at her feet, and she slid her foot over his stomach for the obligatory belly rub.

"How have you been?" Lucas asked.

"Good. Fine. Great, actually." She cleared her throat. *Think of him as an old friend.* "You know. Connor and I bought the pub, and he's the chef, and I run the place. We love it. Things are good."

"And your family?

"Just fine. Sort of. Dad and Gail got married, and they have a daughter. Savannah. She's nine now." Weird, to be telling him about this. Maybe he knew. Maybe he internet stalked her the way she occasionally looked him up on Google. Well. She hadn't in a long time. But she used to.

"Is your grandfather still alive?" he asked.

"Yes."

"How's he doing?"

"He's horrifyingly healthy." Gramp no longer spoke and hadn't in years, and he cried most afternoons, but his body was doing just great. One of God's little jokes.

"How old is he now?"

"Eighty-seven."

Lucas nodded. Didn't say anything else, and she didn't, either. He was the one who wanted to talk, after all.

"Colleen," he began, and his *voice,* damn it, so deep and rumbly and scraped her in all those special places, and it just wasn't fair.

She'd talk. It was safer that way. "Lucas, here's the deal. You're back for a while, and of course we'll see each other, and no hard feelings, okay? I mean, we were young and foolish and all that fun stuff. I'm glad you're doing well, and it's nice for Joe that you're around."

He turned to look at her, and she forced herself to return his gaze, even if her knees were trembling.

"Anything else?" he said.

Why? Why her and not me?

"Nope. Anything else for you?"

"No. Except I'd really like you to leave Bryce alone. Now isn't the time for him to be involved with anyone."

"Whatever you say, God. I mean, Lucas. Sorry. I get you two confused sometimes."

He lifted an eyebrow. "I take that as a 'piss off.'"

"Perceptive of you."

He sighed. "All right, Colleen. Do what you want. You always have."

"And what is that supposed to mean?" she asked. "After all, you haven't been around for roughly a third of my life. Not one letter, not one email, not one phone call. You have no clue about what I always do."

"Did you want me to call you?"

"No. I'm just saying maybe you don't know everything, Lucas."

"I think I know what's best for my cousin. He needs to grow up. He needs to stand on his own two feet and be a man."

"Oh, I love when you talk all Latin machismo."

He leaned forward so she had to look at him now. "His father is dying, Colleen. His mother still hasn't cut the cord, and Bryce hasn't ever had a job for more than two consecutive months. I'm here to honor Joe's dying wish that his son grows up a little, and the last thing he needs is another meddling woman trying to run his life."

"Are you talking about me or Paulie?"

"Definitely you."

"How nice. Well, I spend a lot of time with Bryce, unlike yourself. I might know him better than you think. Paulie is a very nice person. She'd be good for him."

"I'm not debating that. I'm sure she's nice. But distracting Bryce and trying to force some kind of romance—"

"Okay, Lucas. I understand your opinion. I just don't happen to share it." She twisted the silver ring on her right hand. "Is this what you wanted to talk about? Bryce?"

"Yes. Why? Did you want to talk about something else?"

Men. "Nope."

"I get the impression that you want very much to talk about something else. So do it."

"I'm fine." Rufus licked her ankle.

"Colleen."

"I'm good, Lucas. Is there something on *your* mind?"

"I just told you what's on my mind. Can you not be so female and please just address what you want to talk about?"

"I can't *not* be female, Lucas. I mean, not without

the big operation, which I really don't want to have and can't afford anyway."

He threw up his hands. "I don't know whether to strangle you or kiss you."

"Don't you *dare* kiss me."

He kissed her.

God.

God. It was a prayer, as in *God help me,* because Colleen's whole body lit up with flares of light and heat and tiny pinpricks of shock. Lucas was hot and hard and strong, and she wrapped her arms around him and held him just as hard, her mouth opening under his, and yes, yes, *this* was what they were meant to do, this elemental, hard, thought-stealing kiss.

How dare he.

She yanked back. "Hell's to the no, Lucas," she hissed. "You're not here for me. You're back to help your uncle, and then it's bye-bye, Manningsport, back to Chicago and your swanky life there. So don't you dare kiss me. Don't you dare, Lucas. I'm not about to become some little fling you have in between the important chapters of your real life. Been there, done that."

He ran a hand through his ridiculously gorgeous hair. "You're right."

Damn.

Strike that. *Good,* she meant. "Yeah. So just…you know. Remember that. Whatever." She stood up. "Come on, Rufus, let's go."

Her dog, who was lying splayed on the grass like a giant dog-slut, leaped to his feet and trotted up the street.

Colleen followed, furious with herself, furious with

him, her whole body throbbing with need and lust and heat and…and…

Don't go there again, Connor's voice said. *We know how this ends. We've been through this before.*

You'd be stupid to do it again.

CHAPTER NINE

BY THE TIME his senior year of high school rolled around, Lucas Campbell was well aware that girls found him very appealing. He didn't mind. Had the typical fun with the occasional girl, making out in a car or stairwell at school, getting fifteen texts a day from some infatuated sophomore. His school had almost two thousand kids in it, and he was out from the shadow of being Bryce's impoverished orphaned cousin, since Bryce went to a private college prep school (days, of course; Didi would never let him board).

But then they moved from Illinois to the tiny town of Manningsport, New York, a postcard type of place with vineyards and a lake that was a far cry from the mighty Michigan. Bryce had gotten into Hobart (thanks to Lucas dragging his GPA into a respectable range), and Didi took a transfer to her company's branch in Corning so she could be closer to her son.

Lucas, on the other hand, got a full scholarship to University of Chicago. When Didi announced the move to Manningsport, he figured he'd stay in Chicago; Stephanie would let him crash on her couch for a couple of months until he graduated. But Bryce wanted him to come along, already distressed that they wouldn't be at the same college, and Bryce generally got what he wanted.

It was fine. Lucas had no ill will toward his cousin, who was easy to get along with and endlessly cheerful. Come August, they'd be parting ways, and he'd even miss the big doofus, so what was another few months? No big deal.

Until he saw Colleen O'Rourke, that quick instant when their eyes met, and something he'd never felt before slammed into his chest at seventy-five miles per hour.

Under normal circumstances, he would've classified (and dismissed) her as another too-popular pretty girl, same as any other.

But something happened when their eyes locked.

She saw him.

Not just his general bad-boy looks, which he had nothing to do with but which had an undeniable effect. Not just a slide of her eyes up and down his torso.

She *saw* him. Her eyes—her big, wide beautiful eyes changed from smug and amused to…more open somehow. Like something clicked, and she could see his whole life story in one look.

He didn't like it one freaking bit.

By the end of that day, he knew her voice, could tell when she was nearby, because it was the same feeling as when the barometer dropped in front of a storm, that strange, buzzing sensation he'd get before the mighty Midwestern clouds rolled in, churning with electricity and heat. The same feeling as the night he'd put his foot on the rail and felt the train coming, that hum of power.

She felt it, too. He could tell, because she avoided him for weeks.

Couldn't even look him in the eye, the girl who seemed to have a smile and a quip for everyone, universally looked up to by the other girls, universally wanted by the boys.

If she was walking down the hall and he happened to be close by, she'd veer off or stop to talk to someone—the janitor, a teacher, a friend. If he was sitting in the bleachers, watching Bryce play soccer, she made sure to sit far away. She didn't come into Raxton's Hardware, where he'd gotten an after-school job. Only if she absolutely couldn't avoid it would she give him the briefest and most generic smile he'd ever seen.

Ever since his father had gone to jail, Lucas felt as though he was half invisible and half a front. His fellow students in Manningsport were a little awed by his newness, his half–Puerto Rican looks, as most of them were as white as snow. A mixed-race kid from Chicago? Wow! Cool! Bryce saw him almost as a superhero, where the ordinary act of doing his own laundry was regarded with wide-eyed wonder. To Joe, he was a remembrance of the old neighborhood, an obligation to his late brother.

Sometimes he'd watch Bryce and Joe horse around on the perfect lawn of the perfect house, scuffling over the soccer ball, and a sense of longing would almost drop Lucas to his knees—to go back in time so just once more, he could sit on that old blue plastic crate, handing his father tools as he worked on a car.

The memory of that *almost* moment on the train tracks, when he'd almost made it to see his father one last time, almost had been able to tell his father he'd been a good dad, almost had that last time to see his father who had worked so hard, who'd done a very wrong thing for very right reasons…just one more time to see those careworn eyes smile at the sight of his son. He'd almost had that.

Joe tried. But he had a son, and Didi made sure he remembered the difference between son and unwanted relation.

As for Didi, he'd learned early on to stay out of the way. If he joined them for Family Movie Night (Fridays) or Family Game Night (Mondays) or Family Hike (Sunday afternoons), she'd get that corpse-sniffing look on her face, her lips tight, her eyes on him for too long, willing him to disappear. Lucas claimed that he'd rather stay in his room and read, which wasn't untrue. But when he heard them laugh, or even just the sound of Didi's voice, relaxed and easy with him not around… he'd just turn up Bryce's cast-off iPod and try to remember his mother's face.

His sister would call once in a while, mostly to vent about Rich. Things weren't working out, and Steph was up to her ears in babies: Mercedes was one of those high-maintenance types who'd learn to talk back before she could walk, and the twins, Tiffany and Cara, were toddlers bent on taking over the world one broken lamp at a time.

So Lucas's plan was simple. Make good grades, get a scholarship to a school in Chicago, go into a field where he'd make a lot of money, take care of Steph and the girls. Head down, nose clean.

It irked Didi that Lucas was smarter than her own son, but then again, this way, she had a built-in tutor. She made sure Lucas checked Bryce's homework and taught him algebraic theorems and quizzed him in history dates. Between that and his own heavy load of homework, running interference when his cousin hung out with the wrong kids or drank too much, the job at the hardware store and cutting lawns on Sundays so he could save as much as he could, Lucas definitely did not have time for a girlfriend.

He had a plan, and it wasn't to fall in love. He had three months of high school left, three months to spend with kids who'd been together since birth, it seemed. He'd be going back to Chicago soon. He was just passing through Manningsport.

And then prom night came, and for once, he was in the right place at the right time. When he saw Colleen on the dock, being held by that dickless wonder, he felt something bigger and more powerful than anything he'd felt since his father had been led out of the courtroom in handcuffs. He would've died for Colleen O'Rourke that night with a glad heart, no questions, no hesitation.

From that night on, he and Colleen were together. They weren't dating, hanging out, hooking up. They were together. He was locked in from the second he kissed her, something he'd been thinking about doing from the moment he first saw her, something he'd vowed not to do because it was certain that even one kiss would bind him to her.

He was right. The second his lips touched hers, a word came into his head, a word from long ago when his mother was still alive, when Spanish was still spoken at home.

Mía. Mine.

Colleen was his.

They managed to wait until after graduation to seal the deal; the first time for both of them, two kinds of birth control because he was paranoid about getting her pregnant, the way his father had done to his mother. He went as slowly as he could, heart thudding so hard he shook, unable to believe that she'd have him.

It got awkward, they were nervous and inexperienced, and it was amazing anyway, and when he was on top of her and inside her at last, and he was just holding still for fear of causing her any more discomfort than he probably already was, she opened her eyes, those beautiful clear eyes, and just looked at him. Colleen who always smiled and always laughed was serious now, and for one beat of his heart, he thought she was going to say *Get off, leave, this isn't working.*

"I love you," she whispered instead, and the words wrapped around his chest and squeezed hard.

No one had said those words to him in a long, long time.

"Say that again," he whispered, just to make sure he'd heard right, and she laughed, and the sound was even better than her words.

She could do that—flip a switch like that. She'd be laughing with her friends on the green, eating an ice cream cone, and she'd see him walking to the hardware store, and her eyes would change from that slightly knowing, sly smile to unguarded and soft and full of so much that he could drown in it. Or the reverse, too—one July night they were lying on a blanket in the backyard of her house, just holding hands, and Lucas was trying to figure out a way to tell her he loved her, because of course he did, and of course she knew it. But the actual words…they were harder.

Just say it, his brain instructed. *Don't be such an ass. She tells you five times a day. You're gonna blow this, you know.*

But the words stayed locked.

Colleen rolled on top of him, looking at him, and there it was, that soft, gentle gaze that seemed to know every event that had torn off a chunk of his heart—his mom's slurring voice as her ability to speak died little by little, his father's arrest, the phone call that came from the prison at 2:36 a.m., asking if he was the son of Daniel Wakeman Campbell—every jealous thought he'd ever had about Bryce, every lonely minute spent trying to be invisible… Colleen's love erased them all.

But all he could do was look at her, touch her face, and hope she knew.

She smiled just a little, almost as if she was answering his question. "I'm starving," she said, and her smile grew in a flash, and his was born. Because yeah, it felt as if he had never smiled until her.

Her family liked him well enough—except for her father, which was understandable. Pete O'Rourke tolerated him, though, and Lucas appreciated it. Her mom exclaimed over his manners and always made a lot of noise when she was coming down the hall, giving them a warning to keep it clean. Connor watched him at school, and then seemed to mellow, realizing that Lucas wasn't some player out to break his sister's heart.

In late August, she drove him to Chicago, ten hours of them holding hands and barely talking, and dropped him off at the university, took an unnecessarily long time to unpack his meager belongings and walked around campus with him.

Then it was time for her to leave.

"I'll call you in an hour," he said, kissing her for the hundredth time.

"Nah," she said, wiping her eyes. "I'm already over you. It was a passing thing, like a virus."

He waited.

"Fine," she said. "I love you."

"Say it again."

"Say it again," she grumbled. "Not that *you've* ever said it once, mind you."

He kissed her, feeling as if he was saying goodbye to the brightest, best thing that life had ever granted him, and Colleen wrapped her arms around his neck and buried her face against him. "I love you, too," she said, and her back hitched with a sob.

"Adiós, mía."

"God, I love when you speak Spanish. So hot."

Then she got into her car and drove off, tossing him a cheery salute that contradicted the tears that gleamed on her cheeks.

He stood there until her car turned the corner. Kept standing there until she pulled up again, because he'd known somehow that she'd drive around the block to see if he'd left. She got out of the car, laughing, and jumped into his arms again. "Go to your dorm, idiot," she said. "Call me in an hour."

So his plan became more complicated. Stay in college, make good grades, get a job that earned a lot of money, take care of Steph and the girls…and marry Colleen.

For three and a half years, it worked. Whenever possible, in between working as a security guard at a gleaming skyscraper downtown, between fixing Stephanie's car/furnace/pipes and the occasional stint babysitting the girls, working summers for a construction company, keeping his GPA over 3.7, he saw Colleen. He'd hitchhike back to Manningsport when he could, or kick his roommate out for the weekend when Colleen came to Chicago. They called, emailed, instant-messaged, took advantage of whatever form of communication available to them.

She was still his. He was still hers. He wasn't sure why she kept him, but she did.

And then, one weekend when he had scored a plane fare that let him fly to Buffalo-Niagara for seventy-nine dollars, the shit hit the fan.

Because he hadn't been sure he could get the time off from work, he hadn't told Colleen he was coming. Figured it'd be fun to surprise her; she was going to Ithaca College, not wanting to be too far from home, from her elderly grandfather, specifically. Connor was at the Culinary Institute, which was a few hours' drive, and Faith was all the way in Virginia. Colleen put on a cheery front, but Lucas knew she was lonely. She'd told him she'd be home this weekend, and the stars had fallen into alignment with that flight.

He stopped for a cup of coffee at an airport kiosk, tore open two sugar packets, glanced up and saw a familiar figure.

Colleen's father was kissing someone who was definitely not Colleen's mother. Who was, in fact, a redhead dressed in a tiny white dress that just cleared her (admittedly great) ass and who wore high heeled shoes and was wrapped around Pete O'Rourke.

Both of them had suitcases.

Both appeared to be doing a tonsil swab of the other with their tongues.

Mr. O'Rourke broke the kiss, looked up with the smug expression of exactly what he was: an older man with a very hot, much younger girlfriend. Then he saw Lucas. He froze for a second, and—horribly—smiled. "Lucas. How are you, son?"

He'd never called Lucas that before, that was for damn sure.

He took the hot chick's hand and towed her over to where Lucas was standing, sugar packets still not emptied into the coffee. "This is Gail," he said.

"Hi there," she purred.

She was a knockout, Lucas would give her that. Long red hair, creamy skin, and a look in her green eyes that said she knew it.

Lucas didn't say anything.

"Gail, babe, give us a second," Pete said, and Gail gave both men a sultry look and cruised away, ass swinging in a blatant advertisement. Pete folded his arms. "So this is awkward," he said. He gave Lucas a fake smile, his eyes completely uninvolved, like a snake's.

"Yes," Lucas said.

"I think it's obvious what's going on here, so I won't bother saying it's not what it seems. It's exactly what it seems. But it would obviously hurt my family—Colleen especially—to hear about this."

He kept talking. More of the same. *I'm not terribly proud of it... Colleen's mother...haven't been right for a while...just happened...wouldn't understand.*

He made Lucas's skin crawl. The kind of man who thought he was smarter than everyone else, who endured conversation from his wife. *Slick,* that was the word.

But Lucas knew how much Colleen loved him. She was a daddy's girl, but not in a bad way. Just in maybe a typical way, a girl who thought her father was the smartest, funniest, greatest guy around. Steph had felt the same way about their dad. And yeah, with Colleen, Lucas would admit, Pete was okay.

"So I hope I can count on your discretion, son. No reason for anyone to get hurt here."

Lucas gave him a long look. "I'm not your son," he said.

Mr. O'Rourke's eyes narrowed. "True enough. Well, you probably have to get going. I gather you're visiting my daughter."

Lucas didn't bother answering. Glanced over at Gail, who was putting on lipstick to the fascination of a security guard, then back at Pete. Without another word, he hefted up his backpack and walked away.

When he arrived in Manningsport a few hours later, he stopped at the Black Cat, the scummy little bar where Colleen occasionally filled in. Her face lit up when she saw him, and he smiled as she launched herself into his arms.

"I was *just* thinking about you!" she exclaimed, her eyes bright. "You're a sight for sore eyes, Spaniard. Kiss me! Do it!"

He obeyed, and the unclean feeling from the airport faded.

Colleen took him home for a late dinner, and they sat at the kitchen table. Jeanette cut him a slab of cake before helping herself to one, and said how Pete was in Mexico…a conference for commercial property owners.

"You didn't want to go?" he asked carefully.

"Oh, well," Mrs. O'Rourke said, waving her hand demurely. "Pete said it wouldn't be any fun. Just a hotel with a lot of drunk people."

"Dad hates those things. Wouldn't want to drag Mom there and make her suffer, too," Colleen said.

Yeah. What a champ.

All weekend long, it throbbed like a rotten tooth, and every once in a while, he'd reach out and touch the thought. Framed how he'd bring it up to Colleen. *Hey, mía, I ran into your dad and his lover at the airport* or *Hey, Colleen, how are things with your parents?* or *This conference of your dad's, Colleen—it's no conference.*

A hundred times over the weekend, he started to tell her, and stopped. It wasn't his place. Maybe it would blow over. Maybe Pete and Jeanette O'Rourke had an arrangement, an open marriage, whatever.

Colleen drove him to the airport Sunday night, waited with him as she always did, every minute together precious. She lay with her head on his lap, her long black hair glistening under the lights, a smile on her face, eyes closed.

She looked so happy.

"Things are good with your family?" he finally asked.

"Oh, yeah," she said without opening her eyes. "You know. Connor's perfect, Mom's discovered scrapbooking, and Dad... Dad's been working a lot."

Now was the moment.

But the smile on her face...he couldn't. Stroked her hair instead.

"Hey, I have a summer job lined up," she said, practically purring under his hand. "Nurse's assistant at Rushing Creek. Kind of great, don't you think?"

"Sounds perfect."

"So that'll be great. I can work there, take care of Gramp, sock some money away, finish school, and then we can get married and have twelve beautiful children." She smiled more fully and opened her eyes. "Speaking of that..."

Lucas stopped breathing.

"Speaking of what?" he croaked.

"Kids. Marriage. Eternal love and death do us part. Wanna get married this summer?"

"Are you pregnant?" he managed.

She bolted up. "What? No! Oh, I get it. Sorry. Wow, look at your face. Are you having a heart attack?"

"Yes."

She rolled her eyes. "No, babe. Not pregnant. I mean, come on. We use two kinds of birth control." She paused. "But you do want to get married, right?"

He was still digging out of the avalanche of terror. "Uh, sure, *mia*. Someday, yeah." He took a deep breath and looked at her face. Shit. Wrong answer. "What?"

She shrugged. Never a good sign.

"What, Colleen?"

"I thought you wanted to get married. To me, specifically."

This was, unfortunately, one of the few parts of their relationship that stuck a little. Her picture of the future, and his.

To her, there was nothing at all scary or strange about getting married young. Why not? They loved each other. (True.) She wanted to live in Manningsport, preferably down the street from Connor, and have a bunch of kids.

And so did he. Mostly.

Except for the Manningsport thing. He was a Southie. His sister lived in Chicago, not to mention his nieces, and Steph always needed something, whether it was babysitting, or extra money, or a flat tire changed. She was his true family, as opposed to Bryce and Joe and Didi. He hadn't even called them to let them know he was in Manningsport this weekend, not wanting anything to take away from his time with Colleen.

Marriage, sure. Just not now.

Lucas wanted to get through law school, having decided that was the best way to make a decent living. Colleen wasn't materialistic, but Lucas would kill himself before having her live in some shitty little apartment the way Stephanie did, bartending nights while he was in law school. She deserved better than that, and until he could give it to her, they weren't doing anything. He wanted health insurance and sunny rooms and a yard and a dog.

He wanted to provide for his family, and he wasn't going to have one until he could give them a good life. He wasn't ever going to be in the same straits his father had been in. Ever.

"Well, this silence doesn't give me much to go on, does it?" Colleen said, pulling her legs up onto the chair and wrapping her arms around them. She rested her chin on her knees and sighed.

"You know what I want," he said.

"Yes, I do."

"It's you."

That got a little smile.

"Just not yet, *mía*."

"You have this image of me," she said, "as needing a nice car and three acres and a membership at the country club." Her voice wavered a little. "And all I want is for us to be together."

"Attention passengers," came the voice over the PA. "We'll now begin boarding for American Flight 227 for Chicago."

"Crap," Colleen whispered. "We should have these talks earlier in the weekend next time."

He kissed her, tasting the salt of her tears. "I'll miss you," he said. "I'll call you when I land."

"I love you."

The words almost made it out this time. It didn't matter. She knew anyway, and despite her wet eyes, she smiled.

"Say it again," he said.

"I love you. Even if you don't deserve me."

"I don't."

"You kind of do." She stood up and hugged him and kissed him again, sending him off with a smile and a pat on the ass, despite her wet eyes.

Next time, he promised himself. Next time he would definitely say the words. And next time, he'd tell her about her father and Gail.

EXCEPT HE DIDN'T.

How do you break someone's heart? How do you ensure that someone never sees her father the same way again? He just couldn't do it.

So he told himself it wasn't his business. Maybe the affair had blown over by now, anyway. It was the right thing to do, he told himself. Even if agreeing with Pete O'Rourke made him feel unclean. It wasn't his job.

If his conscience knew that was bullshit, Lucas nonetheless stayed mute on the subject. His arguments for doing nothing sounded good enough. For two months, he tried not to think about it.

One April night, he sat at the front desk at the trading firm where he was one of the night security guards, attempting to read a textbook on commercial torts in anticipation of law school, and instead listening to Bernard detail his conquest the weekend before.

"So she's all this and that, right? But I just keep looking at her, she's so hot, let me tell you, a body that would make Jesus weep, okay? And so all these guys, they're trying to get her number or dance with her, but I just stare, and she's all, 'Hey, what you looking at, asshole?' and I'm like, 'I'm looking at nothing,' and she's all pissy now, right, and—"

Mercifully, because these stories tended never to end, a banging came on the front door of the lobby, despite the fact that it was after ten.

"Isn't that your girlfriend?" Bernard asked. "Man, you been cheating on her or something? Yikes. That, or she's pregnant, dude." It was Colleen, clad in a sweatshirt, jeans, flip-flops and a Yankees hat. She was crying.

Lucas ran over, punched in the code for the door, and she hurled herself into his arms, her face unrecognizable with grief.

"*Mia,* what happened?" he asked, holding her hard.

"I didn't know what to do," she sobbed. "I couldn't talk on the phone…so I just came here, I drove all day… he…my…"

"Is it Connor? Is he okay?" Oh, God, if something happened to her twin, it would kill her. Literally, maybe.

"No," she managed, her voice strangled. "It's my father. He—he's…"

"Is he hurt?" he asked, picturing Smug Pete lying in a hospital bed.

"He's—he's…" He heard her take a shaking breath, then another. She pulled back and wiped her eyes with the heels of her hands. "Lucas, he's divorcing my mom! He has some whore on the side, and she's *pregnant!*"

"Gail?" he asked.

Huge. Fucking. Mistake.

She blinked up at him, her face changing. "How… how do you know her name?"

He took a breath. The damage was done—time to face the music. "I saw them at the airport a while ago. He, uh…he introduced me."

Bernard grimaced and tiptoed a safe distance away to the bank of elevators where he'd probably eavesdrop.

The innocent distress that had painted Colleen's face a minute ago slid off, and in its place came a horrible nothingness.

She took a step away from him.

"You *knew?*"

Well, shit. "Yes."

She closed her mouth. Opened it. Closed it again, then spoke. "You saw them together, and you never told me?" Her voice bounced through the huge, vacant foyer.

"I didn't know how to break it to you."

"So you did nothing? Let me sit there like an idiot, thinking my father was the best guy in the damn world, and he was screwing another woman the whole time?"

"Colleen—"

"What was this? A man-to-man agreement or some such shit? You didn't think I'd want to know about this?"

"Okay, look. I should've said something, and I didn't. I'm sorry."

"Oh, you're sorry. Well, that's fine, then. You've been lying to me for—how long? How long have you known? Specifically, Lucas."

He grimaced. "Since February."

"Since *February?*" The last word was a shriek. Bernard peeked around from the elevator banks again and shrugged, male sign language for *Dude, if I could help you, I would, but you're up shit creek, man.*

Colleen's breath was coming in gasps.

"Coll, I think you should calm down."

Again, *such* a dickhead thing to say.

"I should— Wow. Wow, Lucas. Months! You've known for months! Did it ever occur to you that if you'd said something, maybe I could've stopped this? Maybe I could've talked to him, and he would've seen how wrong this was, and I wouldn't have a baby brother or sister on the way right now, did that ever occur to you?"

"Colleen, if you'd just listen—"

"I would've *loved* to have listened a few months ago. Now, not so much."

He took a deep breath. "Look. I know how you worship that guy. Okay? And I didn't want to say anything, since this is exactly what would happen. You'd get hysterical."

Dickhead thing to say. He winced and tried to take her hand, but she pulled it away. Folded her arms and looked out the window, her jaw hard. "I'm going home. Don't call me."

"Colleen, I didn't mean to…" Here came the part where he would beg.

"In case it's unclear, we're breaking up."

Her words sucker punched him in the gut. "What?"

"You have to go to law school, my family's imploding, and maybe we're not the people we think we are."

"I don't even know what that means."

"It means," she barked, even as tears spurted out of

her eyes, "that I thought you were the kind of person I could trust! But no, Lucas, you've been keeping this huge secret from me, and it's about *my* family and *my* father, but *you* decided who gets to be told and who gets to stay in the dark!"

"Colleen, just—"

"I *thought* we were close, I *thought,* despite the fact that you're struck mute half the time we're together, that you loved me! But maybe you don't! Maybe I'm just a habit you don't know how to shake. Same as my father can't shake my stupid, oblivious mother, right?"

"No, Colleen, that's not how it is at all."

"Yeah? Well, do you want to get married, then?" Her breath was ragged.

You have the right to remain silent. "Yes. Eventually."

"I see. Well, I want to get married sooner than eventually." She jammed her hands on her hips, and for the first time, Lucas felt a stir of anger.

"So you're blackmailing me, is that it?" he asked. "I screwed up, I was trying to protect you—"

"Don't even go there. Do you want to marry me, or don't you? Do you want to play the field? Is that it?"

"Colleen, come on." He tried to take her hands, but she stepped back. "There's no one but you, okay? But if you're asking if I want to get married now, at the age of twenty-two, the answer is no. I don't want to live above some garage, I don't want the hassle that goes along with getting married, not to mention staying married. Not right now. I just don't, Colleen. I'm sorry about your father, but…no."

She was quiet for a few seconds. "Take care, Lucas."

And with that, she walked out, and he stood there

like an idiot, her words surreal, hanging in the air like a noose.

"Jesus, man," said Bernard. "She's feisty."

Lucas bolted after her. "Colleen, this is stupid. We don't have to break up."

"Yes, we do," she said, yanking open the door of her Honda. "If you think of being married to me as a hassle, we do. Now, I'm sorry, but I have a ten-hour drive."

"Colleen, don't be irrational." On such a roll tonight, really. But honestly, she couldn't issue an ultimatum just because she was upset. That wasn't how things worked.

"You had a choice. You made it. Goodbye."

Nice. Did she think he was about to drop to his knees and say, "Yes, baby, whatever you want, just don't leave me." For the life of him, she looked as if she was about to rip his heart out of his chest and eat it like an apple. "You're acting like an idiot," he said.

"That's great," she answered. "Who could resist such tender and beautiful words? Really. I'm all choked up. Fuck you, by the way."

She got in the car, slammed the door and threw it in gear, laying down some rubber as she left. Screeched around the corner.

He pulled out his phone and texted her. Slow down and call me later. We're not done.

She may have slowed down. She didn't call.

He called her the next day. When it went to voice mail, he hung up and called the house. Connor answered.

"Is Colleen around?" he asked.

"We're kind of in the middle of something," Connor said tightly.

"Yeah. She told me. Uh…can you have her call me?"

"I'll tell her you called." Connor hung up.

Fine. She was mad, he understood. She could call him when she wanted to. But he wasn't going to marry her because she ordered him to or as some kind of Band-Aid; he'd marry her when they could have a good life together. That had always been the plan, and she knew it.

Colleen had never gone without. Lucas had. He remembered his sister at the age of sixteen, spending hours to get across town, taking three buses to the store that had double coupons once a month. He remembered knowing not to ask for seconds because whatever was left over would be tomorrow's dinner, too. He'd been poor, and he'd seen what a lack of money had driven his father to do, and he was damned if he'd bring Colleen into that life.

As for the situation with her father…that was wretched. He knew this must be killing her, and the only thing he wanted was to help. But he'd called her, and she didn't want to talk, so it was her move.

A week later, Colleen hadn't called him.

Fine. She wanted to take a break, fine, that was great. Smart, even. She had shit going on, and so did he. Classes. Finals. He'd be going to Loyola for law school. Stephanie had found another, slightly nicer apartment and needed him to help her move. Maybe Colleen would realize that all or nothing wasn't the way to play this. Maybe she'd miss him.

It took him a month to snap.

He took a bus to Manningsport and got there at nine-thirty that night with a massive headache from diesel fumes and the rose perfume of the old lady next to him, who hadn't stopped talking since Terre Haute. He stood for a minute on the green, breathing in the clean air, the smell of the lake and recent rain. The town was quiet, and it took a minute for Lucas to acclimate from the roar of the Greyhound bus, the squeal of its brakes.

The Black Cat was open.

Despite thirteen hours of thinking of nothing else, Lucas suddenly wasn't sure what he was going to say. Hopefully, when she saw him, she'd give him that smile and say, "It took you long enough, idiot," and all was fine with the two of them, and yes, marriage now wasn't the best idea, of course she'd wait. She loved him. And this time, he'd tell her the same thing.

Still, he hesitated, not sure if walking through the door was the best plan. From the green, he could see the bar was crowded. Probably, being May, there was some kind of wine thing in town, as there was most weekends during the spring and summer (and fall, and half of winter). Sure enough, there were plenty of out-of-state license plates on the cars parked in the street.

Maybe she wasn't even there. Maybe he should go to her house and throw pebbles at her window, like he had the summer after high school graduation.

He'd take a look inside, see if he caught a glimpse of her.

The windows on the side of the bar showed the pool table and a little open area where people sometimes danced. And sure enough, Colleen was there, and his heart lurched so hard he staggered a little.

She was talking to some guy he didn't recognize, and she was laughing, and *God,* he'd missed her so much, he'd forgotten how beautiful she was even if he had a dozen pictures of her, and it was so *stupid* that they'd gone twenty-nine days without—

Then she kissed him. The guy who made her laugh. Really kissed.

As in, *kissing*.

Lucas stepped back. Kept looking, though.

The guy's hand went to her ass.

She didn't move it.

He wanted to look away, but he couldn't. He wanted to kill that guy, unleash his South-Side talents and go for it. Grab her by the hand and drag her out of there and remind her just who she belonged to, and yes, beg her to take him back.

She wasn't supposed to need reminding. She loved him. So she said, anyway.

The kiss ended, thank God. Another smile. She laid her hand on his chest and said something, giving him that grin—the grin that promised so much, that Lucas had seen countless times, slightly knowing and…and…

Almost without realizing it, he was walking. Past the library. Past the other restaurant. Post office, candy store, antiques, antiques, bakery.

He wasn't sure where he was supposed to go, really. Didi's house was out of the question. He felt as if he'd been sliced open with a blade so sharp he was a little confused as to why his guts were spilling onto the street. *Hey, where's all this blood from? Are those intestines? That'll leave a mark, won't it? Band-Aid's not gonna help that one, pal.*

He spent the night on a bench in the little cemetery, a place where Colleen wouldn't see him just in case she drove past. The sky was black, and somewhere nearby, a stream shushed gently, counting the hours as they dragged past.

The next morning, when the sky was just turning pink, he hitchhiked into Corning and caught a bus to Chicago.

He skipped his graduation ceremony the next week. Started both jobs he'd lined up for the summer. Took his nieces to the beach. Went running along Miracle Mile.

And then one day, he ran into Ellen Forbes, a classmate from college. Also a political science major, also from Chicago itself, though not a Southie, no way. A Cubs fan and everything.

He knew her, of course. Ellen was nice. One time this past year, she'd had a study group at her parents' apartment—a two-story, massive penthouse overlooking the lake. Her parents had been away, but a maid or housekeeper set out trays of food: lobster macaroni and cheese, filet mignon sliders, Greek salad, sweet potato fries. Wine and microbrewed beer. Ellen was cool about it, neither embarrassed by her family's wealth nor stuck-up about it. It was what it was. He mentioned that he worked on a Forbes Properties job the summer before; she said she hoped they treated him well.

She'd always seemed happy. Pleasant. Nice. They were friends, a little bit, anyway. Ate together occasionally, always with other people, too, and took a lot of the same classes. She always said hello and chatted, the kind of easy and graceful conversation he imagined they taught in finishing school, whatever that was. She was headed for law school, too, at Northwestern.

It was about a month after graduation when she came to the construction site where he was working. It was his third consecutive summer working for Forbes Properties, and there she was, talking to a silver-haired guy in a suit—Frank Forbes himself. Lucas waved.

"Hey, stranger!" she called, and he went over, wearing carpenter shorts and an aging T-shirt, hard hat in hand, and met her father.

"Daddy, this is a classmate of mine," she said brightly. "Lucas Campbell, my father, Frank Forbes."

"Good to meet you, son," the man said, shaking his hand firmly.

"Likewise, sir."

"You work for me?"

"Yes, sir. This is my third summer here. Johnny Hall hired me."

"He's good people, Johnny."

"Yes, sir. It's a beautiful building."

Mr. Forbes smiled. "That it is." He turned to Ellen. "Sweetheart, I have to talk with the building inspector. Give me ten minutes, okay, and then we'll grab that lunch."

"You bet," Ellen said. Her father walked away.

"I should get back to work," Lucas said.

"Oh, sure, sorry, Lucas, I didn't mean to keep you." She smiled. "We should grab a drink, since we're both here for the summer. Talk about law school."

"That'd be nice."

"Are you free tonight?"

He hesitated.

"I meant as friends, Lucas," she said gently. "I know you're seeing someone."

"No, no, I'm...not."

Since he'd seen Colleen with that other guy, it felt as if a hard, wooden block had filled his chest, as if that hot, soft place that Colleen had created with her very first glance at him had petrified into something unbreakable.

A beer with a pleasant woman who'd never been anything other than nice? Why not? "Sure. Let's grab a beer," he said.

He met her at a bar near her place. They had a drink. They had another. Two beers for him, two glasses of white wine for her. He paid and walked her home, the smell of chocolate from Blommer's thick in the air. Talked about mutual friends, professors, the usual.

When they got to her place, a town house on North Astor Street, she asked him if he'd like to come up. He said yes. When she offered him another beer, he took it. When she told him to have a seat on her sleek gray couch, he did. Then she kissed him, and he kissed her back, slightly drunk and feeling oddly surreal.

He hadn't kissed anyone other than Colleen in four years.

Colleen, on the other hand, had already moved on.

Ellen was nice. She smelled good. Her lips were soft.

"Do you want to stay?" Ellen whispered.

"I don't have anything with me," he said.

"It's okay. I'm on the Pill." She smiled and kissed his neck.

So he took her to bed for the simple reason that she was nice, and she was uncomplicated, and he was almost unbearably lonely.

The hard place in his chest remained.

In the morning, he thanked her for a nice time and said he'd call her. She smiled, said she had a nice time, too.

Nice. It was the only word applicable. Ellen was nice. They'd had a nice time. He'd been nice, too.

Jesus.

She didn't seem to have any expectations, and she didn't seem needy or desperate. It certainly hadn't felt like his heart might stop because he loved her so much. It had just been sex, and despite the reputation of the twentysomething American heterosexual male, Lucas was finding that just sex and making love were miles apart.

Because he didn't want to be a dick, he called Ellen that weekend. They went to a movie and he held her hand, and when it was over, he apologized. He had to be at his construction job at 6:00 a.m., which was the truth. Maybe they could do this again, since it was all so nice. He kissed her quickly. She emailed him a few days later, saying she was going away for a while with her mom. *Have a great time,* he responded.

Three weeks later after they'd gotten that beer, she called him and said she needed to see him. It would be best if she could come over.

Before she even got there, he guessed. She waited until he'd gotten her a glass of water and sat across from her at his tiny kitchen table before saying the words.

"It appears that I'm pregnant. And I'm so sorry."

"No," he said. "It's…it's not…it's fine." There were probably better responses he could've made, but his mind was a roaring white space at the moment.

Ellen cried a little—hormones, she said, and apologized repeatedly. She'd been on antibiotics a few weeks before, and apparently, that weakened the birth control. He told her it wasn't her fault, just biology. She admitted to being in love with him since freshman year but knowing that he had a girlfriend back home. She wasn't asking him for anything, but he had a right to know that she'd be having a baby, and even though the circumstances were far from ideal, part of her felt blessed.

He looked at his hands for a long minute.

"Let's get married," he said finally, meeting her eyes.

She made some token protestation, but her eyes lit up at the prospect.

Besides, what else was he going to do? Be a baby daddy? Hopefully get some visitation rights? His father had gotten his mother pregnant with Steph, and they'd worked out okay. They'd been happy.

He'd been raised to be honorable, despite how things might've looked from the outside. He'd gotten a girl pregnant, and he'd stand by her.

Just how things had become so badly butchered between him and Colleen…he couldn't think about that anymore. He was going to be a father.

CHAPTER TEN

"MOM, LET'S GO ALREADY!" Colleen bellowed up the stairs of her childhood home. "We're gonna be late."

"This is Satan's plan," Connor said mildly.

"Oh, yeah? Got any better ideas, brother mine?"

"You could set yourself on fire. That'd probably be more productive."

Colleen narrowed her eyes at him. "Look. She's finally interested in meeting someone else. Take a gander, Con. This place is a shrine to Dad." She looked back up the stairs. "Mom! This place is a shrine to Dad, for the love of God! You should redecorate!"

"You're right, Colleen. Maybe I'll just burn the whole house down."

"Is she serious?" Connor muttered. "It's always hard to tell."

"I don't know. You're her favorite."

"Don't burn the house down, Ma," Connor said as Mom emerged (finally) from the bathroom. "And you look very nice."

"Are you ready to go, Colleen?"

"I've been ready for forty minutes," she said. Any outing with Mom tended to be like this. Suicide-provoking, in other words.

"Have fun, you two. You'll be the prettiest ones there," Connor said, securing his position as favorite.

"Thanks, Mr. Cutie Potatoes." Mom beamed.

"You know what would be so great, Cutie Potatoes?" Colleen said. "If you came with us."

"That will never happen."

"Why? You're single!" Mom said. "I want grand-children. Now."

"I'm not going to art class," Connor said. "Is it even art class, or is it just a meat market?"

"It's art class. Please."

It was art class with a side of meat market. *Singles* art class, mind you, and yes, Colleen was trying to trick her twin into coming along. Granted, Colleen loved singles events. Loved them! Singles events were to her what Gaul was to Julius Caesar. She came, she saw, she con-quered. Granted, her search for a sugar daddy had been fruitless thus far. The truth was, she had a soft spot for older men and liked to give them an ego boost by flirt-ing with them. Sharing her gift with the world, that was all. Looking for a serious relationship…not so much.

Mom took a look in the mirror, hoisted a bra strap and sighed. "If only your father hadn't had a *lapse in judgment,*" she began.

"Dad's Lapse in Judgment," Connor said. "Now in its tenth year at the Winter Garden."

"Connor Michael O'Rourke, shut it," their mother said. "You don't have a love that was more than a love and not realize how special and wonderful it was."

"So wonderful, the cheating and the lying," Con said.

"Well, yes, there's that," Mom said. "No one's per-fect."

"Dad's not even close."

"I'm aware of your father's many flaws, Connor. I love him anyway. If he'd come to his senses…"

"Mom," Colleen said patiently, "Dad's been with Gail for ten years. A third of your children's lives. Please get on with your own."

"I'm *trying,* Colleen," Mom said, sighing as only a Catholic could. "If you'd prefer, I'll just be the stupid, aging rejected first wife, traded in for a whore, and I'll start drinking and become a bitter, fat alcoholic. Would that be better?"

Connor and Colleen exchanged a look. "We could give it a try," Connor said.

And that was the weird thing with Mom. She knew Dad wasn't leaving the Tail. Then again, he might well trade her in for a newer model, now that Gail was staring down forty. But he *wasn't* coming back to Mom, and Mom knew this…she just wouldn't admit it.

Colleen looked at her watch. "Okay, Dad's a cheating dog, and Mom's a martyr, and Con, you and I are emotionally scarred for life. Can we get going? Let's find you a new man to smother, Mom. Hopefully, he'll be a good stepfather and get me that pony I always wanted."

"I want season tickets to the Yankees," Con said.

"Oh, me, too. *And* a pony. A black pony named Star Chaser. Also, the Barbie Dream Van."

"And a Foosball machine. And new soccer cleats."

"You two materialistic little monsters," Mom said fondly. "As if I'll meet anyone. Certainly no one as handsome as your father, because if there *are* men like that at this thing, they're all looking for whores like Gail." One more glance in the mirror, one more Catholic sigh. "Fine. Let's go. I suppose it beats staying home and scrubbing the bathroom floor."

"Does it, though?" Connor muttered, and Colleen smacked him on the back of the head as she passed.

Yes, there were times when Colleen wished she and Connor had grown up in a nice clean orphanage. Dad was a complete jerk, but he was the only father she had. Not everyone got the John Holland type, those gentle, faithful, sloppy dads who still had his daughters sit on his knee and remembered not only their birthdays but how much they weighed at birth and what Santa had brought them for Christmas when they were five.

She got Pete O'Rourke.

But Mom was trying, or pretending to try, even if it was so she could have another failure on her list—*Dating: A Complete Joke, Your Wretched Father Ruined My Life/If Only He'd Come Back.*

Thus, Singles Art Class.

Yes.

MANNINGSPORT WAS HOME to the Wine Country Art League, whose offices squatted between the optometrist's office and the pizza place in the strip mall over by the trailer park. Every year there'd be an art show, and since O'Rourke's was one of the sponsors (as was every other business in town, you really couldn't get out of it), Colleen would go, pretend to admire the crooked mugs and plates the same weight and thickness as discuses, the smudgy landscapes depicting—guess what—vineyards—and the still lifes of—guess what—wine bottles and grapes.

But it was kind of cute nonetheless.

And they offered classes. There were other singles things—Singles Shooting Night, which Colleen had gone to with Faith once; she'd had a very good time. Guns and romance, what could be better? There were a few singles wine events in the off-season, but Mom worked at Blue Heron in the tasting room and didn't want to do something work-related in her free time. There was Singles Sailing ("A quick way to drown," Mom said), and Singles Square Dancing ("Where the perverts go to meet"), and Singles Mixology, hosted by none other than O'Rourke's and taught by Jeanette's fabulous daughter ("I'm your mother and everyone will pity me").

And so, Singles Art Class it was.

Paulie was coming, too. After the disaster and near injury of Paulie's first attempt with Bryce and the trip to the shelter (Paulie had hyperventilated in the parking lot), Colleen thought that maybe Paulie needed to practice a little on the opposite gender.

They pulled into the strip mall; Mom waved to Edith Warzitz (whiskey sour, two cherries), who was older than God but apparently looking for love, too. The lovely Lorelei (sweet Riesling to match her sweet personality) waved and blushed…hmm. As soon as Colleen was done with Paulie, maybe she'd try fixing Lorelei up with someone. Gerard Chartier, maybe, because that goofball had been single long enough. Plus he was a firefighter, so all the women loved him. Firefighters seemed to make either wonderful husbands or become man-whores. Therefore, it really was Colleen's sacred duty to fix him up, or he'd wind up dying of gonorrhea.

The Art League looked more like a nursery school than an artist colony, but that was largely because of the quality of the work hanging on the walls. A hand-print turkey? Really?

"Oh, my God," a man said, approaching Colleen. He wore a winter coat, despite the warm May evening, and had orangey teeth. His breath enveloped her in a toxic cloud. "Wow! I never expected to see someone like you at a thing like this! I would love to take you home and have sex."

"Your game needs work, pal. And a little oral hygiene wouldn't hurt," she said.

"And after that, we can hook up?"

"Nope."

"How about some dry humping?"

"Oh, my dear God," Mom said. "Colleen! Do something!"

"Like what, Ma? Shall I castrate him?"

"If you don't, I will."

The man continued to stare. "I don't want to be castrated," he said, raising a tousled eyebrow.

"Then back off, buddy. My mother's menopausal. You never know what might happen."

"I had to try."

"Nope, that's fine. But you've failed." She granted him a smile.

"Is this what dating is like?" Mom asked in horror.

Kind of, yes, Colleen thought. "No! I'm sure we'll meet someone great for you, Ma."

Paulie was just coming in, dressed in white leggings (who knew they made them?), a black tank top that showed off her muscular pectorals and a pink Thneed. It was almost cute, *almost* being the key word.

"What happened to that red sundress we picked out?" Colleen asked. Paulie *had* nice enough clothes; she just didn't wear them.

"It gave me a rash," Paulie said.

"It was cotton."

"I know. Nerves. I had to go for comfort. Sorry, Coll. Besides, check out the sweater. You like the way I wrapped it?"

Colleen suppressed a Catholic sigh. "I do. You look great." Too late for honesty, and Paulie needed the confidence.

Another man, this one dressed in black pants and a yellow turtleneck, approached. He was very pale.

"Ladies, good evening." Based on the accent, Colleen would have to guess that he was Count Dracula.

"Hi," Colleen said. Mom remained silent, clutching her arm in a python grip. "I'm Colleen, this is my mother, Jeanette, and this is my friend Paulie."

"Jeanette, Colleen, Paulie, yes, yes, hello. I am so pleased to meet you." He pushed back his hair, revealing a sharp widow's peak. "You and Jeanette are mother and daughter? And both so luffly. I am Droog Dragul."

The bizarre name sounded familiar. "Have you ever been to O'Rourke's Tavern?" she asked.

"No, I heff not had pleasure. I teach at college. You are student, perhaps? Shall we heff date?"

"Oh, wait! I think you went out with a friend of mine. Honor Holland?"

"Yes! Honor, she is so luffly! And now marrying Tom, my friend! You are going to wedding? We can go as couple, yes?"

"No," Colleen said. "But thank you."

"You are most welcome." He turned to Paulie, who appeared stricken. Colleen pointed to her own face and smiled, then made the sign for *talk* by opening and closing her hand. Paulie's face flushed purple, but bless her, she looked up (way up) at Droog. "How's it hanging?" she asked.

Oh, dear. Well. Brave attempt.

Colleen steered Mom, who was cowering like an

abused dog, to the classroom in the back. Easels had been set up in a circle.

"Is it warm in here?" Mom asked, starting to flutter her shirt.

"You're having a hot flash," Colleen said.

"I don't think so," Mom said. "It's just hot. Wow! They must've turned up the heat. Make them turn it down, Colleen."

"Mom, it's menopause."

"You always think my problems are menopause."

"Hail Mary, full of grace, get my mom on some estrogen, please."

"So?"

"So God better reward me for this."

The instructor came in—Debbie Meering (strawberry margarita), who had painted *Still Life with Grapes #15* out in the gallery.

"Welcome!" she cried, flinging out her arms and hitting Droog on the back of the head. "Let's start by taking a few cleansing breaths…in…and out!…and in!"

"In case we've forgotten how to breathe," Colleen said to her mom, who rolled her eyes.

"I'm so glad you've decided to embrace Art with a capital *A!*" Debbie said. "It's changed my life! No, it has. I've found a side of myself heretofore hidden—"

"That's a word you just don't hear enough," Mom said, and Colleen felt a rush of affection for old Momster. She had her moments.

"Everyone should feel free to tap into their inner gods and goddesses," Debbie continued, "and set free their muses and let their chakras flow! There is no right or wrong here, just Art! With a capital *A!* And of course, our fellow single people! Let loose your true selves, people!"

The students glanced nervously around; Colleen was quite interested to see what the true selves would be like. The Hulk? Wolverine (please, God)? Voldemort? Nope, everyone seemed like their regular selves. Ah, well.

Except for Orange Tooth, Droog the Vampire and a man so old Colleen wasn't quite sure he was alive, everyone here was female. The usual, Colleen knew.

And that was the thing. All the women here were attractive enough. Clean, at any rate. They'd made an effort. Granted, the Thneed choked off much of Paulie's appeal, but still. She was trying. The point was, normal, honest, decent women with good hygiene were always willing to go to these types of events, whereas the normal, honest, decent men seemed to be anywhere but.

"So let's get started by going around the circle and telling everyone why you're here and what you're looking for in a relationship. Bert? Get us started, won't you?"

Bert, the elderly man, was fast asleep in his wheelchair, drooling. Colleen grabbed a paper towel for when he woke up.

"Okay, then, Colleen, why don't you get us going?"

"Sure," Colleen said. "I'm Colleen, perpetual flirt, here with my mom to find me a stepfather."

"And are *you* looking for love?" Debbie asked.

"Can't say that I am, Deb."

"Her first boyfriend just came back to town," Mom offered. "He broke up with her years ago, and she's still not over him. She wants to find someone. A beard. Is that the right term?"

See? Just when she was feeling warm thoughts about Mom, this happened. "Wow, thanks, Mom. I'd deny that, but I'm reeling from the fact that you're so willing to blurt out my personal—"

"And you, Jeanette?" Debbie asked.

"Colleen made me come." Mom looked around at the others in the circle. "My husband left me for a whore."

"Same here," said a woman who had to be eighty if she was a day and was eyeing Drooling Beauty. "An actual prostitute. He said if the dwarf on *Game of Thrones* could do it, then so could he."

"I see. And you, Paulie?" Debbie said, completely unfazed.

"I, uh…well, there's a certain someone who… He… I wouldn't…." Her face blossomed into the fascinating mottled purple. Mom started shirt-flapping in sympathy. "It's a case of, um, unrequited love."

"Unrequited at the moment, that is," Colleen said, giving Paulie a smile.

"Young luff!" chortled Droog. "How wonderful! Eh heh heh heh heh!"

"I… Is my turn over?" Paulie asked.

"It is if you want it to be," Deb said.

"Then it's over." Paulie wiped her forehead with the tail of the Thneed.

The rest of the class took their turns, saying more or less the same thing—"I'd like to meet a nice person for a special friendship, possibly more." So Match.com.

"Okay! Let's get started," said Debbie. "Stanley? Come on in." A man came in, barefoot and wearing a pink terry-cloth bathrobe. "Stanley's our model today, people. Make yourself comfortable, Stan."

Stan stood in the center of the circle, turned so his

back was to Mom and Colleen, and let the bathrobe drop to the floor.

Colleen and Mom recoiled in unison.

She hadn't known it was possible for a man to be so…so…hairy.

And so naked.

And so, *so* hairy.

As in, pelt. As in, he could donate his back hair to Locks of Love.

"I think I found my stepfather," she whispered.

"You are not funny, young lady. I'm telling Connor about this."

"It may kill him." Colleen hunched behind her easel, torn between the urge to pee in terror and hilarity. "Okay, time to make art," she whispered to her mother. "Take a good hard look, Mom."

"I can't. I've been struck blind."

"In my country," Droog said, his tone conversational, "back hair is sign of virility."

"Then, Stan, you must have twenty children," Mom answered drily.

Coll glanced over to Paulie, who was giving off light, she was so red in the face. She was on the other side of the circle. The *front* side, God bless her, which meant she had to see the…parts…of Stan, Stan the Hairy Man. Lorelei sat next to her, chatting away, drawing without a care in the world.

Stan struck a pose, sort of a Mercury pointing to the heavens, and Colleen had to pretend to check her phone to hide her laughter.

"Colleen?" Debbie asked, leaning over her easel. "You haven't even started yet. Is there a problem?"

"Nothing that a week of waxing won't solve," she managed.

"Okay, that's rude," Debbie said. "Bodies are all beautiful, all miracles of a higher power, all representative—"

"Yeah, okay, I'll get started."

Debbie gave her a disapproving look—*no inner goddess for you!*—and moved on.

Colleen took a breath and risked another look at the wizened buttocks and scrawny legs of Sasquatch. A breeze came through the window, ruffling the tufts of hair on Stan's shoulders, and Coll bent down to hide another surge of wheezing laughter.

For the next half hour, Mom Catholic-sighed and sketched and gave Colleen censorious glances. Colleen herself drew several rather adorable stick figures, complete with tufts of hair, trying not to look directly at Stan, specifically at the fronds of armpit hair, which hung down like human scalps. The skin under her eyes grew raw from tears of silent laughter.

"Stanley, thank you," Debbie said at long, long last. "Class, one of the things you may not know is just how physically taxing nude modeling is. If you'd like to tip Stanley, I'm sure he'd appreciate it."

"I think he should pay me for having to look at that," Mom muttered, fishing out a dollar bill. Colleen, unable to make eye contact, handed him a twenty.

She went over to Paulie. To her surprise, Paulie had drawn a pretty good picture of Stan, capturing his beady eyes and balding head, and hunched, criminal posture. "Nice, Paulie," she said.

"Once I got over the shock, it was fun."

"Your first naked man?" Colleen whispered.

"Well, my first in real person. I've watched a little porn."

Colleen bit her lip. "I see. Listen, I'm sorry there aren't more men here to practice on. You never can tell with these singles things."

"No, that's okay! It's nice to do something different." Paulie smiled up at Colleen so sweetly that Coll's heart tugged.

"So I was thinking Bryce should see you on your home turf," she said. "You interested in throwing a party?" The Petrosinsky home was gorgeous, if, er, unusually decorated.

"Sure!" Paulie said. "Yeah! My dad would love that."

"Great. We'll invite everyone." Colleen smiled, squeezed Paulie's rock-hard biceps, reminded herself to work out more and went to find her mom. She was talking to Orange Tooth, who wore a pair of Uggs similar to Colleen's own, though she wore them only in the winter, like a normal person. Colleen overheard Mom say the phrase "lapse in judgment" and rolled her eyes.

"Lorelei, do you know Gerard Chartier?" Colleen asked, figuring she'd scatter a few seeds.

"Oh, sure," Lorelei said. "Kind of a man-whore, right?"

"Mmm-hmm. He needs a good woman to reform him. And I know for a fact he loves your coconut macaroons."

Suddenly, there was a commotion in the corner. Orange Tooth had fallen to the floor, clutching his chest. "Call 9-1-1," he gasped. "I'm having a heart attack and need sixty milligrams of Oxycontin and a bolus of morphine."

"Anyone else thinking prescription drug abuse?" Colleen murmured.

Ten minutes later, the guy (whose name was Calvin) was being bundled into an ambulance. He was talking, sucking hard on oxygen and clutching Mom's hand. Gerard and Jessica Dunn, who was a volunteer firefighter, were talking reassuringly to him.

"Speaking of the heroic man-whore, right?" Colleen said to Lorelei. "Nothing like a guy in turnout gear."

"Absolutely," she sighed.

"Colleen!" Mom barked. "Calvin wants me to go with him. Follow me to the hospital so you can drive me home."

Fifteen minutes later, Colleen got out of her car and walked into the E.R., a place she'd spent many happy hours as a kid, watching Connor get sewn up from his various injuries.

"Heya, Calvin," the intake nurse said. "Back to visit us again?"

"Get me some Oxy, stat," he said. "And not the generic crap. I want the real deal."

"You're grounded, young lady," Mom said as they wheeled Calvin away. Since he still hadn't let go of Mom's hand, she had to go, too, which was cute in a serial killer kind of way. Colleen waved merrily. As Paulie said, it was good to do something different.

But Mom would be really nice to Calvin because Mom *was* really nice, if a little obtuse. As for Colleen, having to wait here in the E.R. with nothing to do, or read...

Maybe she'd call Faith. Nah. It was after nine, and Faith was a newlywed and probably shagging Levi this very moment.

A sweet needle of envy pricked Colleen's heart. Not that she begrudged the happy couple. It was just that everyone seemed to be pairing off these days. Even Connor had a girlfriend, and one important enough to sneak around with. So far, the nanny cam she'd put on his bookshelf had captured nothing.

Honor Holland and the lovely Tom Barlow had hooked up pretty fast, too. The first night Tom had come into the bar, Colleen felt a tiny spark of interest; how could she not, with Tom's blue-collar British accent and goofy smile? But the spark fizzled for no good reason. Just like with Jack. Just like with Greg the waiter from last summer. The damn spark always fizzled.

Except with one guy.

Maybe she understood Mom better than she let on.

Not that she was still hung up on the past. She was happy, she'd gone out with plenty of guys and slept with a few (though not as many as she let people think).

But there were a lot of nights in the past couple years when she lay in bed at night, wondering if she'd ever find anyone who made her feel…special. The way Lucas once had.

Exactly four minutes had passed since she arrived. Maybe she'd go see if Jeremy Lyon was on call. He was always good for a chat.

She walked through the E.R. to the main part of the hospital. Faith's niece, Abby Vanderbeek, was on the front desk, volunteering no doubt, earbuds in place as her thumbs flew across her phone.

"Hey, Abby," she said to the teenager. "Is Jeremy working today?"

"Oh, hey, Colleen," Abby said without taking out the earbuds. She tapped a few keys. "No, sorry. It's Dr. Chu. She's new and schizo, so beware."

"Poop. Any patients I might know?" Colleen asked.

Who knew how long Calvin would need Mom to stand guard?

"I'm not supposed to tell," Abby said. "Confidentiality and all that."

"I'm covered by HIPAA, since I work part-time at the nursing home."

"Oh, yeah, I forgot. Have you seen Goggy and Pops over there?" Abby said, asking about her weirdly named great-grandparents.

"No, they're not in my wing. I heard your grandmother complaining about the food, though. I hid."

Abby smiled and hit a few more keys. "Let's see… how sick do you want them?"

"Very sick. That way I can be an angel of mercy."

"Dude. You're so awesome. Okay, I can fix you up. Joe Campbell's in for dialysis. You know where that is?"

"I sure do," Colleen said. "Thanks, beautiful."

The dialysis unit was on the third floor of the hospital, same floor as the intensive care unit. Last year, Gramp had been here for a week with pneumonia (almost managed to die that time before his pesky and amazing immune system saved him), and Colleen had seen Joe. After she'd gotten Gramp settled and he'd fallen asleep, she'd ventured over to say hi.

She hadn't known him too well back when she was with Lucas, but Joe and Bryce had been a father-and-son fixture at the far end of the bar until six months ago.

Being a bartender—*the* bartender—made her privy to all the town gossip. She'd heard that Joe's wife, the pinched and snotty Didi, hated going to his appointments, and Bryce seemed to be in denial about his dad's condition. Joe was often alone during these long, quiet stretches when his blood was cleaned and rotated back inside him.

So yes, she'd visited. Dialysis took a long time, and it was boring. Three or four times a week, four to six hours at a stretch. Joe was always happy to see her.

She peeked into Joe's curtained area. He was awake. "Time for your sponge bath, Mr. Campbell," she said in her sultriest voice, getting a most rewarding grin from him.

"Which Mr. Campbell are you referring to?" came the voice behind her.

She jumped.

Lucas.

Of course. He raised an eyebrow at her and sat down next to his uncle, a paper cup of coffee in his hand.

He hadn't shaved today. Or yesterday, maybe. And what was it about that? Did they teach this to men in Man School? *Don't shave, fellas. Chicks love that, wondering how it would feel to have your scratchy face in all sorts of places—*

"Lucas, it's you," she said, aware that she hadn't said a word. "I was referring to your much handsomer uncle. Hi, Joe! How are you?" She leaned over and kissed him, and he patted her hand.

"It's nice to see you, sweetheart. I hope you brought me some of your amazing margaritas."

"Wouldn't they kill you?" she asked.

"But what a way to go." He smiled. "You remember my nephew, of course."

"Well, given that we dated for four years, yes, I'm afraid I do." She smiled at Joe. Not at Lucas.

"Have a seat, Colleen," Lucas said. There was a chair next to him.

She tried not to brush against him as she sat down. Tried not to notice that he smelled so good, that clean, outdoor smell even here in the hospital.

She cleared her throat. "So I'm here because my mom's date seems to need a drug fix. These are interesting times in the world of romance." She glanced at Lucas (damn those beautiful eyes), then told the story of the hirsute nude model, and by the end, Joe was laughing so hard he could hardly talk, tears leaking out of his eyes.

"Oh, Colleen, it's good…to see you…sweetheart."

His eyes closed, just like that. Lucas lurched forward.

"He's asleep, that's all," she said.

He glanced at her, frowning, then watched his uncle's chest, which rose and fell with a breath. Another one. Another. "How did you know that?" he asked, sitting back down.

She shrugged. "Lucky guess."

"Did you ever become a nurse?"

"I'm an LPN. Licensed practical nurse. I work over at Rushing Creek. There are a couple dialysis patients there." She paused. "I've visited Joe here a couple times."

"Thank you for that."

She wondered if he knew that Joe came here alone most of the time.

"So you understand how all this works, then?" Lucas asked.

She nodded. "Do you?"

"I watched a few YouTube videos." He looked tired. And worried.

He'd never said too much about life with Joe and Didi. When they were dating, they didn't spend a lot of time with his relatives. There'd been an awkward family dinner in the early days (she seemed to remember insisting on it). Bryce had been as cheerful as a puppy, Didi with that pinched look, Joe amiable and friendly.

But Lucas could say more with his eyes than most people could say in three days.

Then again, that was the kind of thinking that had gotten her exactly nowhere.

Lucas adjusted Joe's blanket, and that tender gesture...damn. Those were the kinds of things that messed with a person's head. She should go before she felt mushier than she did already.

"So where are you staying while you're here?" she asked.

"I got a furnished apartment in town. The old opera house."

"Sure. Faith used to live there. With Levi. Well, across from Levi, then with Levi, then they bought a house. They're cute. The apartments, I mean. Well, Levi and Faith are cute, too. You know what I mean." She closed her eyes as the Tourette's of Terror welled up again, spurred on by the old feelings that had led to her ruination.

She pictured Lucas in the generically furnished apartment, alone, not staying in the big McMansion where the other Campbells lived. The quiet of the green at night. No dog to keep him company.

"Would you like to have dinner sometime?" she heard herself say.

He gave her a long look, then nodded.

"I'm only asking because, well, hell, maybe you're lonely. I collect strays, you know how it is. Plus, you don't know too many people here. But you know me.

And I know you. But it's not a date. It's not romantic, I mean. It's just dinner. We get together and eat."

"Yes, I seem to remember how dinner works." His eyes were smiling.

Her arm was almost touching his, and she had an almost overwhelming desire to put her arms around him and draw his head to her shoulder, kiss his hair and tell him it would be okay. Maybe kiss him on the forehead. Or the mouth. Or the neck. Or the—

Slutty. Very, very slutty, envisioning sex in the dialysis unit.

"Can I ask you a question?"

She swallowed. "Mmm-hmm."

"Why are you so intent on Bryce and Paulie being together?" His voice was low and perfectly pleasant.

She risked another look at him. Damn. His hair was so frickin' beautiful, black and curly, carelessly tousled. If hair could talk, his would say, *That's right. This means everything you're imagining. Run your fingers through me. Do it. You won't be sorry.*

"Colleen?"

"What? Yes. Um, what was the question?"

He smiled, and her uterus clenched. "Bryce and Paulie. Why is that a good idea?"

She cleared her throat and looked at Joe, who was dead to the world. Poor choice of words, actually. Who was sound asleep.

"You won't say anything to Bryce, will you?" she asked.

"No."

And he wouldn't. She could trust him, she knew. No one she'd ever met in her life was as honorable as

Lucas Campbell. "Paulie's loved him for years. She's a really great person, Lucas. Decent and kind and good."

"I'm sure she is."

"Do you remember her from high school?"

He shook his head. "Not really. I remember those chicken ads, though."

"'Thirty-eight ways to a heart attack,'" Colleen said with a smile.

"Doesn't her father have ties to the Russian Mafia?"

"That was never proven."

He raised an eyebrow. "If Paulie's so great, Colleen, why are you fixing her up with my cousin? Why aren't you fixing her up with Connor or Jack Holland or someone with a job and a future?"

"She doesn't want those guys. She wants Bryce." They were whispering, not wanting to wake poor Joe.

"And why does she want Bryce? Because he's good-looking?"

"Well, actually, Lucas—"

"If—and I repeat, if—you manage to get Bryce to date her, what about what happens next? You know how many women Bryce has slept with?"

Her face flushed hotter. A lot, she knew, give or take a few.

"A lot," Lucas said. "He likes the shallow, beautiful type who are only interested in screwing him."

"I know exactly the type of women Bryce sleeps with," she whispered back, suddenly furious. "And yes, they're generally shallow and beautiful, and no, Paulie isn't. And maybe it's time for Bryce to find someone with more depth and character."

"You're going to have a big mess on your hands, and your friend is going to get hurt."

"Right. He might marry someone else when she thought he was in love with her."

He gave her a narrow-eyed stare. "We're talking about my cousin, who goes through life without having to deal with the consequences of his actions, Colleen. If you want to fight about the past, you'll have to do it alone, because I'm not interested."

"Oh, so sorry. I didn't mean to talk about something that wasn't on your agenda."

"You're the one who showed up here, I might point out."

"And you're the one who swans back into town— You know what? Forget it. I happen to think Bryce *should* be with a woman like Paulie. No, she's not some supermodel slut. She's grounded and decent and loyal. And, I might point out to you, Spaniard, I've got a fairly amazing track record when it comes to matchmaking."

"Bryce is going to break her heart."

"Funny, how concerned you are about the hearts of women."

"For God's sake, look at my uncle," Lucas said, his voice low. "Bryce has convinced himself Joe will get better, but he won't. Joe asked me back here so he could see his son settled before he dies. I don't want to have to tell him that Paulie's father had Bryce's body dumped in the lake."

"How *Godfather: Part III*. I think the Chicken King is more likely to cut him into pieces and deep-fry him."

"Bryce needs to grow up. He needs a job, a home, a life."

"And Paulie could—"

"Colleen, he's never had a real relationship in his life."

"Neither has Paulie," she whispered hotly. "And wouldn't it be nice to see first love work out for a change?"

He ignored that. "Leave him alone. Don't manipulate him into a relationship he's not ready for."

"But men are simple creatures, Lucas dear, meant to be manipulated into doing what's best for them."

"Did you manipulate me into doing what was best?" His eyes were hot.

"No," she hissed. "You're my one failure. Ellen Forbes, on the other hand…she had you down cold."

His eyes shut off, all that heat and anger instantly muted. "You're wrong about that."

"Yeah, sure, I'm wrong. You and she are like a Lifetime television movie. Boy from the wrong side of town marries billionaire's daughter. Very romantic."

"Don't talk about her."

That hurt—Lucas, defending his ex-wife. "Fine," she muttered. "Either way, you underestimate your cousin. And Paulie, too. And me."

"Oh, I've never underestimated you, hotshot." He paused. "So you're barreling ahead with this because you're mad that I married Ellen?"

"No, Spaniard, your irritation is just a happy by-product. I have good instincts about people, that's all."

"Use your instincts somewhere else."

"In fact, you were the only man I've ever been wrong about. You and my dad."

His jaw turned to iron, but he didn't deny the comparison. Turned his eyes back to Joe.

"I have to go," she said, standing. Yes. Time to make a regal exit.

Unfortunately, she tripped on the leg of the chair,

landing on Joe, who woke up with a start (and a yelp). Lucas hauled her off his uncle and set her on her feet.

"Joe, I'm so sorry!" she said. "Are you okay? Did I bruise your kidneys?"

"Well, they don't work anyway," he said kindly.

"Any other body parts hurt? Spleen? Liver?"

"Don't worry. I'm dying as it is."

She bit her nail, then stopped. "I'm so sorry."

"It's okay, sweetheart. Most fun I've had in weeks. I love your perfume."

Lucas didn't add his reassurance, she noted. "Feel better," she said to Joe, leaning over to kiss his cheek.

"I already do."

She smiled at him; well, she tried to. Hoped to God, she hadn't hurt the poor guy.

"I'll call you about dinner," Lucas said as she left the room.

"The offer has been revoked," she said. "See you soon, Joe."

CHAPTER ELEVEN

THE AGE OF twenty-two is not generally celebrated as a time of deep wisdom and calm, measured acts.

Almost as soon as she broke up with Lucas, Colleen regretted it.

But the thing about being right most of the time… it was hard to know what to do when you were wrong. *If* she'd been, that was because Colleen was kind of on the fence.

She knew one thing. Everything felt wrong without him.

At first, she'd just been furious. Life was going to hell on a lightning-speed roller coaster. Dad, Mom, Gail, a baby…and Lucas had *lied* to her, had played God, deciding what she should and shouldn't know. What did that say? What if he kept other things from her? What else wasn't he telling her? Say they did get married and he got a brain tumor. Would he keep that from her, too? Huh? Would he?

"Colleen, enough," Connor groaned one night. He was done at the CIA and was working at Hugo's. Colleen was still bartending at the Black Cat, but she'd come over on her dinner break because she wouldn't eat the food at the Cat with a gun to the back of her head. "I can't stand to hear this one more time. *You* broke up with *him*. If you want him back, call him.

Okay? But I can't listen to you *and* Mom complaining all the damn day!"

"Men. You disgust me."

"Really? Is that why you were making out with that guy the other night?"

"Oh, please. That was nothing." Colleen shifted, guilt squirming in her stomach. The guy in question was some dork from Ithaca and, yes, she'd flirted with him. And kissed him. And then told him that while he was cute and she was positive she'd regret it, she couldn't go out with him (that is, have sex with him). Because that kiss had been totally *meh*.

Not like kissing Lucas, when the world seemed to stop, when the world seemed to smile, even, because they were so right together.

Then again, Lucas hadn't been banging on her door, begging to get back in touch with her. One voice mail. One call to the house. That was it. So they were taking a break. Fine. Maybe it'd get his priorities straight. Maybe he'd miss her.

Maybe…and this was the thought that caused a cold tremor of fear to shake her heart…maybe he was relieved. She was, after all, his high school sweetheart. He'd said he wasn't ready for marriage. Maybe…maybe like so many other men, her stupid father most certainly included, he wanted to see if there was someone else out there.

Because he sure didn't try very hard to win her back. She hadn't seen that coming.

Dad had moved in with Gail the Tail. He hired a divorce attorney and started proceedings, and Mom sobbed for twelve hours straight, and Colleen cried with her as the movers took her father's things away, taking with them the memories of her happy childhood.

Connor hadn't been as close with their dad as she had, but this had shaken him, too. Not just Mom's distress, but Dad being so…pathetic. A hot young second wife. Another family. And in case that wasn't enough, a convertible.

But despite that, she couldn't stop loving her father. She was mad, embarrassed, furious…but when she heard his voice on the phone, or even when she saw him, sometimes, just for a second, she'd forget that he was the man who cheated on Mom, and she'd just remember Daddy. The man who taught her to ride a bike and sail a boat, who used to brush her hair when she was little, who read her stories, who let her stay up late and watch scary movies, then sat on her bed when she was afraid to go to sleep.

The Tail got a cushion-set diamond as big as a human eyeball, despite the fact that Mom and Dad weren't even divorced. Dad had shown her the ring, for the love of God.

Oh, and they were having a girl.

Dad invited her over to the new place for dinner to meet his lover/fiancée. "I know you're upset," he said on the phone, and the thinly veiled impatience in his voice chilled her. "But, Colleen, enough. If you're going to come over, and I hope you will, I'd appreciate some civility. Your mother is hysterical crying half the time and screaming the other half, Connor won't speak to me, and I won't put up with a guilt trip in my own home."

It was almost a threat. Another wife; another home; another chance at fatherhood. Another daughter.

In other words, accept or be discarded.

She went to dinner.

The Tail herself answered the door wearing a cropped T-shirt and micro-shorts. Fantastic body, completely athletic and lean and perfectly muscled. Poor Mom. Gail's red hair was pulled into a ponytail, and she looked dewy and innocent. And most horribly of all…young.

"Colleen, at last!" she cried, throwing her arms around her. "I've been dying to meet you!"

Colleen extricated herself. "How old are you?" she asked.

"I'm twenty-six."

"Holy shit."

"I know. We could be sisters." Gail smiled, but her eyes remained cool. Her huge engagement ring flashed.

Dinner was excruciating. Dad was helpful in a way he never was with Mom. Gail waffled between Adorable Ingenue and Experienced Prostitute, biting her lower lip and shooting Dad come-fuck-me looks. Whenever she stood, she arched her back, shoved her nonexistent belly outward and made doe eyes, smitten with the Miracle of Life.

When Colleen got home, she was exhausted. Mom was waiting by the door. "Well? It's just temporary, isn't it? This can't last. He'll come to his senses. This is just a lapse in judgment."

And that was maybe the worst part. Far worse than Mom's occasional and very righteous anger was her hope.

"Mom, why would you even want him back?" Colleen said.

"Why? Because I love him. Because he's the father of my two beautiful children."

"And soon he'll be the father of another beautiful child." She sat down on the tired couch. "Gail has an engagement ring."

Her mother's face went white. "He won't go through with it. He's just having a midlife crisis, that's all. Who even knows if Gail's really pregnant? Or if she is, if it's even Pete's baby?"

The next day, Mom went to House of Hair a brunette with a few streaks of gray…and came back a redhead. Not only that, but her perfectly lovely blue eyes were looking awfully green lately, courtesy of her tinted contacts.

In other words, she looked like a wannabe Gail.

It made Colleen want to cry.

Mom called Dad six or seven times a day on flimsy excuses…"Pete, honey, I'm looking for the screwdriver. Can you come by when you get a second? Pete, do you remember where you put the car insurance papers? Pete, we should talk about the kids. Want to go to Hugo's and see Connor?"

Colleen could only watch in sorrow and anger and misery.

She missed Lucas. God, she missed him.

But he'd *lied* to her. Lucas, who was so scrupulously honest and decent beneath his scruffy, South-Side tough-guy persona, had covered for her father. If only he'd told her about it, maybe she could've talked some sense into her father, because she and Dad, they were too smart for this.

And then Gail wouldn't be pregnant right now. Mom wouldn't be in schizophrenic divorce hell. Connor's mouth wouldn't be so tight, and half the town wouldn't be clucking and gossiping over the O'Rourkes.

And maybe her father would still love her as much as he used to, if he didn't have a replacement daughter on the way.

Maybe her family would still be intact.

It felt as if Lucas had taken that chance away.

But that didn't keep her from missing him, his dark, steady eyes, his workingman hands and low, smoky voice. The feeling of his mouth, his slow smile, and yes, that little-boy-lost shadow that he still carried with him. His voice when he called her *mía*. Mine.

Of *course* she wanted to marry him, more than ever now. Her own family was screwed up beyond repair, but they could make a new family. They'd get married and have a relationship that was ten times better than what her parents had had. Lucas would have a home, a real home, and his sister and the girls could come stay for the holidays, and Connor would be in and out, and he and Lucas would be best friends, and they'd be able to handle anything life threw at them. Including her parents' divorce and her impending sibling.

They were better together than they were apart. He needed her; she made him smile, she made him happy, she made him whole, and he did the same things for her.

It was possible, Colleen thought late at night, that she'd been a little…rash.

But pride kept her from calling him. She wanted that first move to come from him. He was the one who'd lied, and of course she'd forgive him. All he had to do was ask.

And then, one day, he was here. Finally.

It was July, and the town was hosting the Days of Wine and Roses, a garden tour/wine extravaganza. Colleen was helping at the Blue Heron booth; the Hollands had just hired Mom in the tasting room for the season, and thank God for that, since the job was at least a distraction. Faith was home for the summer and had been absolutely stalwart.

The whole town was out, the sun was shining, the green was covered in tents, and mason jars filled with roses adorned every table. Dogs and children ran around in the park across the street, and every business was offering goodies on the sidewalks.

Connor waved to her from Hugo's doorway—*You doing okay?*

She waved back. *You bet. You?*

He raised his chin. *Doing fine.*

Good. She turned back to the wine-tasting table and reached into the cooler for another bottle of the unoaked Chardonnay, which always ran out first.

"Colleen."

She jumped as if electrocuted.

Lucas stood in front of her table. With him was his cousin.

"Hey, Coll!" Bryce said as if he hadn't been at the Black Cat just last night. "How you doing?"

"I'm good," she said faintly. "Hi, Lucas."

"Hi."

He was so beautiful. No, that wasn't the right word. Bryce was beautiful. But Lucas…he was *enthralling,* and dear God, she'd missed that face. His voice. He wasn't smiling, not yet, but that was okay.

She felt a smile start in her heart, warm and full. Finally, he was back.

His eyes dropped. "Can I talk to you?"

"Sure! Um, Faith, I have to—"

"Get out of here, go, away with you," Faith said, smiling. "Hi, Lucas."

"Hey, Faith." He gave her a nod.

"Should I say something bitchy?" she whispered to Colleen.

"Are you capable of it?" Colleen whispered back. She untied her Blue Heron apron and skirted around the table. He was here. Finally, he was here.

"Where should we go?" she asked.

"We could get a drink," Bryce suggested.

"Bryce, I need to talk to Colleen alone," Lucas said. She could smell his nice smell, soap and laundry detergent and sun, and holy St. Patrick, her knees almost buckled with longing, and she felt so damn *right* again that she wondered if she'd just float away.

But yeah, privacy. That would be good because she wasn't going to last long without wrapping herself around him and kissing him with some happy crying possibly thrown in for good measure.

He took her hand and led her off the green, and Colleen felt like a blushing bride leaving the wedding…as if everyone knew where they were going and exactly what they'd be doing. His hand was work-roughened from the construction work he did each summer, and his olive skin was darker than usual from the sun.

The library was closed for the festivities. Lucas took her behind the pretty limestone building, where it was shady and cool and quiet.

"About time you came to see me," she said, and her voice was shaking. "I missed you so much."

"I think you should listen to me before you say anything," he said, not quite looking her in the eye.

A tremor of fear wriggled through her knees. But

no, it was okay. He wanted to go first. That was fine. That was better, really. "Apologize away," she said with a smile.

He looked at her. Still no smile, his eyes dark and fathomless. A second passed. Another. Another. The tremor became a spasm.

"I'm getting married," he said.

It was so…freakish…that she almost didn't understand the words. A chipmunk cheeped from under a dogwood tree, and the sounds of music and people drifted from the green.

"What…what did you say?" she managed.

"I'm getting married, Colleen."

There was something wrong with her lungs, because she couldn't breathe. "That's not funny."

"To Ellen Forbes. I think you might've met her once or twice."

He was serious.

Colleen closed her mouth. "I don't… I don't understand."

He didn't clarify.

Colleen took a step backward. Her legs felt watery. Ellen Forbes. Ellen Forbes. Oh, shit, Ellen Forbes.

Yes, Colleen remembered her. Ellen had offered them a ride once, when they were walking back to campus, pulling over in her little BMW. And while the O'Rourkes were pretty comfortable financially, there was that aura of Money with a capital *M* around Ellen Forbes, and it didn't come only from the last name (though that sure reinforced things).

It came from a blissful ignorance of things as mundane as bills and taxes and budgets and sales, and allowed her the freedom to focus on other things. Her

clothes were preppy and dull and screamed expensive—
crisp white shirt and little gold hoops in her ears, a
sumptuous bag at her side, the designer unfamiliar to
Colleen, who might've been able to recognize a bag sold
at Macy's or Nordstrom, but not from Saks or Bergdorf. Colleen was used to being the prettiest woman in
the room and didn't worry too much about clothes, but
suddenly, she'd felt juvenile and blowsy in her peasant
skirt and tank top, long dangly earrings (from Kohl's)
and scruffy sandals on her feet.

Lucas was marrying Ellen Forbes? *Marrying* her?

"Are you…are you serious?" she asked, her voice
just a whisper.

"I'm sorry," he said, and to his credit, he looked it.
Those dark eyes were all ripped up inside.

"Why?" she asked.

He started to say something, then stopped.

"Lucas…you can't marry her. What about us? I
mean, we had a fight, but you don't have to—"

"I wanted to tell you myself. That's why I'm here.
I'm sorry."

Good *God.*

"You can't marry her," she said, striving to sound
calm. "I love you, Lucas. I always have, since the first
time I met you. I've never loved anyone else."

Shut up, Con's voice said.

Lucas was staring at the grass. "I'm sorry," he said
again.

"Is it her money?"

"No."

"Is she pregnant?" Oh, please, not that.

He looked at her a long minute. Something flickered
through his eyes, and her stomach seized.

"No," he said, and thank you, God, thank you. No, Lucas was paranoid about that.

"Then... I... I don't..." she stammered. "Lucas, please."

"I didn't mean to hurt you."

"Lucas..." Colleen took a shaking breath. Another one. *Hold on. Hang on, it's coming, the thing that will explain this. Yep, here it is.*

He doesn't love you.

No, no, of course he does.

You're the one who wanted to get married. He wanted to wait. Wait for something better, apparently. You were too easy. Too obvious.

Colleen cleared her throat. "I guess I'm just like my mother, then. I hear what I want to hear. See what I want to see."

"I'm sorry."

She wanted to slap his face, but she seemed to be paralyzed. *Get out of here,* Connor's voice instructed, so she turned and walked away, the grass soft, crinkling under her bare feet.

The tears wouldn't come, jammed hard in her throat like a fist.

She walked fast, out of town. Thank God everyone was on the green. The asphalt burned her feet as she went up the Hill, past the Luces' driveway, up to Blue Heron, into the fields, then the woods. A little down the path, and there it was, the place she and Connor had thought was the most magical place when they were little, a stream that led down to the lake, complete with small waterfall. The water was cool and gentle, balm on her dirty, burned feet.

Lucas was getting married.

What was the phrase Dad had used? Moved on. Lucas had moved on.

Wrong again. Wrong about Dad, wrong about Lucas.

And then she cried for the loss of her first love. Cried so hard it hurt, and she understood why they called it heartbreak, because it really did seem as if she was being ripped in half from the inside out.

CHAPTER TWELVE

COLLEEN HAD GONE to college to become a nurse. Yeah, yeah, it wasn't what most would've guessed. But she'd always been good at taking care of people, she thought, and doing it in a way that didn't make her seem condescending or irritable. Her grandfather had gone into a nursing home when Colleen was a teenager, and the staff there made Colleen want to scream sometimes. "Just lift your butt for me, hon," one nurse said once without even waiting for Colleen to leave the room. Or even worse, "Great. Another dementia patient. Just what I needed today," as if Gramp, who'd been an English teacher in his prime, chose to have his brain cells harden and die.

And so Colleen had started helping. Got her certificate as a nurse's assistant when she was seventeen, volunteered and then worked at Gramp's place. Called the patients "sir" or "ma'am," or Mrs. Carter or Mr. Slate. Explained what she was going to do before she started, whether or not they understood her or not.

"Become a doctor," Dad had said when she told her family of her plans. "Why be low man on the totem pole when you don't have to be?"

She didn't want to be a doctor.

She did graduate with a degree in biology, but by then, her family had imploded and she and Lucas were done. Their great-grandmother on Mom's side died, and the twins inherited a pretty nice nest egg. Two weeks after Lucas slammed her with his news, Connor asked her if she wanted to buy the Black Cat, which was in foreclosure, and she said sure. Being near her twin seemed like the smartest move, and she sensed that Connor felt the same way.

They spent the summer gutting the place, and the hard work enabled Colleen to fall into a near-coma each night. The noise of saws and hammers (and the jukebox, one of their first purchases) kept other thoughts at bay. She'd be in charge of management and the bar, Connor the king of the kitchen.

And though she'd never thought she'd end up as a full-time bartender, Colleen loved it. People opened up to her; Connor said there was something about her face that made people spill their guts, and it was an honor, really. And yeah, sure, mixing drinks was kind of fun, too. Tasting wines from the local vineyards, beer from the breweries…before they'd been open six months, O'Rourke's already had a reputation as being the place for the best spirits, best beer and best wine list. And the best nachos, too.

Dad and Gail were ensconced in their swanky new house. Mom was a wreck. Connor was clenched and angry and working sixteen hours a day. Gramp lost the ability to speak, and only Colleen seemed to be able to make him seem content. So she stayed in town, the cheerful one, the fun one. She knew everyone, liked everyone (more or less), remembered baby names and boyfriends, advised on romances, recommended people for jobs, and gave the lonely a place where someone, at least, would be a friend.

Then Savannah Joy O'Rourke was born, and it was love at first sight.

"Why are you still bartending?" Dad asked one night when Gail had gone to put the baby to bed.

"I like it," Colleen answered. She was only here to see the baby and already had her keys in hand.

"You're smarter than that," he said, and the words caused a starburst of anger in her chest. His old mantra, how smart the two of them were. *Guess I wasn't smart enough to see who you really were, Dad.*

"I'm half owner of a successful restaurant," she said coolly. "And yes, a bartender. An excellent bartender."

"I thought you were going to be a doctor," he said.

"Wrong."

"I wish you *were* a doctor, hon," Gail said, slapping on her doe-eyed stepmother smile. "We sure could use a pediatrician in this family! Savannah's not even sleeping through the night yet! I get so tired out carrying her. I think she weighs half of what I do! Babe, maybe I need to start lifting weights, what do you think?" She held up her arm to be admired and fluttered her eyelashes, lest Dad forget that his wife was a Hot Young Thing, or, God forbid, have him focus his attention on his grown daughter.

Colleen kept working at the nursing home, just eight hours a week. She liked the old folks and was glad to be able to help her grandfather. Rushing Creek had several levels of care, and Colleen was one of the few who preferred the sickest patients.

Gramp didn't seem to know who she was anymore, but sometimes when she held his hand, his fingers would curl around hers as if he was telling her he was still in there, and glad for her company, her love. That hurt her heart almost more than the days when he didn't even open his eyes.

Bartending was a nice balance.

Eventually, Colleen always thought, she'd meet the guy who would make her forget Lucas Damien Campbell. She tried. She really did. Sort of. Okay, she didn't try much.

A couple times a year, she'd go out with someone, only to find that he was married or weird or just *meh*. And every once in a while, she'd fool around with some guy, let him kiss her, maybe allow a little groping. Even more rarely, she'd sleep with someone, hoping there, too, that maybe sex would be a great revelation, and the two of them would realize, *Hell's to the yes, we are in love, baby!*

It didn't happen. Her reputation was hugely inflated, but hey. If people wanted to think she was some sort of siren, let them. Better than them knowing she'd never recovered from her first love…like her mom.

"Do you want to go out with me sometime?" Bobby McIntosh asked her one night when Lucas had been back for two weeks. He sipped his O'Doul's (proof that he stashed bodies in his cellar, Colleen always thought).

"I don't, Bobby. Sorry, pal."

"I really like you. You're nice."

"I'm not that nice."

"But you have great boobs."

"That's true. Don't wait for me in the parking lot, okay? I'll have to knee you in the groin if you do."

She pulled a Cooper's Cave for Chris Eckbert, who always left a huge tip (as he should, perpetually guilty for that prom night so long ago when he hadn't stuck up for her), then turned to Levi, who was sitting with

Honor Holland's fiancé, Tom, a sheaf of papers in front of them. Blueprints.

"Hallo, Colleen," Tom said with a smile.

"Hallo, Tom," she returned. *Loved* that accent. "How are the wedding plans?"

"I've no idea, really. Girly stuff, don't you think? I'll just be glad to be married."

"I don't know. Levi here obsessed over napkin colors for his wedding, didn't you, bub?" Levi gave her a tolerant look, and she messed up his hair fondly. "What can I get you, boys?"

"I'll have a beer," Levi said.

"We have seventeen different microbrews," she said. "You'll have to be more specific."

"Dazzle me."

"Will do. Whiskey for you, mate?" She winked at Tom.

"I'll have a beer as well, Colleen, and you've already dazzled me."

"Oh!" she said, putting her hands over her heart. "Levi, why can't you be more like Tom?"

"I'm more the strong, silent type. Also, I'm about to kill myself over these plans," he said.

"Oh, are those the blueprints for the thing?" she asked, tilting her head so she could see better.

"The public safety building, Coll," Levi said. "Your tax dollars at work."

"I voted against that," she murmured, then smiled at him. "I didn't. Faith would've killed me. I'm a huge supporter of all of you goofballs, right, Gerard?"

"Anything you say, Colleen," he said, smiling at her.

"I say you should go out with Lorelei, that's what I say. She's an amazing baker, she's nice and she could reform you. And you know how much you need re-forming, Gerard."

"Yes, master," he said.

"That's what I like to hear." She pulled Tom and Levi their beers (Empire Cream Ale for Tom, Blue Point Toasted Lager for Levi), and slid them down the bar, where they stopped two inches from Levi's elbow. A life skill to be sure. "You treating my friend well, Chief?" she asked.

"Very well," he answered.

"Would you say multiply well? If you know what I'm saying?"

"I think we all know what you're saying, Colleen." He gave her his famed crinkling forehead look. "And yes."

"And you, Tom?" she asked. "Is Honor multiply happy? Hmm?"

"What do you think, darling?" he answered, his grin widening.

"I like your confidence. Just don't get smug."

"Colleen," Connor yelled from the kitchen. "Stop harassing the customers."

"Is anyone feeling harassed?" she asked the bar at large.

A chorus of denials went up from her peeps.

Slipping under the bar, she went into the kitchen, where Brother Dear was hard at work. "What bug is up your ass this time?" she asked.

"Did you know Mom was at the hospital the other night?" he said, flipping the vegetable tempura around in the basket.

"What? Oh, that. Singles Nude Modeling. Yeah, I was there."

"Jesus, Coll. Nude modeling? Did Mom—"

"Listen. She needs a hobby."

"She sent some guy to the E.R. with a heart attack."

"Happens to the best of us."

He gave her a long-suffering look, which she happily returned until Hannah came into the kitchen. "Cheeseburger, medium rare, blue cheese, bacon, mayo—"

"Speaking of heart attacks," Colleen murmured.

"Sweet potato fries, Caesar salad with chicken, nachos grande, salmon cakes and the pasta special," Hannah continued, then bustled back out. Connor's memory was the stuff of legend.

"Out of my kitchen," he said.

"You'll miss me," she answered, pushing through the doors. She slid back behind the bar, got Lorena Iskin another Manhattan without being asked, smiled at Cathy and Louise, who always only had one drink, refilled Jessica Dunn's Chardonnay (on the house, Jess was nice) and turned to check on Tom and Levi.

Lucas was sitting two stools down from them.

Damn. She didn't need this. He'd gotten her all... stirred up at the hospital the other day, being all holier-than-thou. So irritating, so judgmental. So...hot...gorgeous...delicious... Crikey. White oxford shirts were so underrated. His sleeves were rolled up a few times, and his olive skin made her want to take a bite. Those hands...oh, she remembered those hands, yessirree. Those were gifted hands, hard and strong and yet so gentle...and so smart, always knowing exactly where to—

He was looking at her. A corner of his mouth lifted, as if knowing just how tight her special places were becoming.

Time to bring him down a little. She flashed Tom a smile and leaned down in front of him, giving him a view of her magnificent boobage. "How's that beer, Tommy?"

"Cover the goods, please," he said, shielding his eyes. "Engaged to another, hate to break your heart."

Shit, yes, what was she thinking? She jolted upright. "Sorry. So, how are things, you…um, you handsome Irishman?"

Tom flinched. "British, darling. Please."

"Yeah, I knew that," she muttered, glancing at Lucas. "And, Levi, you big strong, gun-toting lawman, you." Ack.

"Don't say that ever again," he said mildly.

"Oh, shush. I'm trying to flirt."

"Why?"

"Life skill."

"Is it, though?" His forehead crinkled at her.

"Bite me, Levi. You guys need some food?"

"I need another architect is what I need," Levi muttered, rustling the blueprints.

"Mind if I take a look?" Lucas asked.

Levi looked over. "Oh, hey," he said. "You went to school with us for a while, didn't you? I'm Levi Cooper. Chief of police here in Manningsport."

Lucas shook his hand. "Lucas Campbell. Bryce Campbell's cousin."

"Right, right. Good to see you. This is my brother-in-law, Tom. Well, almost my brother-in-law. He's marrying my wife's sister in a few weeks."

"Hallo, mate," Tom said, shaking hands, as well. Lucas moved down to look at the blueprints.

Great. Three beautiful men, all in a row. Two spoken for, one…not.

"Are you an architect?" Levi asked.

Lucas shook his head. "A building projects manager out in Chicago."

"Oh, yeah? What kind of buildings?"

"Skyscrapers, hospitals, that kind of thing."

Annie, one of the new summer hires, came behind the bar with a menu for Lucas, her pad in her other hand. "Hi," she breathed, and Colleen envisioned the girl's ovaries exploding. "Can I get you anything?"

Lucas smiled. Annie staggered.

"Go clean the bathroom, Annie," Colleen said sweetly. "I'll take care of Lucas. He and I are old friends." She folded her arms under her chest. "Lucas, can I get you something to drink? Would you like to see a menu? Or are you meeting someone?" Yes. Pretend he was just another customer, as unthreatening as Reverend Fisk, who was eighty-nine years old.

"I'm meeting Bryce," he said. "But I'll have a beer."

"Absolutely. What kind, hon? We have Sixpoint Harbinger, Southern Tier IPA, Sly Fox O'Reilly's Stout, Empire Cream Ale, Naked Dove Bock, Blue Point Toasted Lager, Cooper's Cave IPA, Victory Donnybrook Irish Stout, Stone Vertical Epic, Captain Lawrence Brink Brown, Ithaca Flower Power IPA, Dogfish Head Immort Ale, Sly Fox Maibock, Bud, Bud Light, Miller, Miller Lite, Coors, Coors Light, Corona, Stella, and, in honor of our New York heritage, Genesee."

Her regulars applauded, as they always did, when she recited the beer list in one breath.

"I'll take the Dogfish," he said.

"Coming up."

She went over to the beer taps and filled the glass halfway, then filled the rest with 7Up.

"Enjoy," she said, putting it in front of him.

He took a sip, choked a little, then swallowed. "You like it?" she asked. "Limited release."

He raised an eyebrow. His phone beeped with a text, and he glanced at it and sighed. "Bryce ditch you?" she guessed.

"As a matter of fact, yes," he said.

"Well, then. Don't let me keep you. Nighty-night." She gave him her best smile.

His eyes narrowed. "Actually, I may as well stay for dinner."

"Join us, mate," Tom said, the traitor. Just couldn't trust those Brits; had the War of 1812 taught nothing?

Fine. That was *fine.* Colleen slapped a menu on the bar. "No need," Lucas said, nodding at the chalkboard (which she'd written out that very afternoon, complete with an adorable stick figure lifting a pint). "I'll take the burger special."

It *was* pretty fantastic—an all-Angus beef burger with herbed goat cheese from the Mennonite farm up the Hill, native tomatoes and Vidalia onion on an English muffin and served with an arugula salad and Con's famed sweet-potato fries. As her brother's guinea pig with all house specials, Colleen had it for lunch. It was almost as good as sex.

"I'll have that as well, please, Colleen," Tom said.

"Make it three," Levi added.

She smiled oh so pleasantly. "Coming up, boys."

She went into the kitchen. "Three house burgers, Con. Medium on two—" Tom and Levi were regulars, and she well knew their preferences "—and petrify the third."

"Really?" Connor asked.

"Yeah."

She went out again. Time to schmooze. "Hey, love-birds, happy anniversary!" she said to the Wheelers, who were celebrating their thirty-second. The Murrays were in with their beautiful, red-haired daughters, and Colleen asked the older one how trumpet was going, and the younger one about their new kitten. Bill and Laura Clemson were fighting, but that was nothing new; it was a Friday night tradition. Louis Hudson and Amy Bates, however, were cooing at each other in a dark booth, and Colleen told Hannah to bring them out a crème brûlée, two spoons, on the house. They were engaged, thanks to one Colleen Margaret Mary O'Rourke.

By the time she got back, the three burger specials were just about ready; the two medium burgers were on yellow Fiesta ware; the well-done order was on blue. Colleen lifted the bun to check it. It was dark, all right. Just not dark enough.

"What are you doing?" Connor asked as she put the burger back on the grill.

"It's not well-done enough," she said.

"You said well-done. It's well-done."

"I said petrify. Where's that Chinese sauce?"

"Which Chinese sauce?"

"The fire sauce."

"It's over the sink. Go easy on that. It's vicious. Two drops will bring a grown man to his knees." He turned back to the chicken marsala he was making.

Colleen rummaged through Connor's salt collection; honestly, did a person need seven different kinds? Rock, kosher, sea, truffle, black… Aha! Here it was, the strange little bottle with the dragon on the label and some mysterious Chinese characters. She took it out, checked to ensure that the burger was a hardened, dry, hockey puck of meat, then put it back on the bun. Doused it with fire sauce, then added a splash more on the fries.

She brought the plates out to the bar and set them in front of their respective orders. "Enjoy, gentlemen," she said.

Levi folded up the blueprint of the public safety building. "Lucas will be helping us out," he said. "Project manager."

"That's great," Colleen said easily. "Glad you found someone to help you."

Lucas gave her a long look, picked up his burger and took a bite.

Colleen smiled. Happiness was being in charge.

His eyes began to tear. Sweat broke out on his forehead. He raised an eyebrow, then, she had to give it to him, chewed and swallowed. With great effort. He took his doctored up beer and drank it down. Rested the cold glass against his forehead.

"All right, mate?" Tom asked.

"I'm fine," he wheezed, as the fire sauce had paralyzed his vocal cords a li'l tiny bit.

"How's that burger, hon?" Colleen said.

"Perfect." He wiped his face with a napkin, and Colleen leaned her elbows on the bar and just enjoyed the sight of him, sweating, red-faced, maybe a little closer to death than he had been a few minutes ago.

"I made it special just for you." She smiled sweetly.

"I guessed that."

Then he stood up, slid his hand around her neck and pulled her in for a kiss.

She didn't see that coming.

Didn't pull away, either.

It was a hard, authoritative kiss that seared through her. Good God, the Spaniard could *kiss*. His five-o'clock shadow scraped her just the right amount, and his mouth, oh, yes, that mouth of his, that fallen-angel mouth…and then it was over, and he stood in front of her, dark and sure and steady when she was lucky to be standing, her legs suddenly warm and wonderfully weak, her special places bursting into song. Also, her lips were burning, thanks to the fire sauce, but hey. Worth it.

Then Lucas smiled that pirate's grin full of secrets and fun and cockiness, and her heart was rolling and shaking like a hyperactive puppy.

Oh, man. She was in trouble.

The bar was completely still.

"We should get that dinner sometime," he said calmly, his voice normal now.

"I thought this would count."

"It doesn't."

"Oh. Okay, then," she said, then cleared her throat.

"Thank you for the wonderful meal."

"You're very welcome," she said. "My pleasure."

Then the kitchen door banged open, and Connor tapped Lucas on the shoulder, and punched him in the face.

"I'M NOT SEEING HIM," Colleen said three hours later. "Rufus, tell your uncle Connor he's got his head up his butt." Unfortunately, Rufus was engrossed in a documentary about Yellowstone National Park and couldn't drag his doggy eyes off the family of wolverines on screen. It was ten past midnight, and Connor had demanded an audience to discuss her love life. Which was a joke because there was no love life, of course.

Not yet.

Lucas had taken Connor's anger like a boss; a Southie from Chicago wouldn't be bothered by one punch, no matter how enraged the brother who'd thrown it. Levi, being a cop and all, jumped to his feet, and Tom did, too, but Lucas just said, "It's fine. I earned that." He slid a twenty under his plate, nodded at Colleen and left calmly. Connor glared at his retreating back, then at her, then at Levi, then at the bar in general, then stomped back into the kitchen, where he banged around for the rest of the night before coming for Big Brother Lecture. He'd always taken those three minutes very seriously.

"Colleen, I saw how you were looking at him."

"Yeah, okay, he kissed me. Look. He's back in town because Joe Campbell is dying. Of course I'm going to see him from time to time."

"You know what you are? You're one mattress fire away from becoming our mother."

"I'm not like Mom," she said calmly. "How dare you and all that. Want some ice cream?"

Connor folded his arms and tipped his head back to stare at the ceiling (and pray for patience, Colleen knew). "If you're not dating him, why were you flirting with him?"

"I wasn't." Rufus put his head on her foot, then licked her ankle with his giant tongue.

"Yeah? What was that game with the fire sauce, then?"

"Oh, just a little…signal. A shot across the bar."

"It was flirting. And then you let him kiss you."

She pulled a face. "Yeah. That might've been dumb."

"He's divorced."

"I know."

"Do you want to get back together with him? You gonna move to Chicago? Is he dating anyone back there?"

"I don't know. Look. It was one kiss." Well, then, there was that other kiss, down by the lake. Two kisses.

"One kiss? This wasn't the first time, was it?"

"Look, Long Island Medium, he took me by surprise, okay?"

"Just remember what he did to you last time. I don't think he deserves a second chance, personally. But I'm just your brother. I'm just the one who's been watching you avoid a serious relationship this past decade."

"Where's your wife, huh? Do you have three beautiful children stashed somewhere? No? So don't throw stones. You won't even be seen in public with this mystery woman of yours."

"Don't change the subject." He sat on the floor; Rufus, the whore, rolled onto his back and presented his stomach (and other parts) for admiration. Connor flinched. "You should get this dog neutered."

"He is neutered."

The twins were quiet for a moment. They didn't fight often; well, they bickered constantly, and Mom still complained about it, but they hardly ever really disagreed. "You shouldn't have punched him," she said.

"He broke your stupid heart," Connor grumbled.

There was no lying to her brother.

She'd done her best to hide her feelings last time. She certainly *didn't* want to be like Mom. Didn't want people to know she'd been dumped. She was supposed to be smarter than that.

But Connor knew anyway. Despite her playing it

lightly with most people—*You know how fickle young love is. Hardly ever lasts*—Connor knew.

"I don't want you to get hurt, Collie Dog Face," her brother said now.

"Me, neither."

"Be careful."

She swallowed. "Yeah."

Connor scratched Rufus's tummy another minute, then stood up and gave her shoulder a squeeze. "See you."

"Wait. Who's your girlfriend? Do I know her? Is she a prostitute? I won't judge either of you. Please tell me," she said.

"Good night," he called from the door. Tossed her a grin and left, his feet thumping on the stairs.

CHAPTER THIRTEEN

THE CHICKEN KING lived in a beautiful old Victorian house that had once belonged to Mark Twain's wife's aunt, legend had it. Colleen was here to go over the planned encounter with Bryce. And just to hang out a little because, let's face it, she really liked Paulie.

The blue-and-cream-painted house sat high on a hill in a heavily wooded neighborhood overlooking Keuka Lake. Their driveway was long and shaded, and the house had to have at least twenty rooms.

However, the yard—grounds, really—were littered with giant metal chicken statues in lurid colors, like a terrifying dream you might have as a kid when you're running a very high fever. As the breeze blew, it made a strange whistling sound through the, uh, artwork, making it sound like the chickens were moaning. And those beaks looked mighty sharp.

"Dad collects these from all over the world," Paulie said. "They're beautiful, aren't they?"

"Yes," Colleen said, trying not to look. She'd always been a little afraid of chickens, personally. The polka-dotted statue seemed especially hostile.

Inside, the house was just as beautiful, carefully restored and extremely elegant. Not what you'd picture for the Chicken King; well, no, there were a lot of paintings of chickens on the walls, as well as Mr. Petrosinsky dressed in chicken garb standing next to various local celebrities…and some national celebrities, too. "Is that Meryl Streep?" Colleen asked.

"Oh, her. She's so nice. Loves the Sweet Home Alabama Triple Batter Honey Dijon," Paulie said.

"And Vladimir Putin?" Perhaps the Russian Mob rumors were true, after all.

"Make-Mine-Miami Cuban Spice."

Paulie's bedroom was a Maxfield Parrish–blue, deep and poignant. A dressing room bigger than Colleen's entire bedroom, filled with clothes.

"Yeah, I don't wear much of this," Paulie said. "If you see something you want, take it. You know me. I mostly wear gym clothes." She was, in fact, now clad in spandex shorts that showed her ripped muscles in great detail, and a Cabrera's Boxing T-shirt.

"You shouldn't. You have a great figure. Very girl-power strong. Here. Put this on. My God, it's Armani! Hello, gorgeous! Dog, don't chew on that," she added as one of Paulie's rescue dogs, this one looking like a dirty mop, began gnawing on a boot.

A few minutes later, Paulie frowned at her reflection.

"See how it hugs you here?" Colleen asked. "You look taller and leaner."

"These shoes are killing me."

"Offer it up to God. And this belt is funky and young and surprising. You look incredible!"

"Are you sure? I feel weird."

"It's just an adjustment, trust me. Where'd you get all these clothes, anyway?"

"My dad. He does a lot of online shopping."

"He's single, right?" Colleen asked. Hey. If she was

going to have a sugar daddy, she was going to have one who bought Armani.

"Yeah. Ever since Mom left, you know."

Colleen squeezed her hand. "Okay, so on to Operation Flat Tire. This is how it's gonna go."

"Oh, God. Will this really work?"

"Of course!"

The plan was simple. Bryce was home, a little benign stalking had shown. Joe was at dialysis, Evil Didi was at work. Lucas—not that she was thinking about him too much (pause for laughter)—was out at the public safety building, according to Levi, who'd come to the bar for lunch just half an hour ago.

"So," Colleen said. "You get a flat tire, and heck, what's this? You're right in front of Bryce's house, and Bryce is home! What do you do?"

"Change the tire."

"No, Paulina. You don't change the tire." The pug barked, backing her up.

"Why?"

"Because Bryce is going to change the tire."

Paulie frowned. "Oh."

"You're going to be all feminine and helpless."

"But I know how to change a tire."

Colleen suppressed a sigh. "And that's great, Paulie. But today, Bryce gets to change the tire and help you, and feel very manly and smart, because men like to be tricked into thinking they're in control."

"Oh. Got it." Her face started its amazing sunrise impression.

"No panicking. Just do what I say, and Bryce and you can have a nice conversation."

"What should I say? I feel a little sick. Do I really

have to talk to him? Damn it, this *stupid* deodorant is supposedly extra strength and it's doing squat. Oh, I hate being in love!"

"We all do at certain times, Paulie."

Paulie threw herself down on her giant bed and covered her eyes with her hands. One of her cats jumped up and began kneading her thigh. "I can barely *think* about talking to him, let alone actually talk to him. What if I hurt him again?"

Colleen pondered. "You know what would be great?" she said. "If I could somehow feed you lines. Like Cyrano and Christian. You have a Bluetooth, right?"

Ten minutes later, Colleen pulled around the corner from Bryce's house, Paulie's adorable little Porsche purring behind her. Craftily, feeling a bit like Bond, James Bond, Colleen parked and got out, approaching Paulie's car.

"Okay, babe, this is where you get a flat," she said. She opened up her Swiss Army knife and stabbed Paulie's tire.

"Hey!"

"Relax. Now just drive really slow to Bryce's house, then park, get out and stare at the car, helpless and feminine. That's your job—to appear helpless and feminine, helpless and feminine. Also, mention that you're throwing a party and you'd love for him to come. Now go. Into the car. Drive on, little sparrow!"

With a dubious look, Paulie obeyed. "Can you hear me?" Colleen said into her phone when Paulie was almost there.

"Yeah. Colleen, I don't feel so good." She made a noise that sounded suspiciously like a dry heave.

"You're doing great," Colleen said in her most reassuring tone, the same one that got people who over-indulged to hand over their keys. "Okay, stop. That's his house."

"I know. I've probably driven by a thousand times."

Colleen's heart tugged. "This will work, Paulie. Just try to relax and enjoy it."

From where she stood, Colleen could see her client pull over. This ploy, while definitely on the points-for-difficulty end of what Colleen usually recommended, had worked on her cousin Monica just last year, when Monica had a "bike accident" in front of Fox Den Vineyard. Monica was now married to the Fox Den heir, thank you very much. Colleen had been a bridesmaid, her tenth such gig.

Paulie got out of the car.

"Walk slowly around the car, looking at the tires," Colleen ordered. "He'll be out any second." She glanced at the house. The day was the best of June, bright and lilac-scented. "Okay, squat down and take a look at the tire. Oh, dear, what's this? It's flat!"

"Of course it's flat," Paulie said. "You stabbed it."

"I know, but pretend to be surprised and dismayed."

Paulie hesitated, then bent down. "Oh, shit!" she bellowed. "My tire's flat! What will I do?"

Colleen bobbled her phone. "Down, girl," she said. "Easy on the melodrama, and the volume. You don't want just anyone coming along. And try not to swear."

"Shit, I forgot about that. Okay."

They waited. No one came out of the house.

"He's not home," Paulie whispered.

"His car is in the driveway," Colleen said. "He's probably watching TV or something. Hang on, I'll get his attention."

She picked up a handful of pebbles and walked toward the house, sticking close to the shade from the neighbor's wide maples. There was a thick hedge of lilacs against the eastern side of the Campbells' place, and she eased into it, the clean, perfect smell of the flowers giving her a contact high.

Bryce lived in the basement, she knew. Didi had made it into a full-scale apartment for her baby boy not long after he dropped out of college.

She threw a pebble. Thanks to thousands of games of darts she'd played over the years, she hit the window on the first try, a satisfying *tick* against the glass. "Places, everyone," she whispered into the phone. "He should be out soon."

A mockingbird called from a tree. The wind blew, brushing a lilac bloom across Colleen's cheek. Paulie appeared to be frozen in place. "Check the tire like you're trying to figure out what the heck went wrong," Colleen whispered. "And be prepared to repeat after me, okay?" Paulie squatted obediently, her short skirt fluttering against her thighs.

Bryce didn't come out.

Colleen threw another pebble. Waited. Nada. Another pebble. Nothing.

"My legs are burning," Paulie whispered. "Please let me stand up."

"Sure, sure," Colleen said. Paulie stood, groaning, grabbed her ankle and stretched her quads.

"Put your leg down," Colleen ordered. "You're flashing Mr. Bancroft, and he's kind of pervy as it is."

"Hey, there, Paulie!" called Mr. Bancroft. "Got a problem?"

"Say no," Colleen instructed.

"No! Go away!" Paulie barked.

"Henry! Get in the car," Mrs. Bancroft ordered. "We're already late! Paulie, what's the problem?"

"Nothing! Nothing at all," Paulie said. "I, uh, I... I have a bladder infection and had to stop. That's all."

Mrs. Bancroft paused, shook her head and got into the car.

"Let's cut the improv, okay?" Colleen said as the Bancrofts drove away. "Say only what I say. Now hang on. This time, I mean business." She looked at the pebbles in her hand, selected the biggest one and threw it with slightly more gusto.

The window shattered.

"Shit!" she hissed.

"Shit!" Paulie echoed.

But the broken glass did the trick. After a second, the front door opened, and there stood Bryce, blinking in the sunlight.

"Oh, my God, I see him. Oh, damn it all, he's here," Paulie said, her voice strangled.

"Calm down, calm down. Deep breath," Colleen whispered. "It's showtime. He's a nice guy, you're a nice woman."

"Hey, Paulie," Bryce said as he loped over to Paulie's car. "Everything okay here? Our window just broke."

Paulie inhaled audibly, her breath hitching in her throat. "Oh! Wow. Hi. Your eyes are so...so...blue."

Colleen winced. "Stop that."

"Stop that," echoed Paulie.

Bryce stopped and tilted his head.

"Paulie, relax. Just...just say hi to him."

Another shaking breath. "Hi, Bryce!" she said loudly. "What are you doing here?"

Bryce laughed. "I live here. How about you?"

A squeaky groan came over the wire.

"I threw a pebble, I guess. I think I had a blowout," Colleen whispered.

"I threw a pebble, I guess," Paulie parroted. "I think I had a blow job." She clapped her hands over her mouth. "Out, out! I didn't mean blow job. I never had a blow job. I meant something else. Out. I had a blowout."

"Paulie, calm down," Colleen whispered. "Jesus."

"Jesus, calm down," Paulie said, then wiped her forehead with her arm. "Uh… I… I have a flat tire."

"Bummer," Bryce said, not freaked out in the least by Paulie sounding as if she were possessed by a demon.

"Can you help me change it, Bryce?" Colleen asked.

"Can you help me change it? Bryce? Please? Please help me."

Dear Lord. This was going to be a long afternoon.

THE PUBLIC SAFETY BUILDING, half begun and currently stalled, was in a state of chaos. First of all, every one of the three agencies—police, ambulance and fire—felt that theirs was the most important. Lucas had already changed the plans so the police department office was situated between the fire and ambulance departments, because apparently those two fought the way his twin nieces did over who got to sit in the front.

Besides that, the ventilation had to be specialized, and the alarm system was fairly complicated. It was tricky to make such a functional building also be attractive inside and out, and the builder who'd quit hadn't tried very hard. Lucas had requested the plans, then got to work on the design. He moved the back entrance so it didn't come right into the fire department kitchen, repositioned

Dispatch to the back of the building and reinforced the walls, added some windows on the eastern side so the place didn't look like a crematorium. The town council was falling over with gratitude.

It was nice to be needed.

Funny, how much he really did love construction work. Never minded it a bit in the summertime during college, though back then, he thought it would be temporary.

When Frank Forbes had first summoned him after learning that Lucas had impregnated his angel, it was fair to say that Lucas expected to be thrown from the fifty-fifth story.

Frank Forbes *was* furious. Lucas couldn't blame him. "So you want to marry my daughter, do you?" he asked.

"Yes, sir."

"And why is that?"

"It's the right thing to do."

"The right thing." Frank shook his head. "How do you plan to support them, my daughter and grandchild? You won't be able to work if you're in law school."

"No, sir. I withdrew and got a job with Windy City Construction. I start on Monday. I can join the union after a year."

Mr. Forbes gave him a long look, his jaw knotty. The silence was leaden.

Then he took a sharp breath. "Quit Windy City. You'll work for this company, on construction, because Johnny Hall says you're not bad. You'll earn what all people at your level earn, and you'll have a health care plan, same as all my employees. Windy City has an abominable safety record, and their work is shoddy at best."

Lucas hesitated. "I'd rather make my own way, Mr. Forbes."

"Yes, well, you should've thought of that before you got my daughter pregnant!" he snapped. Then he took another deep breath. "You and Ellen can live in one of my apartment buildings," he went on. "I don't want my daughter and grandchild living in a bad neighborhood, and that student apartment of hers isn't big enough for a baby. You, however, will support your family. You will pay your bills on time, and I will never bail you out financially. You will sign a prenup saying you'll never get a dime of Ellen's trust fund. I will pay for Ellen's law school; you will pay for your family's living expenses. You will give this marriage a real try. If you hurt, mistreat or cheat on my daughter, I promise you your body will never be found. I love my daughter. She's the most important thing in the world to me. Do you understand me, young man?"

"Yes, sir. I imagine I'll feel the same way about my own kids."

Because yes. He was going to be a father, and if some kid from the wrong side of the tracks knocked up his baby girl, he imagined he wouldn't be quite as civilized as Frank Forbes.

Frank looked at him for a long minute.

Then, to Lucas's extreme surprise, he sighed, all the anger seeping out of him like air from a balloon. He walked around his desk and hugged Lucas. "Welcome to the family. I don't like how it happened, but I appreciate the fact that you're owning up to your responsibilities. My daughter is smart, and she says you're honorable and decent. She loves you, and whether I like it or not, you're part of the family now."

You could've knocked him over with a feather. Lucas had expected Frank Forbes to try to pay him off or threaten him. Possibly beat the shit out of him, which, Lucas admitted, he deserved.

Instead, Mr. and Mrs. Forbes took him and Ellen out to dinner that night. They asked about his family, expressed their condolence over the loss of his parents, murmured sympathetically when he told them the truth about his father's criminal activity. In fact, Frank had already run a background check on him and knew full well how both parents died. And again, Lucas would've done the same for his daughter.

A daughter (or son) who was growing in Ellen's belly right now.

Lucas did all the right things. Held her hand, held her chair, asked how she was feeling, went to the obstetrician's office with her. He cooked for her, which she thought was charming, and listened to her when she talked.

He'd always wanted kids.

He couldn't think about Colleen. That was forbidden now. He was with Ellen, and they were starting a family. The only thing to do was be a man about it.

Though it had been thrown together at the last minute, the wedding was at a huge downtown hotel with three hundred and fifty guests, five bridesmaids and an eleven-piece band at the reception. Frank made a speech and referred to Lucas as a fine young man who'd put himself through college, who knew the value of a hard day's work. Hugged him, reminded him to treat Ellen like the princess she was, and seemed to bear him no ill will whatsoever.

Lucas went to work, worked hard, kept his head

down and did what he was told. Came home to the beautiful apartment and talked with Ellen, who really was very nice. Put his hand on her belly and kissed her and smiled at her and slept with her, even if it still felt as though he was cheating on Colleen. If Ellen sensed something was off, she didn't say anything.

And when they'd been married for six weeks, he got the call that Ellen was in the E.R. She wasn't quite at twelve weeks, and the second he saw her face, he knew the baby was lost. Then he gathered her into his arms and kissed her head as she sobbed.

"It happens more than you might think," the doctor said. "I'm very sorry."

He took her home and lay in bed with her, holding her close. "You don't have to stay married to me," she whispered. "I know it was only because of the baby."

He looked at her a long minute. "I'm not leaving you," he said.

He'd been willing to stand by her when she was pregnant with his child; he damn well wasn't going to leave her because of a cruel act of nature.

He grew to love her. Not the way he loved Colleen, no. But Ellen was good and calm and smart. He loved her parents, too—Grace was funny and generous and a little bit bawdy when she had a drink in her, and Frank… Frank was remarkably open and optimistic for a man who ran an empire. One newspaper article referred to him as "the Donald Trump of Chicago," and Frank said, "Kill me now," and laughed.

No, the Forbes family seemed to embody all the good Midwestern qualities—generosity, kindness, optimism and a very touching sense of innocence. "I've found that if you expect the best of a person," Frank told him once, "you generally get it."

"What happens when you don't?" Lucas asked.

"Live and learn. Emphasis on learn."

Lucas had always been a worker, ever since he collected bottles at the age of six to return for the deposit (that story had made Ellen cry). He worked harder and longer than his coworkers, hoping to show he wasn't just some schmuck who was being promoted because of who he was. And he was promoted, moving up through the ranks from construction worker to foreman to project manager.

It was…well, it was good. But it was also hard; he was never far from the knowledge that he owed the Forbes family more than he could ever repay. That with one night, he'd changed the course of Ellen's life…and his, of course. But mostly hers. She was the one who'd endured twelve weeks of morning sickness, and the one whose body had to let go of their baby.

Ellen didn't get pregnant again. She went back on the Pill, which was fine; she went to law school, and then got hired by a big firm. She worked long hours, as did he, and seemed to love it. They didn't talk about kids directly. Ellen didn't seem to want to pursue it just yet. That was fine. They were young. There was time.

But it would've been amazing to have kids, Lucas thought, especially when he saw his nieces. He often thought of the baby who wasn't…how old his son or daughter would be now, what it would be like to have a little one come running into his arms. To tuck a child in at night, straighten out the covers, to kiss a little head and say, "Daddy loves you."

Six years into their marriage, Ellen came home from

her swanky office, took off her shoes and poured herself a glass of wine. "So, Lucas," she said, very kindly. "I think it's time to call it quits, don't you?"

The sorrow he felt was more because he hadn't been able to make it work, rather than because his heart was broken. She'd loved him a lot once, and he'd done his best, and it wasn't quite enough.

The divorce was so amicable, it was almost shameful. He would've preferred some fighting or tears to the calm dissolution of their household. He took only a photo of the two of them; they'd taken his four nieces to the beach, and Mercedes had been fooling around with the camera. He and Ellen had been holding hands, and he said something to make her laugh. It was an indication, maybe, that he hadn't been a bad husband. He hoped he hadn't been.

It was just that his heart belonged to someone else, and they both knew it. They never spoke of it, but it was true just the same.

They went out to dinner the night before their divorce was final, to Alinea, her favorite restaurant, where the maître d' knew them both by name. She ordered a martini; he ordered a beer. They talked about work and her parents, about Mercedes getting the lead in her school play. Ellen had assured the girls that she'd still be their aunt, and Frank and Grace had all four girls for a sleepover and said of course they'd still be Grandpa Frank and Nana Grace, because that's just how they were.

Finally, Ellen took a deep breath. "I hope this won't upset you," she said, tilting her head the way she always did when she had something momentous to say. "But I've met someone."

He put down his beer. "Really." Should probably say more than that. "That's good."

She looked at the tablecloth, started to say something, then stopped. Her eyes filled with tears.

"What is it?" he asked, leaning forward and covering her hand with his own. She was still his wife, even if only for a few more hours.

She smiled and shook her head a little, blinked back her tears. "I don't know if you remember this." She took a deep breath, once again fully composed. "It was sophomore year, maybe? No, junior, because we had that class with Professor Hayden." She smiled at someone she knew, then continued. "Anyway, we were eating in the dining hall, and your girlfriend came in. She surprised you, and you stood up so fast the table practically fell over, but you didn't even notice. And she jumped into your arms and wrapped herself around you and you two were kissing like no one else was around."

The memory stole his breath… Colleen's exuberance, her unabashed happiness and affection.

"That's how this guy makes me feel," Ellen said quietly.

He picked up her hand and looked at it for a minute. She'd already taken off her wedding ring. His was still on. "Then I'm glad for you, honey," he said. "I really am."

Twelve hours later, they were divorced.

Frank took it the hardest. Lucas was the son he never had. Since the divorce, Lucas had stayed on to finish the Cambria skyscraper. But they both knew this was his last project with the company.

He wanted to stay in construction—not to make skyscrapers, but to make homes. He wasn't an architect, but he'd taken several drafting classes over the years and had a good eye. He wanted to be a general contractor, to work on every stage of the house, from the cellar to the wiring to the walls. He wanted to make people the home they'd live in all their lives. He'd earn about a quarter of what he made as a project manager for Forbes, but he had the connections, the experience, the reputation.

That's what waited for him back home. Back in the City of Big Shoulders.

But for now, it was awfully nice to be doing something other than sitting at Joe's bedside or coaxing Bryce into a plan for his life.

That's what he was supposed to be doing right now, in fact.

Instead, he was standing in a field, imagining the house he'd build. It was an occupational hazard; wherever he traveled, he tended to scope out a site. This one wasn't far from the emergency services site; it was on a hill, the lake in the distance, vineyards roping their way down the slopes. The house he'd build here would have lots of windows, cedar planked exterior, a riverstone chimney.

Right. Well. Maybe he could teach Bryce some construction work. That, or gigolo, because the guy had a way with women, that was for sure.

Joe had dialysis, Didi would be denying amputees their claims, and Bryce was presumably home. Lucas got into his car and headed to Didi's.

Both Joe and Lucas were aware of the fact that Didi would undercut any effort to dislodge Bryce from the family home. She gave Bryce an allowance and a credit card, despite the fact that he was thirty-one years old. Castrated him, in other words.

Lucas parked the rental car a few houses down from his aunt's; old habits died hard. Didi hated cars in the driveway or on the street in front of her house; said it looked poor white trash (this with a significant look at Lucas, despite the fact that technically, he was Hispanic and not white).

Bryce's car was in the driveway (Didi's rules didn't apply to him). Lucas knocked, waited and then went in the front door. From the basement, came the sounds of gunfire and explosions. Lucas let himself in and went down the cellar stairs. The apartment was surprisingly neat and airy. Chances were high that Didi had a cleaning woman come down here each week. Big leather couch, a pool table, a bar, a bedroom and a tiny kitchen that Lucas bet was never used.

Lucas waited until his cousin had killed another innocent person on-screen, then said, "Hey, Bryce."

"Dude! Good to see you," Bryce said, grinning up at him.

"How's it going?"

"Excellent. Want to play?"

"Another time, maybe."

"Sure. What can I do you for?" Bryce turned off the game.

"So how are things jobwise these days?" he asked.

Bryce nodded. "Yeah. Well, I do a little work at the shelter and the gym, you know?"

"You ever think about getting certified as a trainer?"

"Maybe. Sure, I guess. I don't know, though. Might not be fun anymore if I had to do it for a living."

"What *would* you like to do for a living, Bryce? You're past thirty now. Maybe living at home is getting old?"

"Are you kidding? It's great."

Technically, they were the same age. It never felt like that.

"I guess I want to see you moving forward, buddy," Lucas said. "You know. Have a career, your own place… you mentioned wanting a family someday."

"Definitely. I love kids."

"But you have to take some steps, Bryce. Those things don't just happen."

"Right, right." He nodded sagely.

"So maybe we could work on that while I'm around." He paused. "I think it'd mean a lot to your dad if he could see you a little more settled, Bryce."

"Yeah. Uh…what do you mean?"

Lucas paused. There was a touching, if somewhat pathetic, innocence in Bryce's eyes. "Bryce, your dad's not doing well. He won't be around much longer."

Bryce stiffened. "Actually, he's doing great. I mean, the dialysis is just as good as a regular liver."

"Kidney."

"That's what I meant. Besides, he'll get a new kidney any day." Bryce started picking at a hole in his jeans.

"He's not on the transplant list, buddy. The cancer ruled that out."

"I'll give him my kidney." Bryce's eyes filled with tears.

"And I'd give him mine, if it would help." Lucas put a hand on Bryce's shoulder. "His biggest concern is you. He wants you to have a great life—"

"I do have a great life. And my dad… I'll talk to him. But he's not going anywhere. I won't let him. Anyway, why are you talking about the job stuff?"

"I have some construction work to do while I'm here.

Maybe you could help." Bryce looked unconvinced. "We could hang out, you know? And you could learn some construction skills, and who knows? You might like it."

Bryce mulled that over. "Okay," he said, grinning. "Sure! Swing some hammers, then grab a few beers at O'Rourke's, go down to the lake, maybe pick up some girls."

Lucas closed his eyes briefly. "Sure. Sounds good. Pick you up tomorrow morning, okay?"

At that moment, the window shattered with a crash, causing them both to jump.

"What the heck?" Bryce said. He ran up the stairs and out the front door, slamming it behind him hard enough to make the house shake.

But the window was on the side of the house, not the front. Lucas went over to it, his feet crunching on the broken glass, and looked outside.

Colleen O'Rourke was standing in Didi's lilacs, staring at the street, talking on the phone.

He opened the door that led to the backyard and, his feet silent on the grass, went up behind her.

Ah. Paulie Petrosinsky was standing in front of her little Porsche, wiping her hands on her thighs. Bryce stood with her, talking amiably.

"Okay, Paulie," Colleen muttered, "I want you to—"

"What are you doing, Colleen?"

She jumped, hitting her head on a branch. "Jesus! You scared me!" she hissed.

"Jesus, you scared me!" Paulie barked, her voice clearly heard from the phone.

"What?" Bryce asked, his voice audible, as well.

"Nothing," Colleen said.

"Nothing!" Paulie said.

For the love of God. "Give that to me," Lucas said.

"No," Colleen said.

"No," Paulie echoed.

Colleen tapped the mute button on her iPhone. "Still good at sneaking around, I see," she grumbled.

He felt a smile start in his chest. Yep. Once or twice (four times, actually), he'd sneaked into her own yard, climbed the trellis to her bedroom and spent a happy night wrapped around her. They'd drawn the line at actual sex, but just barely.

Happy times.

Colleen seemed to be thinking the same things, because her face got pink.

"What are you doing here?" he asked softly.

"I'm trying to help Paulie make Bryce feel manly."

"How?"

"By having her act feminine and helpless," she said.

"Ah. So she has engine trouble?"

"I slashed her front tire. Think Bryce can change a flat?"

"No."

She grinned, and Lucas felt it like an electric shock. Once, Colleen had been the prettiest girl around.

Now, she was beautiful.

And not a girl anymore.

"Don't bug me," she said, tearing her eyes off him. "I have work to do." She tapped her phone, and once again, they could hear the star-crossed lovers from the street.

"So, um, do you know what I should do?" Paulie said, clearing her throat.

"Call Triple A?" Bryce suggested.

"Oh. So you don't know how to change a flat tire?"

Paulie asked, looking rather desperately at Colleen, who pointed at Bryce's back.

"Not really. I never could figure out the jack, you know?" Bryce said.

Colleen whispered, "Tell him you're sure he can figure it out. Be feminine. Be helpless. Make him feel strong and manly."

Lucas rolled his eyes. "Tell me when you've ever acted feminine or helpless in your life."

She looked up at him, her face suddenly stricken. She took a shaky breath. "Lucas, please," she whispered, blinking back tears. "I'm just trying to help my friend. You're right, it's stupid. I just didn't know what else to do." Her mouth quivered.

"Nice try."

She shrugged. "Well, it works on everyone else."

He took the phone, clicked End and put it in his front jeans pocket. "You want it, you have to come get it."

"I will. I'll cut it out with my Swiss Army knife, and I won't be careful of the landscape." She waited. He didn't move. "Lucas, give me my damn phone." She reached for his pocket, but he intercepted her hand.

"You set this up, Colleen. Let them finish it." Her hand was smooth and cool and fit into his just right. Same as always. Because he couldn't resist, he stroked the back of her hand with his thumb, that soft, sweet skin.

"Oh, wow," she sighed. "You're really turning me on." She batted her eyelashes at him, then pulled her hand free. Reached into his pocket.

¡Hola!

She kept her eyes locked on his. Fumbled around… deliberately, he figured. She gave that wicked smile.

Still the same Colleen.

And thank God for that.

He bent his head so that his unshaven cheek brushed hers. "Be careful what you wish for," he whispered. God, she smelled good. Better than the lilacs, even.

"The ego on you could choke a blue whale," she said, yanking her hand (and her phone) free. Her cheeks were very encouragingly red. She tapped her phone; a second later, Paulie tapped her Bluetooth. Command Central was once again established.

Bryce had found the spare tire in the trunk and put the lug wrench on a nut without too much difficulty. "I saw this in a movie," he said happily, giving the wrench a hard turn. It sprang off and hit him in the arm. "Oops. Hang on, let me try that again."

"Tell him how glad you are that you got this flat in front of his house. He's a regular white knight," Colleen muttered into the phone.

"It's so lucky I got this flat in front of your house," Paulie said. "You're a prince, Bryce."

"No prob, dude!" Bryce answered. He seemed to get the lug nuts loosened, but the jack was more perplexing. Paulie waited, cracking her knuckles. Bryce fumbled. Turned the jack on its side to see if it would work better that way, which, shockingly, it didn't. "You know what?" he said. "My cousin's here. I bet he could do this in ten seconds."

"Maybe less," Lucas murmured.

"No, don't let him leave," Colleen hissed into the phone. "Improvise."

"Wait, wait," Paulie said. "Uh…um…here. I'll lift the front bumper, and you change the tire, okay? Count of three."

And sure enough, she hefted the front end of her car.

"She's magnificent," Lucas said.

"Shush," Colleen muttered. "And she is."

"I meant it."

"Wow!" Bryce exclaimed. "You're superstrong. What's your workout?"

"Marine Boot Camp 360," Paulie grunted.

"No kidding! Me, too!" Bryce exclaimed. "How much can you bench-press?"

"Pull the tire off, for God's sake," Paulie said. "I'm gonna pop a hernia."

"It's like watching a porno," Lucas murmured.

Colleen snorted and hit Mute again on the phone, as her protégé apparently couldn't take orders while lifting a small vehicle. "So why'd you get a divorce?" she asked after a minute.

"Maybe I never got over you."

"Ooh. Good line. I'm serious. Why'd you leave that sweet deal of yours?"

"I thought we were having dinner sometime. I'd rather not discuss my marriage in the bushes." That being said, he could see down her shirt. Push-up bra, thank you, Lord. She'd never been shy about showcasing her assets, and times like this, he was grateful.

She seemed to read his mind, because she glanced back at him. Busted. He grinned.

So did she, completely confident.

It suddenly occurred to Lucas that he was single, and Colleen was single, and he'd be in town for—

No. He wasn't here for a relationship, and certainly not one that would doubtlessly be as tangled and intense as his and Colleen's had been ten years ago. She wasn't the fling type.

At least, she hadn't been. She'd been in it with her whole heart, and it came back to him like a tidal wave, what it had been like to be loved by Colleen O'Rourke.

"Stop looking at me like that," she whispered, then cleared her throat. "The whole Heathcliff thing doesn't work anymore."

"You seeing anyone?" he asked.

"Oh, shut up."

Bryce dropped the tire, laughing. It seemed like Paulie's arms were shaking.

"She's gonna drop that on his head any minute now," Lucas observed.

Colleen sighed. "So go help. Be manly and heroic, Lucas. You do it so well."

"You're right," he murmured. "Nice to see you, hotshot. Stop throwing rocks through windows, okay?"

With that, he walked toward the front yard.

"Dude, thank God!" Bryce said.

"Hey, Paulie," he said. "You can put the car down now. I got this."

A minute later, he heard a car start and looked down the street. There was Colleen, behind the wheel of a MINI Cooper convertible.

Hot girl in a red car.

Worked every time.

CHAPTER FOURTEEN

"It's good to see you, Lucas. Even if you did break my baby girl's heart all those years ago."

"Oh, snap," said Bryce, grinning. Mrs. O'Rourke smiled fondly at him.

Lucas nodded. "Good to see you, too, Mrs. O'Rourke." It was *strange* to see Colleen's mother, that's what it was, and even weirder to be back in the house he'd visited when he was Colleen's boyfriend. It hadn't changed much.

"Call me Jeanette. I'm thinking of going back to my maiden name anyway. Come on, I'll show you what I'm thinking." She led the way to the back of the house. "This was his study. Where he called That Whore for phone sex, no doubt. I'd like you to rip it down. Burn it, if possible."

"Better late than never?" Bryce suggested.

"Exactly, sweetheart. It's been ten years. Men. They really suck."

"Not me, of course," Bryce said.

"Well, not yet," Jeanette murmured. "I'm sure you have it in you. Are you seeing anyone, Bryce, dear?"

"Why? You wanna go out sometime?"

Colleen's mother smiled and slapped Bryce's arm.

Jeanette O'Rourke had tracked Lucas down and said she had a project for him. Given that he was trying to train Bryce, and construction hadn't started on the public safety building yet, he agreed to come over and take a look.

The study was typical of 1970s architecture; a long room with a few small windows and some built-in cabinets on one end, and still a shrine to Pete O'Rourke— a picture of him with some minor politician on a golf course, a trophy from high school, a slew of Robert Ludlum novels. A picture of a college-age Colleen, her cheeky smile, gray eyes soft, hair gleaming in the sun.

Seemed like he was staring.

"Maybe you could remodel, rather than rip it down and burn it," he said, turning to Colleen's mother. "Seems a shame to waste the whole room."

"Good point. I could have an art studio, maybe. I'm taking classes."

"What kind of classes?" Bryce asked.

"I paint nudes," she said, giving him a speculative glance. "They pay the models, you know. We're always looking for new talent."

"Cool!" Bryce asked. "How much?"

"Not enough," Lucas said. "Anyway, we could put in some skylights, since you need a new roof anyway, and bigger windows. You'd have great light. French doors on that wall, maybe a little deck."

"Wonderful! When can you start?" she asked.

He turned to look at her. "Are you sure you want me to do this, Mrs. O'Rourke?"

"Jeanette."

"Given my history with Colleen, Jeanette?"

"I'm sure," she said, so smoothly that he was immediately suspicious. "So it'd be you both? You and Bryce?"

"Yes."

She smiled. "I could probably sell tickets. Can you work up some plans? I don't care how much it costs. My cheating bastard husband had to give me a metric ton of money in the divorce. Blood money. Guilt money. Whore money."

An hour later, he'd drawn a rough plan and given her a ballpark estimate. He and Bryce got into the pickup truck Lucas had rented for the duration.

Joe would be glad about this. It was a start, at the very least, and hopefully Bryce would have some kind of aptitude for construction.

They passed a dirt road. He and Colleen had parked there one night, before they'd both gone off to college. He could still remember the impossible silkiness of her skin, the way her eyes went so big and soft when she—

"Did you see my dad yesterday?" Bryce asked. "He's feeling a lot better."

Lucas glanced over at his cousin. "Glad to hear that." Yes, he'd seen Joe yesterday. He'd been asleep, looking smaller somehow.

Bryce had had a cat when they were teenagers, a scruffy old thing he'd found abandoned near the school. He brought it home and kept it in the spare room over the garage, an unfinished space that held only some boxes of old toys. Didi hated cats. But eventually, Bryce had worn her down; the woman didn't refuse him much, and the cat was no exception. It was old and battered, but it had a rusty purr that rattled in its throat. Bryce named it Harley, and the cat loved Bryce. Slept on his bed every night. If Bryce wasn't around, the cat might give Lucas a few head butts, but it was clear he knew where his bread was buttered.

Unfortunately, Harley was old and riddled with health problems, which was probably why someone had dumped him in the first place. Despite the myriad pills Bryce coaxed down Harley's throat each day, despite the vet warning him that the cat wouldn't see Christmas, despite the fact that the cat slept more and more and ate less and less, Bryce just didn't believe the cat was sick. "He wouldn't purr like this if he didn't feel good," he'd say, petting the cat's head, and it seemed almost true.

Until the day the boys had come home from school and found Harley dead, curled up on Bryce's bed.

Bryce had been utterly stunned. Lucas had heard him crying at night, despite his advanced age of sixteen.

It didn't look as if things were going to be much different with Joe. And far, far worse.

"You should spend as much time with him as you can, Bryce," Lucas said now.

"I already do. I mean, I live there, right?"

"Make sure it's time well spent. That's all."

It would've been nice to have been able to do the same with his own father. To have said goodbye, to have held his hand in the last minutes.

But this time, he could be there for Joe. And Bryce, too.

On Wednesday, Colleen stopped by her mother's house.

Mom had called last night to say she was having Dad's study redone, and thank the baby Jesus. The tenth anniversary of Dad leaving had really lit a fire under her. First the nude modeling, now redecorating.

Colleen pulled her car onto the street. There was a pickup truck in the driveway and a stack of lumber piled alongside the house, as well as a Dumpster. Carol

Robinson's white Prius was parked on the street, too; Colleen recognized it from the many open houses she'd been to. Mrs. Johnson's car, too, a monstrous Buick that Mrs. J. (piña colada) tended to drive down the middle of the street, striking fear into the hearts of every living thing.

"Hey, Mom!" Colleen yelled, going into the house. The sound of a power saw ripped through the air, then faded.

"We're out back!" Mom called.

Colleen pushed through the door to the backyard. Carol, Mom and Mrs. Johnson—she was Mrs. Holland, technically, though no one called her that—sat in lawn chairs and were sipping something pink.

"Hey, ladies!" she said, bending to kiss each one. "What's going on here?"

"Just a little healthy observation, Colleen dear," Mrs. J. said. "We're not dead yet."

"Grab a chair," Carol said.

Colleen obeyed. Looked up at the roof. "Is that Bryce?" she asked.

"And Lucas. His cousin," Carol said. "Joe's dying, you know. He has maybe six weeks left. Didn't you used to date him?"

"I never dated Joe Campbell," Colleen murmured.

"Hey, Coll," Bryce yelled.

"Hi, Bryce."

Lucas came into view.

Oh, wow. Wow. He wore carpenter shorts and work boots and a white T-shirt that made his skin seem darker. Blue-collar man and his big, strong...um...hammer. Wasn't there a porno about this? There should be. Someone should make one. Now.

Seeing her, he gave a nod. Maybe a smile.

"That's right," Carol said. "You *did* date Lucas. But he married someone else, right? Lucas! Are you still married?" she yelled.

"Not anymore, Mrs. Robinson."

"I could be single in a few hours," she called. "You like older women?"

"I *love* older women," he answered, getting a chorus of giggles from Team Menopause. Colleen just swallowed drily.

"You gonna tap that, Colleen?" Carol asked. "Because I sure would if I was your age. Even if I was sixty again."

"I'll tell him that," Colleen said. "But personally, I think I'll pass. And where do you get off saying 'tap that'?"

"He's the only boy Colleen ever really fell for," Mom said.

Colleen closed her eyes. "Is there alcohol in those glasses?"

"Not in mine, my dear," Mrs. Johnson said. "Though when the clock strikes five, there'd better be. But yes, these two are drinking."

"Just a little white Zin and 7Up," Mom said.

"That's right. Stab me in the heart. Ladies, have some dignity. At least let me make you mojitos," Colleen said.

"All right," Carol said. "But oh, wait, Bryce is taking off his shirt. Do it, Bryce! Do it!" She giggled most adorably.

"I feel dirty," Colleen said.

"Me, too," Mom said. "Bryce, you make me feel dirty!"

"Jeez!" Colleen squeaked. "Come on, ladies! A little decorum."

But she watched as Bryce took off his shirt, sure. She

wasn't dead, after all. He was pretty, no doubt about it. Washboard abs, nice muscles, she'd seen it all before.

"I'd give that an eight and a half," Mrs. Johnson said.

"Nine," Carol said.

"Nine," Mom echoed. "Colleen, I think you and Lucas should get together again. Why not?"

"Hail Mary, full of grace, please make my mom stop talking."

"I heard he kissed you in the bar the other night."

"Blessed art thou who can change the subject, and blessed—"

"Oh, come on," Mom said, slurping down the rest of her hideous drink. "Don't be coy. Before you know it, you'll be old and your ovaries will be turning to stone, and still I won't have a grandchild." She began fanning herself. "Phew! Is it getting hotter out here? My God. I'm sweating. Colleen, have you ever had a bikini wax? I'm thinking of getting one."

"Holy Mary, Mother of God, pray for us, now and as we contemplate matricide."

"Quiet, you two," Carol ordered. "Lucas! Take off your shirt! Your cousin did! You should, too."

Carol had a point. And it *was* pretty hot.

Lucas looked down at them. His white teeth flashed among that incredibly sexy razor stubble, and Colleen gave what she hoped was a casual wave and not a boneless flop of the hand, as she suspected.

He pulled off his shirt in one smooth move. Colleen stopped feeling her legs.

"Ten," Mrs. Johnson said.

"Ten," Carol and Mom echoed.

Maybe it was his swarthy skin. The muscles in his shoulders and across his chest. His hard, sweaty, delicious torso, not ripped like Bryce's gym-perfect boy-toy body, just…just complete, utter masculine alpha perfection.

"Colleen?" her mother asked.

She closed her mouth. "Nine," she said faintly. "Who wants a mojito?"

They all did. And Colleen could use one, too. Or she could stick her head in the freezer for a few minutes.

So Lucas would be around. She shouldn't be surprised; Mom was hardly a master of subtlety. Bryce was a bar fixture, so sure, Lucas would be there, too. It was okay. She could handle it.

On lust-numbed legs, she stumbled into the kitchen. Checked Mom's fridge, which was filled with fresh vegetables that, if history served, would melt into one big vegetable which would then be thrown away, but not before Mom called to complain about the price of fresh vegetables. But there was mint, and lime, and of course Colleen kept her stocked up with good quality booze.

She poured some sugar and water into a pan and heated it, since Mom didn't have any simple syrup. Took out the white rum, squeezed the limes and rinsed the mint. From outside, she could hear the women laughing and the power saw screeching again.

Seemed as though any minute now, Lucas would come down and see her.

Sure enough, she heard the clump of his boots coming down the stairs.

He'd pulled his shirt back on. Good thing, too, because he looked like sin begging for a taker as it was. A bead of sweat ran from his temple down his cheek, then down his neck. She remembered how it felt to be held in those arms, to lie on top of him and look into those dark, lonely eyes that only ever seemed happy when they were alone together.

Yeah, right. She'd bet Ellen Forbes had made him look happy, too.

"Hey," he said, and her knees went weak. She really had to get a grip.

His voice had always been a wicked weapon in his arsenal, deep and holding a scrape that made her special places throb with every word. "Do you have—"

"Okay, listen," she interrupted briskly, pouring the syrup over the crushed ice. "Before you say something adorable, like, 'How can I get that nine to a ten?' let's be frank here."

"Colleen."

"We had a thing once, it was very lovely, and then it ended when you married someone else after saying you didn't want to marry me. Maybe it was her money, maybe you found out what love really was, I don't care, Lucas. Water under the bridge."

"Colleen." His voice was more forceful now, but she kept talking, grinding the mint leaves with slightly more force than needed. "Yes, I find you attractive. I have a heartbeat, after all, and you're frickin' gorgeous. Yes, you find me attractive, because I am. Even so, I think it would be stupid for us to—"

"Colleen, Bryce shot a nail through his hand."

She looked up abruptly. "Uh...what?"

"Do you have a first aid kit?"

"Dude," Bryce said cheerfully, coming into the kitchen, his hand held aloft. "Total Jesus moment, right?"

The nail went through the webbing of his hand between his thumb and forefinger, and blood streamed down his wrist.

"Oh," she said. "Uh, yes, we do."

Then she fainted.

WHEN HE SAW Colleen's eyes roll, Lucas did try to catch her. Didn't quite make it, unfortunately, not before she cracked her head on the counter. "Jeanette!" he called. "We need you!" He glanced at his cousin. "Bryce, you're dripping blood on the floor. Grab some paper towels and hang on a sec, okay?"

He cradled Colleen from behind. Very uncool to be thinking lustful thoughts, but she smelled like fresh mint and sunshine, and her hair brushed his face. *"Mía,"* he said, pushing her head forward a bit to get some blood flow there. "Time to wake up."

"Connor, why did you punch me?" she muttered, reaching for her head.

He smiled into her hair. "Colleen. You okay, sweetheart?" She sat up straighter and gave him a confused look. "You fainted," he said. "Bumped your head on the way down, too."

"I never faint. Also, you're supposed to catch me. Haven't you ever been to a movie?"

"I broke your fall."

"Not good enough."

"Did she faint?" Carol Robinson asked as the three women bustled into the kitchen like a flock of purposeful chickens. "My daughter fainted once. She hadn't eaten breakfast, it was hot, and I said, 'Beth, why didn't you eat breakfast?' but no one ever listens to me."

"Bryce Campbell, whatever did you do to your hand?" Mrs. Johnson said. "Come here, child."

"Don't you two look adorable sitting there," Jeanette said. "Is it wrong to hope for grandchildren?"

"Mom, I'm injured. Be nice to me."

Jeanette sighed and rustled around in the freezer for a minute, then handed Colleen a pack of frozen Brussels sprouts. Coll went to hold it against her head, but Lucas took it out of her hand and did it for her. She started to protest, but he made that little *tsk* noise that worked with his nieces, and she settled back against him.

He pushed her hair to one side—she had a lot of hair. And it smelled *really* good. And she felt…perfect. His arms were around her, his back to the cabinet, his woman in his arms.

Dangerous thinking, that. Especially after her little speech.

"What do I have to do to get that nine to a ten?" he whispered against her ear, and she shivered.

"You always hit on injured women?"

"You're the first." He smiled.

"They're adorable together," Carol said. "Are you Spanish, Lucas? You look like a pirate."

"I'm half–Puerto Rican."

"Ooh. That's so exotic," Carol said, and he had to smile. Manningsport wasn't exactly a melting pot.

Mrs. O'Rourke was standing in front of the freezer, flapping her shirt. "Colleen, you didn't turn on the heat, did you?"

"No, Mom. I didn't turn on the heat." She sighed, the movement sweet against his chest.

"Now hold still, Bryce my darling," Mrs. Johnson said, grabbing his hand.

"What are you gonna do?" he asked. "Oh, dude! A little warning next time."

Mrs. Johnson held up the nail. "You children today. So careless. Now hold on, this might sting a little." They watched as she poured hydrogen peroxide on Bryce's hand. He took it like a man.

"You're brave, Bryce," Colleen said, earning a smile from his cousin.

"He has a high pain tolerance," Lucas murmured against the sweet spot just behind her ear. "Comes from being dropped on his head as a baby."

"You know who else has a high pain tolerance?" she asked, still talking to Bryce. "Paulie Petrosinsky. She's totally badass."

"Oh, yeah?" Bryce said. "Did you know she can pick up a car?"

"I do know," Colleen said. "That is hot, my friend."

"Stop matchmaking," Lucas whispered, his lips touching her soft little earlobe. Good enough to bite.

She turned her head a little. "Can you stop nuzzling me?" she whispered. "I realize you don't get this close to many women, but it's getting pervy. You, me, the Brussels sprouts, Team Menopause watching."

He nuzzled her again, smiling as her breath hitched.

Mrs. Johnson wrapped up Bryce's hand in gauze. "Is your tetanus shot up to date?" she asked. "You don't want to come down with lockjaw."

Actually, Lucas wouldn't mind Bryce coming down with lockjaw. His cousin had not once paused for breath this entire day. Reluctantly, he disentangled himself from Colleen and stood up, then offered his hand and pulled her to her feet. "You good?" he asked.

"I'm fine," she said. Her cheeks were pink.

"Eat something," he said. "Come on, Bryce, let me take you to the doctor. I'll be back tomorrow, Mrs. O'Rourke."

"Jeanette," she said, rubbing an ice cube on her chest. "Bye, boys."

Colleen walked them to the front door, the Brussels sprouts still in place. "See you, Coll!" Bryce said happily, loping to the pickup truck.

Lucas turned to Colleen. "See you around, hotshot."

"Don't play with me, Lucas," she said tightly.

His smile evaporated.

"You're not back in Manningsport for me, and I'm betting that as soon as Joe dies, you'll be back to your life in Chicago. And that's fine. But the kissing and the flirting and the nuzzling…it has to stop. I don't have a problem with you, I really don't. You're a good guy. I know that. You're very welcome at O'Rourke's. You're welcome at my mom's house. But you left me."

"Actually, you left me, *mía*."

"Yeah, right. I didn't marry someone two months after our first fight. And don't call me *mía*." She seemed to realize she still had the bag of vegetables on her head and lowered her arm. "You broke my heart, Lucas," she said. "It was a long time ago. But I'm not dumb enough to let history repeat itself. So don't mess with me. Are we clear?"

He looked at her a long minute, the noise of the chattering women in the background, the birds twittering in the bushes outside. And as much as he would've liked to tell her yes, sure, he'd leave her alone, he couldn't.

Colleen had a pull on him. That same sense he had when he first laid eyes on her in that classroom so long ago, that locked-in feeling, as if he'd waited all his life to see her…that still pulsed between them.

She felt it, too. She licked her lips, and the pink

stained her cheeks again. He could swear he heard her heart beating.

"What seems clear," he murmured, stepping a little closer so that they were almost touching, "is that this is going to happen. You and me. It's just a question of when."

She looked at him a long minute. Then she pressed her forefinger into the hollow at the base of his throat, gently, forcing him to take a step back.

Closed the door in his face. Didn't slam it; just closed it.

Lucas found he was smiling all the way to the truck.

CHAPTER FIFTEEN

IN THE THREE weeks he'd been in Manningsport, Lucas had had no success in pinning Bryce down on his hopes and aspirations, careerwise. Nope. That was a black hole. Lucas, on the other hand, was acting as project manager for the public safety building, had been asked to consult on a new wing for the senior citizen community and was putting on a new room for Colleen's mother. A couple had asked him about building a superdeluxe chicken coop for their free-range chickens, and while Lucas didn't particularly want to be building that sort of structure, he'd sketched out a plan for them nonetheless.

It had always been that way. Work found him.

Work cowered from Bryce. And his cousin, let's be honest, excelled at laziness. Bryce had been rather thrilled with his injury, and while it had been a little on the gruesome side, it really was something that he could've taken care of with a couple of Band-Aids, rather than the wad of gauze he was currently sporting.

Since construction was clearly not going to work (Bryce had knocked a pallet of shingles off the roof, lost his hammer seven times and dropped his phone into the roofing tar before mishandling the nail gun), Lucas had talked to a few people, studied Craigslist and had gone over to Didi's to rouse Bryce out of bed for a little swing through town.

First stop, the firehouse.

Lucas had become friendly with Gerard Chartier, winning the man's loyalty when he agreed that fire services outranked the other two. (Lucas had also told Levi that police services were the most important, and agreed with Kelly Matthews that EMS clearly came first. Hey. It made everyone happy.) At any rate, Gerard told Lucas they were hiring five new people; apparently there'd been a big house fire up at Blue Heron, and the good people of Manningsport had agreed to fund a paid department.

Perfect job for Bryce's type. Bryce was in great shape, liked people and…and…well, maybe he'd make a good firefighter.

Bryce seemed suitably awed as Gerard gave him the talk, staring in childlike wonder at the fire trucks. Lucas felt the same way. Every little boy wanted to be a firefighter, after all.

"This would be awesome," Bryce said. "Not to brag, but I have already saved someone. Lucas? Remember? When I saved you?"

"Yep." At Gerard's questioning look, he added, "I got my foot caught in the train tracks, and Bryce knocked me free."

"In the nick of time, too," Bryce said happily. "So what do you have to do to qualify?"

"There's twelve weeks at the fire academy," Gerard began. "Firefighter I, Firefighter II—"

"Whoa. There's school?"

"Yeah. You learn about hazardous materials and how to contain them, incident command system, blood-borne pathogens. Oh, and you have to be an EMT, too, but that's easy. Just a six-week class."

"Bummer. That's really not my thing." Lucas's head jerked back a little. "But thanks for your time, Gerard!" Bryce shook the firefighter's hand vigorously. "See you at O'Rourke's!"

"Bryce," Lucas said as they crossed the green, "what's the problem here? Is it fire academy? Twelve weeks will go by like that."

"I'm not going back to school," he said.

"It'd be fun," Lucas said.

"Yeah. I mean, jumping out of windows and rescuing dogs and stuff? *That* would be fun. Hazardous material containment? No way."

"You're not stupid, Bryce," he said, though he did sometimes fear that his cousin had taken a sharp blow to the head. "You could pass, I'm sure." Especially if Lucas tutored him.

"You're probably right," his cousin said blithely. "I'm just not interested. Plus, it might interfere with my work at the shelter."

"You'd have health benefits, vacation…"

"You know, the more I think about it, the less I want to do it. I mean, what if I got hurt on the job? I could be disabled for life."

"Or not."

"No, it's a good thing I thought this through. Kinda dodged a bullet there."

Lucas closed his eyes briefly. Once Bryce made up his mind, there was no talking him down.

Their next stop was the bakery. Lorelei, the owner, had advertised for an apprentice baker; apparently she supplied quite a few of the local restaurants with bread and desserts. "Hi, guys!" she said with a sunny smile. "Bryce, what happened to your hand?"

"Oh, it's nothing," he said, proudly holding up the heavily bandaged extremity. Honestly, amputees used less gauze. "Put a nail through my hand when my cousin and I were doing this job up on the Hill."

"You poor thing," she said, melting a little as Bryce stepped closer to show her his boo-boo.

"You're looking for help, Lorelei?" Lucas asked.

"Yes! Do you know anyone?"

"Bryce might be interested, right, buddy?"

"Sure," Bryce said amiably.

"Really?" Lorelei said, blushing. "Wow. That'd be… that'd be great."

"So long as I don't have to get up too early," Bryce said with a wink.

"Bryce," Lucas warned.

Lorelei wrung her hands. "Actually, you'd have to be here at four."

"That's not too bad," Bryce said.

"Really?" Her face lit up again.

"No, not at all. I'd get a dinner break, right?"

"Four in the morning, Bryce." Lucas sighed.

Bryce looked incredulous. "You actually wake up at four?"

"No," she said. "I wake up at three-thirty."

"Man! Hey, you going to Paulie's this weekend? We could hang out, maybe." Code for hook up, of course.

And that was another thing.

Colleen's little matchmaking plan.

The Petrosinskys were hosting a cookout, and half the town—almost literally—had been invited.

The bell over the door rang, and speak of the devil— the gorgeous, gray-eyed devil—in she came, along with Faith.

"Hi, Lorelei!" Faith said with the same joy expressed by those reuniting after decades of war. "Got any chocolate croissants today?"

"I sure do," Lorelei said. "Hi, Colleen!"

"Hello, good people of Manningsport," she said. "And, Lucas, always such a delight to see you. Got a sweet tooth?"

"For some things, I do," he murmured.

"Oh, my God, are you flirting with me? Give me a second to take off my panties, and I'm yours. Lorelei, I'll have one of those black-and-white cookies, okay?" But she was blushing, and didn't look him in the eye.

Faith was already halfway through her pastry. Rumor had it she was eating for two, and Lucas smiled at her. Good old Faith. "What are you boys doing today?" she asked.

"Just hanging out," Bryce said.

"Bryce is looking for work," Lucas said. "Got anything at the vineyard, Faith?"

"Actually, Bryce has already tried working for Blue Heron," she said. "It didn't quite work out."

"Afraid not," he said amiably. "I was in the tasting room. I got a little drunk, I guess. Honor fired me after my first day. She's kinda scary, isn't she?"

"You passed out behind the bar, Bryce," Faith said, a hint of admonition in her voice.

"Yeah, I guess so." He shrugged happily. "You guys make great wine."

"What kind of work are you looking for?" Colleen asked.

"Something creative and where I can make my own hours and help people," Bryce said, and Lucas rolled his eyes.

"I can get you a job," Colleen said.

"Really?" Bryce shot Lucas a nervous look.

"Sure."

Lucas waited. Colleen raised her eyebrows, looking at him and not Bryce.

Ah. He got it.

"Bryce, go get a cookie," he said. When Bryce was out of hearing range, he turned back to Colleen. "What will it cost me?" he asked.

"You agree not to meddle with him and Paulie."

"Are we going to have this argument again?"

"No."

He narrowed his eyes at her. Waited.

She raised an eyebrow.

"Fine. It's a deal," he said. At least he could tell Joe his son had a job, and that was something.

"Okay, Bryce," Colleen said. "Come with me. Faith, back in ten minutes, hon."

She took Bryce by the arm and towed him out of the shop. Lucas followed. A couple was approaching the bakery, a little baby strapped to the woman's chest in a complicated harness.

"Colleen!" the woman cried. "How are you?"

"Oh, hi, guys! Look at her! She's so beautiful!" Colleen peered at the baby. Lucas did, too. Cute little bugger, a tuft of black hair on the tiny head, perfect little ears. Colleen let go of Bryce, and he wandered a bit down the street, eating his cookie.

Colleen turned to Lucas. "Lucas, meet Jordan and Tate Lawrence, and their beautiful little girl, Colleen."

"We named her after Colleen," the guy explained, grinning. "Since she fixed us up."

"There'd be no little Colleen without *this* Colleen,"

the woman added. As if on cue, she reached for her husband's hand.

"You two are so cute together!" Colleen gushed with a significant look at Lucas. "Have a great day!"

She waited until the little family went inside. "*Another* couple I can claim. I should be a professional. Want me to find someone for you, Lucas, dear?"

"Pass."

"You know how many babies there are in Manningsport named Colleen?" she asked smugly. "Seven. *Seven,* Lucas. That's one one-hundredth of the population, named after me with joy and gratitude because I fixed up Mommy and Daddy, and that even includes two boys."

"Boys named Colleen?" Bryce asked.

"No. One is Colin, the other is Cole, but we all know who they're talking about. Me. Come on. Bryce! Come! Over here, across the street. In we go."

Window boxes, which seemed required if you were a shopkeeper in Manningsport, spilled over with blue and orange flowers. The pink-and-gold sign said Happily Ever After. "To the dress store?" Bryce asked.

"Yep." She opened the door and ushered them in. White dresses. Pink couches. More white dresses. Lots of sparkle.

A woman about their age came into the foyer, and her face lit up. "Colleen! How are you?"

"Hi, Gwen! How's it going?"

"Fantastic," the woman said. "Can I get you some wine? Coffee? A foot rub? Clean your house for you?" She and Colleen laughed merrily.

Colleen gave Lucas a smug smile. "I've sent a bride or two Gwen's way," she said.

"Or two? Or a dozen, more like it! Honestly, your dress is going to be free when the day comes."

"And I'll pick out a winner. Anyway, Gwen, I'm wondering if you can help me. Bryce here is looking for work."

"Really?" Gwen asked with a frown. Bryce smiled. So far, no objections from him.

"I know how busy you are," Colleen said.

"That's true. But I'm not sure about, um, a straight guy."

At that moment, the door to a dressing room opened, and a woman came out in—surprise—a wedding gown. Very poufy, and so tight you had to wonder how she'd sit down. Then again, Lucas knew enough about women to know that comfort was pretty low on the list when it came to dressing up.

"Hey. How *you* doing?" Bryce said. "You look amazing."

"Um…hi. Really?" the woman said nervously. "I'm not sure."

"Are you kidding? This is…yeah." He nodded appreciatively.

"I do like it," the bride said, fluffing the skirt as she looked in the mirror. "It's just that I'm not sure. There was this dress I saw in Buffalo—"

Bryce shook his head. "I don't know what that one was like, but this one just rocks it. Your guy is really, *really* lucky. Wow. You are *beautiful*."

The bride glanced at Bryce and smiled. Looked back at herself.

Gwen and Colleen exchanged a look.

Ten minutes later, Gwen had sold an eight-thousand-dollar dress and Bryce had a job.

Okay, so it might not be the profession Lucas would've picked—bridal-gown consultant—but he wasn't about to argue.

"This is so awesome, guys!" he said as they emerged into the sunlight. "And I get to look at beautiful women all day!" He held his hand up for a high five, and Colleen obliged. "Hey, I gotta run. Gonna go wash some doggies at the animal shelter." He loped off down the street.

"You can thank me now," Colleen said.

"Thank you, *mía*."

Alongside the store was a little alley where they'd kissed once, before they'd been sleeping together, when things were still new. She had taken him by the hand and pulled him in here one summer night, that bittersweet summer between high school and college, and kissed him until his entire being throbbed with wanting her and he couldn't form actual thoughts, reduced to the primal state of one need, with one girl.

This one.

He reached out and pushed a lock of hair behind her ear, trailing his finger along her earlobe.

"Knock it off," she said unconvincingly, her voice husky.

He leaned in closer, nostalgia and present-day wanting getting the better of him.

Then her phone buzzed, and she jumped two feet backward. "Sign from God," she said. "See you around, Spaniard."

With that, she ran across the street to the bakery, to the safety of pastries and her friend.

CHAPTER SIXTEEN

ONE OF THE best things about Manningsport—aside from the vineyards and the green and the lake and the cute downtown and Lorelei's cranberry-orange muffins, and O'Rourke's, of course—was the town softball league. It was fifty-three years old and had the unusual tradition of mixing players of all ages and both sexes on the teams. It was fiercely competitive, however. Hey. It was New York.

To play on the team, you had to try out. In other words, you had to be *good*. Connor, Colleen and Savannah played for the O'Rourke's team—Savannah was the youngest player in town history to make the team. The kid could *hit*.

And it was nice because Colleen and Connor got to play with their little sister. There weren't too many occasions when the three of them did something together, as Connor kept his distance from Dad and Gail. The Friday night dinners were about it, so when it was game night, both Con and Colleen took the night off to demonstrate the O'Rourke supremacy.

Tonight, however, Stoakes Candy Store was short a player. As manager, Coll had made the great sacrifice and offered to play for the competition. She donned the candy store shirt; the Stoakes team's slogan was an insipid *Stoakes Candy & Baseball: A Sweet Deal*. Not nearly as cool as her own team's: *O'Rourke's: Smiting the Rest of You Since 2009.* Because yes, they were always the town champs. Colleen was pretty great at baseball; Connor was better, and though it was Savannah's first year, she had first round draft pick written all over her.

Savannah played in the regular Little League, too, but she loved the game and begged Dad and Gail to let her play on the town league, too. The more baseball, the better. At first, people had been kind of sweet to her, throwing soft pitches last summer…right up until they had to hit the dirt to avoid her wicked line drive. At the ripe old age of nine, Savannah could throw out a runner attempting to steal second. Her batting average was .378 this year, and that was hitting against grown men. On-base percentage? Please. .479.

It was a balmy night, Monica and Hannah were running the bar, Rafe manning the kitchen, though Con would go by later to obsess and micromanage and irritate their sous chef. Dad and Gail were here to see Savannah; Dad had not yet missed a game. Well, he hadn't ever missed one of Savannah's games. He'd missed plenty of hers and Con's back in the day.

Mom was also here, cheerful as the Angel of Death at a wedding. She stood directly in Dad's line of vision and had on one of her familiar expressions—*Hello, my name is Rejected First Wife.*

"Hey, Mom, what are you doing here?" Colleen asked, going over to the bleachers, Rufus at her heels.

"I'm here, Colleen," Mom began in that slightly defensive and regal voice she always used when lying, "to support you and your brother. And that sweet little girl from church. She happens to adore me."

"Really? What's her name?"

Mom gave her an irritable look. "Sherry."

"There's no Sherry here, Mom."

"Yes, there is."

"No. There's not."

"The Irish one. You know."

"Shannon? Shannon Murphy?"

"Yes, that's the one. Adorable girl."

"She's eighteen."

"Fine, Colleen. Mock me. We'll see how your memory is when you're fifty-four." Mom paused. "There's that child. Is she really qualified to be here?"

"Savannah? My sister? Is that the child in question? And yes. She's really good."

"When does this get started? And how long does each round last?"

"Inning, Mom. Baseball has innings." She muttered a prayer for patience to St. Gehrig of Lou. How could one live in the Empire State and not be a baseball fan? Colleen herself had a photo in her bedroom of the mighty Jeter going into the stands (July 1, 2004, Red Sox/Yankees, greatest game ever, and one she watched repeatedly whenever the YES Network reran it).

A man approached, and Colleen did a double take.

"Hello, there, Jeanette. So great to see you again."

"So good to see you again," Mom said as he kissed her cheek, and Mom gave Colleen a smug look. "You remember Stan, don't you, Colleen?"

"Uh…yes. You look…different with clothes on." It was Stan, Stan the Hairy Man. So those singles things *did* work, after all, and holy shitake, Mom had a *date*. So that's why she was here. She wanted Dad to see.

Colleen couldn't help feeling a little bit proud.

"Sweetheart," Mom said loudly, "not only is Stan *artistic,* he's a *doctor.*" An arch look of triumph accompanied the statement. "We met again last week when he did my colonoscopy."

"That's…beautiful."

Stan smiled. "Your mother's preparation was perfect. Utterly clean. I haven't seen such a gorgeous colon in years."

"She gets that a lot," Colleen murmured. Stan was wearing a white dress shirt, and she could see his Neanderthal-style chest hair all too clearly. "Connor! Over here, buddy!" This was far too good not to share.

Her brother gave her a look. *What fresh hell are you luring me into now?*

She smiled. *You don't want to miss this.*

"Nice meeting you, Stan," Colleen said. "I have to run. I'm playing for Stoakes tonight, Mom. Cheer for me!" She kissed her mother's cheek and loped off with Rufus. "Ask how they met," she told her brother in passing.

There was Savannah, standing with Dad and the Tail. Colleen sighed.

Being an attractive female was nice, granted, and Coll had no problem enjoying it. She knew she was pretty, and appreciated her good genes. But Gail… Gail advertised sex. Tonight she was wearing a dress that barely cleared her ass. The dress was so low cut her lacy white bra showed, not to mention half her boobage. Two years ago, she'd gotten implants, and the new boobs stuck out at an angle that defied God and nature.

Maybe Gail, who was no longer as young as she'd been when she was the Hot Young Thing, was afraid of losing Dad.

Not that he was such a prize.

At the moment, he was goofing around with Savannah's hair, pulling a strand, then pretending he wasn't when she turned around to see. Both of them were smiling and laughing, and Gail would occasionally look at them and smile, her red-painted lips a bit ghoulish in the natural light.

"Hey, Yogi!" Colleen said, using the nickname her sister loved. "Ready to kick some patootie? Hi, Dad. Gail."

"Why are you in a candy store shirt?" Savannah asked.

"Oh, they're short a player, so I'm on their team today. It's okay. I'm still rooting for us." She winked at her sister.

"How are you, Colleen?" her dad said, glancing over her shoulder. "Marian! Good to see you!" Yes. Schmooze the mayor.

Gail tossed her shiny red hair. "Listen, Colleen," she said, her voice already tight. "About Savvi playing…" Gail was the only one who used Savannah's sappy nickname, and insisted that it end in an *i,* preferably topped with a heart. "This is her last game. We'll be focusing on cheerleading from here on out."

Savannah looked at the ground.

"Oh, yeah?" Colleen said. "Do you like cheerleading, hon?"

"I guess," Savannah muttered.

Colleen gave her father a sharp look. He returned it blankly.

"Cheering will be a better sport for you, sweetie pie!" Gail said. "You look really pretty in that little outfit, too. Stand up straight, Savvi. It makes you look perky."

"Well, you look great in catcher's gear, too, Savannah," Colleen said. "Very kick-ass."

Gail narrowed her eyes, then looked away in distaste, as if Colleen were a shmooshed porcupine rotting on the side of the road. Colleen narrowed back. But now wasn't the time to argue, not in front of Savannah, not in front of the crowd, which was thick tonight with tourists and townies alike.

Motherhood obviously hadn't given Gail the type of daughter she'd thought she'd preordered. She'd wanted a gorgeous little doll, a girly-girl who loved clothes and nail polish and long hair…ironically, a little girl like Colleen had been. Not a sturdy tomboy who'd asked for a poster of Jorge Posada for her last birthday.

"Okay, Dad, Mother Gail," Colleen said, earning another glare. "See you later! Come on, Savannah, let's go."

"Go get 'em, tiger," Dad said, and Savannah grinned over her shoulder. "I'll be watching!"

Colleen felt the familiar pang. She should be more like Connor, who'd given up on Dad long ago.

"Collie, I don't know if I should be a cheerleader," Savannah said mournfully. "Some of the girls are mean."

"How are they mean?"

Her sister swallowed. "They just are. The way they look at me." Her voice dropped to a whisper. "Someone said I was fat, and no one talked to me at tryouts."

Colleen's jaw clamped tight. "You're not fat, sweetheart. You're strong."

"I'm chubby."

"Honey, people come in all shapes and sizes."

"I wish I looked like you."

The words were stated with such hopelessness that Colleen stopped and dropped to her knees. "Savannah, you're wonderful. Do you know that? You're so funny and smart and I love being with you. I always have. You also happen to be absolutely adorable. You're my favorite person in the whole world." She smiled. "Don't tell Connor, he'll get jealous."

Savannah smiled, but her eyes stayed sad.

"And Dad's crazy about you. No one wants you to be anything but exactly who you are."

Except Gail-the-Tail-Chianese-Rhymes-with-Easy-Hyphen-O'Rourke. Savannah's *mother*.

"I wish I could keep playing baseball," Savannah whispered.

"I'll talk to them," Colleen promised. "We'll see what we can do, okay?"

Paulie Petrosinsky was coming onto the field. Perfect. A role model of physical strength in an unconventional package. "Over here, Paulie!" Colleen called. "Do you know my sister? Savannah O'Rourke, meet Paulie Petrosinsky, my friend."

"What's up, kid?" Paulie said, fist-bumping Savannah. "Word on the street is you're the best player in town."

Savannah's face lit up. "Thanks," she said.

Well, well, well. Colleen owed Paulie a drink on the house.

The three of them went into the dugout, where the rest of the team was assembled, pulling on gloves and cleats. "Coll, wrong shirt," said Kelly Murphy, Shannon's sister and part of the Murderer's Row of the O'Rourke offense.

"I know, I know," she said. "I have to play for Stoakes tonight."

"You gonna throw the game?" Bryce asked, coming down the steps to the dugout. Paulie's face began its burn.

"I won't have to, because we're so superior. Gang, today we have a new player. Paulie, welcome!"

"Hi, Paulie," everyone said. Connor cocked an eyebrow, all too aware of the matchmaking in progress.

"Bryce, would you help Paulie with her glove? She's never played baseball before." A lie, but hey.

"Seriously, dude? This is gonna be fun," Bryce said. "I bet you're a natural."

The goal had been secured: a physically close moment. Paulie had been instructed to ask for help as much as possible.

Bryce gave the glove a tug, his hand on Paulie's wrist. "Looks good!" He slapped her shoulder and trotted out to the mound.

"He touched me," Paulie whispered, her breathing fast and shallow.

"Okay, don't faint. I have to go. Keep an eye on Savannah for me? She's a little blue." Plus, if Paulie was good with kids, as she seemed to be, Bryce could see her as the potential mother of his children.

It was hard to be in charge of the world, Colleen mused as she trotted out to the shortstop position. Savannah was clearly dejected. Gail kept gesturing from the bleachers…probably some horrid advice like "suck in your stomach." It was throwing off Savannah's game.

And if Gail had her way—which she usually did—it would be Savannah's last.

Dad watched his youngest intently, cheering every time she came to the plate. The poor kid struck out twice. "Good try, baby!" Dad called both times. "You'll get 'em next time!"

Colleen looked away. Paulie had been instructed to high-five Bryce every time he got a hit (he was really good), so Colleen had to keep an eye on that. She was also watching Connor to see if he was giving any significant looks to anyone, because he just wouldn't crack and tell her who his mystery girlfriend was. He was clever, too; he'd erased his texting history on his phone, which she had stolen that very morning. Damn that twin telepathy thing.

Mom kept braying with laughter at whatever Stan, Stan the Hairy Man said, then looking over at Dad, who wasn't watching, which caused Mom to laugh more and more loudly until she sounded like a laboring mule. *Brahahaha! Brahahaha!* In between innings, Coll texted her. Quiet down, you're trying too hard.

Her phone chimed with the answer. I don't know what you're talking about. Another donkey bray.

Sigh.

In the second inning, Colleen led off with a double, then watched as the next three runners struck out. In the fifth, she walked and again didn't score, since Stoakes's offense would've had trouble hitting a beach ball.

Then, in the eighth inning as Colleen was walking back onto the field, Lucas appeared with Joe and Didi.

As usual, Didi Campbell looked pissed off about something. Bryce loped over and said hello, then returned to the dugout, as O'Rourke's was up.

Lucas helped Joe sit; he'd brought a camp chair, which was good, because the bleachers were uncomfortable. Joe didn't look so good; his skin was dark and he was moving slowly. The evening was cool; Lucas had brought a blanket, too, and tucked it around his uncle, then sat next to him on the bleachers and said something, making Joe laugh.

He was an awfully good nephew.

Her heart wobbled dangerously.

He glanced up, and Colleen looked away fast.

Savannah was coming up to bat. She wiped her eyes with the back of her arm. "Time!" Colleen called, and ran over to her sister. "Honey?" she whispered, kneeling down. "What's wrong?"

Savannah pressed her lips together. "It's my last at bat, that's all," she whispered, and a tear streaked down her chubby little cheek. She glanced toward the dugout, obviously afraid that her tears would be noticed.

Colleen squeezed her shoulder. "Oh, sweetheart. I'll talk to them. I told you that already. Don't cry."

"Do you really think you can change her mind?"

"Please. Who do you think you're talking to? Does anyone say no to me?"

Savannah gave a watery smile. "I guess not."

"Of *course* not!" Colleen glanced over at her father; he was standing, looking concerned. She'd take him aside later and force him to let Savannah stay on the team. Cheerleading was fine; in fact, Colleen herself had done a little in middle school. It just wasn't for Savannah. "Now come on. I want you to knock it out of the park, okay?"

"Okay." Savannah wiped her eyes once more. "Don't tell anyone I was crying."

"Gotcha. Here, let me pretend to check your eye." Colleen examined Savannah's eye solemnly. "It looks clear to me," she said in a regular voice.

"Everything okay?" the umpire said.

"She had something in her eye. We're all set now. You ready, Yogi?"

Savannah grinned. "Yeah. Thanks, Colleen."

Coll ran back to her spot between second and third. She felt warm, suddenly, and the back of her neck prickled.

Lucas was watching her, his eyes steady on her, and for a second, it felt as if they were the only two people here.

"Stee-rike!" called old Mr. Holland, their home plate umpire.

Colleen smacked her fist into her glove and gave Savannah a smile. Big Frankie, the pitcher for Stoakes and a lug-headed jock, wound up and threw again.

"Stee-rike two!"

Lucas was still watching her.

He'd always had a way of looking at her that went right into her bone marrow, making her skin thrum and buzz.

The crack of the bat made her head snap back to the game. Line drive to the gap, Coll could catch it in three paces, but she'd be damned if she was going to. She took two strides and made a dramatic, full-out lunge for the ball, pulling up an inch short and hitting the dirt hard. The ball flew past her and into the outfield, rolling into no-man's-land.

The crowd roared. Savannah rounded first and chugged toward second—*hurry, hurry*—and Shannon Murphy scored. Colleen picked herself up and watched as Lefty Moore streaked after the rolling ball. People were screaming and yelling as Savannah hit third and kept going, and Colleen's toes curled—an in-the-park home run, that *never* happened, let alone to a nine-year-old girl.

Lefty fired the ball to Colleen. She caught it and threw it home, timing it so the ball hit Evan Whitfield's glove just a second after Savannah's foot hit the plate.

"Safe!" Mr. Holland shouted, and everyone on both sets of bleachers was on their feet, cheering and screaming and whistling. Connor ran out of the dugout and scooped up their sister, giving Colleen a subtle thumbs-up.

Savannah's sweet face shone as the entire O'Rourke's team swarmed her. Con hoisted her up on his shoulders, and the rest of the team—the fabulous Murphy girls, Bryce and Paulie, Ned Vanderbeek, everyone, all high-fived her, cheering and hooting. Con said something, and Savannah turned and tipped her hat to the crowd, getting another roar, and Colleen guessed this was pretty much the best day of her little sister's life.

"So close, Colleen," said Emmaline Neal, the third baseman, with a knowing smile.

"Quite a dive," Robbie Mack added, slapping her on the butt. From the stands, Faith pointed at her and smiled, then continued clapping.

"Nice try, Colleen," Jeremy called from first. She held out her hands in the "whatcha gonna do" gesture and grinned.

So, sure. She'd thrown the play. She was a good player, and Savannah's hit had been catchable, especially by the town's best shortstop. But it was worth it, and her teammates knew it. Just about *everyone* knew it except Savannah, and Colleen felt a rush of love for her town. No one would ever tell Savannah that she'd been handed that hit.

Then Dad ran over to home plate, and Savannah wriggled down from Connor and jumped into her father's arms. "Daddy, Daddy, did you see that?"

"Are you kidding? It was amazing!" he said. "My little girl hit a homer! I'm so proud of you, baby!"

Colleen waited for him to glance over at her with that same fond smile she was getting from people on both teams.

It didn't come. He only had eyes for Savannah.

Colleen's happy bubble deflated a little. She looked away.

"Okay, okay, batter up," Mr. Holland said, and Paulie picked up the bat and came to the plate.

Colleen assumed the position, bending her knees. But she kept looking over at Dad. Savannah was in the dugout, still accepting congratulations from the team, chattering in amazement, her eyes bright, gesturing wildly, completely at home with her peeps. Dad kept looking over at her, beaming and pointing—*Who's my girl?*—and accepting some backslaps of his own for having raised such a little prodigy.

He still didn't look at her.

Did he not know? She could've had Savannah out easily. Did he not know that she'd deliberately given the little girl a great moment to cherish, especially because his shallow trophy wife was fixated on some stupid idea of what a little girl should be like? Did Dad truly not get it? Did he—

And then there was a crack, and a thunk, and Colleen was suddenly down on her knees, and holy sphincter, her head! She clapped a hand to the spot that was just *yelping* in pain and saw the baseball at her feet.

She'd been hit in the head with a frickin' ball.

"Ouch," she said faintly.

What would Jeter do? Colleen picked up the ball and tossed it to Robbie, who fired to first. Runner was out.

And so was she. The dirt rushed up to greet her, and all was quiet.

BEING CARRIED OFF the field had a certain élan to it. A certain horrifying, embarrassing, completely unsexy élan.

Marian Field, the mayor of Manningsport, insisted that she go to the hospital, Jeremy concurred, and the volunteer EMTs, half of whom were at the game, couldn't have been happier, as they loved pain and misery, especially the accidental kind, since it would give them something to brag about at O'Rourke's.

So she was put in a neck brace and on a backboard, which was ridiculous and more uncomfortable than a baseball to the head. And now she was just lying here like that dead porcupine, Ned Vanderbeek holding an ice pack on her head and trying not to laugh.

Lucas was holding her hand.

It was a disturbingly wonderful feeling.

She kept jerking it away. He kept scowling and taking it back.

"Can we please get this show on the road?" she asked, pulling her hand free for the eighth time. Gurneys. So not her. She tried to get up, and Lucas gently pushed her back down.

"The patient is combative," Ned Vanderbeek said, grinning.

"I'll give you combative, little boy. Lean in closer."

"Stop whining," Lucas said, taking her hand again.

"I'm not whining. I'm demanding. And why are you acting all possessive and concerned? I got bumped in the head. Big deal."

"You got knocked out cold. Second time this week."

"Yeah, well, I also made the play, didn't I?"

"Fine, you're Derek Jeter," Lucas snapped. "And you're going to the hospital. The end."

"Oh, so bossy and alpha male. I think I'm having an orgasm."

Ned choked.

"You're the one who's always collapsing around me," Lucas said. "Just come out with it. You want me to take care of you."

"Jeez! The ego! How do you both fit in the same car?"

He grinned, and the orgasm became a possibility. She scowled, then looked around for help. "Jeremy! Please let me go home! I need a drink and my dog. Where is he, by the way?"

Connor appeared in her line of vision. He scowled at Lucas but didn't punch him and looked down at her. "Nice play, Collie Dog Face."

"Finally, someone appreciates me. Do you know where Rufus is?"

"Here."

Her dog's shaggy head appeared, and he began licking her maniacally. She scratched his ears with her free hand. "Who's a good boy? It's you, Rufus-Doofus! You're the good boy! Yes, you are!"

"So that was kind of fun. You went down like a side of beef," Connor said, because despite the fact that he was an adult, what was better than having your twin sister get hurt?

"Laugh it up," Colleen said. "It will never top the time you sliced open your scrotum when we were six." Connor, Lucas and Ned winced in unison. Good.

"Be right back," Connor said. "I hear the ice cream truck."

"Bring me a Mr. Nutty."

And now Paulie was here, her face scrunched in concern. "Coll, I am so sorry! Really! You okay?"

"Oh, sure. Nice hit, by the way. Next time, I'll try to catch it with my glove instead of my head." She pried free of Lucas's grip once more and patted Paulie's muscular forearm. "No worries."

"Hey, bud, can you hold this?" Ned asked, handing the ice pack to Lucas. "I see a girl I like. Sarah! Hey! How you doing?"

Lucas smiled down at her and put the ice pack back on her forehead, pushing a strand of hair behind her ear. "You look cute," he said.

Her special places crooned. "You're a pervert."

"I could be."

"You guys make the best couple," Paulie sighed with gusto. "Totally romantic."

"No, it's not, Paulie." Colleen closed her eyes.

It *was*. Lucas was the first person she saw when she woke up; granted, she'd been out all of five seconds, but his worried face was looking down at her, and she could've sworn he called her *mía*.

That nickname was dangerous.

So what if he was divorced now? He'd be leaving soon, and she'd be smart to remember it. No matter how good he was making her feel.

"Where's my child?" Mom pushed through the crowd, the smell of Jean Naté foreshadowing doom and despair. "Baby! You poor thing!"

Colleen heaved a Catholic sigh. "Hi, Mom."

"My precious girl! Oh, Lucas, hello, dear. How nice that you're tending to Colleen. The new windows look fantastic, by the way." And back to Colleen. "Are we going soon? I'll ride with her," Mom announced with great overtones of martyrdom. "I'm her *mother*, after all."

Her twin was back, eating a Mr. Nutty ice cream cone. "Where's mine?" she asked.

"Ran out of cash," he said, taking a bite. "Hey, Ma."

"I'm going to the hospital with your sister. Are you coming?"

"Connor, do not let her come with me," Colleen hissed. "I will kill you in your sleep if you let her come with me."

"Ma," Connor said patiently. "She doesn't want you to go. I'll go."

"Of course I'm going! You're my *daughter*. You're my first priority." Mom was scanning for Dad, eager to win the Concerned Parent award, not that there was any competition. "Oh, and Stan had to leave. Ulcerative colitis, very messy." Mom groped for her free hand, hitting her in the sore spot on her head.

"Ow!"

Lucas's hand tightened on hers. Was he about to laugh?

She yanked both hands free from both irritating people. "Gerard," she said to the big guy, "don't I get to pick who comes with me?"

"It's usually next of kin, usually. How much is nine times seven?"

"I don't know. I've never known."

"Her IQ is somewhere around room temperature," Connor said.

"Just for that, you can't ride in the ambulance, either," she said. "Gerard! Can we please get going?"

As always, it seemed as if the ambulance corps had to work on their novels or something. Emergency services has been ruined by iPads…she could've sworn that Jessica was looking at dresses on ModCloth.com. Jeremy, who'd been great the first few minutes after she'd come to, was now manipulating Carol Robinson's right arm, earning plenty of giggles and squeals of delight.

"What's twelve times nine?" Gerard asked.

"Can we stop with the math?" she snapped. "I want to get this over with and go home. Oh, hey, Levi. Where's Faith?"

"I'm right here," Faith said. "You okay? Want me to come with you?"

"That'd be great. Thanks, pal."

"Oh, hang on, I have to puke. Be right back."

"Next," Colleen said as Faith bolted, Levi on her heels.

Gerard patted her leg. "Ready to take a ride?"

"I've been ready for thirty minutes, Gerard."

"Are you complaining? Because I can tell Ned to hit a lot of potholes on the way to the E.R." He checked something on his iPad. "Hey, Yanks are up by five. So who's going with you?"

"I am," Mom and Connor said in unison.

Lucas looked at her. "I am," he said.

"He is," Colleen agreed.

CHAPTER SEVENTEEN

THE CHAIRS IN the waiting room were ridiculously uncomfortable. That, and Connor O'Rourke glaring at him made for a long evening.

When they got to the emergency room, Colleen sent Lucas to wait, and the nurse glared at him until he obeyed. He didn't like being away from her, and he didn't like how quiet she'd gotten in the ambulance. She seemed fine, going through her shtick with Gerard, but there was something else going on, too.

Things were getting complicated.

For a long time, he'd very effectively put aside his feelings for Colleen. From that moment when Ellen had told him she was pregnant, he gave up the right to think about Colleen, and certainly to miss her.

But those feelings ran under his life like a subterranean river, and every once in a while, something would crumble, undermined by the current. He dreamt of her smiling with those clear, dark gray eyes, that wise, knowing smile, and he'd follow her into an empty room, thinking finally, finally they were together again…and then he'd jerk awake, and hear Ellen's soft breathing and remember that he had a wife now. He'd taken vows. He couldn't betray that with memories of someone else.

But.

She was always there, that river of dark, fast water.

"So you're working for my mother, and you're nosing around my sister," Connor said, speaking at last. They'd been waiting for more than an hour now.

"He does beautiful work, Connor," Mrs. O'Rourke said mildly. She was reading *People* magazine. "Which you would know, if you ever came over. Oh, dear. Justin Bieber broke up with his girlfriend. Sad. Connor, what did you think of Stan?"

"He's very hairy." Connor resumed the death stare.

Lucas didn't care. He was here, and he'd be here until he could see that Colleen was okay.

He'd seen her watching her father, not paying attention to the game, and a prickle of warning went through him. Almost before Paulie hit the ball, he was on his feet, somehow knowing Colleen was about to be hurt, and Jesus, her head stopped that ball cold, and then she was on her knees, and for the love of God, made the damn play. And then she went down as if she were dead.

Then he was kneeling at her side, and someone yelled, "Don't move her!" He didn't; he just put his hand on her back to see if she was breathing, and thank the sweet Christ child, she was. "*Mia?* Sweetheart?" he said, his voice rough.

"Ow," she groaned. "My head! Why did you hit me, Connor?"

Jeremy Lyon checked her, and Levi called it in. Her little sister had been crying, and both Gail and Pete O'Rourke hustled her away.

A concussion was serious business these days. Especially when it happened on town property. When Lucas was a kid, he'd fallen out of the second-story window of Tommy O'Shea's house and was out cold for ten minutes. His biggest concern was the wrath of Mrs.

O'Shea, who'd told the boys to be silent during her soap opera. "Got a pretty good lump," his father had said when Lucas had gone to the garage to show him. "Get some ice on it."

Now, though...9-1-1 and ambulances and doctors. Probably a good thing.

"Why are you even here?" Connor snapped.

"Because he *cares*, Connor. Back off," Mrs. O'Rourke said. "They may be getting back together, right, Lucas?"

"You're not getting back together with my sister," Connor said.

"Oh, please," Mrs. O'Rourke said. "He's her first love. And you know how powerful that can be, Connor."

"Save me," Connor muttered.

A tiny Asian girl came into the waiting room. She looked to be about thirteen, but she wore a white doctor's coat and had a stethoscope around her neck. "Hi! I'm Dr. Chu! How's everyone tonight?" She waited for an answer. "Is everyone here for Colleen O'Rourke?"

"Yes," Lucas said.

"I figured. It's a superslow night. She's the only one here. I was watching *Game of Thrones* on my phone before she came in, and I was like, yay, finally! A patient!"

"I'm her brother, and this is our mom," Connor said. He didn't bother to explain Lucas.

"Excellent! Are you twins? You guys look totally alike."

"They're twins, all right," Mrs. O'Rourke said. "Connor weighed eight pounds, three ounces, and Colleen was seven-fourteen."

"You're a champ!" Tiny Asian Girl said. She looked at him. "And you're the husband?"

"He's *not* the husband," Connor growled.

"Her first love," Mrs. O'Rourke said.

"Aw! Totally romantic!" the doctor said. "Well, she has a closed head injury, which is a cool way of saying, whoopsy, concussion! Right? We just wanted to observe her for a little while, make sure she didn't puke or anything. That can be a bad sign. But she's fine! No emesis—that's medical speak for puking—and no signs of disorientation. She turned down the CAT scan, which is totally what I would do, too. Why expose yourself to radiation for a bump on the noggin, right?"

She beamed at the three of them, and, getting no response, looked back at her clipboard. "She needs someone to watch her tonight and just do a couple checks, wake her up and see how she feels. If you can't wake her up or if she seems confused, or if she stops breathing, *most definitely* call 9-1-1, okay? No Motrin or aspirin for forty-eight hours. Just an ice pack. Do you have any questions?"

"How old are you?" Connor asked.

"I'm twenty-three. Almost twenty-four. Graduated early, kind of a prodigy, not to brag. Any other questions about Colleen? She's totally pretty, by the way."

"People say she looks like me," Jeanette said.

"Really? Okay, yeah! I see it! Great rapport with family, check! Well, I think we're done here, people, so it's, like, back to the beheadings for me!" She practically skipped off.

A nurse wheeled Colleen into the waiting room. "Someone's ready to go home," the nurse said.

"And guess who it is? I'll give you a hint. It's me," Colleen said, pulling a face.

"How do you feel?" Mrs. O'Rourke asked.

"Fine."

"I'll stay with you tonight," Mrs. O'Rourke announced. Lucas tried not to smile as Colleen flinched.

She looked at him. "Um… Lucas can take me home," she said, and something moved in his chest.

"*I'll* take you home," Connor said.

"Lucas will take me home, bossy-pants. Right, Lucas?"

"Right."

"The doctor said you need someone to stay with you tonight," Connor stated.

"Nah."

"Connor, she wants *him* to stay with her," Mrs. O'Rourke said. "So they can make amends."

"I'll stay with you," Connor said.

"No one's staying with me," Colleen repeated.

"I'm staying with you," Lucas said.

"Fine! Lucas is staying with me," she snapped. "For an hour. Now can I please get going? I want to take a shower."

HE DROVE HER to her house and followed her up the stairs to the second floor. There was a note taped to the door.

We walked Rufus. Sorry about the puking. Call me when you get home. xoxox Faith

Added in different handwriting was Next time, use your glove. Levi.

Colleen smiled as she read it.

"You have nice friends," he said.

"I certainly do." She unlocked the door and went in, and he followed. A deer walked into the kitchen. Check that. It was her giant dog, who bayed a few times, then aimed straight for his crotch. Lucas wrestled the beast's head away, which resulted in the dog collapsing as if shot and rolling over on his back.

"Impressive," Lucas murmured. "You should probably get him neutered."

"He is neutered. Okay, I'm gonna take a shower."

"Call me if you need me."

She rolled her eyes, winced and left the room.

Lucas took a look around. The apartment had high ceilings and tall, narrow windows. The kitchen walls were painted warm yellow, the chairs were red and blue, and it was cheerfully cluttered, pictures on the fridge, a bowl of peaches on the counter, a few catalogs, the dog's tartan-plaid leash. The living room had a fireplace filled with white birch logs and a nice view of the street. Her furniture was cheerful: a polka-dotted chair and a soft-looking red couch, a coffee table with a small bookshelf underneath.

Family photos, mostly of her and Connor and Savannah, were everywhere. Here was one of her and her cousins, a whole bunch of them. Colleen at age twelve or so on a sailboat. One of Rufus and Savannah, lying on the floor, the girl using the dog as a giant pillow, reading a book. A bride—Faith—hugging her, both of them laughing.

That thing moved again in his chest.

All these years, Colleen had stayed in this little town. She seemed to be friends with everyone—Bryce and Levi and the British guy Tom and just about everyone he remembered from high school. She worked with her twin. Adored her sister, that was clear.

Colleen was tied to this community in a way that Lucas couldn't imagine. Sure, he was a Southie, but his time away had made him suspect in the eyes of those who'd stayed. He didn't belong anymore, and that was fine. He'd left when he was fifteen, after all. When he and Ellen divorced, he'd moved from the Gold Coast neighborhood (and where Lucas had always felt like an impostor) to an apartment building near Irving Park.

But even though he knew Chicago like the back of his hand, sometimes he got lost driving home. Not because he didn't remember how to get where he was going, but because he wasn't sure where he was supposed to be.

Rufus gave a little moan and stretched out his paws. The dog had to be more than six feet long.

The water shut off in the bathroom, and he heard the sound of the curtain moving. "You hungry, Colleen?" he asked.

"No," she said, cracking the door a little. "I ate before the game. But I'll probably lay waste to some Ben & Jerry's, even so."

She came out a few minutes later, wearing white cotton pajamas and looking like a freakin' supermodel.

"Feeling okay?" he asked.

"A lot better." She checked her answering machine. "Ooh! Sixteen messages, and ten more on my cell. I feel like prom queen."

Except she hadn't gone to her prom.

The memory flickered across her face, too. Before he could say anything, though, she pressed the button to listen to her fans expressing their concern.

Her face fell with each message. She checked her phone, too. Then she walked over to her computer, touched a key and scrolled through her emails.

"Well. I guess I can return those tomorrow," she said. There was a small note of sadness in her voice.

"Come sit down," he said, taking a seat on her sofa. She did. Didn't look at him, just curled into herself and stared straight forward.

He put his arm around her—dangerous, that—but he was helpless not to. Pulled her against him, even though she resisted a little.

She fit the same as she always had, the feeling old and new at the same time.

"That was quite a play you didn't make today," he said.

"You mean stopping the ball with my head?"

"I meant the one before that." He kissed her damp hair. "You're a good sister."

He heard her swallow thickly. "Did my father check on me?" she asked in a small voice. "While I was out?"

Lucas hesitated. "He knew you were okay."

"In other words, no." Her breathing hitched. "Ah, shit," she whispered. "I'm jealous of a nine-year-old. My father's a prick, and I still want him to pat me on the head and tell me I'm a good girl. How stupid is that?"

"It's not stupid. It's human."

"What's wrong with me?" she asked. "I have this thing for men who reject me." Her dog came over and put his enormous head in her lap. "Except you, Rufus."

She wiped her eyes with her sleeve, then extricated herself from him and the dog and went over to the phone. Dialed in angry jabs. "Hi. This is the other daughter, the one who went to the hospital. Yeah. Whatever. Put Savannah on." She took a shaky breath, then changed her tone to chipper. "Hey, sweetie! No, don't cry, really. I'm perfectly fine. They don't let you use your phone in the E.R. No, no. I'm home. Yep. Rufus is taking good care of me. I'm gonna eat ice cream and watch movies. Okay, honey. Hey. You did great tonight. I was so proud of you." She smiled. "You bet. Nighty-night."

She hung up and stood there for a second, looking into space. "Lucas," she said carefully, "I can't fall in love with you again."

The words hit him hard. As if sensing that, the dog shifted his giant head to Lucas's leg and licked his chops.

"And yet, I can't stay away from you. You're horribly irresistible. It's very embarrassing." She gave a half smile, but her eyes were serious.

He lifted Rufus's head from his lap and went to her. "Colleen," he began, and he didn't know what would've come out of his mouth then, but his phone rang.

Damn it.

It rang again, and he pulled it out to silence it.

"Answer it," she said.

"No."

"It might be Joe." She took a step back and picked up her own phone and started texting.

He sighed, took his phone out of his pocket and looked. *Ellen.* He glanced at Colleen, who was still tapping away at her phone. "Hey," he said.

"Hi, Lucas. How are you? How's Uncle Joe?"

"Holding his own, more or less."

"Good." She paused. "So I'm coming to town next week. I think I might have a lead on something for you, divorcewise."

"Great."

"Got any idea on where I might stay?"

He looked at Colleen. "I'll email you some places." He paused. "You okay to fly?"

"Sure, sure. So okay, I'll let you know when I'm coming in. It'll be good to see you."

"You, too. Thanks for calling."

He hung up. Looked at Colleen. Her face was neutral.

"The wife?" she asked, though it was obvious she knew who it was.

"The ex-wife."

She nodded. "So. Back to what I was saying. Thank you for driving me home. But we shouldn't…get involved. Even if you're very gorgeous and so am I and all that."

"I think we should talk, Colleen," he said.

"Faith will be here any minute. Pajama party. Girls only, I'm afraid."

"Colleen—"

"Lucas, you have a life back in Chicago. I have one here. It's just stupid to get all tangled up. I… I can't do that. I only have flings. Since you, I haven't had a real boyfriend. Just flings. And that's fine. I like it that way. I'm kind of a slut, in fact."

He remembered her kissing that other guy, and the long-ago memory still ached, like a bruise that had faded but not quite healed. "I doubt that," he said.

"Well, read the bathroom walls, then." She swallowed, and shifted her gaze to outside the window. "But I don't think I could have a fling with you."

"*Mía,* don't—"

"No, please. I mean, as irresistible as you are, I'd get hurt, you'd leave, I'd hate you again, and I don't hate you now, and I'd rather not hate you ever again. Okay?"

The door to the apartment opened, and in bounded a

golden retriever. "Did someone call a landscape architect and her faithful puppy?" Faith said. She came into the living room, cradling four pints of Ben & Jerry's in her arms. "Oh. Hey, Lucas."

"Faith."

She looked back and forth between them. "Um… want me to go?"

"No," Colleen answered. "He was just leaving." She turned to Lucas. "Thank you very much for staying with me. See you around."

She was right. He'd be leaving again. Soon. Whatever he found himself thinking whenever he was around her was just that. Thought. She was being the smart one here, and he should be grateful.

"I'm glad you're okay," he said, and with that, he extricated himself from the golden retriever, who was attempting to mount his leg, and left.

CHAPTER EIGHTEEN

"THIS FOOD ISN'T worth eating," Joe said, pushing back his plate.

"Give it a try, unc. It's not that bad." He pushed the Cream of Wheat back, and Joe took a spoonful and grimaced.

"I'd kill for a Big Mac," he said.

"And the Big Mac would kill you," Lucas answered.

"But what a way to go," Joe said. "All that gorgeous sodium." He grinned, a shadow of the old Joe.

He was at Lucas's rented apartment in the old opera house—a nice change of scenery, he'd said. But the climb to the second floor seemed to take the last of his energy. Dialysis was supposed to make him feel better, but *better* was a relative term when you had cancer on top of kidney failure.

Joe pulled out his pocket watch. Lucas used to love seeing it when Joe came to Chicago to visit, hearing the story of their ancestor and how he'd fought so bravely at Antietam, how the watch was given to him by the major whose life he'd saved. Being the older son, Joe had inherited it from his father. Too soon, Bryce would have the watch, who hopefully would have a son or daughter to give it to someday, as well.

"I need you to handle some things," Joe said now. He

frowned. "I called Ellen. Hope that was okay. I couldn't remember if I talked to you about it."

"She called me."

"Good. Well. Didi's idiot brother is our lawyer, and obviously I can't trust him." Joe idly stroked the pocket watch. "I sold an app a couple months ago, and I want Bryce to get it for a nest egg."

"Good for you, Joe." Lucas smiled.

"Yeah, it was fun. Remember 'Rat-Whacker'?"

"How could I forget?"

"Well, this is slightly more sophisticated." His smile faded. "Ellen said she'll check on that for me. But about the funeral... Bryce won't be up for it, and Didi will do whatever she thinks will win her the most social points."

"What would you like done?"

"I love that old stone church. Trinity Lutheran. And for the eulogy, I thought it would be nice if...well. I want Bryce to do it."

For a second, Lucas had thought Joe had been about to ask him. But obviously, his son would make more sense. "Of course."

"And here are some songs I want played at my wake. None of those drippy hymns, okay?" He handed Lucas a list. U2, the Stones, Pearl Jam, and Lucas had to smile. Unc had great taste in music.

And now for the harder questions. "How do you want it to be at the end, Joe?"

His uncle sighed. "Well, as little pain as possible. I'd like you boys to be there. And I'd like Didi not to be."

"What about Steph? She'd definitely come if you wanted her to."

"No, that's fine. She's got the girls. You two will be enough."

It was hard to answer.

"You know what I miss?" Joe said, looking out the windows. "Sailing. Big Macs and sailing."

"Do you still have the boat?" Lucas asked.

"No, no. We sold that a while ago. Didi said...well, hell, I have what? A month left? Let's not waste it by talking about Didi." He was quiet a moment, listlessly stirring his bland lunch. Then he looked up at Lucas. "You look just like your dad, you know. Except for the eyes. Those are your mother's eyes."

Lucas gave a half smile.

"Do you remember her?" Joe asked.

"Not a lot."

"Well, she was the most beautiful woman I ever saw." He paused a second. "Guess I'll be seeing both your parents before long."

The words made Lucas's stomach twist. He knew Joe was dying.

It didn't mean it would hurt less to lose him, the last link to his father, his affable, easygoing uncle who'd only ever been kind.

"How's Stephie doing?" Joe said, changing the subject. "She coming to visit?"

"She is," Lucas answered. "You'll get to see all four girls, too."

Joe laughed. "Fantastic. They're firecrackers, those girls. It'll be nice to have you all together. You know what? I want to have a picnic, all of us Campbells. What do you think?"

"Great idea," he said.

"Would it be all right to ask the Forbes contingent? I feel like they've been family these past ten years."

"Sure."

Joe took out his phone and dialed. "Hi, Didi. Yeah, sorry, whatever, I'm dying, what can I say?" He rolled his eyes. "Look, I want to have a picnic. Steph and the girls are coming to… No, I haven't forgotten. Yeah. Fine. No, I thought just us… Oh. No, I— Yeah. Okay. Whatever. Hanging up now." He put the phone down. "She says it's too much work, we should just go out for dinner, and if we're doing a family picnic, her pack of hyenas has to be invited, too. Though she didn't use that phrase, exactly."

"I'll take care of it. I'm seeing another lawyer about your divorce tomorrow," Lucas said. This one was someone who specialized in complicated cases. "Didi never deserved you, Uncle Joe."

"Word, nephew. Word."

"Did you ever ask her for a divorce before?" he asked.

Joe nodded. "When Bryce was about eight. She said she'd move so far away I'd never see him. We signed a prenup, did you know that? At the time, I was the one who was supposed to make more money. But I signed one, too, and as luck would have it, she became the breadwinner." He sighed. "And then your dad died, so things got more complicated."

Two boys to raise, in other words, instead of just one. So Joe had stayed. For him *and* for Bryce.

"I'll take care of things, Joe. Don't worry about anything."

"I know you will, son."

At the word *son,* Lucas had to look down at the table.

"Ah, Lucas. You know what they say," Joe said, covering Lucas's hand with his own. "Only the good die young."

THE NEXT DAY, the news wasn't what Lucas had hoped to hear.

"I do understand, I really do," the attorney said. "But given the time frame, it's probably not possible. If it were uncontested, that would still be tricky, though I know a judge who might do it, given your uncle's health. As it is, though, I can't see it happening."

Lucas was in Ithaca to see the attorney, who'd been recommended by an old college friend. New York required a yearlong separation, and Joe didn't have nearly that much time. The law didn't make exceptions for a man who just wanted to die without being shackled to his bitchy wife.

The lawyer frowned. "Think we could prove cruel and inhuman treatment?"

"Probably," Lucas said, thinking of Joe's dark little room off the kitchen.

"Being a bitch doesn't necessarily equal cruel and inhuman," the lawyer said, reading his mind. "Has she had an affair that you know of?"

"No."

"Too bad." She sighed. "I wish I could help you."

So that was that. Too freaking bad, because Lucas wouldn't have minded seeing the look on Didi's face when she was handed divorce papers. And the look on Joe's when he could be free of his pinched, sour wife.

Well. He'd be free soon enough.

Lucas walked out to the parking lot. He had to check in on the public safety building; the foundation had been poured, and the framing was well under way. He could also bring Bryce to Jeanette O'Rourke's house and get him started on some sanding—the bridal store job was only part-time. Hopefully, Bryce could handle that without injury.

His phone rang. "Hey, Joe. What can I do for you?"

"I hate to bother you, but I was wondering if you could come get me. I'm at dialysis, and Didi's an hour late. She's not picking up on her cell or at work."

He sounded exhausted. "I'm about an hour away," Lucas said. "Bryce isn't around?"

There was a pause. "I called you first. I'm sorry. I should've thought."

"No, no problem. I'll call him right now and call you back." Someone would have to help Joe into the house and into bed. A cab wouldn't cut it, if Manningsport even had cabs.

He hit Bryce's number on his contacts list. It went right to voice mail, indicating the phone was off. Called the house phone; the answering machine picked up. "Bryce, if you're there, pick up the phone. It's Lucas."

Nothing.

Shit.

Lucas rubbed his jaw. He only had one option. A second later, he made the call.

"O'Rourke's, home of the best damn nachos on the face of the earth," she sang merrily.

"Colleen, it's Lucas." His voice was tense, even to his own ears.

"Everything okay?" she asked instantly.

"My uncle's stuck at dialysis, and I can't reach Bryce. Is he there?"

"No, sorry, he's not. I can go get Joe, though, if that's what you need."

He paused only for a second. "That'd be great."

"You bet. Connor! I have to run out. Have Monica come in and cover for me, okay?"

"Thank you," Lucas said. "I'm in Ithaca, but I'm on my way."

"Don't drive like a maniac," she chided. "I'll take good care of him."

"I know."

There was a pause. "Okay," she said, and her voice was softer. "See you later."

"COME ON, YOGI," Colleen said to her sister. "We're off to be angels of mercy."

"Okay," Savannah said instantly, sliding out of the booth where she'd been drawing. "What's an angel of mercy?"

"It's us. My friend is sick, and he needs a ride home from the hospital. And boy, is he gonna be happy to see you. He loves kids. Especially the smart, nice kind."

They got into the car, stopped to get Rufus (Joe loved Rufus, and who didn't?). The dog climbed gently over Savannah in the backseat, making her sister laugh; the kid adored the monster.

The hospital was fifteen minutes away. Colleen kept up a stream of chatter, but her heart felt tight.

Poor Joe.

And poor Lucas. He'd sounded so...worried. Worried and clenched and...and grateful.

That warm, dark chocolate voice of his should be illegal.

"Stay in the car, Rufus, boy. Come on, Savannah, let's go find our pal."

Colleen didn't waste any time getting up to Dialysis, and there he was, looking small in the uncomfortable chair in the waiting room. He was sleeping. He must've looked a lot like Lucas's father, because she could see the resemblance to Lucas, the strong jaw and straight nose. Bryce and Lucas could've passed for brothers themselves.

She went over and knelt next to him. "Hey there, handsome," she said softly, winking at Savannah, who looked a little worried. Joe opened his eyes, momentarily confused. "Did someone call an escort service?"

"Colleen," he said, smiling. "It must be my lucky day. And who's this beautiful girl?"

"This is my sister, Savannah," she said. "Savannah, meet Smiling Joe Campbell, the nicest guy in the world."

"Hi," she said.

Ten minutes later, they were helping Joe into his front door, Rufus trotting around the house to sniff the good spots. She'd left a message for Bryce, but hadn't gotten a call back.

"Can you handle the stairs?" she asked, as Joe had struggled in just from the car.

"My room's off the kitchen," he said.

Lucas's old room.

Colleen peeked in. Not a lot of memories here, as they'd always gone to her house whenever possible (or the backseat of her car, or the no-tell motel in Rutledge). But she'd been in here, of course. And it was still basically a big closet. No window.

This house was frickin' huge. Living room, family room, den, sunroom, kitchen, dining room, laundry room, and that was just on the first floor.

And Joe was in a storage room where his nephew had once been banished.

"Let's get you settled on the couch," she said, taking

Joe's arm. "There's a gorgeous breeze today, and this room's a little stuffy."

"Sounds good," Joe said, his voice weak.

They helped him into the living room, which was stiff and formal. Chintz fabric everywhere, like a giant Laura Ashley explosion. Savannah thoughtfully got a pillow and a blanket, and Rufus, who was an archangel in disguise, sat next to the couch like a guardian.

"I always thought it'd be nice to have a dog," Joe said, petting Rufus. Within seconds, he was asleep.

"He sleeps in a closet?" Savannah whispered as they went into the kitchen.

"I know," Colleen said. "His wife is a big poopyhead."

"We should make him a cozy spot," Savannah offered. "I'm good at that."

Colleen paused. "Let's do it," she said. "Cozy spot commencing."

An hour later, the sunroom was transformed. A multicolored sign hung over the doorway... Joe's Cozy Spot, courtesy of Savannah taping five pieces of paper together and discovering a stash of Magic Markers in a kitchen drawer.

"Looks great," Paulie said, lying on the hospital bed. She closed her eyes. "Very comfy." Rufus nudged her shoulder with his nose, hoping to climb on, and Paulie smiled.

Because yes, the troops had been called in. Colleen needed help moving furniture, and she needed it fast. She was afraid Didi the Poopyhead would come home and have a fit, which Colleen guessed she was entitled to do, being that this was her house and all.

But it was Joe's house, too. The man was dying, and

it was absolutely ridiculous that he was crammed into that sad, dark little room.

It'd be nice, too, having Paulie do something nice for Bryce's father. She'd been here five minutes after Colleen made the call. They'd moved the coffee table and two big comfy chairs into the storage room and brought out the hospital bed. There was still a couch and chair, and the big TV, and best of all, the view of the pretty yard, of trees and sky and birds and whatever wildlife might wander in.

Much better than four walls.

Savannah had wandered the house like a little thief, lifting whatever she thought might brighten Joe's spirits—a picture of him and Bryce from years ago, a Yankees sign from Bryce's apartment downstairs, some throw pillows from one of the empty bedrooms, a blue glass sun catcher from the dining room.

"Who's this?" the girl asked now, coming back in with another framed photo. "Is that Joe?"

Colleen looked at the picture, her heart snagging. "Yep. That's Joe there, and that looks like his brother. And that's Bryce, and that's Lucas."

Even in the picture, you could see which brother had toughed it out, and which had an easier life. Lucas's dad and Joe were practically twins, but Dan Campbell was leaner and rougher-looking. The kind of guy who could handle himself, as the saying went.

Like father, like son.

The boys must've been about ten in this picture, and they were at a ball game. Bryce and Lucas were all cheeky grins and big eyes. Killer lashes, both of them.

It was quite uncomfortable, sometimes, how much they looked alike.

Colleen hadn't seen many pictures of Lucas as a child. None, now that she thought of it.

He'd been beautiful. Skinny and absolutely beautiful.

"Hey."

Colleen jumped. "Hi. You're back."

"Sorry it took so long. There was construction." His eyes took in their handiwork. "Hi, Paulie."

"I'm resting," she said amiably from the bed. "How you doing, Lucas?"

"Good." He looked down. "Hello, little girl who plays great baseball."

Savannah grinned. "I'm Savannah. Her sister."

"Yes. You look a lot alike."

Savannah's face lit up, and Colleen felt another healthy chunk of her heart melt.

"We did some re-org," Paulie said, getting off the bed. "Your uncle's sleeping in the other room."

"It looks great," Lucas said. He looked at Colleen, and there he went again, saying everything without words. "How was he feeling?"

"I'm great," Joe said, emerging from the living room. "Oh, Lord, what have you done? Joe's Cozy Spot? What on earth? Ladies, thank you! This is beautiful!" He went over to the bed and got on it. "What a wonderful cozy spot."

"Would you like a comfortable pillow?" Savannah asked, offering the red velvet.

"I'd love a comfortable pillow," Joe said. "Thank you, sweetheart."

At that moment, the front door opened, and into the kitchen came Didi and Bryce.

"Hey, gang," Bryce said affably. "Are we having a party?"

Didi's mouth was disappearing, her eyes narrowed, hands on her hips. "What's going on here?" she asked, looking as though she smelled raw sewage.

"We figured Joe could use a change of scenery," Lucas said.

"Mom, this is Paulie Petrosinsky," Bryce said. "How's it hanging, Paulie?"

"Hi," Paulie said, her face igniting. "Um, nice to see you, Mrs. Campbell."

"Aren't you the Chicken Princess? From TV?"

Paulie's face grew even more red, and Colleen made a note to use dishwater in Didi's drink the next time she came into O'Rourke's. "The power behind the chicken throne, right, Paulie?" she said. "Mrs. Campbell, Paulie is chief operating officer of her father's franchise."

Didi wasn't impressed. "I'm still not sure why any of you are here."

"Well, you forgot to pick me up, Didi, I had to get a ride from someone," Joe said.

"And who gave permission for them to rearrange my house?"

"I did," Lucas said, and Colleen felt a little thrill at the dark edge in his voice. So Heathcliff. "Joe deserves better than the storage room." He looked at his uncle. "I'm sorry we didn't think of it before."

"Totally great idea," Bryce said. "Dad, we can watch baseball in here, if you fall asleep, you won't have to schlep off to your room."

"Does anyone care what I think?" Didi asked, putting on a wounded look. "This is my house, too! It's my money that supports us. It's my hard work…" Her eyes widened with terror, and she staggered back a few steps. "Oh, my God! What the hell is that? Help! Bryce, help!"

Everyone looked around. "It's just a dog," Bryce said. "Chill, Mom."

"Get that thing out of here!" Didi commanded. Rufus, sensing fear, felt fear himself and barked back.

"Stop! Get it out!"

"Don't yell at him," Colleen said. "You're scaring him, and he's likely to attack when threatened." Granted, the last thing Rufus had attacked was the bacon she'd left out on her plate last week, but that bacon had been asking for it. "It's okay, Rufus. Don't mind the scary lady."

His tail wagged, sweeping the remote and several doodads from the end table.

"It's destroying everything!" Didi said. Rufus barked again. "Get it out!"

"Come on, Rufie," Savannah said. "Wanna go for a ride? In the car? You wanna go in the car for a ride?"

Rufus leaped at the magic words, crashing against Joe's bed (which only made him smile), jumped onto one of the chairs, barking with joy, then raced through the house to find the door that would lead him to his beloved pastime.

"I'll wait outside, Collie," Savannah said.

"Okay, babe. Thanks."

"I'm sending you a cleaning bill," Didi bit out. "Joe needs quiet. He can't stay here. Lucas, move all this back to your old room."

"Ellen and her parents are coming to visit," Lucas said, and a little jolt of jealousy shot through her. "They want to see Joe. Can't imagine what they'd say if he was in that dark little room in the back."

Didi paused. The woman had always been an ass-kisser, Colleen recalled. "Fine," she said. "I have a migraine. I'm going to lie down."

With that, she tap-tapped across the tiled floor and stomped up the stairs.

"Sorry about that," Bryce said. "She's under a lot of stress lately."

"No, of course," Paulie said. She reached out as if to pat his arm, looked at Colleen for approval. Colleen nodded, and the pat was meted out, Paulie drawing in a shaking breath.

"Thanks, Paulie," Bryce said. "So, Lucas, is Ellen really coming to visit? That's great."

So great, Colleen thought, then chided herself for being petty. "I should get going," she said. "It was so nice seeing you, Joe. See you, Bryce."

"Colleen, Paulie, I don't know how to thank you," Joe said. "But I'll think of something. Tell your sister she's my new best girl, okay, Colleen?"

"You bet."

"See you at the gym, Paulie," Bryce said. Paulie responded with a huge (and adorable) smile. Colleen smiled, too. Her matchmaking skills were working. Again.

"I'll walk you out," Lucas said. He held the door for them, and they went out on the porch. Savannah was throwing a ball to Rufus, then running to catch up to him. They went around back, the dog barking joyfully, and Colleen hoped the sound hurt Didi's brain.

"Well, I'll let you two make googly eyes at each other," Paulie said. "See you around, big man." She punched Lucas in the shoulder hard enough that he rocked.

"You're good people, Paulie," he said, giving her a kiss on the cheek. "My cousin's lucky to know you."

Well, well, well.

Paulie's eyes filled with tears. "Shit, Lucas, thanks.

That means a lot to me." She socked him again, gave a watery smile and ran out to her car.

Savannah was conveniently in the backyard, judging from the sound of Rufus's barks.

"We can probably pass on the googly eyes," Colleen said, clearing her throat.

He wrapped her in his arms and hugged her against him, tucking her face against his beautiful, smooth warm neck. "Thank you," he whispered, and her entire side electrified.

"Oh, you know," she said, her voice wobbling. She tried to pull back, but he just held her tighter.

"Have dinner with me tomorrow," he murmured, his lips so close to her ear. "I promise not to break your heart."

Her heart thudded fast and hard. He smelled so good. Felt so right. Tasted so— *Down, girl,* she told herself, resisting the urge to bite his neck. "I can't tomorrow. It's the party. The Petrosinsky thing."

He pulled back, his eyes so dark and liquid and beautiful, those soulful Latin eyes. "Then soon."

Rufus came bounding into the front, Savannah right behind, and crashed against them, practically dislocating Colleen's knee. "Oh, my God, are you guys kissing?" her sister asked.

"Not quite," Lucas said, letting her go, and Colleen took a shaky step back. "Not yet."

"You slay me, Spaniard," she whispered.

"I do my best." He smiled, and that just about sealed the deal.

She was in serious trouble.

CHAPTER NINETEEN

COLLEEN HAD FELT that Bryce needed to see Paulie on her own turf, where, one hoped, she'd feel more confident and secure.

The Petrosinsky home looked gorgeous in a French surrealism, circusy kind of way…the chicken statues loomed large and ominously cheerful around a yellow-and-red-striped tent on the lawn, and dozens and dozens of chickens were roasting over a huge barbecue pit. There was a table full of salads and summery foods, a lemonade stand, a full bar. A band played the grotto—yes, there was a grotto—and the Crooked Lake shimmered in the distance.

Colleen had picked out a dress for Paulie to wear, part of the "I'm a Girl" campaign, and then done her makeup (subtly, just some mascara and lip gloss to give her strong features a little more femininity) and hair, which was a bit of a challenge. But the dress was really cute—yellow and cheery, a full skirt that swished and swirled and showed off Paulie's chiseled legs. It seemed to be working; Bryce had ambled up to Paulie right away, and, as instructed, she'd led him off on a tour of the many chicken statues that dotted the grounds, her adopted dogs following joyfully.

The sound of a rooster cut through the air; right. Ronnie Petrosinsky was having a crowing contest.

Lucas didn't seem to be here yet. Should she be having dinner with him at all? Would they end up in bed? Just the thought made her knees buckle.

It didn't help that every spot in town seemed to hold some wicked-hot memories. *Wicked* being the operative word. The first time she'd let Lucas put his hand up her shirt. The first time she'd taken his off. The first time, period, when she'd told him she loved him, and it seemed like his heart might break at those words.

She sighed, either with longing or frustration or nostalgia or lust or all of the above. Her special parts needed attention. This was a problem.

She needed a drink. Some wine would be nice.

"Sangria?"

"Connor, just when I'm ready to auction you off to a home for unwed mothers, here you are, redeeming yourself." She took the glass, glancing around at the other guests.

"Looking for Lucas?" Connor asked. "Because you're stupid and want your heart broken all over again?"

"Nice weather, isn't it?"

"Coll…"

"I don't want my heart broken, Connor. No."

"Stay away from him, in that case."

"Where's your date, brother mine?"

"She's not here. Are you kidding? With you *and* Mom here? Not to mention Dad and Gail."

Sure enough, there was Mother Dear, tossing back a white Zinfandel and 7Up, her signature cocktail. "You think she drinks that just to punish us?"

"I do, yes," Connor answered.

Colleen took a sip of the sangria. "So this mystery

woman, Con, she must be dying to meet your beloved twin."

"Not really."

"She is. Admit it."

"We've been on three dates, Colleen."

"Sex?"

"No comment. And you'd better not be sleeping with Lucas."

"Really! So you're doing it. Good. Is she blonde? I bet she is. She is, isn't she? Lovely. You know, Con, for a while, I thought you were gay. Figured you and Jeremy would make a great couple—"

"Okay, fine. I'll shut up about Lucas if you'll shut up about everything else."

She smiled over the rim of her glass. "Deal."

"Just don't come crying to me when he—"

"You know what? I'm gonna go talk to Mom. It's come to that." She walked over to their mother. "Hi," she said with a dutiful kiss.

"There's your father and That Whore."

"Yes." Savannah was somewhere, then; Colleen scanned for her sister. Hopefully, she'd be off playing with some other kids; but more likely, she was hiding inside, eating in secret so Gail wouldn't chastise her, poor kid.

Stan, Stan the Hairy Man was nowhere in sight. "No date for you, Mom?" Colleen asked.

"No," Mom said, not taking her eyes off Dad and Gail. "That Stan was quite unappealing, it turns out. A little too fascinated with his work. All he could talk about was infected bowels and intestinal parasites."

"And that put you off, did it?"

Her mother still stared at Dad, who was excellent

at not seeing his ex-wife. His hand was on Gail's back, just above the legendary ass.

Poor Mom.

"Here's the thing, Colleen," Mom said slowly, and Colleen braced for bitterness. "I never got over him. I should have, I wanted to, I know he cheated on me and I know he's completely over me, but I still love him."

There was no bitterness. And no false naïveté, either, no "lapse in judgment" excuse. It was, horribly, just a fact.

"I'm sorry, Mommy," she whispered, squeezing her mother's hand.

"I'm a laughingstock."

"No, you're not! You're great. They love you at Blue Heron, and you have a lot of friends, and—"

"No. I'm a laughingstock, a menopausal idiot who didn't know her husband was cheating and made every excuse in the book for him."

Mom's eyes were full of tears, which made Colleen's eyes fill, too, because if there was one thing she couldn't stand, it was her mother crying. "You deserve better than Dad."

"Well, where is better? I'm ready for better! That hairy colon doctor wasn't exactly better, asking me about how many times a day I—"

"Hey, Jeanette, how's it going?" It was Bryce. He leaned in and kissed her mother. "You look as gorgeous as always. We're just bringing out the watermelon."

We seemed to mean *Paulie,* who held a giant watermelon in each arm. And for some reason, she'd donned a yellow Thneed.

"How's it hanging?" Paulie asked, jerking her chin at Mom.

"I thought we talked about wardrobe," Colleen murmured as Bryce continued to flirt with her mother.

"It got chilly," Paulie said.

"Fine." Those watermelons had to weigh fifteen pounds each. "Let him carry one of those and feel manly and stuff," Colleen suggested in a whisper.

"Manly, right. I get it. But his hand is really hurt."

Sure enough, Bryce's hand was still bandaged to boxing-glove proportions. "He can hold a watermelon, Paulie. Give him a chance to be strong and helpful. Right? Remember? Girl/boy stuff?"

"You're gonna dance with me later on, right, Jeanette?" Bryce was saying. "I've had a crush on you for ages."

"You're adorable, you know that?" Mom said, much cheered. "Oh, there's Mrs. Johnson, probably gloating about Faith being pregnant. There's Carol, too. She has eleven grandchildren, Colleen. Eleven." She leveled the famed Catholic martyr look over her shoulder. Colleen merely raised an eyebrow.

"Bryce," she said, turning back to the project at hand, "help Paulie out, okay? What a champ you are, Paulie, but heck, those must be getting heavy."

"No, they're fine," Paulie said. "Oh! Wait, I mean yeah, they're pretty heavy. Really heavy. So heavy. Uh, Bryce maybe you could hold one of my watermelons?"

"You bet."

Perfect. Colleen smiled as Bryce fumbled for a watermelon, Paulie's face practically bubbling as her blushing took hold. All good, Bryce groping in the general area of Paulie's chest.

She left the young lovers and headed inside to look for Savannah. The sound of her father's fake laugh floated over on the breeze, and Colleen looked in his direction. He saw her…but instead of a smile or a nod, he gave her the drive-by glance, his eyes passing over her but not acknowledging her in any meaningful way.

Her chest felt hollow.

When she was little, Colleen had been prone to stomach bugs, and Dad would sit on the edge of her bed and read to her. Mom would get the sympathy pukes if she was too nearby, so it was just Dad and his good smell, his starched shirt and steady voice that marked those nights, making them almost fun, the vomiting aside.

Dad laughed again.

She couldn't remember the last time they'd had a real conversation.

Swallowing the lump in her throat, she headed inside. The house was quiet; everyone was outside, and who could blame them? It was a beautiful night.

She heard a voice. *The* voice, as it were. Impossibly deep, with that rumble that scraped her special places in a most satisfying and yearnful way.

Lucas and Savannah were sitting on a curved-back sofa. He was reading to her… *The Wind in the Willows,* a book Colleen had read over and over as a kid. Lucas had on a pair of glasses; that was new. And hot. He looked sinfully well-educated, like a professorial Lucifer. And she felt like the slutty college girl who was about to offer whatever it took for that B to become an A.

"'But Mole stood still a moment, held in thought. As one wakened suddenly from a beautiful dream, who struggles to recall it, but can recapture nothing but a dim sense of the beauty in it, the beauty!'"

Lucifer—er, Lucas—was a good reader. Savannah

was pressed against his arm, looking at the pictures. She could read to herself, of course. Then again, if Lucas had offered to read Colleen something…anything…the instructions on how to use her three-in-one remote, for example…she'd fall over herself saying yes. Especially if she could cuddle with him on the couch. Naked.

"Hi, Collie!" Savannah said, catching sight of her.

Colleen jumped guiltily, then feigned surprise. "Hey, you two," she said.

"Want to see the secret room I found?" Savannah asked, wriggling off the couch.

"Um, maybe we shouldn't—"

Savannah was already running up the stairs.

Lucas stood and slipped his glasses into his shirt pocket. "After you," he said.

"Right," she breathed. She went up the stairs, Lucas close behind her. Could he see up her dress? Was she wearing nice underwear? Well, of course she was, she was Colleen Margaret Mary O'Rourke, after all, but—

"Up here!" Savannah called. There was another staircase, this one not so ornate as the first, going to the third floor.

At the top of the stairs was a little hallway. "Sweetheart, we probably shouldn't be sneaking around the house," Colleen began.

"Oh, come on," Lucas said. "It's fun. Where's your sense of adventure, *mía?*"

"I guess I'm a grown-up now," she said, cocking an eyebrow.

"So? Grown-ups can have a sense of adventure," Savannah said, opening a door. "Look! You can see everything from up here! We can be like Harriet the Spy."

The room's ceilings slanted down; though it was finished, it was still the attic, and hot and musty in this weather, too. It held a few cardboard boxes; otherwise, nothing except for two small dormered windows.

But yeah, the view was great. Especially for spying. The picnic guests seemed to be having a blast, and why not? The band was playing, smoke rose up from the chicken pit and Keuka glittered in the distance, white sails sharp against the cobalt water.

Colleen felt Lucas behind her, and she had to resist the urge to back into him, feel his arms around her, pressing against his—

You really are trashy, said her brother's voice in her head.

She focused on the crowd below. There was Faith, distinguishable by her red hair. Rufus and Faith's dog were romping joyfully around, making toddlers scream with joy (or terror, maybe). And oh, nice. Bryce was pushing a youngster on a swing—looked like Cole Richards, one of her namesakes. Paulie was there, too, visible thanks to the yellow Thneed. The band started playing in earnest now—"Devil with a Blue Dress On." Mr. Petrosinsky had spared no expense. Hopefully, it'd pay off for Paulie.

"It smells so good down there," Savannah said wistfully.

"Are you hungry, honey? Want to eat with me?"

"Hi, baby!" As if summoned by those words, Gail appeared in the doorway. "There you are! What are you doing? Spying?" She walked over. High heels, even though it was a picnic.

"Hi, Gail," Colleen said.

"Colleen." She gave Lucas a big, bleached smile. "Hi there. I don't think we've met."

"We have," Lucas said. He didn't offer more.

"Mommy, I'm hungry," Savannah said, tugging Gail's hand. "Please let me get a hamburger. Please? And potato salad? I love potato salad."

"Sure, baby. No bun, though, okay, and maybe a green salad instead of potato. Carbs, remember?" She flashed the teeth at Lucas again. "We have to watch our figures, especially if we're going to be cheerleaders!"

"I don't think *we're* going to be cheerleaders, Gail," Colleen said. "I mean, I just don't see Lucas doing all those flips. I'm past thirty, and you're what, forty-two now?"

"Hardly, Colleen," Gail said sharply. "I'm thirty-five."

"Really? They're doing great things with Botox these days. You should check it out."

"Mom," Savannah said, whining now.

"Don't pull on me, Savvi!" Gail sang, batting the two-inch eyelash extensions that sat like tarantulas on the end of her eyelids. "You know how it is, Lucas. Kids."

She turned, smoothed her dress over her ass and sa-shayed to the door, swinging her hips so violently that Colleen was surprised she didn't fall over.

"Thanks for reading to me," Savannah said over her shoulder.

"My pleasure," he answered, his voice all rumbly.

Gail and Savannah left, the door closing behind them.

It was hot up here. Also, she was here with the Prince of Darkness, which made it hotter still.

Maybe it was having her mom admit her feelings, seeing her still hung up on the guy who'd left her for someone else. Like mother, like daughter, after all. Falling for Lucas again…hell, she already was. And if she wasn't careful, soon she'd be just like Mom, drawing hairy naked men in order to fill up her days.

Lucas was looking at her, doing the fallen angel thing.

She took a deep breath, the air close and dry. "Thanks for being sweet to my sister."

"She was hiding under the couch when I came in."

Colleen's heart pulled. "Really?"

"Yeah. Eating cookies."

Damn. "Gail's had her on a diet for years already. She has food issues."

Lucas made a noncommittal noise.

"How could she not? To Gail, everything is about how you look. Savannah's a little pudgy. Big deal. She'll outgrow it. I was pudgy when I was a kid."

"I find that hard to believe."

"Well, I was. A little. Not really. Fine, I wasn't. So what? What's it to you?"

His mouth pulled up in one corner. "Nervous, Colleen?"

Damn it! That dark, scraping voice. He used to call her from college and talk dirty once in a while, and my! God! The things that voice *did* to her!

"I'm not nervous. I'm just…irritable. I love Savannah, and I don't want to see her either obese or anorexic or hating the way she looks because she's got Gail for a mother."

"Good thing she has you, then."

She looked at him sharply. "Are you being sarcastic?"

"No."

He just looked at her, saying nothing more, and a

breeze drifted through the window, rustling the maple leaves across from them, ruffling his beautiful, thick hair. His eyes always held so much more than what he managed to say.

Well. That's what she'd always thought, anyway, and look where that got her. A woman who was the town flirt, who was probably unhealthily attached to her brother and still didn't trust men, who hadn't had a real relationship in ten years.

"Wow, look at the time! I'm starving," she said, reaching for the doorknob. It stuck, so she tugged it, and the damn thing came off in her hand. Huh.

She tried to put it back, but it was one of those old glass things, and the metal rod was still stuck inside. She shoved it in again, but it fell off immediately. Tried again. Wiggled it. Nothing. "Lucas, can you fix this, please?"

He came over—did he stand this close to everyone? Glanced down at the doorknob in her hand and said, "You broke it."

"No, I didn't. It slipped out. Just put it back."

"It's broken, Colleen."

"Can you please just try to fix it, Lucas?"

"Yes, *mía*. I'll try, just for you."

He knelt on the floor and you know, sigh. He was *kneeling* at her *feet,* and if she didn't knock it off with these thoughts, she was going to slap herself. Hard. Lucas pushed the doorknob onto the, uh, shaft, gave it a shove, then tried to turn it. Once again, the doorknob fell to the floor with a thud. "See?" he said.

"Yeah, yeah." She banged on the door. "Hello? We're stuck in here. Can you open the door?"

They waited. Nothing. Lucas smiled, as if she'd just agreed to sign over her soul.

He stood in one graceful move. "This gives us a chance to talk."

"We're not going to talk."

"I thought we needed to talk."

"So talk to yourself, then! Talk away, Lucas! Jeesh! It's too hot in here. It's like one of those Swedish saunas where they kill people. Who can talk?"

It's hard to believe you were once so good with men, because you are now officially a babbling idiot. She went to the window. Great, plenty of people down there, and a little cooler.

"Hello! Hi! We're stuck up here! Hello!" Nope. Apparently, the band was too loud—"Let's Spend the Night Together," perfect—and not one person looked up. *Connor, get your ass up here,* she thought, hoping the psychic twin thing would work this time.

Twilight was falling softly over the party, the sky a beautiful shade of slate blue.

"Sit, Colleen," Lucas said. He was already on the floor, his back against the wall, long legs crossed. Jeans. White shirt. That skin, that beautiful olive skin.

She sighed again and obeyed, crossing her arms grumpily. She sat kitty-corner from him. *The better to see you, my dear.*

A faint smile played on his mouth. He had a perfect mouth. Full and perfectly shaped and just a little sulky.

You really have it bad, Connor's voice informed her.

"No kidding," she muttered.

"Excuse me?"

"Where'd you get the bracelets?" she asked, nodding her chin at the little woven strands around his wrist.

"Tiffany made this one for me. Cara did this one. My nieces."

"I remember." Hard to believe those girls would be, what…thirteen? Fourteen?

Lucas had always been a sweet uncle. And now he wore his nieces' friendship bracelets, the kind that would have to stay on until you cut them off, which Colleen knew he wouldn't do.

Dangerously appealing.

"You seem happier," she said unexpectedly, and while she honestly wouldn't have wished him to be miserable, the acknowledgment stabbed her.

He shrugged.

"Are you still working for your father-in-law?" Hey. Google didn't exist for nothing.

"Ex-father-in-law. And yes, though I won't be doing that much longer."

"Starting your own company?" she asked.

"Yes. How did you know?"

She tugged her skirt to cover her knees. "It just seems like a better fit for you. You're a loner. Or you were."

"And you, *mía?* Are you happy?"

"Don't call me *mía,* okay? I might think all sorts of deliciously romantic things and start writing your name in my notebook." She glanced out the window to the leaves of the big maple, which were rustling in the wind. "Yes, I'm happy."

"You never…" His voice trailed off.

"Never what?" she asked a bit sharply.

"Never got married? Never came close?"

"Lucas, I'm insulted you never stalked me on Facebook."

"No, I never did."

And why would he? He had a life, a wife, a different time zone. He lived in the City of Big Shoulders, he was Frank Forbes's son-in-law.

"You haven't answered the question," he said.

She pursed her lips. "I thought I came close once. With you. Otherwise, no."

"But you're happy?" he asked.

"Why? Trying to soothe your guilty conscience?"

"Because I always hoped you were."

Well, shit. Her cynical heart gave a tug. He always had a way of cutting through her usual shtick with that wretchedly effective weapon—sincerity.

"I'm happy," she said. "The bar is great."

"The heart of the town, it seems."

"Thanks." She sure hoped it was. That was kind of the point. "I work at the nursing home a little."

"I saw you there on Thursday."

"You did?"

"I'm consulting on a new wing. You were with your grandfather. I didn't want to intrude."

Gramp had been having a bad day. Completely unresponsive, only accepting a sip of water if she held the glass to his lips, like a baby bird.

The noise from the party floated up to them, laughter and music, in little waves on the summer air.

She cleared her throat. "And your marriage? Was it good?" Crap. This talking stuff was very difficult.

His eyes were so dark. "For the most part, yes."

Ah, shit. She was going to have to ask. It was the elephant in the attic, after all. "Lucas," she said, and her voice shook a little, "why her and not me? You said you didn't want to get married so young. Was it who she was? Her family? The money? I won't judge you. I just want to know."

He didn't answer right away. "She was pregnant."

The words seemed to suck the hot air out of the attic completely, leaving nothing to feed her lungs.

Maybe she'd always known. She'd asked him that that horrible day, and she still remembered the pause before he said no. For nine months, she waited to hear news of a baby, not proud of it, but waiting and waiting.

No birth announcement. Back then it had been a relief.

But now… "I'm so sorry," she whispered.

He nodded once and looked at the floor. "Thank you."

For a few minutes, they didn't say anything else. Colleen surreptitiously wiped her eyes.

Lucas was looking at her again, his face somber. "I came to see you," he said. "After you broke up with me. I couldn't stand it anymore."

She already knew why he never followed through.

"You were with someone else," he said, his voice quiet. "It seemed like you were serious about breaking up. I went back home, ran into Ellen a few weeks later, slept with her. One time. And that was that."

"I asked you, though. When you came back, I asked if she was pregnant."

He nodded again. "She didn't want anyone to know, outside of her parents. I didn't… I didn't want to hurt you more than I already was. And I had to respect what Ellen wanted." He paused. "She miscarried about a month after the wedding."

"I'm so sorry," she said again.

He gave her a small smile. "Me, too."

Colleen swallowed.

Ellen Forbes had gotten pregnant, and Lucas married her. That was completely in keeping with his sense of honor and responsibility...and the fact that he was a family man.

And she knew without him speaking the words what the loss of that baby must've meant to him. Lucas, who would have made the best father. He never would have left Ellen, not after that kind of shared sorrow.

"Did you love her?" she asked.

"Yes. Of course."

He never had said that to her—"I love you." The thought came unbidden, and it filled her throat with tears. Lucas looked at her, his dark eyes liquid. He reached out and wiped her cheek because it seemed a tear had slipped out.

"Then why did you get a divorce?" she whispered.

He looked at the floor, then up at her. "Because I didn't love her enough," he said.

She kissed him then, of course she did, because those words, they broke her heart, sliced it in a sweet, hot cut. The kiss was soft and tender and almost shy, as if she was kissing him for the first time again. His heart had been broken, too, she realized, if not by her, then by that sad, helpless loss. And Lucas had lost so much in life.

Her hands slid through his hair, that gorgeous, thick, waving hair, and her mouth opened. He dragged her across his lap to hold her, one hand cupping her face. His arms were safe and strong, pulling her against his solid chest, and the kissing changed now, harder and less sweet and more wonderful, because it had always been like this between them, that raw heat that practically lifted her off the ground with its force. All she wanted was this, and she wondered how she'd lasted so long without him, without the hot, red force that made her heart shudder. The scrape of his cheek, the heat of his hands, the way they fit together, made her shake.

Slow down, slow down, slow down, her brain chanted.

She pulled back, her breath shaking out of her. His eyes were heavy-lidded, his breath coming hard, and he looked at her the way no other man had ever looked at her.

Mine.

"Not bad, Spaniard," she said, and he laughed, that low, smoky sound. She always could make him smile.

"Oh, *mía,* what am I going to do with you?" he whispered, pushing a strand of hair behind her ear.

"Again with the *mía.* I'm not yours. I'm a rental."

"Doesn't feel like it."

The words caused a sunburst in her chest. "I'm definitely writing your name in my notebook."

He smiled, but his eyes held a note of worry. "I'll be going back to Chicago soon," he said.

That dampened the moment a bit. "Right. I know."

"But I can't seem to stay away from you, either."

"No."

There was a pause; her heart counted out the beats.

"Should I leave you alone, Colleen?" he asked.

He was giving her a chance to back out, or at least, to stall. And yes, she felt as naked and vulnerable as a newborn kitten. She should ask him about the future. She should go slowly, make sure this time, not jump—

But last time, she'd had the whole future mapped out. The house, the kids, the plan. Maybe this time, she could just...be.

His black eyes were half-closed, and he looked more like a Spanish pirate than ever, about to claim his woman.

"No. Don't leave me alone," she said, and his mouth

was on hers again, his hands sliding under her dress to her hips, pulling her closer, his tongue sliding against hers, and this was it. He was the one, and she knew it, no matter how scary it was, how big and deep and easy to get lost in, she was simply, undeniably his.

The door banged open, and there was Connor. "Coll, where have you— Oh, for the love of God."

Colleen hurtled off Lucas's lap and straightened her skirt.

"Great! This is just great," he said, turning his back. "Paulie and Bryce are missing, and you two are up here, making out." He gave them a second, then turned back with a disapproving look. "The Chicken King wants you to help find his little princess, Coll. Mind getting your ass in gear?"

THERE WAS LOGIC, Lucas thought as he followed the O'Rourke twins downstairs, and there was…this.

It didn't make sense to get involved with Colleen. She wasn't a quick, sweet summer romance. She was forever. And he'd be leaving in too short a time, back to his life in Chicago, where he'd worked so hard to build something. A life. Friends. A career in which he was respected. He had family there, Steph and the girls, Frank and Grace.

And Ellen was, arguably, his best friend.

Colleen was Manningsport. She was the heart of the town, and she wouldn't leave, and he wouldn't stay.

He didn't want to hurt Colleen again; he hadn't wanted to hurt her ever.

But they were adults now. They could talk about things better. They could make something work.

Until Lucas had met Colleen, everything had always been…tainted, somehow. Complicated. His father had been a good man, and yet he'd dealt drugs. Ask the mother of a meth addict how good a man Dan Campbell was. Lucas's memories of his mother were that she was too sick, too fragile, and he always had to be careful and quiet. Steph…of course he loved Steph, but until the past five or six years, she'd been something of a screwup. Bryce was the good-hearted idiot, and Joe was the uncle who couldn't quite stand up to Didi. Ellen was the woman he'd made a life with because of their circumstances, and try as he might, he hadn't made that work.

But Colleen had been perfect. Pure in the sense that…well, hell, he didn't know exactly, but that's what it felt like.

You didn't just turn your back on that.

"Where is my daughter?" Ronnie Petrosinsky asked. He looked furious, as if Paulie were a fifteen-year-old who'd just slipped off with a college senior. "Is she with that idiot friend of yours?"

"I'm not sure, Mr. Petrosinsky," Colleen said. "But they're both adults."

"They're not adults!" the man yelped. "That Bryce is a complete loser, and my daughter is a very innocent and protected person, Colleen! I am not a happy man! If Bryce is compromising her, he's in for a world of hurt. You think the Chicken King becomes king without a lot of bloodshed?"

Colleen bit her lip, trying unsuccessfully to look contrite (and not laugh, Lucas thought). "No, no. I respect that, Mr. Petrosinsky. But the little chicks have to leave the nest sometime, right?"

"Wrong!"

"But I don't think they'd do anything—"

At that moment, a door slammed and in came Paulie and Bryce.

Paulie's sweater was on inside out, and her face was pink. Bryce, too, was sweaty, grinning ear to ear. "You're about to get killed," Lucas murmured.

"Dude! Having a good time?" Bryce said.

"Paulina! Where have you been? What have you been doing?" her father barked. "What did he do to you?"

"Hey, Dad. I was showing Bryce the gym."

"She can bench-press my weight," Bryce said. "I mean, she can *literally* bench-press me."

"And you thought I'd drop you," Paulie said, beaming.

"You were lifting weights?" Ronnie said.

"Yeah," Paulie said. "Well, I was lifting Bryce." Her face flushed, and she shot Bryce a little smile. Bryce returned it.

Well, well, well.

Colleen caught Lucas's eye and lifted an eyebrow in an unmistakable "told you" expression. Had to hand it to her.

"Bryce," Mr. Petrosinsky said. "You can leave now."

"Dad!" Paulie said. "He's my friend. Don't kick him out."

"Thanks, Paulie," Bryce said with a warm smile. "You rock, girl!"

"Bryce, get out." Ronnie turned to Paulie. "You. No more gallivanting with this joker. Understand?"

"Dad," Paulie said, "I'm thirty-one years old."

"Not with this goofball, you're not."

Lucas scrubbed a hand over his face to hide a smile.

Bryce looked confused. "Dude—"

Ronnie's head snapped around to glare at Bryce. "I am not a *dude*. Do I look like a cowboy? Because I'm not. You are forbidden to see my daughter." He turned to Paulie. "You want a husband? I'll find you a husband. Dmitri's been working for me for years." He glanced at Bryce. "He's in charge of slaughtering. You get my meaning, pal? Paulie, if you want to get married, Dmitri will marry you."

"Whoa," Bryce said. "No one's talking marriage, Mr. P. It's not like that." He glanced at Paulie. "I have a girlfriend."

Oh, shit. Lucas closed his eyes.

"What?" Colleen blurted. "No, you don't."

"Sure I do," Bryce said. "That chick from the bridal store? The bride? She left her fiancé, and we've been dating. She's totally hot."

"Bryce…" Lucas sighed.

Poor Paulie. Her hands went over her mouth, then dropped. She turned stiffly and walked out of the room, but as she reached the stairs, she bolted, her face twisted with crying.

Damn it, Bryce, Lucas thought. *Just once, it'd be nice if you could get it right.*

"Uh-oh," Bryce said. "Well, shit. I feel bad now."

"Out," Ronnie said.

Lucas turned to Colleen. "Happy?"

"Oh, bite me," she said, gnawing on her thumbnail. "Don't even start."

He looked at her a minute. "I'll call you."

She glared at him. "Okay. If you don't, beware. I'll spit in your beer again."

Again.

That was his girl.

CHAPTER TWENTY

"IT'S NOT YOUR FAULT," Paulie said, tears leaking out of her eyes. "I never had a chance with him. At least we got to hang out a little, though." She took a shuddering breath and reached for the Chicken King bucket. Rufus, who hated when people cried, gave a moan of sympathy (and chicken-lust) from where he lay with Paulie's pug and two of her cats.

"Paulie, I'm so sorry. I had no idea." Colleen patted her friend's calf. "I talked to Gwen, and apparently she fired him his second day."

"It's okay. Really." She smiled, then choked a little, then resumed eating. Hey. comfort eating. No judgment from Colleen, that was for sure.

It was the day after the party; the Chicken King had banned Colleen from his princess's room the night before, though Colleen had been up until 2:00 a.m. talking to her on the phone. This morning, Mr. Petrosinsky had barely let her in, and Colleen couldn't blame him.

"You want a wing?" Paulie asked thickly. "It's Haitian JooJoo Spice, deep fried twice for deliciousness."

"No thanks." It was nine o'clock in the morning. The chicken did smell good, though. Rufus agreed, licking his scruffy chops. He put his head on Paulie's shin and gave her his best "they're going to gas me in an hour" look. As usual, it worked; Paulie gave him a chunk of chicken, which he inhaled.

"Paulie..." Colleen paused. "Maybe Bryce isn't good enough for you. Have you thought of that?"

Paulie took a tissue and blew her nose so loudly Rufus jumped. "No. I haven't because he is. He's funny and smart and nice and generous."

"You sure? You're not just hoping he's all those things?" She winced as she said it, not wanting to disillusion Paulie. But Bryce had done what he always did—picked up some shallow, attractive woman for sex, rather than see that Paulie was worth ten of them.

"You should see him at the animal shelter, Colleen," Paulie said, wiping her eyes. "He's so dedicated! I mean, it's a crap job, literally, and he doesn't care! He talks to the dogs while he does it, says things like, 'You deserve a nice clean place, don't you, pal?' And he's gotten every single animal adopted since he started there. Even that smelly old Boxer with the hip dysplasia who bit everyone. Lorena Iskin took him, and the dog is like a new person."

"No, he's good at that. He got me Rufus, after all. But maybe—"

"His problem, Colleen, is that he doesn't *feel* like he's worth anything. When he was a kid, he always had Lucas around, being perfect. Then there's his mother, basically telling him all he should do is live with her forever and be a mama's boy. His father was always just the fun dad, never making him stay in college or get a job. That's why he takes the easy way out. Because no one believes he can do the hard way."

Wow. "Except you."

"Yeah." Her eyes filled again. "It's not just those blue

eyes." She took another wing. "Though they don't hurt the cause, either."

Colleen took a deep breath. "You know what? I don't think this bride person is going to last. Let it run its course, and we'll—"

Paulie tossed the chicken bone in the bucket. "No. I'm done. I don't want to keep embarrassing myself. I have some pride. He doesn't want me."

The words stabbed right through Colleen's heart. "Paulie, don't give up."

"It was a good try," she said with a sigh. "And I really appreciate your help." Paulie looked at the bedspread (fuzzy yellow chicks with pink flowers in their beaks, utterly adorable). "So you and Lucas seem to have something going on."

"We don't have anything except a past," Colleen said.

"That's not how it looked to me."

"Well, I'm about to be stupid and get my heart broken again, if it makes you feel any better."

"Oh, please," Paulie said, grabbing a piece of chicken rather violently. Rufus and Mrs. Tuggles looked at it with great hope. "Don't be an idiot, Colleen. Do you know what I'd give to have someone come alive when he saw me? I mean, yeah, it would be so amazing if it was Bryce, but anyone! Anyone, Colleen! And you have this beautiful pirate of a man who looks at you like you're naked and covered in Krispy Kremes! So what if things didn't work out the first time? So frigging what?"

Colleen closed her mouth. "Right," she whispered.

Paulie gave her a hard shove. "Get out. Go rock that man's world. You owe it to the rest of us who'd sell body parts for just one kiss from a guy like Lucas. Or Bryce. So just go and stop trying to protect yourself from a little heartbreak, because you know what? Just once, I'd love to be heartbroken because someone loved me and left me, instead of heartbroken because I never got on that train at all."

COLLEEN'S THOUGHTS WERE muddled at work. She had the lunchtime shift today, and O'Rourke's was mobbed with tourists and locals alike. Rafe was in the kitchen, singing opera, serenading her whenever she came in. She went through the motions, joking with her staff, ruffling the hair of children, asking out-of-towners which vineyards they'd visited, suggesting places to go if the forecast for rain held up.

Around two, when the crowds had left for the vineyards or sails on the lake or a nap, Colleen was wiping down the bar as the blender screeched, pulverizing more watermelon for the cocktail of the day (watermelon mojitos, terribly delicious). The only customers were a family of Swedes at a booth in the back, Victor Iskin, who came in every afternoon for a little mental health break from his wife, and Prudence and Carl Vanderbeek, who were pretending to be strangers meeting over a game of pool, despite the fact that they'd been married almost twenty-five years.

The door opened, and in came her father.

That was a rarity. He usually only came here to pick up Savannah, and then he texted from the parking lot.

"Hi," she said.

"Hey. Is Connor here?"

"No. He's at the farmer's market."

"Oh." Dad stood there a second.

"Have a seat," she said. "Want something to drink? A menu?"

"No, Colleen, I'm not here for food. I ate already."

Yes, of course. He never did come in here, a fact that both relieved and irritated her. "Well, sit down. You're making me nervous," she said.

"I'm divorcing Gail."

Shit.

The Swedish father came over and handed Colleen the bill. "Thank you so much," he said.

"Bye!" the children chorused, beautiful little blonds all. The beautiful mother waved, as well.

"Bye, guys!" Colleen said. "Come again!"

She waited until they'd left, then turned to her father. "Wow."

"Things have cooled off between us—"

"Dad, who cares? What about Savannah?"

He gave her a frosty look. "What about her?"

"Does she know? Is she handling it okay?"

"We haven't told her yet. She'll be fine."

"She better be, I guess. God forbid her emotional state gets in your way. Do you have a younger mistress on the side?"

"Colleen, don't make everything about you, okay? I waited till you and Connor were grown to divorce your mother. I think you'd be over it by now." He paused. "I wanted you to know."

With that, he turned and left.

Colleen unclenched her jaw. Note how he didn't answer the question about a girlfriend, the ass.

Savannah was going to be wrecked. Colleen pulled out her phone and sent her sister a quick text: Thinking of you, Yogi! How's your day going? xoxox

A second later, the answer came. I miss you too! That party was fun! Guess what? I lost three pounds!

Colleen closed her eyes. A nine-year-old shouldn't have to worry about weight issues. Can't wait for Friday, she texted back. Love you!

The bar phone rang, waking up Victor. "O'Rourke's, home of the finest watermelon mojitos in the known universe."

"It's Lucas."

The rush of heat was fast and thrilling. "Hey."

"Dinner tonight?" There were hammers in the background; he must be at her mom's or the public safety building.

"Okay."

"Name the place."

"Mine."

"Got it. Seven?"

"Great."

She hung up. World's shortest phone convo, but hey. He never was good at talking in the first place. She was going to sleep with him tonight. Or, more likely, not sleep with him. It was time.

Connor came in through the back, his arms laden with whatever he'd picked up at the farmer's market for today's special. He took one look at her face and stopped. Scowled. "I don't want to hear about it," he said. "I warned you."

"Thanks for the brotherly concern. Dad and Gail are getting a divorce."

"Oh, shit," her brother said. "Poor Savannah."

"I know. Dad's being his prickish self."

"Why would today be any different?" He pushed through the swinging doors to the kitchen, where Rafe was wiping down the counters.

"Ciggie break for the beautiful people," Rafe said,

tossing the dishrag into the sink and grabbing his back-pack. He zipped out the back door.

Colleen sat on the stainless steel counter. "Get off," Connor said. "Some people care about where their food is prepared, unlike you."

"I once ate a Reese's Peanut Butter Cup I found on the sidewalk," she said. "Yet here I am, still walking the earth."

"Doesn't make you less gross. Come on, off." He shoved her toward the stool and sprayed down the counter, full of martyrish zeal.

"I don't like Gail, God knows," Colleen said, "but I don't see Savannah being better off with them divorced."

"I imagine you asked Dad why they were splitting up."

"Yeah. He didn't answer. My money's on Hot Young Mistress 2.0." Poor Gail. Her whole identity was being hot young mistress/wife...and even if she wasn't quite as young as she used to be, she was still a helluva lot younger than Dad.

Poor Gail. That was a new thought.

"Con," she said, "you ever miss the old Dad?"

Her brother stopped his anal-retentive cleaning and looked up. "What old Dad? He's always been a prick, Coll." He gave her shoulder a squeeze as he passed to the sink and began rinsing cilantro.

"Not always."

"He was. He just liked you more, so you didn't notice."

"Doesn't seem that simple." She looked at her brother's face. He was in the Food Zone, hypnotized by the smells and textures of his work. "Why did you get all the Zen genes?" she asked.

"Also the smart genes, don't forget."

"Is that what your woman tells you? Oh, by the way, I figured out who it was."

"Did you?"

"Julianne from the library."

"Nope."

"Damn. Okay, I'm leaving. Monica and Hannah are both on tonight, and that dopey Annie. Have a good one."

He looked up. "Be careful," he said after a beat.

"Yep. No drinking and driving, no unprotected sex."

"And no tuna fish."

"Got it."

"Are you cooking, or is he?"

"I am."

"Poor Lucas."

"Hey, why don't *you* cook for us? I can come pick it up just before seven."

A jaundiced look. "No, Colleen. I'm not making you two your pre-sex meal."

"It might be a postsex meal."

"You disgust me."

"Fine," she said. "I don't need you. If you can read, you can cook. You don't need to go to the CIA." She stuck out her tongue and smacked him on the back of the head as she left.

"By the way, I won't be coming home tonight," he called. "Because I don't want to hear a damn thing."

"That's fine by me. Go to her, your ladylove." She paused in the doorway. "Is it Lorelei? Because I thought Gerard and she would be perfect together."

"Get out of my kitchen. And be careful."

"No tuna for anyone!" she called as she left.

THE PROMISED RAIN started to fall around six.

The apartment was quiet; Rufus and she had gone for a run earlier, and her dog seemed to be in a coma, out cold in front of the couch. No music because Colleen needed to concentrate. She didn't spend a lot of time cooking—what was the point of owning a chef-brother if you couldn't eat for free? But for this night, she wanted to make her man a meal.

"If you can read, you can cook," she repeated aloud, then surveyed the groceries she'd bought. Tonight's menu was meant to impress, yes. To start, beet, almond and goat cheese salad, followed by braised scallops in a white wine reduction over celery root and potato puree and topped with fresh dill; a roasted carrot and parsnip side dish topped with freshly grated Romano cheese; and vanilla bean crème fraîche pudding topped with fresh raspberries.

She may have overcommitted.

Frowning, she checked the recipes she'd pulled up online. Damn. The carrot thing had to cook for three hours. Really? Were carrots worth cooking that long? Honestly, that smacked of hubris, didn't it? *I, the lowly carrot, formerly growing in the dirt, demand three hours in the oven.*

Speaking of vegetables with attitude…the celery root was grotesque and vaguely homoerotic, somehow. The produce guy at the market had to show her where it was. Thirty-one years old, and Colleen had never seen a celery root before, despite having a twin who viewed cooking dinner on the same level as performing open-heart surgery on a child in the middle of a field after a plane crash.

Ah, well, time to get to work. Because raw seafood made her sick to her stomach, she figured she'd cook the scallops first. Melted the butter (not hard at all!), opened the container and dumped the nasty little creatures in. Speaking of nausea, she hadn't talked to Faith in eighteen entire hours.

She found her phone, wandered out on the little balcony and called her pal. Faith and Levi's house was on the next block, two houses down, so their backyards almost adjoined.

"Hey!" she said when Faith answered. "I'm looking at your house. If I get a telescope, I could totally spy on you two."

"The good stuff happened an hour ago, the second that man walked through the door," Faith said, a smile in her voice.

"Le sigh. How's my godchild?"

"It's official, by the way. We told my dad. There were tears."

"Oh! You Hollands! Please ask your father to adopt me, since he threw me over for that slutty housekeeper."

"I'm telling Mrs. J. you said that."

"Don't you dare." She could hear Levi's voice in the background.

"So what's going on with you and Lucas?" Faith asked. "Don't think I didn't notice that you two were missing for an hour at the picnic yesterday."

"Um…he's coming here for dinner."

"Is that code for sex?"

"Probably." There was no probably about it. "Am I being stupid, Faith?"

There was a pause. "I can't imagine you'd be stupid."

"That pause concerns me." She glimpsed Mr. Wong in the yard next door doing tai chi (or swatting a mosquito in slow motion). "I might be stupid. This isn't a sure thing at all, him and me."

"Is it ever? I mean, Jeremy and I were a sure thing."

"Extenuating circumstances, pal."

"And then, for a while, I thought Honor and Tom weren't going to make it, and look at them. Hey, are you bringing Lucas to the wedding next weekend?"

"I don't know. Should I?"

"Yes! So romantic! Levi, don't you think Colleen should bring Lucas to Honor's wedding? He does."

There was a funny smell out here...someone was burning leaves or trash. "I should probably go," Colleen said. "I have to do stuff. Food stuff. I also have to change into slutty underwear."

"Have fun," Faith said. "You're not stupid."

Colleen smiled. "Thanks, hon. Talk to you tomorrow."

She turned, froze, then bolted.

It wasn't leaves that were burning. It was scallops.

She yanked the frying pan off the burner. The smell was thick, but not quite acrid. More of a tarry, oily smell. "Sphincter," she muttered.

Well, great chefs were innovators, right? She dumped the scallops onto a paper towel, let them cool a bit... crap, the carrots and parsnips needed to get cooking, didn't they? She grabbed another pot, filled it with water, figuring she'd boil them a bit to soften, then roast them. Not to mention the stupid puree. Whose idea was this whole thing? Would it have been so hard to go to a restaurant?

She chopped the carrots and parsnips, figuring they'd

cook faster that way, and threw them into the pot. Turned back to the scallops. She'd just trim off the burnt bottom edges. But wait, weren't blackened scallops kind of good?

Time to call for backup. "Hey, Con," she said.

"We're slammed. What's up?"

"Blackened scallops—delicious?"

"They're great. Bye."

Perfect! Necessity, the mother of invention.

Who said cooking was hard?

AN HOUR LATER, right on time, a knock came at the door.

Shit. "Don't come in!" she yelled. "Not yet, don't come in! And don't look through the window, either! I will gouge your eyes out if you do. Sorry! That sounded mean. I didn't intend it that way."

"Is there a nice way to say 'gouge your eyes out'?" Lucas asked, his voice full of laughter.

That voice was foreplay incarnate. She damn well better have the same effect on him, or life was just not fair.

But first, she had to feed the man. She wasn't ready to fall into bed (give her an hour). And before they could eat, she had to get rid of the, er, evidence. She resumed flapping the dish towel at the window, trying to dispel the thin veil of smoke layering the kitchen. Who knew roasting beets was so hard? How dare they be hard? It wasn't like they were the world's most popular vegetable.

Rufus wandered into the kitchen, started to snuff at the scallops, then hung his head and slunk away. Perhaps not a good sign.

It didn't smell so good in there. She dashed around,

grabbing scented candles from various and sundry sur-
faces throughout the apartment.

Lucas knocked again. "Colleen? Everything all right?"

"Stop bugging me! I know you're here! Just...give
me a sec."

"You sure you're okay?"

"Yes! Why would you even ask that? It's fine. Just...
I'm changing, that's all." And yes, she had to change because at the moment, she was wearing a now-filthy, beet-
stained, scallop-stained, everything-stained O'Rourke's
T-shirt with the sweatpants she'd stolen from Connor last
month and hemmed by hacking off four inches at the
bottom, and it wasn't as sexy as it sounded.

The smoke could dissipate on its own. She had to
beautify. She yanked off her shirt, tripping over Rufus.
"Sorry, baby."

"Did you say something?" Lucas asked. He may have
been laughing.

"Shut up! Just wait for me!" The shirt caught on her
hair clip, tugging painfully, and she whacked her knee
on the door frame, then staggered into the door so that
it slammed into the wall.

"Colleen?"

"I'm *coming!* Just keep your pants on."

Seven minutes later, she was slightly sweaty but
totally gorgeous, please God. Tight black dress, hair
down (if perhaps smelling of charred mollusks), some
lip gloss, long silver earrings, barefoot because she'd
spilled some boiling water on her foot and her slutty
shoes were a bit painful to begin with.

Oh, crikey. She needed a nap. And possibly the fire
department.

But no, no, Lucas was here. Her one and only love,

etc., etc., and yes, she was excited about that. It would've been nice if she had time for a shower, but hey. What was a girl to do? She opened the door.

"Hi," she said, trying for dew-kissed and sultry, and her voice did sound huskier, thanks to the smoke inhalation from earlier. "Come on in." Rufus began his Serenade of the Visitor. *Ah rah! Ah rah! Ah rooroo rah!*

"It smells so good in here," Lucas said. "Were you burning feathers?"

"Hush, boy. It'll be delicious. I had a slight fire. It was nothing. Wine?"

"Sounds like I'll need some." He held out a bouquet of yellow roses.

"Thanks," she said.

They were her favorite. He remembered.

Le sigh.

Lucas surveyed the kitchen. "Wow. Look at all this. Did you just make dinner for China?"

"You want to eat tonight or not?" she asked. But yeah, okay, she was seeing the kitchen through his eyes. Plates, pots, bowls, spatulas, three frying pans, a Dutch oven, several whisks and three cookie sheets. Oh, and the baseball bat she used because she couldn't find a rolling pin.

"How many people are coming tonight?" he asked.

"You're it." She poured some wine and downed it, then refilled her glass and got him one. "So. What's new? Oh, shit, I forgot about those *conceited* beets! Go in the living room and stay out of my way. Sorry! I meant that in a nice way. Get. Go. Come on, I'm losing the war here."

"Do you want help, Colleen?"

"No! Just get out. Scratch my dog's stomach."

He left, Rufus following, and Colleen yanked on an oven mitt, grabbed the beets out of the oven (they looked like charcoal briquettes, for the love of God, maybe jacking the heat to five hundred hadn't been wise). The Pyrex dish slipped from her hands and clattered against the oven door, spilling half the ashen vegetable.

"I'm fine!" she called. "Do *not* come in here."

Forty-five minutes later, feeling as if she'd just fought off an army of rabid mountain gorillas, she sat down at the table. "Beet salad with goat cheese and roasted almonds over a bed of arugula," she said.

Not that she was hungry, not after seeing all this food for the past eternity. But hey. Maybe she'd feel better after she started eating.

She tried to cut a beet. It was harder than perhaps it should've been. She had sawed off the burnt parts, and they were the requisite color of blood, but they weren't exactly tender. She kept trying. Nope, nothing. More pressure, perhaps? The knife snapped, her hand thunking down on the table, clattering the dishes.

Lucas raised an eyebrow—Prince of Darkness, Sardonic Edition—but said nothing.

Well, how about an almond? Harmless creatures, almonds. Except this one appeared to be petrified. Onto the goat cheese. That, at least, was delicious. A little clot of it fell off her fork and shot right down into her cleavage. Colleen opted to pretend that didn't happen.

Lucas smiled.

"And how was your day, dear?" she asked.

"Wonderful." He tried to cut a beet, failed and took a bite of arugula, chewed, winced and washed it down with a lot of water. Sue her. It wasn't arugula season, and yes, fine! It was bitter. "How's Paulie today?"

"Sad. Hungry." She tried another almond. Crikey, the thing was as hard as a pebble. Hopefully her molar hadn't just cracked. "How's Bryce?"

"Unemployed once again."

"Yeah, I heard about that." From the kitchen came a popping sound.

Damn it! She'd turned up the heat under the scallops to warm them up, as she maybe cooked them a tiny bit early (like, two hours too early). "Back in a flash."

Scallops, she learned, could be both leathery, burnt and yet still undercooked. The celery root and potato puree was the consistency of water; perhaps she shouldn't have boiled the ingredients quite so much, but she'd been trying to speed things up. The carrots and parsnips were okay, if you liked tasteless, rubbery vegetables.

Ah. Here was one small scallop that was only charred and not raw. She ate it, cringing at the carbon flavor, and heard the unmistakable crunch of sand.

"This is delicious," Lucas said. "Maybe we can go out for cheeseburgers later on."

She closed her eyes in defeat. "Okay, it's a disaster. You're very welcome."

"I'm very grateful. You get an A for effort. Next time, I'll cook for you instead."

She peeked at him through her lashes.

When the Prince of Darkness was smiling, women everywhere should lock up their special places.

A hot, electric ripple spread through her, nearly painful, it was so intense.

Her special places weren't going to be locked up, nuh-uh.

"I did have some success with dessert," she said.

"Then let's have dessert."

"Shall we leave ground zero and eat in the living room?"

"Sounds good."

He picked up the wine and their glasses, and she took a few candles that were failing to mask the odor of char, and set them on the coffee table. It smelled better in here, at least, and it was cozy and neat, except for the magazine Rufus had apparently eaten and regurgitated at some point when she was wrangling veggies. She sighed and went to the kitchen, returning with the paper towels.

"Let me do that," Lucas offered.

"Just sit there and look pretty."

The rain had picked up, and it was such a lovely sound, the patter and tap, the occasional car passing. Rufus crooned at Lucas and splayed himself obscenely.

Colleen ignored her slutty pet (though she knew the feeling) and went into the kitchen, washed her hands twice in the crowded sink, then got two servings of pudding from the fridge and put the berries on top. Beautiful. At least they'd have this. She might suck as a chef, but she could handle dessert. The necessities in life, that was the theory.

Carrying the ramekins into the living room, Colleen decided that all was not lost. There was Lucas, sitting on the floor in front of the couch, idly scratching her dog's belly. "You're allowed on the furniture, you know," she said.

"I'm good here," he answered.

Yes, he was. He'd be even better in her bed.

She swallowed a bite of pudding, which unfortunately had a raspberry in it. An unchewed raspberry. Some very racy choking ensued.

"You okay?" he asked.

"Fine," she wheezed, grabbing a tissue to wipe her streaming eyes. "Good, good. It's all good. If you can choke, you can breathe." She choked again, involuntarily. "See?"

He waited until she was breathing more or less normally, then resumed eating the pudding. Which was excellent, thank you very much.

A flash of lightning lit up the living room, and thunder rumbled in the distance, and shit, Rufus hated thunder. On cue, he bolted upright, knocking Lucas's pudding onto the floor and racing straight for Colleen's womb.

"No, boy! No! Calm down! It's okay!" She oophed as he head-butted her abdomen, seeking shelter. "Off, boy. Down."

Roooo, he moaned, shuddering.

"Hang on," Colleen muttered, trying to stand, which was not that easy, not with a hundred and sixty pounds of terrified mammal on her lap. "I have a tranquilizer for him."

Ah rooo rooo rooo, her beloved pet moaned.

"Come here, boy," Lucas said, standing up. He hauled the dog off her, and she got up and scrambled for the kitchen. For the love of St. Patrick…the mess in here seemed to have grown. It would take weeks to clean up.

She found Rufus's meds, took a scoop of peanut butter and went back to the living room. "Here you go, boy. Sleepy time. That's a good puppy."

He licked obediently, his eyes still tragic, and she knelt down and hugged him. "Good puppy. Good boy. Come on, let's go to bed." She led him into the bedroom, told him to lie down, then stroked his giant head until his pretty eyes closed.

Doggy all set. God bless the vet who'd prescribed those drugs. They worked fast and wore off fast, just what you needed for a thunderstorm. Alas, her black dress was now covered with rough gray fur, but that was the price of dog ownership. Dry-cleaning bills up the wazoo.

Lucas had cleaned up the pudding and was sitting back in front of the couch. "Come sit over here," he said, patting the floor next to him.

"Yeah, one sec," she said, sitting on the floor on her side of the room. Because the truth was, she was starving, and she, at least, had some pudding left. She shoveled a few bites into her mouth (sustenance for the exertion to come, please God) and watched him.

He hadn't shaved today, and a faint smile played in his eyes. His hands—his big, beautiful hands—rested in his lap, and his shirt glowed in the flickering light of the candles.

It was time. Adrenaline flooded through her arms and legs—and special places.

And yes, Colleen O'Rourke knew what she was doing in the old boudoir (or living room, whatever). Granted, most of what she knew she'd learned with this man in front of her, but maybe she could show him a thing or two.

She maneuvered to her hands and knees and started to crawl toward him, like in that hot movie whose title was eluding her right now. Her knee cracked (he probably didn't notice) and her hair fell into her face (sexy? Or just blinding?). She pushed it back with what she hoped was a come-hither smile (but her knee kind of hurt, actually), lost her balance and sort of tilted (just a little, maybe not noticeable?) jostling the coffee table.

And because this night had been against her from the

start, two of her lemon-scented candles (which cost seventeen dollars apiece), fell, and there was a small flare of light (because she'd just started a fire).

"Oh, come on!" she yelped. "This is so unfair!"

Lucas grabbed a throw pillow and smothered the flames. The pretty blue throw pillow that Rufus liked best, the one with the ruffles on it. Ruffles which were now melting, adding to that dee-licious burnt smell her apartment seemed to be sporting. She dumped her wine on top of the pillow, and there was a hiss, some foul-smelling smoke, that was that.

Lucas checked under the pillow. "Fire's out."

"Oh, good. At least we won't be dying tonight. Something to celebrate."

He checked the melted pillow, then looked at her.

Time to admit defeat. She sighed, sitting back on her heels. "I usually do better than this," she said.

"I don't want to hear what you usually do," he answered. Then he cupped her face in his hands and kissed her, and oh, his mouth, and the sound of the rain, and the memory of them together, the way they fit, the softness of his mouth and the scrape of five-o'clock shadow, the good clean smell of him.

He pulled her closer, his hands going into her hair, tugging gently so her neck was exposed for his kiss, the soft scrape of his teeth in the sweet spot just above her collarbone, and she shuddered with the feeling. Her hands were under his shirt, clever hands, and his skin was hot and smooth and velvet. Colleen seemed to have forgotten how to breathe, because shallow little gasps were coming out of her, and she kissed him, hard, urgently, wrapping her arms around him and pressing against him until he lowered her to the floor, shoving the melted pillow aside.

And my God, how it felt to have him on top of her, at last, again, finally. He was so hard and solid and incredible that her whole body was just one aching, throbbing pulse, and finally, finally, they were together again, Lucas and Colleen, the way it was meant to be.

He stood up and pulled her to her feet and led her to the bedroom. Thunder rumbled and shook the house, and Rufus snored gently from his bed.

And then, all of a sudden, Colleen was nervous.

Even though she'd been with him so many times in the past, even though she was far from inexperienced with men, even so. This wasn't men. This wasn't some guy.

This was the only man who'd ever meant anything to her.

He sat on her bed and looked at her, his Spanish eyes black and unfathomable in the dim light of the fading day. Turned her hand over and kissed the soft side of her wrist, and looked at her again, his thumb sliding over the spot he'd just kissed, and suddenly, Colleen realized her eyes were full of tears.

"I missed you," she whispered, and he stood again and kissed her softly, softly, then wiped her tears away and kissed her again.

"Oh, *mía*," he whispered. "I missed you, too."

Then he unzipped her dress and pushed it off her shoulders, the fabric skimming against her skin to the floor. His hands were callused and warm and thorough, skimming her skin, unhooking her bra and sliding it off. His mouth lingered on her neck, her shoulders, and her blood felt slow and heavy and sweet.

This was love. This was what had been missing all the other times, when she tried to find what she and Lucas had.

No wonder nothing had worked. No one else was him.

She opened her eyes, realizing that he was waiting. Then he smiled, just a little, and that smile blossomed in her heart in a warm, heavy wave. She sank down on the mattress and pulled him down with her, her hands going to his belt.

"Vanquish me, Spaniard," she whispered, then bit his earlobe, and the sound of his laugh was like the sound of thunder, reverberating in her heart.

CHAPTER TWENTY-ONE

AROUND MIDNIGHT, Lucas woke up. The rain had stopped, and a cool breeze fluttered the curtains. From the dim glow of the streetlight, he saw that Colleen was sound asleep on her stomach, mouth slightly open, possibly drooling, her lashes smudged on her cheeks, hair matted and tangled. Utterly beautiful, in other words.

Ten years ago, he'd married another woman. Shattered Colleen's heart and walked away, leaving the shards scattered behind him.

And yet here he was, staring at her. He pushed her hair back from her face. She groaned a little and swatted his hand, then rolled over, presenting him with her shoulders and more matted hair.

She smelled like lemons, despite her foray into arson this night. He leaned his forehead against her neck and just breathed her in. Kissed her shoulder once. Then again. Then a third time.

This got a little sigh.

Her dog's tail started thumping on the floor.

He put his arm around her. Her breast fit into his hand perfectly, soft and plump and—

"Hey, creepy man, stop fondling me."

"No can do, *mía*. You were meant to be fondled."

She rolled over and before she even opened her eyes,

she was kissing him, wrapping herself around him, pulling him against her, his generous, beautiful, smiling Colleen, and he didn't waste time, just pushed her on her back made her laughter turn into a gasp, and then a sigh, and then his name on her lips.

And when she was once again smiling at him, her cheeks flushed and her skin glowing, he said, "Get dressed, hotshot. I'm starving."

With Rufus draped over the entire backseat of the truck, they headed to the nearest Chicken King, which was open until 2:00 a.m., and ordered a bucket of Texas Cowboy Big 'n' Hearty Extra Spicy ("made with real lard!") from the beleaguered teen behind the counter. Colleen directed him to a spot way up on top of a hill, in a field where tree frogs sang from the nearby woods and an impossible number of fireflies winked and flitted.

He grabbed one of the drop cloths he kept in the back of the truck, as well as the blanket he'd grabbed from her apartment, and set up a picnic, shooing Rufus away from the food.

They ate and watched the fireflies, the sliver moon giving just enough light. From somewhere not too far away, an owl called and was answered. There was a sweet smell to the air, and the chicken was fantastic, if taking years off their lives.

It was one of those perfect moments in life, like the time before his mother got sick, when the family had gone to the lake and he'd swum underwater for the first time, surfacing to hear Stephanie cheering and his parents clapping. The time he'd hit a grand slam his freshman year of high school off the opposing team's best pitcher, one of the few games his father had been able to make. The first time he kissed Colleen, and known what he'd been trying not to know—that she was The One.

The One smiled at him now, and took another bite of the life-threatening chicken, then wiped her hands on one of the many wipes supplied by the Chicken King. Lucas lay down with his head in her lap, her hand idly stroking his hair, and it was like it had been back then, when she was the only thing he had that was real and unconditional and his.

She'd have to come back with him to Chicago. She just would. She could be happy there. She'd have to be.

"You know anything about constellations, Spaniard?" she asked, looking up into the sky.

"No."

"Me, neither." She smiled, then lay down next to him. The dog cantered over and flopped down next to her, putting his head on her hip. "So about…this. Us."

"Yes. About that."

She took a deep breath, then let it out slowly. "Let's not overthink it this time."

"What does that mean?"

"I don't want to read too much into this."

"Colleen—"

"Let's just have now. Because this is pretty damn perfect, and I don't want to ruin things by making plans."

He propped himself up on an elbow to see her face. She looked serious, but not unhappy.

She reached up and touched his lips, traced them, and a little smile came to her own. "It's not that I don't love you, Spaniard," she said. "It's just that I'm smarter now."

"What do you mean?"

"I mean, seize the day. Or the woman. Live for today. Look both ways crossing the street. Don't use your teeth as tools." Her hand went to his hair, tugging a strand. "I don't want to ruin whatever we have together by looking too far down the road. I know why you're here, and I know you're not going to stay, and I don't want to think about that right now." She looked away and scratched her dog's head.

"Colleen, you could always—"

"Shh. Don't you know I'm the queen of flings? Enjoy me."

His smile dropped. "This is not a fling," he growled.

Her eyes filled with tears. "Be careful what you say to me, Lucas," she whispered.

"This is not a fling," he repeated.

"You don't have to—"

"Colleen. This. Is not. A fling."

"Fine. You're a bully, you know."

He kissed her then, softly, and tasted her, and she opened her mouth to him, her hands fisting in his hair.

"If you break my heart, I will sic this vicious dog on you," she said against his mouth. "And then I'll sic Connor on what's left of you, and then I'll bring your remains to the Chicken King, and he'll—"

"Do you ever stop talking?" he asked, and gave her mouth something better to do, and they kissed, and kissed, and kissed more, tongues and teeth, lips and whispers, and yes, a smile or two as well, and he slid his hand under her shirt, feeling the soft skin of her breast, relishing the quick intake of breath.

"I haven't stayed out all night with a girl for a long time," he said.

"How about with a boy?"

He laughed. "Not with a boy, either."

"You remember the time we went out on my father's boat and fell asleep and woke up in Urbana?"

"I remember your black bra," he said. "The one with the little pink flower in the front." He undid the button of her jeans.

"And the time in Chicago, when we watched the fireworks. We stayed out all night then, too."

"I don't remember the fireworks. I do remember you doing something you'd never done before that night."

She blushed. "Do you? I have no recollection of that event."

"I'd be happy to help you remember. It involved you, me, your mouth—"

"Fine, fine, I remember. And I might be tempted to relive it if you're a good boy."

"I'm *very* good. I thought I proved that. Twice."

"Oh, man. The ego on you is— Oh. Okay." She finally stopped talking as he slid his hand into her jeans.

Lucas turned his head and looked at the dog. "Go away," he said, and Rufus gave him a wounded look and heaved himself up.

"You hurt his feelings," Colleen whispered.

"He'll live," he said. "But if I can't get you naked, right now, I might not."

She tugged his shirt off over his head. "Then shut up and put up, Spaniard." She grinned. "And stop laughing or someone's gonna hear us. This is public property, you know. We could get arrested for lewd acts."

"Let's give it our best shot," he said, pulling off her jeans.

A good while later, after he'd worshipped her sufficiently, when she was trembling and weak and her eyes were closed, Lucas felt her breathing slow, felt her grow heavier against him and covered her with the blanket. The stars burned and blazed overhead, the night was soft and dark, and at this moment, he couldn't think of a single thing he wanted that he didn't have right here.

CHAPTER TWENTY-TWO

WHEN COLLEEN GOT into her car later that week, she was humming. Because yes, life was good. Life was actually kind of perfect, in fact. Rufus seemed to agree; he put his cement-block head on her shoulder to better see where they were heading.

Happiness. Bliss, maybe. She'd forgotten what it was like to be with a man who really…knew her. In the years she and Lucas had been apart, her dealings with men had been frivolous, by and large. It wasn't that she hadn't wanted to meet someone; she had. It was just that she could tell within about ten seconds if there was real potential.

There never had been, and she'd made sure that on those rare occasions when flirting progressed to actual physical contact, it wasn't with someone who was going to get hurt. She'd left the hometown crowd alone, in other words. God forbid she'd had a thing with Levi, for example; she saw him almost every day, and now the guy was married to her best friend. Tom Barlow had been extremely appealing, but within seconds, she could see that he was (a) in need of a friendly bartender buddy, and (b) not really emotionally available…unless your name was Honor Holland, which Colleen's was not.

And so, Greg the waiter from Hugo's last summer and his type. A fling. And flings, Colleen now admitted, hadn't been worth the effort, really. Because there was sex, and then there was Lucas.

Lucas, who took his time. Whose smile alone could weaken her knees and get the special places purring. Whose hands were strong, whose body was warm and solid and—

"Sphincter!" she yelped, jerking the wheel of her car. "Sorry, Rufie."

The street was mobbed with cars. Was there a funeral or something? A wedding? Bar mitzvah? How did she not know, she who knew everything?

Oh, man. Her mother's driveway was full, and Lucas's truck was boxed in. Rufus gave a joyful bark—Grandma, always good for some bacon—and cantered into the backyard.

Sure enough, Team Menopause was in full force in the backyard, and indeed, their number had multiplied. Mom, Mrs. Johnson, Carol Robinson, Laura Boothby, Cathy and Louise. Guess those two being lesbians didn't mean they didn't appreciate some good-looking men. Faith was here, as well.

"Shouldn't you be ogling your hot husband?" Colleen asked.

"He's on his way over. Traffic control," Faith answered. "I'm supposedly picking up Mrs. Johnson so we can all have dinner, but she's not going anywhere, she says."

"Not till I have to," Mrs. J. said, jerking her drink away from Rufus's enormous and thieving tongue.

Bryce Campbell was pouring a day-glow lime-green liquid from a pitcher. Shirtless. Louise was tipping him. "Hey, Coll!" he said cheerfully.

"Has Chippendales relocated?" Colleen asked.

"Oh, don't be such a prude," her mom said. "It's Lucas's last day." Mom gestured with her plastic cup to the roof.

There he was, in full blue-collar glory. And though he'd made her quite happy—multiply happy—just last night, Colleen felt her entire female anatomy squeeze and swell and blossom and bark.

"Hey," he said.

"Oh, my God, that voice," Carol said. "Lucas, say my name. Say, 'Carol, you're still a fine-looking woman.' Do it."

"I thought you had Jeremy Lyon for that sort of thing," Colleen said.

"Leave me alone, Colleen," Carol said. "I have to get my jollies somehow."

"Carol, you're still a fine-looking woman," Lucas said with a pirate grin. Carol squealed, giggled merrily, then held up her empty glass for Bryce to refill. He obliged, winking at Colleen.

"Oh, Colleen," Carol said, "I have a house for you to look at. This one might actually be perfect, and it's not even listed yet. I thought I'd give you first dibs."

For some reason, the words gave Colleen a twinge. "Where is it?" she asked, sneaking a look at Lucas. He was kneeling on the roof, doing something at the base of the chimney.

"It's on Ivy Lane. The Lowensteins' place."

"Oh, that house is very charming!" Mrs. Johnson exclaimed. "The roses, the hydrangeas, the little sunroom in the back!"

Colleen knew the house, a little fairy cottage made of stone. It did indeed have a beautiful garden, and a shady front yard. And a brook in the back. "Thanks, Carol. I'll take a look."

"That should do it, Jeanette," Lucas said. "I'm done here."

A chorus of boos and protests went up from Team Menopause. "You didn't even take off your shirt," Carol complained.

Lucas sighed. "It's tough, being objectified like this," he said.

"Boo-hoo-hoo," Colleen called. "Just do it, Spaniard."

He grinned, sighed, obeyed. Got a hearty round of applause. "Ten," Mom called.

"Ten," Carol and Mrs. J. echoed.

"Nine and a half," Colleen said. Didn't want him to get cocky.

"Jeanette, do you have a license for this?" Levi Cooper approached, shaking his head. "Ladies, I'm disappointed in all of you."

"Take off your shirt, Levi," Carol said. "Let's see what you got."

"Inappropriate, Carol," he said, his eyes resting on Faith. "Hey, beautiful."

"Love," Jeanette sighed. "Mrs. Johnson, you're so lucky to have a grandchild on the way." She gave Colleen a pointed look, then turned her eyes to Lucas. "I wouldn't object if you knocked up my daughter, Lucas."

"Okay, everyone's cut off," Colleen said. "Levi, do a quick sobriety check, will you, buddy?"

Bryce approached her, pulling on his shirt. "Coll, got a minute?" he asked.

"Sure, bud." They went a few yards away from the ladies (though not before Laura Boothby had tucked a ten into his pocket). "So, uh, the whole Paulie thing. I feel really bad about that."

Colleen sighed. "Yeah. She likes you a lot."

"I guess that's why she adopted all those animals," he said, frowning.

"Yep."

He gave her a sad smile. "Not lot of people really like me."

"What are you talking about? Everyone likes you."

He shrugged. "Yeah, I guess. Just…you know. Not when they get to know me and find out I'm just…good-looking and stupid. No one ever gives me a second thought."

"Bryce! You're not stupid."

"Oh, come on. Did you ever give me a second thought?"

He had a point.

"I got fired from the wedding dress place," he said. "And the bride went back to her husband. Fiancé. Whatever. She wasn't really that fun, turns out."

"For what it's worth, Bryce, Paulie really does like you. Not just because you're beautiful. And she doesn't think you're stupid."

"Well, she does now, I bet," he said. "Anyway, I just wondered how she's doing. I called her the other day and said I hoped we were still friends."

"What did she say?"

Bryce fiddled with a button on his shirt. "She said I had some growing up to do. But she was really nice about it, too. She didn't lecture me."

"Do you think she has a point?"

"Probably." He sighed. "Well. I should go. See you, Colleen." He walked away, and Colleen couldn't help feeling a little sorry for him.

"So, hotshot."

She looked behind her, and there stood Lucas. "Spaniard." The slow curl of warmth unfurled in her stomach.

"You busy later?" he said, pulling on his shirt. Pity.

"I'm always busy," she murmured.

"You want to come over when you're not? Set my apartment on fire this time?"

"Is that a metaphor for sex?"

"Mmm-hmm."

"Then yes."

He grabbed her, gave her a quick, hard kiss, copped a feel and went off, smiling over his shoulder.

Le sigh.

Fifteen minutes later, when Team Menopause had been wrangled out (and Levi had ticketed Carol for parking in front of a hydrant), Mom gave Rufus his third piece of bacon, put her hands on her hips and gave Colleen a look. "So? Are you staying or what?"

"Aw. That's so sweet, Mom. Why? You have plans?"

"As a matter of fact, yes." Rufus stole a fourth bacon strip, then licked Mom's hand.

"Strip clubs with Carol?"

"No, I have a date."

"Stan, Stan the Hairy Man getting a second chance?"

"No, that's over. He sent me a picture of his junk, and if you thought his back was hairy—"

"Hail Mary, full of grace—"

"Oh, stop."

"You stop. Please. I beg you to stop."

"Fine." Her mother looked at her watch. "I do have a date, and you must have plans with that Lucas. Are you getting married, you two?"

"We're in a purely physical relationship right now."

Her mom raised an eyebrow. "Sure."

Colleen shrugged, looking away. "I don't know, Mom. I'm not looking too far down the road."

"Carpe diem and all that?" Mom asked.

"Exactly. Don't eat tuna."

Mom gave a faint smile. "Well, off with you. Time to go. Get out. Bye, honey. Don't forget your dog." She walked Colleen to the front door. "You never come over anymore."

"It's hard to feel welcome when you're about to hurl me down your front steps—" The doorbell rang. "Could this be the mystery man?" Colleen exclaimed. She opened the front door. "Hi, I'm the daughter." Her smile froze, then dropped. "But I guess you already knew that."

Her father stood on the stoop, holding a bouquet of flowers.

"This isn't going to end well," Colleen said.

IT WAS UNEXPECTED, her parents told her. Early days yet. Just testing the waters. But obviously they had a history.

"I know you have a history!" Colleen snapped. "I *am* your history!"

It was so frickin' weird to have them both in the newly renovated yoga studio/artist garrett/greenroom/whatever the heck Lucas had built. The last time they'd been there all together was when Dad had stonily informed them about the Tail and her pregnancy, Mom sobbing hysterically, Connor white-faced.

Connor, at least, was at the bar. Lucky bastard.

"I thought you'd be happy about this," Dad said.

Colleen eyed him, started to speak, then stopped. "I don't know how to feel," she said. "You can't just undo everything, Dad. You have Savannah now. Ten years have passed. And are you and Mom together? Or are you just jealous because she started dating?"

He looked at Mom, whose expression didn't betray much. "I've always loved your mother."

Colleen snorted.

"It's true."

"Loved her enough to cheat on her. Loved her enough to make her a laughingstock while you and your disgustingly young wife moved to a bigger house in the same town because you didn't even have the decency to move ten miles away, enough to—"

"Okay, Colleen, we know where you stand," Mom said. "I appreciate your concern and understand you have to express your emotions, but maybe you could do this in a more positive and healthy way."

"You need to stop buying those self-help books."

"I've found that kickboxing works well."

Colleen sighed. "I have to go see Gramp. Your father, Dad, in case you forgot. Come on, Rufus."

It would be nice, she thought as she drove to her shift at Rushing Creek, to have a normal family. Like Faith—the three siblings, the perfect father, the lovely stepmother, a niece, a nephew. Instead, she had her whackadoo parents, a stepmother who wore clothes in the style of Child Prostitute and a mute grandfather whose poor body just wouldn't give out. She had Savannah, at least, and Connor.

And maybe she had Lucas, too.

But that was a dangerous thought. For ten years, she'd done pretty well not getting her heart broken, and not breaking anyone's. And not heartbroken...not *ruined*...that was a whole lot better than the alternative.

CHAPTER TWENTY-THREE

A FEW NIGHTS LATER, Colleen twisted her hair up, pulled down a few wisps and put on her Swarovski crystal earrings that Con had given her for their birthday in a rare fit of thoughtful metrosexuality. Tonight, she wore a long red dress (because you know what they say about women in red dresses), high in front and low in back, the fabric falling in a silky rush to her toes. It was a halter top secured at the back of her neck, so hopefully Lucas could give one tug later on, when they were alone, and remove said dress in a hurry. Or a not-hurry. Nice and slow. His mouth could follow the fabric…and hopefully, he hadn't shaved today, because she quite loved the scrape of his beard against her skin, the contrast of his smooth, full mouth, the hot, wet slide—

"You almost ready?" Connor bellowed up the laundry chute, which served as a magical portal between their apartments.

"I've been ready for twenty minutes," she lied. "Are *you* ready? Are we picking up your date? You may as well tell me who she is."

"She's not coming."

"Connor! I hate you."

"I hate you more," he said, grinning up the chute. "Get in the car."

She dropped her wet towel on his head, closed the

chute door. "Bye, pal," she said to Rufus, who was mournfully chewing his plastic bone. "I love you more than Connor. A lot more." With that, she went downstairs, the heels of her strappilicious sandals tapping away.

THE BARN AT Blue Heron Vineyard looked incredible this night, the sky a beautiful slate blue, fairy lights in the trees, and the flowers! Hydrangeas everywhere, and ivory roses—Laura Boothby had outdone herself. Candles flickered, and the wine-bottle light sconces glowed, and it was so romantic and beautiful that Colleen found herself getting choked up.

Good for Honor, going all out for her wedding. She deserved it…all those years of living with her dad, holding down the fort and running the corporate end of Blue Heron Vineyard. Most of the town did business with Honor, who would make a fine president if the mood ever struck, and everyone had a soft spot for Tom, the transplanted Brit who was so devoted to Charlie, the teenager who was his best man. Especially her own self, who had met Tom his first night in town this past winter. Sure enough, Tom gave her a grin and a wave.

Aha! Connor was talking to Jessica Dunn. "Hey, Jess!" Colleen said. "Are you Connor's mystery woman? If so, we should talk."

"Hail Mary, full of grace," Connor muttered.

"It's nice to see you, too, Colleen," Jess said drily.

"That's a yes, isn't it? I knew it. Listen. I'll make a great sister-in-law, you can put that in the plus column to help balance out Connor's many flaws. And I want you to know I've been dropping hints about you for years."

"We're not dating," Jess said.

"Damn!" Colleen said. "Well, you have my blessing if you change your mind. Just saying."

They took a seat close to the front; Jessica worked at Blue Heron, after all.

And so did Mom. All the Blue Heron staff, full- and part-time, had been invited, but Mom "had plans." And *plans* probably meant something with Dad. Something icky.

She hadn't told Connor about their parents in a rare episode of twin secrecy. First of all, he'd be furious. Secondly...well, she kind of hoped this was a flash in the pan. Mom would sort it out and realize Dad was still...still...whatever.

But of course, Colleen could relate.

How many people want another chance with their first love?

Speaking of first loves... She stood on her tiptoes and scanned the crowd.

"Looking for me?" came that voice. Busted.

"No. I'm looking for Mr. Holland. I've been in love with him since I was eight." She turned, her breath stopping. "You look unfairly handsome, Spaniard," she said, and yes, her voice shook a little.

He didn't answer, just let his gaze drift down her body, then back up, his eyes dark as...as...as coffee or something, she wasn't doing too well in the rational thought department. Suffice it to say, one look from him was reducing her to a puddle.

He took her hand and kissed it. Soon, Colleen thought, she'd be dead of lust. And what a way to go.

They took a seat with the other guests. Tom and Charlie stood up at the front with Reverend Fisk and a shorter, older version of Tom who must be his dad, all the way from England.

Then the music started, Jack Holland walked Mrs. Johnson down the aisle, and the bridesmaids followed—Faith, Pru and Pru's daughter, all looking beautiful in shades of lavender.

And then came Honor on her father's arm, and Colleen glanced at Tom. It was her favorite thing to do, to see the groom's face when he first saw his bride, and Tom did not disappoint. He looked stunned, then covered his mouth with one hand, and, bless him, welled up. Charlie, his best man, put his arm around Tom's shoulders and smiled.

Honor looked amazing, and Colleen felt a little proud of that, having done her makeup earlier that afternoon. She glowed, she really did, smiling at Tom, those nice dimples of hers. She looked so in love that tears came to Colleen's eyes, too. And her dress was fantastic—an ivory, Regency-style gown, utterly romantic and soft, unstructured, flowing softly to her toes. She wore her mom's pearls, Honor's trademark jewelry, and matching earrings, all very subtle and classic and lovely. And hey! She was barefoot, her pink-polished toes peeping out from underneath the dress. Very nice touch, Coll had to admit.

Then Mr. Holland kissed the bride and shook Tom's hand, wiped his own eyes and sat down, and the ceremony began.

Lucas held her hand throughout, and try as she might, Colleen couldn't help a few wedding thoughts of her own. Marriage thoughts, even better—the ordinary, wonderful days that she and Lucas could have… maybe in that little stone house Carol had mentioned the other day, waking up late on a Sunday morning, making French toast and drinking coffee on the slate patio. A black-haired baby or three. It would be so wonderful.

Then Tom kissed his wife and the crowd cheered.

All night long, Lucas was a perfect date. They didn't talk about Bryce and Paulie, which was nice, him not pointing out that he'd been right all along. He flirted with her, kept giving her those hot Latin looks. He danced with her (not the paso doble, as Colleen suggested, making him laugh, but he was pretty good nonetheless).

"How's Joe doing?" she asked as they danced to Louis Armstrong's "What a Wonderful World." "I saw him at the hospital the other day."

Lucas's eyes darkened. "Not too well. The cancer's pretty fast-moving."

Her eyes grew wet. "I'm so sorry."

"It doesn't look like he'll get to divorce Didi."

He'd told her about that. Five attorneys had said the same thing. Colleen put her head against his shoulder. Poor Lucas, about to lose someone else. "You know what you should do?" she said, pulling back to look at him. "Threaten her reputation. She'd hate for anyone to know Joe wanted a divorce, even if he couldn't get one. Especially Bryce. Maybe she'd do it if you said you'd keep it quiet. She could spin it however she wanted after he…passes away."

Those pirate eyes smiled, and a second later, his mouth followed. "You're a genius, Colleen O'Rourke."

"I get that all the time," she said.

"I bet you do."

"I also hear 'extremely pretty' and 'quite hot in the sack.'"

"I'd attest to that."

"So would—"

"I don't want to hear about that," he growled. "The only thing I want to hear is that you never got over me."

"Well. You can think that if you want."

"It's true."

She smiled. "Let's say that it is for the sake of your huge Latin ego." She put her head on his shoulder again. Guilt twinged in her knees, and her smile faded.

She *had* slept with other men. Not that many, but if Lucas knew—

"Ladies and gentlemen, it's time for the best man's toast," the DJ said, and any further thoughts were cut off. She was with Lucas at a wedding, and he loved her. She was almost certain. She pushed any other, more complicated thoughts aside.

They toasted the bride and groom and had cake, and after Connor and she had done the electric slide, and when Emmaline Neal (St. Germain and vodka) had caught the bouquet, Lucas finally turned to her and said, "Come home with me."

It was a command…a velvety promise of deliciousness.

Colleen grabbed her brother's arm. "Walk Rufus for me?" she asked.

"Oh, gross. Listen, Campbell," Connor growled. "Break her heart, and I'll kill you. I mean it. The last time, you just—"

"Okay, okay, thank you for sharing," Colleen said. "Bye, Con."

They said goodbye to the happy couple and the Hollands, and then went off into the soft, sweet night air. A rumble of thunder came from across the lake, and a flicker of lightning lit the low-bellied clouds. Rain later tonight.

"It's nice that you and Connor are still so close," Lucas said as they drove down the Hill into town.

"Oh, yeah. How could we not be?"

"The flight from Chicago's just over an hour."

"I remember." Buffalo-Niagara to O'Hare—how many times had she made that flight?

But wait a sec. What was he saying?

They were here, in front of the opera house. Lucas got out, opened her door and smiled. She tried to return it.

The flight being an hour…as in she could visit? Visit him? Visit Connor?

Well. They could talk about it inside. Or not. Maybe this was the exact conversation they should avoid.

They walked up to the second floor, and Lucas turned to her and kissed her, his hand on her neck. "I had a very nice time tonight," he murmured.

"Your nice time is about to get better," she said.

"Glad to hear it." He opened the door, stood back. He always had such nice manners. Those parents of his had done a good job.

She went in, then leaped back in surprise, a little squeak escaping her. Someone was already here.

Someone blonde. Someone female.

Someone pregnant.

"Ellen," Lucas said. "I didn't expect you."

CHAPTER TWENTY-FOUR

AH, SHIT. The last thing Lucas wanted was the tension that instantly coiled between the two women, but there it was in the middle of the room, like a snake.

"Anyone want something to drink?" he asked. Very uncool to have his pregnant ex-wife sitting on his couch. "Colleen?" Her face was white.

"I'm fine, thanks."

Ellen stood up. "I already helped myself." She looked at Colleen. "I'm Ellen Camp—Forbes," she said. "We met when you visited Lucas in college."

"Yes, I—I remember. You're expecting. I didn't hear that. Congratulations."

Ellen smiled. "Thanks. My fiancé and I are really thrilled."

"You're engaged?"

"Yes. Getting married September first, the twins are due in late November."

"Twins?" Colleen squeaked. "Wow. Mazel tov."

"Thanks." She smiled. "Lucas, I'm really sorry to be here. There was a screwup at the bed-and-breakfast, and they double-booked my room. The other couple was already there. I called you, but you weren't picking up. The innkeeper knows the owner of this building, so she let me in when I told her who I was." She paused. "I thought I could stay in your second bedroom for tonight."

Great. Lucas glanced at Colleen, who stood there, silent. Not good. Not good at all.

"Yeah," he said, suddenly realizing he hadn't spoken. "Of course you can stay here."

"I'm obviously interrupting your plans. I'm sorry." She smiled again at Colleen.

Colleen seemed to snap out of her funk. "No, no, that's…it's fine. I'll talk to you soon, Lucas. Uh, Ellen, it was nice to see you." With that, she turned and left. Fast.

Lucas glanced at his ex-wife. "Be back in a few minutes. I'll just walk her home."

"Take your time. I'm really sorry about this."

"No, no. These things happen. Make yourself at home."

By the time he got out on the street, Colleen was halfway across the green. He ran to catch up to her, took her arm. She shook him off.

"So your ex is coming to visit. Thanks for the warning."

"Colleen, slow down. It's not a big deal."

"Really? It is to me. And hey, she's pregnant. Wow." He pulled her to a stop. "*Mía,* don't—"

She made a hissing noise. "Now is not the time for *mía,* Lucas."

"Why? What's wrong?"

She stopped in front of the Civil War monument and sighed the universally recognized *men are idiots* sigh of the female. "Lucas. First of all, the woman you threw me over for is here."

"I didn't—"

"And second of all, she's engaged. And pregnant."

"Right. Why is that a problem?"

Another disgusted look. "So you only...wanted..." Well, shit. She was crying.

"Colleen," he breathed. "Sweetheart."

"Oh, shut up! Don't sweet-talk me! How dare you sweet-talk me! So she moved on, she found someone else, she's having a baby—and even then, did you ever think about me? No! Not until I was directly in your line of vision."

"That's so far from the truth, it's almost funny."

"Really? How long have you been divorced?"

"Officially?"

"Yes! Officially!"

"Two years." He paused. "And three months."

"So why didn't you call me two years and three months ago? Or two years ago? Or a year ago? Or six months ago? Why is it only now, when Joe needed you and Ellen is breeding twins with some other guy, that you even bothered to think of me again?"

Women. He could really use a decoder ring where they were concerned. "It wasn't because I didn't think of you. It was because I didn't feel like I had any—"

"Don't bullshit a bullshitter, Lucas. You know how many times I've seen men sling those smarmy lines? A trillion and six, okay?"

"Colleen, don't make this into something it's not. Look. We're together now, you and I. Aren't we?"

"I'm not the one with the pregnant woman in my apartment, Lucas!"

An older couple was walking their dog and gave him a sharp look. "Everything okay there, Collie?" the man asked.

"Not really, Bob, but thank you!" she called. "Hi, Sue. Hi, Muffin."

Lucas waited until the couple was inside. "Yes, Ellen is in my apartment. Should I ask her to sleep in the alley?"

"You—I—it's—you know what? Bite me. Go to your ex-wife who's perfect in every way and not messy or emotional or just a stupid bartender."

"You're not a stupid bartender. Colleen. Settle down."

"You know why I think you're with me, Lucas? Because I'm here. You're here for your uncle, you're sad, and hey, what's this, it's that girl you used to be with, and lookee here! She's still single! And easy, apparently, because it only took you what? Three weeks to get into my pants?"

"Four plus."

"Four plus. Wow. I'm a regular chastity belt. All I am is convenient, Lucas. Your wife divorced you and found someone else, and only now are you interested in me. And you're not even here for me. And I knew that. I'm an idiot."

"Colleen, this is ridiculous." Poor choice of words, perhaps, because she answered with her middle finger, then turned and stomped away.

"You're not convenient," he called at her retreating back. "You're extremely inconvenient, Colleen!" Nothing. "I'll call you tomorrow when you've had time to calm down."

And again, not the smartest thing to say. This time her gesture was more creative.

With a sigh, Lucas scrubbed a hand through his hair. This had been a pretty fantastic night until fifteen minutes ago.

Well. Ellen was indeed back at his apartment, and she was an attorney, and his dying uncle needed an attorney, and Colleen could just...just...

She couldn't really believe she was convenient.

He ran the two blocks to her apartment. There was a light in her window, though the first floor was dark. Hopefully, her brother wasn't about to come out and beat him up.

"Colleen!" he yelled up at her window.

No answer, though the giant dog's head appeared in the window.

"Colleen!"

"Quiet, or I'll call the police!" she barked. "This is a nice neighborhood." She yanked up the screen and stuck her head out, then glanced next door. "Sorry, Mr. Wong. My idiot boyfriend. Do you have a gun? Just to scare him or maim him slightly."

"Sorry, Colleen," the neighbor called. "I'm antigun."

"That's a pity. Sorry for the noise." She turned back to Lucas. "What?"

"Don't be mad at me, you inconvenient woman."

"I am mad. Leave me alone."

"Can I call you?"

"No. I'm about to start power-eating Ben & Jerry's. Leave me alone."

"What kind?"

The question brought a smile to her lips, which she quickly smothered. "Peanut Butter Cup."

"I like Coffee Heath Bar myself."

"So go get some and choke on it."

He grinned. "Sleep tight, *mía*."

"You're not off the hook just because you're pulling a Romeo, Spaniard. You're about to break my heart again. I can feel it."

"You're wrong."

"Go away." She pulled her head in and lowered the screen. "Call me tomorrow."

BACK AT HIS APARTMENT, Ellen had made herself some scrambled eggs. "Eating for two. I plan to milk that every second of this pregnancy, by the way." She took a bite and smiled. "Sorry about ruining your night. Is she okay?"

"She's fine," he lied.

"Still so beautiful."

He didn't want to talk about Colleen with Ellen.

They had discussed Colleen once before, because to not talk about her, ever, would've made it seem like more. Which it was, but what was he supposed to do? He'd wanted their marriage to work, figured he'd burned bridges with Colleen forever and wasn't going to moon after his high school sweetheart when Ellen had been nothing but open and decent and nice. So he told his wife about Colleen, and said that it was a typical young love situation, very intense until it burned itself out.

He lied, in other words.

"Tell me about Joe," she said, taking out her razor-thin laptop. "How's he doing?"

"He's still getting dialysis," Lucas said. "He…he maybe has a few weeks."

She gave him a small smile. "Okay," she said. "Here's what I've got on the divorce issue." She paused. "My dad misses you, by the way."

Lucas gave a nod. "The Cambria's almost done," he said. "I talked to the interior designers yesterday."

She gave him a tolerant look. "That's not what I'm talking about at all. He loves you like a son, and nothing will change that. Not even Steve."

"No, I guess not."

"Well," she said with a smile. "You'll be back in Chicago soon."

For some reason, the words sounded vaguely...smug.

CHAPTER TWENTY-FIVE

SINCE LUCAS WAS busy with his ex-wife, and Uncle Joe, and Bryce, and the public safety building, and making sure his hair was beautiful and wavy and arrogant and whatever else occupied his time, Colleen did what she always did when she was stressed. She cleaned.

"Oh, shit," Connor said when he saw her scrubbing the bar with her beloved citrus-scented Clorox Clean-Up. "What did he do? Should I kill him?"

"It's tempting," Colleen said. "How's the lovely Jessica? You sure you two aren't dating?"

Connor leaned on the part of the bar she'd already cleaned. "So you don't want to talk about Lucas and how I told you this wouldn't end well, and how—"

"Hey, placenta hog. Just because you were born three minutes sooner doesn't mean you know everything."

"Are you sure? Because I do. Where you're concerned, anyway."

"Hi, guys." Savannah came into the bar dressed in an ill-fitting, too-short skirt and lacy top, Gail's credit card at work, no doubt. Her eyes were swollen and pink. "Mom said I should stay here because she's at the lawyer's." With that, their little sister burst into sobs.

When both Connor and Colleen had said soothing things and àdministered a slab of Rafe's caramel cheesecake, Colleen took Savannah back to her place. Rufus would make her feel better, or die trying.

But Colleen remembered what it had felt like to have her family life crumble, and hell, she'd been a lot older than Savannah. Everything would change for her sister—holidays, weekends, home life, maybe even home. Where was Gail even from? Colleen didn't think it was New York.

She painted her sister's nails (Zombie Skin Gray) and let Savannah do her toenails (Flirtini Fuschia). They watched an episode of *SpongeBob,* and Savannah fell asleep on the couch, Rufus keeping guard.

Poor kid; she was exhausted from crying. Colleen stroked her sister's wispy hair, kissed Rufus on the head and went to the kitchen. She'd make peanut butter cookies, Savannah's favorite.

Being in the kitchen made her recall her cooking fiasco last week. Lucas had cleaned up the entire kitchen while she was sleeping. Forget the roses he'd brought— *that* was romantic.

She wondered what he was doing now.

When the first batch was done, a knock came on the door. It was her stepmother.

"Hi," Colleen said.

"Hi." Gail didn't look so hot. She was dressed in the usual jeans, cut so low you could practically see her cesarean scar, and a cropped, silky shirt. She wore the requisite heels, but there were circles under her eyes. "Connor said she was here."

"Yeah. She's sleeping on the couch. Worn out from crying, I imagine."

"Is that an accusation, Colleen? Because I'll have you know, I don't want this divorce."

"It's not. Come on in. Want a cookie? They're still warm."

Gail gave her a suspicious look, but sat at the table, and Colleen put five cookies on a plate and poured her a glass of milk. "Thanks," Gail muttered.

Colleen took a breath. "Listen, I'm sorry for Savannah's sake that this is happening."

"But not for my sake, of course."

Colleen raised an eyebrow. "No. Not for your sake. Keep in mind that you're the home-wrecking whore who broke my mother's heart ten years ago."

"Sorry I left my scarlet letter at home."

Well. That was surprising—a literary reference from the Tail.

"Don't look so surprised," Gail said. "I can read, you know." She paused, taking a cookie from the plate and breaking it in half. "I think he's seeing someone else."

And of course, Dad *was* seeing someone else, namely Mom. Though Colleen saw doom painted all over that one, there was certainly some poetic justice at work.

Gail put half of a cookie in her mouth and chewed. "I know you hate me, Colleen," she said. "I know I was the other woman. But I love your father. I was very naive ten years ago."

"Really? Because I think you came out of the womb with a calculator in one hand and a pair of Manolo Blahniks in the other."

Gail sighed and ate the other half. "Fine. If you want to think of it that way, go ahead. But it hasn't all been fun, you know. You think I'd choose a guy with two grown kids? You think I wanted to be a slut?"

"Who put the gun to your head, Gail?"

"He didn't tell me he was married. Not for a long time."

Shit. That did sound like her father, didn't it?

"And by then, the damage was done. I was in love with him. He said he was in the process of getting a divorce, and I believed him. And then I got pregnant. I know you don't think so, but I love Savvi. She's everything to me." Much to Colleen's surprise, Gail's eyes filled with tears.

"Then why are you trying to make her into a Barbie doll?" Colleen whispered. "The diets, Gail! The cheerleading and the horrible clothes."

"I want her to be..." Gail's voice trailed off.

"Pretty?" Colleen said.

"She *is* pretty! It's not that. I want her to...belong. To be popular and happy and fit in. She's overweight, Colleen, and you and Connor stuffing her full of nachos and pie and cheeseburgers doesn't help. It just makes me the bad guy. Do you know the statistics on childhood obesity?"

Colleen felt a stab of guilt. "She's not obese, Gail. She's chubby."

"Ten more pounds and she's medically obese, according to her doctor," Gail whispered vehemently. "You like to think of me as the evil stepmother, and you do it very well, but the truth is, I'm trying to keep my daughter healthy. I broil her fish and make her salads and take her for hikes and walks. We don't all have your metabolism."

"But you can't make her into your image, Gail. She's her own person."

"I know that! I've taken her to gymnastics and tap and karate, and the only thing she likes is baseball, which isn't exactly an aerobic sport. Cheerleading would get her moving, at least." She grabbed another cookie. "And now she's stress-eating. And so am I. These are fantastic." Gail gave a muffled sob, spewing crumbs, and tears spilled over.

Colleen handed Gail a napkin and took out the next batch of cookies, moving slowly. Okay, yeah. Savannah was overweight, and maybe a little more than just chubby. And Colleen *did* like to spoil her with the food she never got at home (and so did Connor). Taking her for a swim now and again might be a better way to spend time with their sister, instead of just movies and popcorn and Milk Duds (though if you couldn't have Milk Duds once in a while, what was the point of living?).

Still, she wasn't used to being wrong. It was an itchy feeling.

"What can I do to help, Gail?" she asked as Gail polished off the last cookie.

Gail didn't look at her, only folded up her napkin into a tiny square. "Maybe you could just…put in a good word about me once in a while. With Savannah. I don't want her to feel like there are battle lines, the O'Rourkes on one side, and me on the other."

Shit. That was exactly how it had always been, after all. Not that Gail had helped the cause, but still. Connor and Colleen had never befriended the Tail and never wanted to.

Maybe Gail had always clung to Dad not just to prove she was the hottest thing on earth, but because she didn't have anyone else. And Colleen Margaret Mary O'Rourke, famed for being friends with every living creature in Manningsport, had never once offered friendship.

Colleen cleared her throat. "You bet. You know how much I love Savannah. I'll make sure she doesn't feel caught in the middle." She paused. "And I'll make sure we throw some vegetables her way, too."

"Thanks." Gail wiped her eyes and looked down at the table.

"But let her stay in baseball. She's so good, Gail. She's scholarship good. Drop the cheerleading—I'll take her to kickboxing with me. Maybe Tom Barlow will let her join his boxing club, even though it's for high school kids. I'll talk to him."

"I appreciate that," Gail whispered. "Can I have more of these?" She pointed to the empty plate.

"Coming up," Colleen said.

Yep. Savannah's mother needed a friend, and even though it went against God and nature, Colleen was going to be that friend.

BUSINESS AT O'ROURKE'S was freakishly slow that night, and thank God for it because it had been mobbed for the past two months. Everyone needed a break. Colleen sent Monica home, put Annie behind the bar to serve the four people there, and poked her head in the kitchen. Her brother was cleaning the grill.

"Close up, brother mine," she said. "And then come join the girls and me so we don't have to talk about you behind your back."

Faith, her sister Pru and Emmaline Neal were sitting at the Girls Night Out table, and Levi and Jeremy Lyon were in a booth, nursing beers, though Levi kept shooting his wife those hot sleepy looks of his.

"Levi, enough!" Colleen called. "The testosterone

is choking me, okay? No wonder Faithie's knocked up. Jeremy, can't you distract him?"

"I'll do my best, Coll," Jeremy said.

"You should try working with him," Emmaline said. "He calls her constantly. 'How you feeling, babe? You need anything, sweetheart?' It sickens me." She smiled at Faith, then looked over at Levi. "You're a horrible boss," she added.

"Then quit," he answered easily. "Jeremy would hire you in a heartbeat."

"That's true, Emmaline," Jer said. "I pay better, too."

"But can I carry a gun in a doctor's office?" she asked.

"It does tend to send the wrong message," Jeremy said.

"And speaking of love," Faith said.

"Oh, are we gonna talk about Carl and me?" Prudence asked. "I have to say, doing it in a car was a lot more awkward than I remembered. My back started to spasm when he—"

Faith put her hand over her sister's mouth.

"When he what?" Colleen asked.

"Don't answer," Faith said. "I wanted to talk about Paulie. What happened with her and Bryce, Colleen?"

Colleen sighed. "One of my rare failures."

"Bryce Campbell?" Jessica asked.

"Yeah."

"He's kind of a slut, isn't he?" Emmaline said.

"Yep."

"Poor Paulie," Faith said. "She's so nice." She sighed. "Well, how are things with you and Lucas, Coll?"

"Let's talk about Connor instead, how's that? Does

anyone know who he's seeing? Other than his blow-up doll?"

"I'm right here," Connor said.

"Really. What a shock." At that moment, her phone rang. She looked at it. "It's Lucas. I'm going to make him wait because I'm just not the type to throw over my friends for a guy— Con, where are you going?"

"I'm leaving. I have to call my mystery woman."

"I'm tapping your phone."

"I have to go, too," Emmaline said. "*Ink Wars* is on. See you around."

"Me, too," Prudence said. "It's RPG night at the Vanderbeek household. Abby's sleeping over at Helena's house, thank God."

"What's RPG?" Faith asked.

"Role playing game," Pru said blithely. "Professor Snape and McGonagall." She gave a lurid wink.

"*Harry Potter?* You're ruining *Harry Potter?*" Faith yelped. "Is nothing sacred anymore?"

"Not ruining anything," Pru said. "Enhancing."

"I just threw up in my mouth," Faith said.

"Have fun, Pru," Colleen said as Pru, married for twenty-some-odd years, sauntered off. "You have to admire the creativity," she added.

"I admire nothing," Faith said. "So. You and Lucas. Spill. Why didn't you take his call?"

"I'm mad at him."

"Why?"

Colleen didn't answer right away. "I don't know," she admitted. "I just… I wonder if we're only sleeping together because we're in the same town. Because it's convenient. His ex-wife's in town, and I understand that she was part of his family for years, and he was part of hers, but I'm still seething with jealousy. Oh, and she's engaged and pregnant, but she and Lucas are still best friends forever, apparently. She's staying at his apartment."

"Oh, dear," Faith said.

"Exactly. That's bad, right?"

"No, I was just murmuring over the seething part." She paused. "Why is she staying with him?"

"Because the Black Swan double-booked."

"Oh, yeah. They did that in January, when Liza and Mike came out for the wedding, remember? Anyway." She took a sip of water. "Is he staying here after Joe… passes away?"

"No." The thought of him leaving made her throat clamp shut.

"Would you move to—"

"No." She took a shaky breath. "Not that he's asked. I mean, we haven't talked about it, because…well, shit, Faith, I don't know. I'm afraid. The truth is, I'm ridiculously inexperienced with serious relationships. Tell me what to do."

"Me? I've had two relationships, and they're sitting in that booth over there."

"Well, what do I know?" Colleen whispered. "I'm the queen of flirting but I haven't had a boyfriend in years. I've fixed up dozens of people, and I give out advice like Dr. Phil, and what has that ever gotten me? I'm thirty-one years old, I've been in love once, and I'm utterly terrified that Lucas is going to break my heart, same as last time."

And much to her surprise, Colleen burst into tears.

CHAPTER TWENTY-SIX

"UNCLE JOE, you handsome devil." Stephanie bent down and gave Joe a big hug, then kissed his cheek and wiped off the red lip imprint. "Girls, remember Uncle Joe?"

The older girls gave out hugs with good-natured duty. Chloe, on the other hand, stared him down. "I'm sorry you're dying," she said solemnly.

Didi looked as though she'd just stepped in a Rufus-sized pile of dog shit. Joe, on the other hand, laughed. "Thanks, honey. For a minute, I thought I'd already died, because you girls are as pretty as angels. You, too, Ste-phie!"

Lucas's sister and kids—and Frank and Grace Forbes—had flown in that morning and taken a limo from the airport straight here, to the park by the lake, where you could reserve picnic areas and grills.

"Frank, Grace, I would've been *happy* to have had this at our house," Didi simpered, shooting Lucas a death glare. "If only I'd known you were coming. Of course, our place is nothing like yours, but we think it's sweet, and I would've *loved* to have had you." That hadn't been the case when Didi thought it was just going to be the Campbells, of course, and Lucas had taken a small modi-cum of pleasure in denying his aunt the opportunity to kiss up to his former in-laws.

"This is perfect," Grace said. "Ellen, honey, sit down and drink something."

The girls ran and splashed; Lucas had bought some little balsa-wood boats at the hardware store, and in the face of good old-fashioned fun, the electronic devices were cheerfully forgotten. Didi cooed over Ellen and tried to act rich, mentioning her Coach bag and how you had to pay for nice things, of course Grace knew all about that, no, it wasn't as if Didi and Joe were anywhere nearly as comfortable as Grace and Frank, of course not, but they did all right, not that she was bragging, but New York wasn't a cheap place to live, and she was smart with her finances, not Forbes-smart, of course not, no, but she admired quality. Ellen caught his eye and gave the slightest grin; both she and her mother were too polite to do anything more than that.

Frank and Joe talked and laughed, Joe doing his best to act robust. He'd sleep like the dead after this.

An unfortunate choice of words.

"Get out of the way, little brother," Stephanie said with an ungentle shove. "I always made these better than you." She took the spatula from him and checked the foil-wrapped sandwiches he was grilling—chicken and ham and pickles, replicas of the cubanos Joe always used to get from Diego's in the old neighborhood when he'd visit.

"Aren't these bad for him?" Steph asked quietly.

"Yep."

She nodded, and a tear fell onto the grill with a small hiss. "So how much time has he got?"

"The dialysis can keep him indefinitely," Lucas answered. "But the cancer's spreading, and he wants to get while the getting's good. Or at least, before it gets horrific."

"Can't blame him, I guess." Steph swallowed thickly, then added more mustard to the rolls. "How's Bryce holding up?" she asked, nodding over at their cousin, who was hurling the girls into the water, much to their shrieking delight.

"He's Bryce. He won't talk about Joe actually dying, and he won't let Joe talk about it, either."

Steph's mouth wobbled. "I wasn't as close to Uncle Joe as you were, obviously, but he was—is—so sweet. I wasn't ready for how old he looked." She wiped her eyes subtly, then waved to Mercedes, who had eyes like a hawk. "When are we having the talk?"

"A little later."

For now, Joe could eat a few bites of regular food, take a few sips of beer, and be with his family. There was salad and coleslaw and ribs and watermelon, and chocolate chip cookies from the smiling woman at the bakery, as well as a cooler full of iced teas, soda and beers, and a bottle of wine for Grace; a Blue Heron dry Riesling, sold to him by Colleen's mother this very morning.

A couple hours later, when they had all eaten and Joe had taken a nap on the lounge chair in the shade, Lucas asked Bryce to take the girls out on one of the tour boats that ran every two hours.

"Don't you want to come, Uncle Lucas?" Chloe asked.

"I'll stay here and talk to the grown-ups," he said.

"Then I want to stay, too."

"We're talking about banking. It's very boring."

"I love banking."

"Good," he said. "It's high time you had a job. But for now, off you go."

"Chloe, don't be a twit," Mercedes said, taking her little sister by the hand. "We're being ostracized."

"Nice word," Lucas said.

"Thanks. I'm in AP English."

"Yes. You've told me seven or eight times now." He winked at her, and she smiled as she walked away.

"Come on, girls," Bryce said, scooping up a twin under each arm. "I hope you don't fall overboard. You know there's a monster in this lake, and it *loves* little girls." They shrieked obligingly, and if Bryce wondered why he was the only adult going out on the lake, he didn't ask about it.

When they were off, Lucas got Ellen another bottle of water. Didi was asking about Ellen and Steve's wedding and trying to finagle an invitation in her unsubtle way. "Will you have many guests? Oh, I just love Chicago in September! I haven't been since that wonderful party your parents had in—"

"Why don't we get down to business?" he interrupted, sitting between his sister and Ellen. Joe gave him a nod and folded his hands. "Didi, I'll get right to it. Joe would like a divorce."

Her sycophantic smile froze, and her head jerked back a fraction. "That's…that's…" She shot a nervous glance at Frank and Grace, who stared back impassively. "Very funny, Lucas."

"It's not a joke."

"Of course it is! I wouldn't divorce my sick husband!"

"I want to divorce you, however," Joe said.

Didi's face was white, and for a second, Lucas almost felt bad for her…right up until he remembered that she'd stuck Joe in that dark, windowless room where he used to sleep.

"Didi," Ellen said, her hand on her stomach, "New York State law says that a couple has to be separated for six months before they get a divorce."

"He'll be dead in six months," Didi said. "Probably long before."

Grace Forbes closed her eyes briefly, the only indication of her disapproval.

"We know a judge who'll push it through, so long as you don't contest it," Ellen continued.

The Forbes name was far-reaching, after all.

"I *will* contest it!" Didi snapped. "What would people think if I divorced Joe a month before he died? Is this some ploy to cut me out of your will, Joe? Not that I need your pathetic life insurance—"

"My money's in a trust for Bryce until he gets married," Joe said calmly. "Lucas is in charge of it until then."

"I doubt very much he'll ever get married. He's not the type. And a trust fund? For twenty thousand dollars? Why bother?"

And so Joe told her how Apple had bought his new app for $1.5 million.

Didi's face bloomed with red. "I'll fight this," she hissed.

"The will is iron-clad," Ellen said calmly, pushing her blond hair behind her ears. "And remember that prenup? You don't get any proceeds from Joe's intellectual property. No judge in the world would have a problem with that."

In other words, the prenup that had forced Joe to stay with Didi was now biting her in the ass. It had a certain karmic justice to it.

"Didi," Lucas said, "Joe's going to file the papers

one way or another, even if he dies before a divorce can go through. If you fight it, I'm guessing that everyone will wonder why that nice Joe Campbell wanted to get away from you so badly."

"But—"

"But if you grant him an uncontested divorce," Lucas said, "he'll keep it quiet, and no one will have to know. Not even Bryce."

"So? I think Bryce *should* know that his father is behaving like an ass!"

"Didi," Grace said in her gentle voice, "I understand how shocking this is. And honestly, I think it's awfully bighearted of you to even consider it—"

"I'm *not* considering it!"

"—granting the father of your son his last wish. Even if it seems hard to comprehend, since you've been such a loving wife all these years."

The sarcasm was lost on Didi.

"But if this is Joe's last wish, it seems so...*uncouth* to disregard it."

Didi's eyes flickered. Colleen had been right. Reputation was everything to Didi.

This was, of course, why Grace and Frank were here. That, and to say goodbye to Joe.

"And of course, we'd still think of you as part of the family," Grace went on, giving Lucas a wry glance. "We'd hope you'd still come visit for New Year's and such."

Didi's expression turned speculative.

She'd always loved that New Year's Eve party, after all. She glanced at Joe, and Lucas could practically see her doing the math. Bryce would have his own money, enough for his own place. He wouldn't live in his mother's basement anymore, not with more than a cool million in the bank.

But if she got invited to the famous Forbes New Year's Eve party, she could find some rich guy. After all, there was no accounting for some people's taste.

"It's stressful, I'm sure," Frank said. "Once all the paperwork is filed and the dust has settled, you should plan on spending some time at the lake house for a little rest."

That sealed the deal. The Forbes lake house was more like a compound, acres and acres of waterfront property in Wisconsin, several wooden boats and a live-in housekeeper. Triumph shone in Didi's pale eyes. "That's so generous of you, Frank," she said. "I'd love that. But only if it's what Joe wants."

LATER, WHEN THE details had been agreed on and Didi had left, and after Steph took the girls back to Lucas's apartment, where they'd be spending the night, and Ellen and her parents had headed back to Chicago, Lucas wheeled Joe down to the dock, Bryce alongside him.

"Push me in," Joe said merrily. "Save me the trouble."

"Dad, don't even joke about that. You look great. What are we doing down here?"

"I thought we'd take a sail," Lucas said. "If you don't mind going out on the water again, Bryce."

"No, not a bit. I love boats."

Carol Robinson owned a rarely used sailboat, and when Lucas asked if he could take his uncle out on it, she only charged him a kiss on the cheek. "Use it, use it!" she said. "That Joe is a nice man."

He and Bryce lifted Joe into the boat, which was a sweet little sloop. Lucas wasn't a great sailor, but he was good enough to take the boat out; Colleen had taught him back in the day. The past couple of years, when his divorce created too many solitary nights, he'd taken some lessons, too.

The sun was setting, that time of evening when daylight seemed reluctant to go, and filled the air with golden light. Joe sat in the bow and immediately closed his eyes, Lucas in the back with his hand on the rudder, his cousin next to him. The sails caught the wind and the boat slid out into the deep blue water.

Lucas looked at Bryce. "Everything okay?" he asked.

"Sure. Just… I don't know."

Maybe the reality of his father's condition was dawning on him. It was hard to believe it hadn't yet.

"I miss Paulie," Bryce said.

Not what Lucas expected to hear. "She's a good person."

"Yeah. Doesn't judge and stuff."

They rounded Meering Point. A bunch of kids were playing under a waterfall, their gleeful shrieks carrying on the wind. "Bryce," Lucas said after a minute, "you ever think you sell yourself short?"

Bryce gave him a questioning look.

"You've got more going on than you think," Lucas continued. "You're like your dad. Heart of gold, not a mean bone in your body. Why do you think you're so good with animals? And kids? You saw how the girls love you."

"Yeah, they're great." He picked at a hole in his jeans.

"Maybe you need to believe in yourself a little more."

"Easier said than done," Bryce said.

Lucas paused. "Why?"

Bryce shrugged and glanced at his father, who appeared to be sound asleep. "I don't know, Lucas. Maybe because I'll never be as good as you."

Lucas blinked.

"I mean, not that there's a competition. You have a great job—"

"Which I'm leaving."

"—you married a Forbes—"

"And divorced a Forbes."

"—and you never left Chicago. Dad thinks you walk on water." He paused. "That's why he sent for you. To take care of me, right?"

"Well, not the only reason. But yeah, he's worried about you. He wants to see you settled."

Bryce swallowed. "Settled how? Married with kids?"

"I think you could start with getting a job, buddy."

"Doing what?"

"Doing anything. No shame in hard work." The boat was really skipping along now, the waves slapping sharply against the hull.

"My mom says I should wait till I have something I'm totally into. No need to do grunt work."

"You can start out with grunt work. I did. Lots of successful people did. Right? Paulie's father used to clean chicken shit, if you believe his commercials."

Bryce pondered that. "Don't you think it's better to be unemployed and kinda cool, or have a job doing grunt work?"

"Bryce. You're thirty-one years old. Being unemployed is not *cool*. Get a job."

He nodded. "Yeah, I guess." He paused. "Maybe Paulie would think…well. That I grew up a little."

"Do it. Show her you're worth a second chance," Lucas said.

"I don't even know if I like her that way."

"Have you ever missed a girl you'd broken up with before?"

"Nope." Bryce glanced at him and smiled. "But Paulie's not my usual type."

"What *is* your usual type?"

"Slutty and beautiful. The fling type."

Lucas laughed. Colleen had said something like that, too. "Maybe it's time to try something else, then. Have some faith in yourself, Bryce. You can be good at something other than video games and dog adoptions, you know." He squeezed his cousin on the shoulder, and Bryce smiled.

"Yeah. You're right, dude. Thanks for the pep talk."

"It's what I'm here for. Now go sit with your father."

Joe woke up as his son sat next to him, and he put his arm around Bryce's shoulders. Bryce kissed his father's head, and the two sat in the breeze, the sun making the water quiver in the shimmering light.

Lucas turned his head, sensing that this was the goodbye Joe so wanted with his son.

He would've given a lot to have been able to say goodbye to his own father this way…or any way. To have felt his father's arm around him once more, to have held his hand when he finally slipped away, instead of knowing he died alone on a cold cement floor in the prison basement in a state he'd never seen except through bars.

He would've given anything to have been able to just have seen his father's face once more.

But at least Bryce would have that. And if Lucas couldn't have been there for his father, he was here for Joe.

CHAPTER TWENTY-SEVEN

ONCE AGAIN, Colleen was indulging in a little Clorox therapy, this time in the ladies' room of O'Rourke's.

Things hadn't been right between her and Lucas since two weeks ago, when Ellen the Perfect had swept into town in all her pregnant radiance.

They weren't fighting. It was more like there was a tremor in the Force.

Because a judge had apparently been a member of the same secret society at Yale as Frank Forbes, Joe Campbell was now quietly divorced. Lucas had thanked her for the idea…but still, it couldn't have been done without perfect Ellen. Not that Colleen was insecure or jealous (cough). No, Ellen was completely nice and classy and engaged and preggers, and why the hell did she bother Colleen so much, anyway? Ellen was back in Chicago now, as were Lucas's sister and nieces. They'd come into the bar to say hello and stayed for dinner, and Colleen had had to go into the office and cry for a second—the girls were so big! Once upon a time, she and Lucas had babysat Mercedes and the infant twins. She'd never even met the fourth one.

Didi had gone off to visit a friend in Boca and would stay for the duration. It had only cost Lucas about four grand, he'd told her, and it was money very well spent. Joe could now die in peace.

The loo was now spotless. With a sigh, Colleen returned to the bustle. But all through the evening, she obsessed. Worried, fretted, mulled and, ironically, tried not to think about Lucas.

Their time together was drawing to a close. They were still sleeping together, but it was almost too much—the intensity, the meaning, the poignance. Soon, one of these times would be their last. Or not. Or they'd try a long-distance thing.

But without saying the actual words, Lucas had made it clear: Manningsport was not his home. Chicago was. Manningsport was where he had lived for a short time and no more. A place that meant nothing to him, and everything to her.

She wasn't going to leave.

Not that he had asked, mind you.

At the end of her shift, she called the nursing home to check on her grandfather.

"Hey, Coll," said Joanie. "He's a little restless right now."

"I'll pop over, then," Colleen said.

A half hour later, she was sitting at Gramp's bedside, holding his hand, talking about her day, the specials Connor had whipped up, how she'd taken Savannah for a swim in Keuka and how cold and clear the water had been. "I remember how you told me about you and Gran, taking a row in the moonlight on your honeymoon," she said. "You said she looked like an angel, and you could hear a whip-poor-will calling." Gramp didn't respond, but she hoped he could picture it, those long-ago days with the love of his life.

But then, she ran out of things to say. Rufus, whom she'd brought in for company, was lying on the floor, twitching in sleep. Aside from his sighs (it sounded like a pretty good dream), the place was quiet.

Gramp made a whimpering sound, and Colleen kissed his hand. Rufus's tail thumped the floor as if to reassure the old man. "I'm still here, Gramp. Don't worry."

Connor came to visit about once a week, more than anyone else except Colleen herself. The other O'Rourke cousins felt—perhaps legitimately—that their visits did nothing more than confuse Gramp, because the staff did report he'd be agitated afterward.

Dad never came. Once, Colleen had brought Savannah, but Gail and Dad had both had fits over it…exposing their innocent flower to the ravages of time, etc., etc. So it was just Colleen. She sometimes thought that if she could, she'd move in to Rushing Creek because she and Gramp had always had a special bond.

Her grandfather pulled his hand away and rubbed his forehead, his classic move when he was agitated.

"So I'm in love again, Gramp," she said, more so he could hear her voice than anything else. Well. Except it was good to say out loud. "Same guy as last time. Dumb, huh? No live and learn here. He'll be leaving pretty soon. We try not to talk about it. I think he wants me to live in Chicago, and I want him to stay here, and neither one of us is going to get our way."

No answer.

She adjusted her grandfather's blanket. "You're right. Live life for the moment. Eat dessert first. I brought you some cookies, by the way. Peanut butter. Your favorite."

"Hey."

She jumped. Lucas stood in the doorway. Hopefully, he hadn't heard her. "Hi. What are you doing here so late?"

"I'm on my way out, actually." He paused. "They just admitted Joe to Hospice. He took a turn for the worse this afternoon."

"Oh, Lucas. I'm so sorry."

"He's sleeping now. Pretty doped up. He had a bad coughing fit and brought up some blood, so he discontinued dialysis and…" He ran a hand through his hair. "It won't be long."

"I'll look in on him."

He gave a ghost of a smile. "He always liked you." Another pause. "How's your grandfather?" he asked.

"The same as ever."

Lucas went over and took Gramp's hand. "Hi, Mr. O'Rourke," he said. "It's Lucas Campbell. Good to see you again, sir."

"Liar," Colleen said, though her eyes were full.

Gramp turned away and closed his eyes. Pulled his hand free and rolled onto his side. "He'll sleep for a while now," she said. "That's my cue to leave."

She roused her dog, and she and Lucas walked down the silent hallway.

"Is that your bike?" Lucas asked.

"Yep."

"Can I drive you home?"

"I have a headlight and stuff. A reflective vest." It was a mile to her house, and Rufus could use the run (though he was even now flopping down on the floor once again). And at this hour, she'd be there almost as fast as she would if she took Lucas up on his offer.

"What I meant was," he said, his voice scraping her with sweet, dark yearning, "can I drive you to the opera house, and will you stay over, Colleen, in my bed, and let me make love to you?"

He wasn't smiling, which made it all the more devastating.

"Okay," she whispered, and he kissed her then, a gentle, long, tender kiss, and it was all she could do not to cry because she knew the clock had almost run out.

A FEW NIGHTS LATER, Lucas stood outside O'Rourke's, hoping to grab a quick dinner and a glimpse of Colleen before returning to Rushing Creek to sit with Joe, who was winding down. Mostly, his uncle slept, but if he was awake, he liked the company…and Bryce had been avoiding him, which Lucas just couldn't understand.

What the future held for him and Colleen, he didn't know.

She was trying to be her normal self, cheerful and flirty and wry, but there was something in her eyes that didn't bode well, and when he asked her about it the other night, she just put on a smile and kissed him, and no amount of coaxing could get her to open up.

That was a problem because he needed to get back to Chicago, finish the Cambria building and leave Forbes Properties behind for good. Not Mr. and Mrs. Forbes, not Ellen, not completely. But he didn't want to be attached to them in any way other than the occasional visit. He'd been a part of their family once, and he knew that Frank especially would want to keep up with the dinners, the sails on Lake Michigan. They'd invite him for the holidays, same as always, but things were changing. He didn't belong there anymore.

Steph and the girls had a different relationship with Frank and Grace (and Ellen, for that matter; the two women had become best friends, however unlikely a pairing—Steph the single mom with her tattoos and piercings, Ellen with her WASPy good looks and quiet money). But an ex-husband, an ex-son-in-law…no.

Ellen would be married soon. There'd be another son-in-law, and two babies, and while Lucas knew he'd failed Ellen on some deep, emotional level despite his best efforts, and he couldn't resent the divorce in any way, there was still a feeling that he was once again on the outside looking in.

Time to do his own thing, with the woman he'd fallen for in one glance. Time to set things right.

But her idea of right and his were very different, and it was becoming apparent just how big a problem this was going to be.

He went inside, and she looked up right away as she made a martini, expertly pouring the vodka, adding a squeeze of lime. A quick smile, the same kind she gave him lately whenever she'd been quiet too long, flashed across her lips. "Hello, Spaniard," she said as he sat down. "What can I get you?"

He didn't answer right away, and a faint blush crept into her cheeks. "Whatever the house special is, and a beer."

"I'm the house special," she said, raising an eyebrow.

"Then I'll have you," he said.

"I want the house special, then, too," said the guy sitting one stool down.

"She's taken," Lucas said, not looking away from Colleen.

"Cajun crab cake sandwich with Hungarian cucumber salad, coming up," she said. "And, Greg, I appreciate the sentiment." She pulled two glasses from the overhead rack and filled them both with beer. "Since you didn't specify, Spaniard, I gave you what he's having. The Ithaca Flower Power IPA."

She went into the kitchen, stopping to admire a baby. Probably one of the Colleens or Colins named for her.

"You guys together?" the guy, Greg, asked.

Lucas gave him a slow look. "Yes."

He pursed his lips. "Well, good luck. Hope you don't catch anything."

Lucas was dragging him across the floor by his shirt before he was even aware that he'd moved. The noise of the bar barely wavered, though Tom Barlow, back from his honeymoon, did hold the door.

"Jesus, man!" Greg yelped. "What the hell are you doing?"

Lucas let him fall on the sidewalk, and Greg scrabbled up, his hands in front of him. "Just calm down, okay? Christ. I figured I'd give you a warning. She's slept with half the guys in this town. Myself included."

"Don't come back here."

"Who's gonna stop me?" he asked.

Lucas took a step closer, and the little asshole hesitated, then turned and fled.

He went back inside, his heart thudding. "Well done, mate," Tom said. "Whatever it was he did, I'm sure he deserved that." Lucas nodded, then went back to the bar and drained his beer.

Colleen came back out. "Where's Greg?" she said, frowning.

"He had to leave," Lucas muttered.

Now granted, he knew that Colleen hadn't been celibate for the past ten years (no matter how nice that would've been to imagine). But it didn't mean he felt good, hearing that kind of shit.

"Lucas threw his ass out," Gerard offered.

"Why?" Colleen asked.

"Because he was rude," Lucas answered.

"I see. So he told you I slept with him?"

"I'd rather not discuss this in a bar."

She sighed. "I own this bar, Spaniard. Try not to be too retro, okay? Sorry I wasn't sitting home alone, knitting bandages for injured soldiers as I waited for you to come back to me."

He gave her a hot look. She returned it, then went to the end of the bar to get someone a drink.

"Hi, Lucas." Faith wriggled onto the stool next to him, Levi at her side. Probably a good thing Levi hadn't been here five minutes ago, or Lucas might be on his way to the new holding cell at the police station. He took a breath and unclenched his jaw.

"The public safety building looks incredible," Levi said. "Went up fast."

Lucas nodded. The job had been easy compared to a fifty-seven-story skyscraper, and had gone without significant hiccups. As soon as the painters were done, the three emergency departments could start moving in.

"Hi, gorgeous!" Colleen said, leaning over the bar to kiss Faith. "How's my godchild percolating in there?"

"So far, so good," she said happily, and Levi touched her cheek.

Lucas remembered that feeling. The awe of having a baby on the way, the protectiveness over your woman.

The broken feeling in his chest when he saw Ellen, white and sobbing in the hospital.

He said a quick prayer that Faith and Levi wouldn't know that sorrow. No one deserved that. And while he was at it, that Ellen and Steve's twins would be healthy and hearty.

Colleen plopped his plate in front of him with a clatter, deliberate, he was sure. Probably another hearty dose of whatever evil hot sauce she'd used on his burger that time.

Then she reached over and messed up his hair. "Faith, have you ever seen hair as beautiful as this?" she asked, and just like that, she was done being mad.

"I'm partial to blonds myself," Faith said. "But no, I haven't. Unless it's yours."

"I'd ask you to stop sulking, Spaniard," Colleen said, leaning down so he could get the full power of the view down her shirt, "but I think it's kind of hot."

He took a bite of the sandwich. It was excellent. No burning esophagus anywhere.

"Hey, bro!" Bryce stood in front of him, beaming. "Guess what! I got a job!" He offered his fist for a bump.

Lucas obliged. "Doing what?"

"Hi, Bryce," Colleen said. "You want a beer?"

"Yeah! I'm celebrating! I'm employed."

"That's great," she said, glancing down the busy bar as she pulled him an IPA. "What will you be doing?"

Bryce sat down and accepted his beer. "Menopause Boot Camp," he announced proudly.

Lucas choked. "Wow. What does that entail, exactly?"

"Coll, it was your mom who gave me the idea," Bryce said. "You know? All these old chicks starting to fall apart, complaining about their creaky knees and hot flashes, and I'm like, 'Girls, you need to get out there a little more, get the blood flowing, right?' and your mom says, 'Bryce, if the instructor looked like you, I'd do it.'

So I'm like, 'Dude, what an awesome idea!' And she got all those other chicks to sign up. Isn't that great?"

"I think my grandmother just joined that class," Faith said.

"She did!" Bryce said. "What do you think, Lucas?"

As ever, his cousin wanted his approval. "Sounds good, buddy. You'll be great at it." He paused. "You need insurance and waivers and a place and all that."

"I know," he said. "Carlos Mendez said if I started working on getting certified as a personal trainer, he'd let me work out of the gym, so long as my clients joined." He paused. "I'm not good at that much, but I know how to work out, and I like women." He smiled and shrugged.

"Good for you, Bryce," Lucas said.

"I think it's genius," Colleen said. "You could also call it Women Who Love Looking at Bryce. Half the town would join."

"You could be grandfathered in," Bryce said with a wink, and Lucas wasn't sure, but for a second, Colleen looked almost…stricken.

But a moment later, she was laughing at something Faith said and flirting with an old guy in a flannel shirt.

Hannah O'Rourke came out of the kitchen. "Collie, Connor wants you."

"Roger," she said. She went into the kitchen, attracting a good amount of male attention, Lucas's included.

At that moment, his phone buzzed. Rushing Creek.

"You'd better get here as soon as you can, Mr. Campbell," said the nurse. "It looks like it's time."

"WE SHOULD TELL my mom," Bryce objected as Lucas towed him down the hallway toward the hospice wing. "I'll call her now."

"There's no time," Lucas said. Didi and Joe had kept the divorce from Bryce as if he was a fragile eight-year-old. "Come on, buddy."

For the past eleven days, Lucas had spent a lot of time in this room. He'd brought in photo albums, meticulously kept since Bryce's birth onward, and listened as Joe told him who was who in the pictures, or described where they'd been—*here's the one from the Cascades... this was in Zion National Park. Oh, the river walk in San Antonio! And here's when we were in France.*

The room felt different now, heavy with the sound of Joe's labored breathing. His uncle's face was puffy, and he appeared to be sleeping.

Bryce hesitated in the doorway.

"Joe? We're here," Lucas said. He went to his uncle's bedside and took his hand, gesturing for Bryce to come closer. Bryce stayed put.

"Hi," Joe whispered. He opened his eyes with effort, and saw Bryce. "Hi, honey-boy," he said.

Bryce took a shuddering breath. "Hey, Dad."

"Come on over here," Joe said, and Bryce obeyed, tears sliding down his face.

"Oh, Dad. Please don't die." There was a note of panic in his voice, poor kid. Bryce sat down in the bedside chair and took his father's hand.

"I'm sorry about this, son," Joe whispered. There was a rattle in his breathing now.

Lucas moved to Joe's other side and put a hand on his shoulder. "What can we do for you, Joe?" he asked.

He hadn't been able to say goodbye to his own father, but he was here now.

His uncle looked up. "Lucas..." He closed his eyes

for a moment. "Would you mind…leaving Bryce and me alone?"

Lucas blinked. He glanced at his cousin, who was sobbing softly, his head on his father's arm. "Um… sure. Of course." He paused, leaned down and kissed his uncle's forehead. "Thank you, Joe," he whispered. "For taking me in."

But Joe's eyes were on his son, and so Lucas had nothing left to do but obey, the door wheezing shut behind him.

The hallway was dark and quiet. A nurse went by, her eyes kind.

He could call Colleen. She'd wait with him.

He had no one else, after all.

Instead, he just stood there. After a while, he sat, looking at the closed door, and it was hard to breathe because of the pain in his chest, like a cold, thick spike had been driven through it.

He'd call Steph after it was over. Didi, too, and Ellen. He'd do what needed to be done, what Joe had asked him to do, and then he wanted to leave this little town and not come back, because all he'd ever been here was an outsider, an impostor.

Except with Colleen.

The door opened, and Lucas lurched to his feet.

"He's gone," Bryce said. "He's really gone."

He burst into racking sobs, and Lucas opened his arms and hugged his cousin.

He could see Joe in the bed, undeniably still.

"I got to tell him about my job," Bryce wept, "and he said he was proud of me, and I was an entrepreneur, like him, and I'd do great."

"Good. I'm glad."

"You know what else he said?" Bryce said wetly, pulling back to mop his face.

"What's that, buddy?"

"He said I was everything he ever hoped for in a son." Bryce's face crumpled again.

"Hi," said the kindly nurse. "Do you need some more time with your dad, boys?"

"He's my dad," Bryce corrected. "Not his."

And that about summed it up.

CHAPTER TWENTY-EIGHT

COLLEEN HAD JUST come out of the shower and was contemplating a binge of Ben & Jerry's to help resist the urge to call Lucas. He had shit going on and didn't need her bugging him with stupid texts like Thinking of you! or Hey, wanna come over? And it was 1:33 a.m. He could well be asleep, and it had hurt her heart to see how tired he looked earlier.

Yep. Ben & Jerry's it was, the only two men who'd never let her down. Vanilla Heath Bar, or Peanut Brittle? Peanut Brittle it was, the crystal meth of the ice cream world. She'd bought eleven pints last week, terrified that Faith would hit the market first and clean them out.

Rufus lumbered to his feet. *Ah rah! Ah rah! Ah rooroo rah!* he bellowed in his mighty baritone. Sure enough, a knock came at the door.

She tossed the ice cream back in the freezer and opened the door.

It was Lucas, and those pirate eyes were unbearably sad.

"Oh, honey," she said, and wrapped her arms around him because it was written all over his face.

"He's gone," Lucas said. He let her hold him, but he seemed…lost.

Ah rah! Ah rah roo! her beastie said.

"Come in," she murmured. "Are you hungry? Want a drink?"

"No. Colleen—" He stopped. She waited.

He didn't continue.

Rufus, however, began his typical "are you a boy or a girl" investigation. "Okay, Rufus, no. Go away, boy."

Her dog obeyed. Lucas, however, just stood there.

Shit. A white-hot brand of fear and guilt rammed through her heart. He knew. Oh, sphincter, he knew. Maybe she should've told him before, but—

"I need to tell you something."

She swallowed, her throat so dry it clacked. She wished she was wearing something other than a Tweety Bird T-shirt and a pair of boxer shorts.

"Um…want to sit down?"

"No." He just looked at her, then rather shockingly cupped her face in his hands. "Colleen…the only thing that's ever really been mine is you."

God. The words hit her like a sledgehammer. A good sledgehammer. "Oh, Spaniard," she whispered.

"When I was a kid, I only remember my mom being sick, and then my dad worked all the time, and Steph was always out with some guy. And then when I came to live with Didi and Joe—" He scrubbed a hand through his hair. "I didn't belong there, and Didi made sure I knew it."

"Lucas," Colleen whispered, tears slipping out of her eyes. "I know Joe loved you."

"He sent me out of the room tonight. At the end."

No. No, that was just not fair. *Oh, Joe, why did you do that?*

"I always thought if I was…good enough, quiet enough or helpful enough, I'd earn a place, you know?

But I didn't. And then it hit me, hard...the only thing I've ever had that was really mine was you, Colleen. Bryce got everything handed to him, he had a home and parents who loved him and did everything for him, but once I met you, it didn't matter. I had you. You were everything to me, and I ruined it."

"Well... I ruined it, too," she whispered.

"No. You were upset, and you deserved to be. I handled everything wrong. I should've tried harder and done better by you, and I've regretted it every day for the past ten years. You're mine, Colleen, and I'll do better this time."

"Lucas..." she said, but it was the only word she managed to get out.

He kissed her then, and she kissed him back with everything she had, wrapped herself around him, his hot skin and Spanish eyes, and though he'd finally said everything, almost, that she wanted to hear, finally, finally, there was a cold trickle of dread slicing through the sunburst his words had caused.

But that didn't matter, she told herself as she led him to bed, to comfort him, to show him how much she loved him. That was nothing, and this—he—was everything.

CHAPTER TWENTY-NINE

HUNDREDS OF PEOPLE came to Joe Campbell's wake. He had never been a mover or shaker in this town, not the type to join the school board or be a volunteer EMT, but the man had no enemies, either.

Bryce was doing okay; heartbroken, but able to smile and shake hands. Didi was there at the head of the room, accepting condolences with her son. She had a brittle smile on her face that most people attributed to grief, rather than pissiness.

Lucas and Stephanie and the girls came next, and that was it for family. Well, aside from Ellen Forbes and her parents, and her fiancé, all sitting in the second row of chairs. Which was nice, of course. Far be it from the Forbes contingent to do anything other than what Emily Post recommended. *Should we all attend the wake of my ex-husband's uncle?*

But of course! Especially if you're on good terms.

Which Ellen and Lucas certainly were.

As if reading her mind, Lucas looked over to her and smiled.

He loved her. Still hadn't said the three magic words, but please. That was just a technicality. And good God, she loved him back.

"Hey, beautiful," said Gerard, giving her a hug so mighty that he picked her up. "Have I thanked you for fixing me up with Lorelei? That woman can bake, let me tell you."

"Well, so can Norine Pletts, so if things don't work out with Lorelei, you can try her. Seventy-one years young."

"I'll keep that in mind," Gerard said.

The four horseman of the Holland family were here with their spouses, except for horrifyingly single Jack, who'd stopped in earlier. (Colleen reminded herself to do something about that; his gene pool was too good to waste.)

Everyone knew Bryce, of course, and Lucas had become a part of the community, thanks to handling the public safety building. There were Marian Field, the mayor of Manningsport, and Everett, her son. Victor and Lorena, also bar regulars, had been quite friendly with Joe. Connor gave her a look—*Hang in there, you're doing great.* She smiled back gratefully.

As usual, Con had read her mind. It was awkward, being the once and future girlfriend, as it were, not quite the other woman, but somehow feeling that way. She didn't belong in the reception line (though she would've been if Lucas had asked), but she wanted to be here nonetheless. Every time she thought of what he said the other night, about feeling so…alone…her heart broke again.

The only thing I've ever had that was really mine was you.

They'd work. They had to. They'd figure something out.

The wake was supposed to end at eight; it was quarter of now. The line had dwindled, and Grant Jacobs, the funeral director, was now standing in the back of the room, giving the subtle sign.

Hopefully, Lucas would be able to come to her place tonight. Probably not, though, not with his sister and nieces…and the Forbes contingent. All Colleen wanted to do was comfort him. Have him lie on her couch with his head in her lap, or rub his shoulders, or make him smile however the hell she could. Her heart felt swollen and achy with love.

"Hey," came a voice to her left.

"Paulie! How are you? I haven't seen you in so long," Colleen said, giving her a hug. Granted, *so long* was anything over a week in Colleen's book, but Paulie hugged back hard, making Colleen wheeze a little.

"How's he doing?" she asked, jerking her chin in Bryce's direction.

"He's taking it hard." They both looked at Bryce, who was indeed weeping at the moment. Poor kid. Lucas put his hand on his cousin's shoulder and said something, and Bryce nodded.

"I'll go say hi, then," Paulie said. "Um…come with me? These things are so freaking awkward. Can I say 'freak' in a funeral home? I was thinking the other word. Saved at the last second, I guess. Shit, I'm babbling. Oh, great, I just swore."

"Easy, girl." Colleen gave her biceps a squeeze.

"Yeah." Paulie sighed. She looked nice, if a little stiff, in her black dress. "It's just my heart is breaking, looking at that." Her eyes filled as she looked at Bryce.

"He'll be glad to see you. Come on."

They went up to Joe's casket, and Colleen swallowed the lump in her throat at the sight of Smiling Joe Campbell, who would never again sit at the end of the bar, nursing his Empire Cream Ale. Paulie put her hand on Joe's shoulder and wiped her eyes.

"Paulie," Bryce said. "Hey."

"I'm sorry for your loss," she said, and offered her hand. Bryce enveloped her in a hug, bending down since Paulie was so short, and burying his face on her shoulder. "Aw, buddy," she said. "You were a great son."

Bryce's shoulders shook with a sob.

Dang it. Colleen seemed to be crying, too.

Bryce straightened up. "Sorry," he said, wiping his eyes. "It's so good to see you." He turned to his mother. "Mom, you remember Paulie Petrosinsky."

"I'm sorry for your loss, Mrs. Campbell," Paulie said.

"Thanks." Didi looked over Paulie's head and shot Mr. and Mrs. Forbes a smile. "Bryce, would you get me some water, please?"

"I'll do it, Mrs. Campbell," Colleen said. "Bryce, you must be tired. Why don't you sit down for a few minutes, catch up with Paulie?"

"Cool," Bryce said. "If you don't mind, Paulie, that is."

"Hell, no, not at all," Paulie said.

She wasn't blushing. No, she looked entirely normal.

"How about that water, Kathleen?" Didi said.

"It's Colleen, Mrs. Campbell, and you bet." Far be it from her to be impolite at a wake.

She went to the watercooler in the back, filled a cup and turned to see Stephanie Campbell standing in front of her. "Hey," she said.

"Hi, Steph."

"Nice seeing you and Lucas back together, and that's all I'm gonna say. See you tomorrow." She smiled, gave Colleen's shoulder a squeeze, then herded her children out the front door.

A sisterly blessing. She'd take it.

When Colleen returned to the front of the room, the Forbeses were gathered around, and Colleen stood there awkwardly with the water. Didi wouldn't make eye contact, as she was too busy ass-kissing. Colleen waited. Lucas was talking to Ellen and her fiancé, Steve, and damned if Colleen didn't feel like the waitress once again.

"Excuse me, please," she said pleasantly, and Mr. Forbes leaped back.

"Oh, I'm so sorry, my dear," he said.

"No, not at all," Colleen said. "Here's your water, Mrs. Campbell." She forced a smile, then drifted toward Lucas. Or maybe she shouldn't. Maybe she should go. Crap, this was awkward.

"So I'll see you at the benefit next week, right?" she overheard Ellen say.

"I think so," Lucas said.

"Great. I'm so sorry we can't stay for the funeral," Ellen said. "But you know I'm thinking of you."

"I appreciate that," he said, shaking Steve's hand. "You guys have a safe trip back. Make sure you get enough rest, Ell."

"You should talk," she said. "Don't think I missed the fact that you were limping. Get some ice on that knee."

Knee? Which knee? Lucas had a problem with his knee?

"She has eyes like a hawk," Steve said, pushing some hair behind Ellen's ear. "But he's right, baby. You should get your feet up."

Not just one, but two men, basking in Ellen's pregnant glow.

Bryce and Paulie were still in a tête-à-tête. The Hollands had left; most people had, and she didn't want to stand around like a lump, watching Lucas kiss Ellen on the cheek (but bugger and damn, she did catch that out of the corner of her eye). She went to the back of the room and texted Savannah. How's everything? I'm at a wake. What are you doing?

A few seconds later, she had her answer. Mom & I r doing pedis. Fun!!!

That was nice. Mother-daughter time. Great! she texted back. Have fun, sweets! Tell your mom I said hi.

Oddly enough, she and Gail were becoming…well, not friends. Allies, maybe. They'd had a glass of wine the other night at O'Rourke's, the first time Gail had come in alone. Gail had asked for her opinion on letting Savannah do the travel league for baseball in the fall (which Colleen had been all for).

They hadn't talked about Dad. If Gail suspected he was dating his ex-wife, she didn't say anything, and Colleen appreciated it.

"Mia."

Colleen jumped. "Spaniard. How are you holding up?"

"Good. Things seem to be winding down here." He picked up her hand and kissed it. Twice.

He looked so amazing in his suit, a dark gray with a white shirt and dark red tie. He needed to shave. Colleen reminded herself to stop lusting in a funeral home, but he made it hard, that gorgeous mouth, those tragic eyes, so dark and deep…and maybe, there was a little glow of happiness in there, too. Maybe, just maybe, she had something to do with that.

"Hey, you two," said Bryce, approaching with Paulie.

"Paulie," Lucas said. "Nice to see you again."

"You, too," she said, punching him on the shoulder. He punched her back, lightly, then took Colleen's hand. Bryce smiled. "So you guys are really together again, huh? Good. I'm so glad Coll and me hooking up didn't bother you, bro."

Colleen's heart stopped. Literally. She felt the blood drain to her feet, then flood back up as her pulse shot into the danger zone.

She didn't dare move.

No one else did, either, except Bryce, who waved to someone.

"Excuse me?" Lucas said very, very quietly.

"What? Oh, Colleen and me," Bryce answered, and oh, sphincter damn and blast, Colleen's legs turned to water.

"What do you mean, you and Colleen?" Paulie asked, her brows coming together.

Realization dawned on Bryce's perfect face. "Oh. Uh…um…nothing?"

Colleen looked at Lucas, then immediately wished she hadn't.

This was very bad. Very, very bad.

"Did you guys…date?" Paulie asked.

"Well, I wouldn't, uh, call it dating," Bryce said.

"This isn't really the time," Colleen began, her voice tight and strange.

"No, no," Lucas said. "What *would* you call it, Bryce?"

"Uh, um, I mean, we slept together, but—"

More silence, and then Paulie barked, "Are you *kidding* me?"

Lucas was granite-still.

"This definitely isn't the time," Colleen whispered.

Paulie's mouth was open. "You *slept* with *Bryce,* Colleen?"

And the thing was, Paulie's inside voice was more of an outside voice, and Didi and the minister and Mr.

and Mrs. Forbes froze, and the song on the speakers was "Yellow Ledbetter" by Pearl Jam, for some reason, and who knew what that song was about, anyway? Sounded like the guy was speaking in tongues.

Focus, Colleen. "Um… I…" Colleen couldn't seem to get her mouth to work.

What could she say, after all?

"This is—you know what?" Paulie said. "This is not my problem. Bryce, sorry about your dad. Lucas, see you around." With that, she left.

Colleen swallowed. "Um…"

Lucas was glaring at Bryce, who gave her a panicky glance, then looked back at his cousin. "Lucas, bud, uh, remember the time I saved you?"

Then Lucas looked at her, and man, Colleen wished he hadn't, because those black eyes were burning into her, and *so* not in a good way. "Let's talk about this in private," she whispered.

"No need," he said. He stood there a horribly long second, then turned and he walked out, dragging her heart behind him.

"I have a bad feeling about this," Bryce said.

She turned to him. "Bryce…"

"Shit, Coll, I'm sorry. I mean, I just…my dad and stuff, I guess I was feeling sentimental."

"It was one time, and we both agreed never to mention it again! And come on! It wasn't exactly meaningful."

"Ouch," he said.

She realized they were at his dad's wake, after all, and put her hand on his arm. "Sorry."

Bryce gave a half smile. "No, no, you're right. It wasn't. I really am sorry."

She took a deep breath, which did nothing to slow her heart rate. "Well, it's done. I should go. Hang in there, Bryce. I'll see you at the funeral."

"Thanks," he said. "Sorry again, Coll."

And she knew he was. Bryce was a gentle idiot.

But not as much of an idiot as she was.

SIX YEARS AGO, for no good reason, Colleen typed *Lucas Campbell, Chicago* into Google.

She couldn't help it. Every once in a while, she did it. He didn't have a Facebook page, or Twitter, like a normal person. But he *was* married to the daughter of one of Chicago's most prominent citizens, and there was mention of him once in a while.

She'd seen their wedding write-up in the Chicago newspaper online. The bride was attended by her closest friend from Miss Porter's School, the article said, as well as the groom's sister and eldest niece. His twin nieces served as flower girls. The groom's best man was his cousin, Bryce Campbell. The reception was held at The Drake, where guests were treated to music by the Moonlight Jazz Orchestra. The renowned Sylvia Weinstock designed the cake. The bride's dress was custom-made by Isaac Mizrahi, a family friend. The couple had met in college. Lucas Campbell was a proud son of the South Side and worked for Forbes Properties in construction—so much for law school, Colleen had thought, and why bother when you could marry into one of Chicago's wealthiest families?

But it didn't seem right. It didn't seem like him.

Then again, she didn't really know him as well as she'd thought.

After that, she vowed not to look ever again. Bryce

was living out of town at the time, and Joe was kind enough not to mention Lucas when he came into the bar. If she didn't want to hear about Lucas, she didn't have to.

Her iron resolve lasted about eight months, until her birthday when she drank an entire bottle of Blue Heron Chardonnay by herself, and looked up baby announcements on Google.

Nothing.

She looked again every few months after that, because for some masochistic reason, she wanted to know if Lucas had become a father. She didn't want to be slammed with that news when she was working at the bar, because she knew she wouldn't be able to hide how she felt.

But there were no baby announcements. Not for two years, and Colleen finally stopped looking.

But she couldn't help thinking about him. She and Faith discussed many times the unfair power of first love. After every guy who turned out to be less than Lucas, after every wine and roses festival that marked another year of not being with Lucas, Colleen missed him so much it felt as if her soul ached.

And then late one snowy night when she was practically alone in the bar, without any good reason, she looked him up on Google again, and boom. The *Chicago Sun-Times* came through.

He was laughing in the photo, and so was his wife. They looked gorgeous, her blond hair, his black. Ellen wore a yellow gown with chunky diamond studs in her ears, and Lucas, damn him to hell, looked like a high-class pirate in his tux, just slightly dangerous and utterly, horribly beautiful.

Lucas Campbell and Ellen Forbes-Campbell enjoy comments from the master of ceremonies at the annual Lurie Children's Hospital gala, the caption read.

Colleen couldn't look away, even though the picture made it feel like a branch was being rammed through her chest.

She still loved him.

What an idiot she was. She still loved a man who was having a marvelous time with his *wife,* far, far away.

She closed the site, deleted the browser history so Connor wouldn't know how pathetic she was, and went back into the bar, and there sat Bryce Campbell. For a second, he looked so damn much like Lucas that she shuddered with missing the boy who'd once treasured her.

"Hey, Bryce. What can I get you?"

She pulled him a beer, and they chatted. Bryce was sweet. Easy. Uncomplicated. And there on a night when no one else was around, when Bryce had nowhere better to be and neither did she, it was nice to have a friend.

He walked her home, as the snow was heavy, and it was courtly of him. As he stood in front of her house, looking up at the sky, he asked, "You ever wish you left this town, Colleen?"

"Not really," she said after a beat. "But yeah. Once in a while."

"I never really thought I'd end up here. At my parents' house. I always figured I'd be... I don't know. Cooler. Smarter."

She wasn't sure what he was asking, but he looked so sad. She reached up and brushed some snow from his hair. "I think you're fine the way you are, Bryce," she said.

Then he kissed her.

Oh, sure, she knew it was insanely stupid. But then, on that quiet, lonely night, when if you looked at him a certain way, you might mistake Bryce for Lucas… when she had seen proof that Lucas was happy without her—well, shit.

Two lonely people. A snowstorm. A few beers. The combination doesn't usually lead to the smartest decisions in the world, and sure enough, forty-two minutes later, Colleen hated herself.

And, to his credit, Bryce kind of hated himself, too.

"This was probably a mistake," he said, pulling his clothes back on.

"Yeah. No offense. But yes."

"You're really nice, Coll."

"You, too."

"Just…" His voice trailed off.

"I know." She wanted a shower, her skin was crawling so bad. Not because Bryce was disgusting…because it was so wrong. "Bryce, if we could just forget about this, I think that'd be best."

"Okay. Yeah. Definitely."

"Don't tell Lucas," she whispered.

"Jesus, no. Listen. It's already forgotten, okay? I'll see you around."

"Okay. Thanks, Bryce."

And that was it. Meaningless, mediocre, mistake. Bryce was no Lucas. Not even close. Worse than being a vengeful act on her part, it was pathetic. Colleen O'Rourke, who was supposedly so smart about relationships, and so good with men, had been reduced to abject loneliness and shagged a guy who reminded her of her first love.

As for Bryce, well, he was all foam and no beer. He was an "Oh, look, shiny!" type of guy, and she'd been shiny.

So Colleen spent a miserable month or two. Bryce still came into the bar, and bless his heart, he really did seem to forget about it. There were no lingering looks, no simmering chemistry (please), and no signs of resentment whatsoever.

Eventually, Colleen shook it off. It was a *lapse in judgment,* that old familiar phrase, and not one she was going to make again. Time to get over Lucas Campbell. She'd find someone else, eventually. No harm, no foul, and no one had to know about it.

Until today.

First stop was the Petrosinsky home. Paulie's father answered the door.

"What did you do now?" he barked. "She's power-eating a bucket of Double Deep-Fried Buttermilk Bossy."

"I'm so sorry, Mr. Petrosinsky."

"Come in," he said wearily. "Go talk to her." He held open the door, and Colleen sidled past the statue of a rooster dressed like a butler and went up to Paulie's room. The door was open, and there was her friend, bucket in hand, eating, crying and watching *Terminator 2* on her enormous TV.

"Paulie?" she said.

Paulie wadded up another tissue and tossed it toward the trash, where it joined its many brothers. "Come on in," she muttered.

Colleen tiptoed closer and sat on the edge of the

massive bed. "I'm so sorry I never said anything," she whispered.

Paulie gave her a watery glare, then glanced back at the TV. "Want some chicken?"

There was probably no better person on earth than Paulie Petrosinsky, and Colleen's eyes filled with tears.

"Thanks." The chicken was horrifyingly good. She chewed and swallowed, watching Arnold's motorcycle outrun the 18-wheeler.

"I'm sorry I made a scene," Paulie said. "It's just… embarrassing. Like I could be with Bryce when he could get someone like you. I was shocked."

"Paulie, you're ten times better than I am."

"Yeah, right. Look in the mirror, Colleen."

"Looks are meaningless."

Paulie snorted. "Right. If I looked like you, Bryce would be climbing me like a tree."

"My looks have gotten me nowhere," Colleen said. "I'm pretty, so what? I'm single, and I've had one meaningful relationship in my life, and everyone thinks I'm the town slut and I let them. In fact, I *like* them thinking that. It's better than knowing I'm kind of a wreck. Whereas everyone takes one look at you and they know how decent you are."

"Decent. A very decent virgin, so cry me a river," Paulie said, taking another piece of chicken. "Have some more. This batter is made with crushed Frosted Flakes."

"No wonder it's so good," Colleen said, taking another massive breast. "Paulie, I didn't say anything about Bryce because it was a mistake. A one-time mistake."

"Was it because you were mad at Lucas? Because it seems like a really shitty thing to do."

Colleen swallowed. "No. It was because I was lonely.

I loved him, and he was married, and I was still stuck." She paused. "And really, really lonely."

"I know that feeling."

"Paulie, I'm so sorry it hurt you."

The other woman sighed and flopped back on the bed. On-screen, the cool, newer terminator stuck his arm into a nurse, killing her. "Okay. I accept your apology, Coll. I mean, it sucks, picturing you beautiful people bumping uglies, but I appreciate you trying to get me with Bryce. I really do."

"He misses you."

"Whatever."

"I mean, don't give up hope."

"I already have. Hope sucks." Paulie sighed again. "Think Lucas will forgive you?"

"I can't really picture that right now." She lay on the bed, too. Paulie took her hand and squeezed it, then handed her the box of tissues.

She didn't deserve a friend like Paulie. But man, she sure would like to.

"Paulie?" she whispered.

"Yeah?"

"I'm so sorry about sixth grade. I wish I'd done better by you."

Paulie was quiet for a long minute. "Well, no one else had the guts. I mean, yeah, I hated you for a while. But I watched you. You've always been really nice."

Colleen swallowed and wiped the tears that were trickling into her hair. "Thanks."

"Now get off my bed and let me wallow. Shouldn't you go talk to Lucas?"

"Oh, probably."

"Then get out of here." She sat up and handed Colleen another slab of chicken. "Take this for the road."

IT TOOK ALL the courage she had to knock on Lucas's door. Still, her hands were shaking. Legs, too. Throw heart on the list as well, because it was beating so fast it felt like a hummingbird's wings, and Colleen wasn't 100 percent sure she wasn't about to faint.

The door opened. It wasn't Lucas. It was Mercedes. "Hey, Colleen!" she said. "How's it going?"

"Hi," she said. "Is your uncle here?"

"Yeah. Hang on. Uncle Lucas!" she bellowed, making Colleen jump. "Your girlfriend is here!" She turned back to Colleen. "Sorry, but you guys are totally obvious."

"Oh."

Mercedes gave her a strange look—*Weren't you good at conversation once?*—and then left, and there he was, filling the doorway with scalding vats of testosterone.

"Got a minute?" she whispered.

"No."

"Please, Lucas."

It actually felt like his eyes were burning her. He turned, said something to Stephanie, and stepped into the hall.

"Can we go somewhere more private?" she asked.

"No."

Not a great start. Then again, he had reason to be furious.

He stood with his arms folded, looking at her, his face blank.

Colleen took a deep breath. "Okay, well, this is very awkward." She started to gnaw on her thumbnail, then put her hand down. "Um…so yes, I did sleep with Bryce once. It didn't mean anything."

"It means something to me."

"Right." She took a shaky breath. "It was a long time ago, Lucas."

"Does that excuse it?"

"No. I'm sorry," she said. "I'm *so* sorry, Lucas. I wish to God I hadn't done it, we both do, Bryce and I, and it really meant—"

"There are plenty of men to sleep with in this town, Colleen. From what you've told me, you know that very well."

Her head jerked back. "Ouch."

"I'm not judging you."

"Really? Feels that way. I feel quite judged."

"But my *cousin*." His voice was like acid.

"Well, it wasn't just your cousin, I mean, it wasn't *because* he was your cousin, but also, yeah, he wasn't the only one that I, uh…" Great. Here came the Tourette's of Terror again. "What I mean is, he wasn't—"

"I don't want to hear about all the men you've slept with, Colleen!" he barked. Someone in the apartment across the hall muted the TV. Couldn't blame them.

She twisted her hands together. "I'm sorry," she whispered. "I really am, Lucas. But don't forget you were *married* at the time. Married! It's not like I cheated on you."

"This entire summer, you haven't said a word. You *knew* this would matter to me. You had to know, but instead, you let me make an idiot of myself."

She stopped and swallowed against the sharp knot in her throat. "How does being with me make you an idiot?"

"I think that's been answered tonight. At the wake.

In the funeral home. In front of the minister. And my former in-laws."

She went to bite her nail again, then clenched her hands. "I'm truly sorry, Lucas. I'm not perfect."

"No, that's not on my list of adjectives for you right now."

"Okay, stop being mean! It was wrong, I know that, believe me. But I was just trying to find someone after *you* got married."

"You broke up with *me,* Colleen. Remember? It was get married or get lost, your way or the highway."

"Don't you quote *Road House* to me. I've seen every Patrick Swayze movie ever made."

He gave her a look that glittered with fury. "That's your problem, Colleen. You can't take anything seriously. Not us, not Bryce, nothing."

"I'm sorry! I'm nervous! I'm taking this very seriously!"

"You slept with my *cousin.* You're the only one who knew what Bryce did to me."

"You mean, how he saved your life?"

"Everything I had, he wanted, and God forbid Bryce had to go without anything. Even you."

"I'm not an ice cream cone, Lucas. It's not the same."

"He took away my last chance to see my father, Colleen! And my God, he *slept* with you!"

"Okay, okay, let's just…let's just settle down. What about what you said the other night? About us? That matters, too, doesn't it?" She bit her thumbnail, the small sharp pain the only thing feeling real right now.

Lucas almost smiled. Not in a good way. "You mean, how I said you were the only thing that was really mine?"

"I meant—"

"Because I guess I was wrong about that, wasn't I?"

"Right. I'm a slut."

"I didn't say that."

"You didn't have to."

He didn't answer, but his eyes weren't exactly brimming with forgiveness, either, and Colleen felt the last of her hope leak out of her. Paulie was right. Hope sucked.

"Well, you have a great time being holy and perfect, Lucas. Good luck with that."

His eyes were flat.

"That was sarcasm. You're not perfect, you know. You never told me you loved me. Ever."

"Good thing, too, isn't it?"

Her heart, which had taken so damn long to heal over, split right in half again. Without another word, she turned and left before she started sobbing.

She knew he'd ruin her all over again. And she'd been right.

CHAPTER THIRTY

"DUDE, YOU'RE NOT MAD, are you?" Bryce asked for what had to be the thirtieth time.

"I don't want to talk about it," Lucas said through gritted teeth, willing his hands not to curl into fists. Didi smirked.

They were in the limo en route to the church for Joe's funeral.

"Because you know…it was just sex."

"Shut up."

"And Colleen, you know how she is. She kinda gets around."

"Do you *want* me to beat you up, Bryce?" he growled. "On the day of your father's funeral? Because if you say another word, I will." He paused. "And don't say that about her."

Bryce slumped back against the seat of the limo. "Sorry."

"She is something of a tramp," Didi said.

"Didi, shut up, or you can walk the rest of the way to church. I'm the one paying for this funeral, after all."

At the mention of money, Didi's eyes narrowed. "Really, Lucas. No need to be rude."

He didn't bother answering.

"Mom, you should stick around," Bryce said. "You really going to Wisconsin tomorrow?"

"Bryce, sweetie, you know how I am. I'd rather do my grieving privately. And I had vacation time to use up."

Lucas suspected she was already on the prowl for a new husband. Play the widow card ASAP. She wouldn't be around for the reading of Joe's will, either. Bryce was still unaware of how much he'd inherit, and that Lucas would be trustee.

Lucas wouldn't need to stick around, either. The will was straightforward, with only a sealed letter from Joe addressed to Bryce.

There was no letter for him.

They pulled up to the church. Bryce and Lucas were both pallbearers, along with four of Joe's friends, two from college, two from Manningsport. They slid the casket from the back of the hearse and lifted it, carrying it slowly into the cool stone church.

This was the last thing he'd do for Joe. He was leaving after the funeral, and honestly, he'd be glad to get away.

The church was packed. There were Steph and the girls, all of them weepy. Faith and Levi, Tom and Honor. Gerard and the pretty woman from the bakery. Everett and Emmaline, the Manningsport cops, and the mayor. The woman who lived on his floor and watched *Game of Thrones* all the time. Jeremy Lyon, who'd been Joe's primary doctor, and Jeremy's boyfriend, whom Lucas had met one night at O'Rourke's. Paulie Petrosinsky, wearing a long black sweater that dangled almost to the floor, stood in the back, as the church was packed. She gave him a sad smile, and he nodded in return.

Everyone had loved Smiling Joe.

And there was Colleen, sitting with her family—her mother, Connor and her little sister.

He looked away.

They set the casket down, and the minister began. Mercedes did a reading, from the Bible, and Stephanie read a sad poem by Robert Frost.

Then it came time for the eulogy. Bryce stood up, took his notes from his pocket with shaking hands and went onto the altar.

He cleared his throat. Took a deep breath. "My dad… my dad…my dad was…"

And then Bryce was crying so hard he bent over. He tried to get control of himself, failed, and just clung to the podium, sobbing.

Any anger Lucas had toward him—over Colleen, over Bryce's easy, shallow life, over the love that was so endlessly showered on him and that seemed so taken for granted—evaporated.

Bryce was just a big kid. A big, sweet, dopey kid who wasn't sure how to be an adult.

Lucas got up and went to his cousin. "Hey, buddy," he said softly, putting his arm around Bryce's shoulders and pulling him away a few steps. "Hey. You can do this."

"No, I can't," Bryce sobbed.

Lucas pulled him into a full hug. "Sure, you can. You need to. For your dad, and for yourself."

Bryce wiped his eyes on the heels of his hands. "Will you do it for me?" he asked. "Read what I wrote?"

"No. This is yours. You can do it."

Bryce looked at him with his blue eyes, so like Joe's, swallowed and nodded.

Then Lucas squeezed his shoulders and sat down again, stepping over Didi without looking at her.

Bryce took a shuddering breath. "Man, this is hard," he said, and a sympathetic laugh rose from the congregation. "My dad was...well, he wasn't perfect," Bryce said. "He made mistakes. He was kind of lazy. But he loved me. He loved his family, and he loved the White Sox." This got a few laughs. "He always wanted what was best for me. I can't remember a single time my dad was mad at me, or yelled at me. Maybe he should have. I mean, I got away with murder."

Another laugh, and Lucas felt himself smile a little, too.

"My dad just didn't have it in him, though. He was never impatient, and he always seemed to be smiling. He was smart, too, a lot smarter than he let on. He probably could've done more with his life, but he was content with what he had."

Steph leaned forward. "Sounds like Dad," she whispered.

Lucas had been thinking the same thing.

"The best thing about my father, though," Bryce continued, "was that he always saw the best in people. He wasn't fooled by what was on the outside. He knew who the good guys were." There was a long pause. Bryce was no longer crying, though...he was looking toward the back of the church. Staring.

Then he looked back at his notes. "I have a lot to do if I want to be even half the guy he was," he said. "But I'm gonna try." He looked to the ceiling. "Thanks, Dad." His voice broke again. "I'm gonna miss you for the rest of my life."

Then Bryce left the altar and walked past the first

pew and kept going until he reached the back of the church. He went straight to Paulie, whispered something, and took her hand and kissed it.

"Let us pray," said the minister.

THE RECEPTION WAS held at O'Rourke's, as Joe had requested. There was a sign on the door: Closed for Private Function. Colleen's cousins were manning the bar, but she was there, making sure things got done, giving directions, bustling in and out of the kitchen. She looked different, her hair pulled up into a sleek twist, a high-necked, sleeveless black dress.

She wasn't smiling. More than anything, that was the difference.

He tried not to look at her. Visions of her kissing Bryce, pulling off Bryce's shirt, underneath Bryce— no. He couldn't go there. Not now. Last night, he hadn't slept a minute, tormented by those same thoughts, but today was about Joe.

Drinks were flowing, toasts were made, food was served. Someone put the jukebox on, and it became festive as people told stories about Joe.

His uncle would've loved this.

Bryce looked happier, too. Lucas checked in on him from time to time, told him the eulogy was perfect. He had an arm around Paulie, who was attractively flushed. "Good to see you, Paulie," Lucas said as Bryce listened to one of the college friends telling him about a prank Joe had pulled.

"Good to be seen," she answered.

"Thanks for giving him a second chance."

"It's more like a fourteenth chance, but I think he could be worth it this time."

Lucas smiled. "I hope you're right. You deserve a great guy."

"Are you hitting on me?"

"I don't think I'm that smart."

"Yeah," she said, gesturing with her Genesee to Colleen, who was hefting a crate of glasses. "What are you gonna do about that?"

"I don't know." He felt his blood pressure rising.

"All I can say is," Paulie continued, "she's been a good friend. And in her own special way, she's a ball of insecurities, Lucas, but so aren't we all, right?"

"Right." Seemed as if he was looking at Colleen again. And she was looking back. She nodded at something someone said, then started over, weaving her way through the crowd.

"Hey, Paulie," she said, biting her thumbnail. Her eyes were on him, though.

"Hey, girlfriend."

"Hi, Lucas. Bryce. Um…it was a lovely service." She seemed on the cusp of saying more, but Didi shoved past her.

"Bryce," Didi said, "I need a word with you." She elbowed her way past Paulie and took her son's arm.

"Sure, Ma."

Didi whispered into Bryce's ear.

Bryce jerked back. "No way, Mom. You have it backward."

"I doubt it very much, Bryce."

Bryce looked at Paulie. "No. You're definitely wrong."

"Bryce," Didi said, her voice getting harder, "do you really want to be with someone called the Chicken Princess? You can do better."

Paulie's face went purple with embarrassment. "Excuse me," she said with terrible dignity. She turned to leave.

"Don't you move a muscle," Bryce said, gently grabbing her arm and pulling her closer. He turned to his mother. "No, Mom, I can't. Paulie is a great person. You have no idea what you're talking about."

"Trust me, I do."

"No, you don't," he said sharply. People were quieting down around him. "You judge everything on how much it cost or how it looks. Where have you been these past two weeks while Dad was dying? What kind of a wife leaves then, huh? Paulie has been a great friend to me, and if I want to date her, I will."

"Don't be like your father," Didi said, her voice dripping with contempt. "Befriending every loser who comes along."

Bryce stood up straighter. "You couldn't give me a higher compliment, Ma. And you're the one who's losing."

With that, Bryce took Paulie by the shoulders. "I'm sorry about that," he said, and without further ado, he kissed her. Hard. Paulie's hands flapped a little (like a chicken, Lucas couldn't help thinking), then settled on Bryce's waist. Bryce pulled back, then kissed her again, more gently this time.

Lucas looked at Colleen. She was smiling, just a little, at Bryce and Paulie, and for some reason, it sliced him in half.

It was time for him to go.

CHAPTER THIRTY-ONE

COLLEEN WAS CLEANING the bar the next morning at ten, indulging in the healing powers of Clorox Clean-Up, when a knock came at the door.

It was Bryce.

She opened it. "Hey," she said.

He looked…great.

And he was wearing the black Thneed.

In a weird way, it had a certain metrosexual charm on him, dangling over his tank-top T-shirt and gym shorts.

"Well, well, well," she said. "Does that sweater mean what I think it means?"

He grinned. "A gentleman doesn't kiss and tell."

"So ironic to hear you say that."

He grimaced. "That's why I'm here, actually. I wanted to apologize for ruining things with you and Lucas."

She sighed. "No. I should've told him. But I figured it would only hurt him, and here we are, hurt anyway."

"Can I fix that?"

"Can you? Because that would be great."

"He left yesterday."

Sphincter. She figured he would, but damn and blast, the words made her eyes well anyway.

"I also wanted to thank you for helping me notice Paulie. She told me about it last night."

"Well. You're a lucky guy, Bryce. She's a really, really great person."

"I know."

"I like how you told off your mom, by the way. High time."

"Yeah. It felt kinda good. I'm moving out, by the way."

"Not into the Chicken Palace?"

"No, no," he said. "Too early for that. I'm taking Lucas's apartment in the opera house. Talked to the landlady this morning. Now that I have a job and stuff."

Connor came in. "Hey, Bryce. Sorry again about Joe."

"Thanks, man." Bryce's eyes filled, but he slapped the counter and stood up. "I should get going. Got Menopause Boot Camp in fifteen minutes."

"Mom's in that, by the way," Colleen told her brother.

"You're a saint, Bryce," Connor said.

"Word, brother. Word." With that, he smiled again and left, the Thneed tails flapping rakishly behind him.

"Don't just stand there," Connor said. "Get to work, you lazy whore."

"Heard about Bryce, did you?"

"I've known for years."

Her mouth wobbled. "Not one of my better moments."

"How's Lucas taking it?"

"He's back in Chicago."

"Ass."

"Yeah. Well. I love that ass."

"You need to get a life."

"*You* need to get a life. Has anyone told you you're

unhealthily attached to me, brother mine? What's today's special, by the way?"

"Whatever my heartbroken sissy wants."

She paused. "Just when I'm ready to put you up for adoption, you go and say something like that. Turkey club, crispy bacon, and that horseradish and basil mayonnaise I love. See? You *are* good for something."

THE NEXT WEEK crawled by. Colleen went running with Rufus in the town conservation land where her pup could put his ridiculously long legs to use and gallop through the meadows, returning covered in pollen and happiness. She took Savannah for a private boxing lesson with Tom Barlow, and her sister was elated afterward. Then they watched *Harry Potter* and ate veggies and hummus, with just one small brownie each afterward. Gail had a point about how Colleen spoiled Savannah with food, and Colleen was trying to do better. Not to be a Nazi about it…just to be more aware.

Lucas didn't call. Didn't email. Didn't text. Didn't send flowers, didn't send a dead squirrel in a box.

She started to write to him a dozen times. Stood in the shower, talking aloud, trying to find the words that would make everything right.

The words didn't come.

Paulie came in for happy hour on Tuesday. She looked the same—love hadn't changed anything about her on the outside, which was oddly reassuring. "So the whole Chicken King's virgin daughter…" Colleen said.

"The title no longer applies," Paulie said, holding her hand up for a high five.

Colleen laughed. "Think you guys will work out? Now that you've seen him up close and personal?"

Paulie pulled a protein drink from her gym bag, twisted off the cap and took a chug. "Pour a little vodka in that, what do you say?" she suggested.

With a wince, Colleen obliged. Worse than Mom's 7Up and white Zin.

Paulie took a sip and sighed with satisfaction. "Things are great," she said. "Bryce is the sweetest man on earth. He cooked me a cheeseburger last night, heated up some French fries, and guess what? He inherited a shitload of money, and he's donating a huge lump to the animal shelter. He could've bought a Maserati or Porsche, but no, he put some in a nice mutual fund. *And* he's taking classes to become a real trainer." She chugged some more of her unusual cocktail. "Seems like everyone kind of underestimated him."

"Except you."

"Except me." She smiled proudly.

"He seems smitten."

Paulie's smile was so bright that it could power a good-sized car. "I'm doing my best. Got any sex tips for me?"

"Not me, sister. My advice days are over. But you know who would? Prudence Vanderbeek. She's in the back booth there with Honor. Go on, ask her. You'll make her day."

WHEN SHE COULDN'T avoid it any longer, Colleen went to see her mom. Dear old Mother had been silent lately, not using her typical guilt-trip tactics of stopping by the bar looking homeless, or texting things like Have you been in an accident? I haven't heard from you in weeks. Is this still your phone number?

The silence was not reassuring.

She pulled into the driveway, and woe unto her, saw Dad's stupid Porsche Cayenne, meant to advertise his lowering testosterone levels and thinning hair. Well. She may as well face both parents at once.

She went inside. "Hi, Mom!"

"Don't come in!" Mom said. "Your father's naked."

"Oh, come on! Haven't I had enough psychological trauma for one summer?"

"I'm *painting* him," Mom said. "Don't get your panties in a twist. It's safe now, come in, sweetheart."

Feeling very much like Sisyphus shoving his rock, Colleen approached. "Hello, parents."

"Hello, Colleen."

"Dad. Nude modeling, huh? I would've thought the car and another divorce would cover your male menopause."

He cocked an eyebrow. "She asked me to pose, and I wanted to make her happy."

"Better late than never."

"What can I do for you, Collie?" Mom asked. She wore a paint-smeared, oversize shirt, leggings and bare feet. Two inches of gray roots showed on her head. She looked relaxed, which wasn't the typical case when Dad was around.

"So let's cut to the chase," Colleen said. "Are you guys really getting back together? Is Gail the Tail over?"

Dad didn't answer.

"Would it be a bad thing, honey?" Mom asked carefully.

Colleen looked at her father a long minute. There was no going back to the vision of her father as some kind of rock star among fathers. He was a shallow, selfish man.

He always had been.

The realization lifted a weight off her heart. Oddly enough, she suddenly felt fond of her father. That being said…

"I think you could do a lot better, Mom."

"Thanks a lot, Colleen," her father said wearily. "I think I deserve a little more gratitude, having raised you and put you through college, but I suppose it's more fun to demonize me."

"'Demonize' sounds cooler than you deserve," she said. "No, Dad. You're a man who doesn't appreciate what he has, and thinks he has carte blanche to pop in and out of people's lives when he feels like it."

"Thank you for that assessment."

"I have more," she said. "You were a crappy father to Connor and me. You were condescending toward Mom, and you only paid attention to us when you felt like it, not when we needed it. And the second the Tail got pregnant with Savannah, all we were was inconvenient."

"You were also adults."

"That doesn't mean we didn't miss you, Dad. Even if you were an ass and remain an ass to this day. So far as I can tell, you have one redeeming quality. You're great with Savannah."

"Gee. Thanks."

"You're welcome. Anyway, I'm just here to say hi. I love you both, even if you drive me crazy. Mom, let's have lunch this week, okay? Get back to your disgusting hobbies, you two."

"Wait," Mom said. "Wait a second." She was frowning, looking at Dad. "Colleen has a point."

"What?" Dad asked. "What point?"

"For ten years," Mom said slowly, "I would've given my right arm to have you back. I loved you, I missed you, and I would've forgiven anything." She looked around the studio, which was so much brighter and cleaner and happier since Lucas had redone it. "But Collie's right. I deserve better." She looked surprised. "I don't think I want you anymore, Pete. These past two weeks have been a little…boring, actually. I'm sorry."

"Wait a sec," Dad said. "All this renaissance woman thing you've been doing, the painting and the new clothes… I thought that was for me."

"Of course you did," Colleen said.

Dad ignored her. "I thought getting rid of my stuff and making this ridiculous studio was to get my attention, and you did, Jeanette! You succeeded. You've become an interesting woman, and I still find you attractive."

"Dad, the thing is," Colleen said, "she's always been an interesting woman, and she's always been attractive, dummy. You just stopped noticing. Come on. We can walk out together."

"I don't understand," he said.

"I'll see you around, Pete," Mom said. "We'll always be Colleen and Connor's parents, after all. No need to be uncivil. Maybe we can even be friends."

"I don't want to be friends," Dad said. "I want—"

"Dad, no one cares," Colleen said, taking his arm. "Let's go."

HER FATHER CAUGHT up with her a week after Mom had dumped his scrawny white Irish ass, knocking on her door on her night off, just as she was digging into a pint of Ben & Jerry's. "Come in," she said.

In the three years she'd lived here, he'd never been over to visit.

"Cute place," he said.

"Thanks. Have a seat." She paused the Bradley Cooper movie she had been about to watch (for the fifth time) and told Rufus to get his nose out of Dad's crotch. The dog reluctantly obeyed, then trotted off to her bedroom for a power nap.

"What's up, Dad?" she asked, taking a bite of the ice cream.

"I just wanted to say hi."

"Really. Why?"

"Because, Colleen," he said irritably, not looking at her, "I'm trying to be a better father."

"How nice. I accept expensive gifts. Cars, for example. Islands."

"Can you be serious?" He sighed and ran a hand through his salt-and-pepper hair. "Look. I thought I was a pretty good father, up until the divorce."

"Up until the cheating, you mean."

"Yeah. Whatever."

"You ever hear that expression? The best thing a man can do for his children is love their mother?"

"No. But let me finish, okay?" He fixed her with a look. "I was always very proud of you and Connor. You were good kids. Smart and funny. I guess I didn't show that enough."

"True."

"It was hard to know how to deal with you after the divorce. I was afraid you'd cut me out of your life completely, so I tried to get ready for that. Connor did it right away, and I was steeling myself for losing you."

Much to Colleen's shock, her father's voice broke.

"I know I disappointed you, Collie. I didn't know how to deal with it. Gail was pregnant, and I had to focus on that." He bowed his head. "I was always grateful that you took to Savannah. Babysat her and all that. I got to see you that way."

"Dad…" She cleared her throat. "You can see me other ways, too. We can have lunch and go for a run and that kind of thing."

"Really?"

"Yes. Of course."

"Connor…he still can't tolerate me." Her father's eyes filled with tears.

Colleen reached out for her father's hand. "Keep trying," she said.

"I'm very proud of you two. I really am."

"Thank you."

Her poor father. Yep. Poor Dad. Emotionally strangled by testosterone and trying to be fabulous.

Nice that he'd been force-fed a dose of humility, and by Mom of all people.

"Want some ice cream?" she asked. "You can stay for the movie, too."

He gave her a grateful look. "Don't mind if I do."

CHAPTER THIRTY-TWO

THREE WEEKS BACK in Chicago, and Lucas was still edgy and irritable. Sitting at his computer in the apartment he'd lived in since the divorce wasn't as rewarding as he'd imagined it would be. His desk was impressive, his Mac expensive, his chair comfortable. The apartment was immaculate, thanks to the cleaning lady who came in once a week.

But aside from the photos of his nieces and a few of their drawings on the fridge, the place was…soulless, and Lucas wondered how he'd missed that. The furniture was fine, the walls were off-white, the kitchen counters were granite. Everything was new and still rather shiny.

Not like the opera house apartment, with its hundred-year-old floors and the smell of bread from Lorelei's Sunrise Bakery. And not like Colleen's old Victorian with the tall, narrow windows and crotch-sniffing dog. And red couch. And soft bed.

Yeah. No. Best not to think those thoughts.

He'd left Forbes Properties for good; the only thing left was the building dedication, and who really cared about that stuff? Lucas was proud of the building and how smoothly it had gone up, but he wasn't the architect, and he wasn't the owner. He'd always love the

Forbes family; he'd always stay in touch, but his time was over.

Steph would be working for his new company, which would finally get his full attention now. He'd already been approached about general contracting a senior housing development and a corporate headquarters on the outskirts of town.

But it wasn't what he really wanted to do. He wanted, simply, to build houses for regular people. Steph rolled her eyes at this because of course the big money was in bigger properties—strip malls and shopping centers. But strip malls wouldn't be the kind of thing he would proudly point out to a future son or daughter and say, "See that Dunkin' Donuts and the Supercuts? Daddy built that."

Not that he was going to be a father anytime soon.

The image of the meadow back in Manningsport kept inserting itself into his brain, usually around two in the morning. Where the porch would face, the way the deer would wander through the yard. How he could build a slate patio in the back so sitting out there, you'd hear the sound of the river that led to Keuka. The maple tree that would be perfect for a swing.

There was no meadow on a hill in this area; there was only flatness. And heat. Two months away, and the heat of the Midwest got baked into him like never before, and he found himself thinking about the nights in New York when it had been cold enough to sleep with a blanket to keep you warm.

Or a woman.

Or a woman and her dog, more accurately.

And then thoughts of Bryce and her would slice through that pretty image.

His buzzer rang, and Lucas got up from the computer. Crap, it was already dark, and he still hadn't eaten. "Hello," he said in the intercom.

"Hey! It's Bryce."

Speak of the devil. "Come on up."

Lucas hadn't heard much from him since the funeral, other than his shock that he was now a wealthy man. If he was smart (and Lucas intended to make sure he would be), Joe's money could keep Bryce modestly comfortable for life.

He opened the door, and there was his cousin.

"What's up, bro?" Bryce said, hugging him.

Bryce had brought a six-pack, which was a first. "Sorry I didn't call. I wanted to see you. Just jumped in the car and drove to the airport, grabbed a cab here."

"That's fine," he said. "How are things?"

They ordered a pizza ("Nothing like Chicago pie," Bryce said happily) and opened a couple beers. Lucas listened as Bryce told him his plans for the future; he was getting his personal trainer's license and was thinking about possibly opening a women-only gym (which would be a frickin' gold mine, let's be honest). Still washing dogs and finding them homes. He and Paulie were still together, really happy, having lots of fun. Didi was back in Manningsport and kind of a pain, always dropping by unannounced, but Bryce hadn't given her a key, so at least she couldn't come barging into his place at the opera house.

"Sounds like things are good," Lucas said, clearing their plates.

"Yeah, so I might need you to free up some money from my trust fund," Bryce said. "For the gym. I'm working on getting a business plan. Paulie and her dad are helping me, and you're smart about that stuff. Maybe you could take a look?"

"You bet," Lucas said.

"Thanks." His cousin paused. "So about...you know. Colleen. You over that, dude?"

Lucas looked at his beer and didn't answer for a minute. "Did it ever occur to you that..." He broke off. *That I loved her,* he'd been about to say.

Bryce gave a sad smile. "Yeah. It occurred to me. But you were gone and married and living the life, right? And Colleen and I were still in Manningsport, and the thing was, I always liked her, from high school on. I mean, I'm a straight guy. Straight guys love Colleen. Gay guys, too, probably."

"So you had no problem taking her to bed."

Bryce sat back in the leather chair and looked at him. "You ever wonder what it was like to be your cousin? You were the smart one. The cool one. You were from the South Side, and that was all my dad ever talked about, the good old days, life in Chicago. I was some spoiled kid from the 'burbs."

"My life wasn't really that great, Bryce. Mother dead, father in prison, remember?"

"And still you were better at everything. I don't know if you remember that first day of school in Manningsport, walking into that classroom. And there was the prettiest girl in town, and she was staring at you like she'd been blind up until that second."

Lucas remembered, all right.

"She was the one mistake you made, wasn't she? Leaving her, marrying Ellen?"

He didn't answer.

"So yeah," Bryce said. "I hooked up with her, but to

be honest, I have no idea why she hooked up with me. Even then, it was pretty obvious she was still hung up on you. She just looked so lonely that night."

The thought made his chest hurt. Colleen, who was always so bright and smiling—lonely, even with her twin, her friends, her sister. Lonely, because he made her that way.

His eyes stung suddenly.

"I'm sorry I did it," Bryce said, and his voice was gentle. "I took advantage of her being sad. I think I just wanted to see what it'd be like to be you, just for a little while. Obviously, it didn't work."

Lucas looked at him, the cousin who'd always looked up to him, who'd always wanted what he had.

The cousin who had risked his life to save him, that day on the tracks.

"Are we okay, Lucas?" Bryce asked.

Lucas got up from the couch and hugged him. "Yeah. We're fine."

"Good. Because there's another reason I'm here." He reached into his backpack, pulled out a small box and handed it to Lucas. "This is for you."

Lucas opened it.

It was Joe's silver pocket watch. The Civil War watch, handed from father to son for five generations now.

Warm and heavy in his hand, the watch's curling design was faint but still legible. Lucas opened it. The numbers were elaborate and old-fashioned.

On the inside of the cover, the engraving read *To My Cherished Son from Your Loving Father.*

"This is your watch, Bryce," Lucas said, clearing his throat. Could his cousin honestly not want this? "It's been passed down from father to son since the 1860s."

Bryce pulled a piece of paper from his knapsack and handed it over. "About halfway down."

Lucas took the paper, the sight of Joe's blocky handwriting giving him a pang.

Lucas won't need anything, but take care of him anyway. I want him to have the Civil War watch, Bryce. I hope you don't mind, but he deserves it. He's always been such a good son to me, and a wonderful brother to you.

    Make sure you stay close with him. I always missed my own brother so much. Picture me with your uncle Dan, okay, son?

There was more, but Lucas couldn't see it, because suddenly his eyes were full of tears.

Maybe Joe hadn't sent him out of the room because he hadn't wanted him there. Maybe Bryce just needed to get his father's final blessing, when Lucas had had it all along.

LUCAS AND STEPHANIE took Bryce out for breakfast the next day at Lula's, then put him in a cab to the airport.

"I love that idiot," Stephanie said. "Granted, I couldn't spend more than a day with him, but he's sweet. Gorgeous, too. Man! We have an amazing gene pool, us Campbells."

"Yeah," he agreed.

His sister fixed him with an irritated stare. "What's the matter? You look like the dog died, and you don't even have a dog. This is about Colleen, isn't it? So she screwed Bryce. Get over it."

"It's not just that."

"Oh, God. You men. You irritate me. I'm so glad I'm a lesbian."

"Are you?"

"I could be. By the way, I hate to tell you this, but I'm staying with Forbes. Frank doubled my salary and gave me a promotion. Sayonara, sonny."

He threw up his hands. "Wow. Thanks, Steph. Family loyalty and all that."

"Please. I'm a single mother."

"Yes, I vaguely remember."

She rolled her eyes. "You know how Frank is. The job offer includes college tuition for the girls and a month of vacation to start. I already have the Rolls Royce health benefits, that freaking amazing gym, and now a wardrobe allowance at Bergdorf. You can't do that for me, youngster."

"Mom and Dad would be extremely disappointed in you, you materialistic monster."

"Talk to the hand. The face is planning to take the girls to St. Croix." She folded her arms. "Besides, you don't want me working for you. I'd take over in about half an hour."

"True."

"And now you're free to leave and go back to Manningsport."

He hesitated. "I can't."

"Why?"

"Because (a) I hate it there, and (b) you're here. You and the girls."

"Well, (a) you're insane, because that place is fucking paradise, not to mention much better weather, and (b) have they not invented phones? FaceTime? Skype? Planes? Trains? Automobiles?"

"I see you'll really miss me."

She hugged him hard. "Get out of town, Lucas. Go get married and make me an aunt, for crying out loud. I gotta run. Chloe has a half day. Love you, bye, sorry I took a better offer, call me from New York." She pecked him on the cheek. "Oh, by the way, I thought of your new slogan." She paused for dramatic effect. "Campbell Construction—It's Time to Come Home."

CHAPTER THIRTY-THREE

ANOTHER FRIDAY NIGHT happy hour at O'Rourke's, and Colleen was doing her thing. Con was in the kitchen. They'd already sold out of the tuna tacos. The Hollands took up two tables, and the fire department was having another of their "meetings," which seemed to involve a contest for the filthiest joke involving a hose or a pole or both. Jessica Dunn was ahead by a mile.

Connor had broken up with his mystery woman. He wasn't heartbroken, and Colleen once again had high hopes for Jess. Even now, Connor was giving her the eye. About time he listened to his sister.

Mother Dear was on a date in the back of the pub (drinking her disgusting white Zin and 7Up) and discussing art with Ronnie Petrosinsky. Poultry art, specifically, though Mom was still extolling the thrill of painting nudes. Savannah had just left with Gail; Gail was debating whether or not to take Dad back.

As for Bryce and Paulie, Coll was thinking she'd wear violet as maid of honor, because it seemed as if those two were just a matter of time.

Lucas would be best man, of course.

Best not to think of him, but her throat tightened just the same.

"Colleen, would you make me one of those grapefruit gimlet thingies I had last time?" Louise asked, and Colleen snapped back to attention.

She made drinks, pulled beers, wiped up spills, flirted with the patrons and made sure Monica and Hannah didn't need help bringing out orders. She called Rushing Creek to check on Gramp. Joanie, his favorite nurse, said he was sleeping comfortably.

Maybe Coll would stop by later.

She turned to check on Jessica and the gang to see if they needed anything, and there was Lucas.

For a second, it seemed as though she was imagining him, his dark eyes and curling hair and rough, fallen angel beauty.

But no, Carol Robinson walked past him, patted his ass, and said, "Hi, hottie," and he smiled a little, not looking away from Colleen, and good God, the smile just nailed her to the spot.

He didn't say anything.

He didn't have to. He was here.

"I'm sorry," he said, and her eyes filled with a rush and spilled right over. "I'm very, very sorry, *mía*."

That word never failed to get her, and he damn well knew it.

"Well, then," she whispered. Couldn't manage anything else.

"Forgive me," he said.

The bar was quieting, and Colleen realized that yes, she had four beer glasses in her hands and hadn't moved, and this was quite unusual, and maybe people were catching on, and what was she wearing, anyway, heck, it didn't matter, probably, at least there was the push-up bra, because every day there was a push-up bra, and Lucas was *here,* and he was sorry.

She wasn't sure she'd ever be the same.

"I love you, Colleen," he said, and no, she wouldn't be the same, not ever.

Then Hannah took the glasses from her, but still Colleen couldn't move, but her breath was jerking a little, and those tears just kept slipping down her cheeks.

Then Connor was there, behind the bar with her, and he put a protective arm around her shoulders. "What do you want?" he growled.

"I want to marry your sister," Lucas answered, his eyes on her still, those deep, dark eyes that always said so much.

Connor bristled. "Over my cold, dead, stiff—"

"Oh, shut up, Connor," she said, and with that, she scooched up on the bar, swung her legs over and then Lucas had her in his arms, and she was crying and laughing, and Lucas's face was against her neck.

"I love you," he whispered. "Let me come home to you, *mía.* Marry me. I'll beg if I have to."

"It's so tempting, but you know me," she said. "I'm easy."

Then she kissed him, and a cheer went up from the gang, and Colleen held her man tight, the one she'd been waiting for, the only man she ever loved.

She pulled back, and Lucas wiped her eyes and kissed her forehead, and Colleen turned to the crowd. Faith was crying, Tom Barlow winked, Mom was blowing her nose into a napkin.

Then she kissed Lucas again and felt him smile against her mouth, and hugged him hard.

She looked over to see her brother smiling, albeit grudgingly *I guess I can live with it.*

Thanks, brother mine.

"Drinks are on the house!" he called.

EPILOGUE

IN THE GREAT tradition of the O'Rourke and Campbell families, Colleen got pregnant before she got married.

The Hollands had offered her the beautiful stone barn for her wedding, but Colleen wanted it held on the land she and Lucas had just bought—a couple of acres of hilltop meadow, Keuka glinting dark and blue in the distance, the vine-covered hills of Blue Heron to the east. Next week, construction would start on their home; they hoped to be in before the baby came. But for today, there was a white tent on the property, and Rufus galloped around the field, chasing Faith's dog and Paulie's fat little pug and dirty-mop dog.

It was a sparkling October afternoon, the sky a heart-wrenching blue, the red and gold leaves glowing on the hills. It would be a simple wedding—a tent, a justice of the peace, lots of good food (nachos, of course) and drinks and music.

Savannah was her maid of honor, and Bryce was best man, Faith and Paulie were bridesmaids. Mom had a date—Ronnie (he'd given them a lifetime pass for free chicken at any Chicken King franchise, and Colleen seemed to have a craving for it, now that she was six weeks knocked up). Dad and Gail were there in the second row, right behind Mom, not quite back together, not quite separated.

All the people Colleen loved, except one.

Gramp had finally slipped away, about two weeks after Lucas proposed. Colleen and Connor had been there, and Dad, too, Colleen with her head on Gramp's chest, crying quietly because even though it was more than his time, and she firmly believed he'd be in a better place, she'd miss him terribly.

It occurred to her, late that sad night as Lucas held her close and stroked her hair, that maybe on some level, Gramp had waited for her to be taken care of. That maybe he knew she and Lucas had finally found their way back to each other, and felt he could leave her now. That all this time when she'd been taking care of him, he'd been taking care of her, too.

But while pregnancy was making her weepier than normal, today was a happy, happy day.

"You look pretty, yadda yadda," Connor said. But his eyes were a little teary, too. "You ready?" Because yes, he was giving her away. No one else could do the job.

"I was born ready," she said, and he grinned and rolled his eyes. "Con?"

"Yes, Irritating Sister?"

"I'll be your best woman when you finally listen to me and marry Jess."

"You're such a pain."

"I love you," she said, eyes filling.

"I love you, too, idiot. Come on. Your song is playing."

And there he was, Lucas Damien Campbell, smiling at her. The boy she'd loved from the second she saw him, the man she'd waited for her whole life, the only one for her, and the sun was shining, and she was laughing, and all was right with the world.

* * * * *

ACKNOWLEDGMENTS

I have been blessed with the wonderful people who have built my career. At Maria Carvainis Agency, Inc., thanks to Madame, Elizabeth Copps and Martha Guzman for all they do for me. I am extremely grateful as well to everyone at Harlequin who gives my books so much thought and care, especially Susan Swinwood and Margaret Marbury and the fabulous sales team. Thank you, thank you, thank you!

Kim Castillo at Author's Best Friend and Sarah Burningham at Little Bird Publicity, what a joy it is to work with both of you!

For the use of their names in the Blue Heron series, thanks to Gerard Chartier, Lorelei Buzzetta, Gail Chianese (she's actually very nice), Dana Hoffman (ditto), the Murphy girls, the Hedberg family and the many readers who offered up their names.

Thanks again to attorney Annette Willis for her help understanding divorce law. My longtime friend, Stephen Wrinn, DC, shared his experiences of dialysis with me—thank you, Steve! Thanks also to Mighty Jeff Pinco, M.D., for fielding my bizarre and sometimes creepy medical questions.

Thanks to Robyn Carr and Jill Shalvis for their love and friendship, and to authors Simone Elkeles and Julie James, who helped me with some facts about the Windy

City. For the laughter, wine and inspiration, thanks to Shaunee Cole, Huntley Fitzpatrick, Jennifer Iszkiewicz, and Karen Pinco, great writers all, but even better friends.

I am blessed with a wonderful family: to my brother Mike, owner of Litchfield Hills Wine Market—I'm so glad you don't own a hardware store, because then I'd never see you. Thanks for all your help, Mikey! To my sister Hilary and my sister-in-law, Jackie, I love you both so much. And of course, eternal love and thanks to my mom.

To readers Lorelei Buzzetta, Diana Phung and Barbara Wright, your thoughtfulness and friendship mean so much to me! Thank you for all the little things!

In the Finger Lakes region of New York, I am hugely indebted to the helpful, warm, wonderful people at Finger Lakes Wine Country and Steuben County Conference & Visitors Bureau, and especially to Sayre Fulkerson and John Iszard at Fulkerson Winery.

To my husband, daughter and son—I love you three more than I could ever say.

Finally, thanks to you, dearest readers. I wish I had the words to tell you what an honor it is to have you spend a few hours with my books. I am so grateful.

HARLEQUIN
PLUS

Try the best multimedia subscription service for romance readers like you!

Read, Watch and Play.

Experience the easiest way to get the romance content you crave.

Start your **FREE TRIAL** at
www.harlequinplus.com/freetrial.